Fire Rush

Also by Jacqueline Crooks

The Ice Migration

Fire Rush

Jacqueline Crooks

JONATHAN CAPE
LONDON

1 3 5 7 9 10 8 6 4 2

Jonathan Cape is part of the Penguin Random House group of companies whose addresses can be found at global.penguinrandomhouse.com.

First published by Jonathan Cape in 2023

penguin.co.uk/vintage

A CIP catalogue record for this book is available from the British Library

HB ISBN 9781787333635
TPB ISBN 9781787333642

Typeset in 12/16pt Fournier MT Std by Jouve (UK), Milton Keynes.
Printed and bound in Great Britain by Clays Ltd, Elcograf S.p.A.

The authorised representative in the EEA is Penguin Random House Ireland, Morrison Chambers, 32 Nassau Street, Dublin D02 YH68

Penguin Random House is committed to a sustainable future for our business, our readers and our planet. This book is made from Forest Stewardship Council® certified paper.

Dedicated to Kirsten and Paul
Gratitude, always

I had thought of walking far from the terrible
Knowledge
Of flames. Spathodea. From ghost-ridden
Trumpet Tree. From personal
Disaster. God's binding judgement. Drunken mystery

And wisps of smoke from cockpits crying lonely
Lonely

But walking in the woods alternating dark with
Sunshine
I knew
Nothing then of cities or the killing of children
In their dancing time.

Olive Senior, 'Cockpit County Dreams' in *Talking of Trees*

BOOK ONE

The Crypt: Underground November 1978–November 1980

If sound is birth and silence death, the echo trailing into infinity can only be the experience of life, the source of narrative and a pattern for history.

Louis Chude-Sokei, 'Dr Satan's Echo Chamber: Reggae, Technology and the Diaspora Process'

I

Follow the Smoke

One o'clock in the morning. Hotfoot, all three of us. Stepping where we had no business.

Tombstone Estate gyals – Caribbean, Irish. No one expects better. We ain't IT. But we sure ain't shit. All we need is a likkle bit of riddim. So we go inna it, deep, into the dance-hall Crypt.

'Come, nuh,' Asase calls. Pushing her way down the stairs. High-priestess glow. Red Ankara cloth wound round her hair like a towering inferno.

Asase is the oldest, twenty-five, a year older than me and Rumer.

Rumer is nothing like her red-haired Irish family. My gyal is dance-taut, tall with a rubber-ribbed belly – androgynous. Blonde, she dyes her hair Obsidian Black, stuffs it underneath a knitted red-gold-green Rasta cap.

We squeeze past chirpsing men. Stand in front of the arched wooden door. Suck in the last of the O2.

I follow Asase inside. My gyal follows the smoke. Beneath barrel-vaulted arches. Dance-hall darkness. Pile-up bodies. Ganja clouds. We lean against flesh-eating limestone walls near two coffin-sized speaker boxes that vibrate us into the underworld.

Runnings: the scene goes the usual way; a Rasta pulls Rumer which is good because that's the only kinda man she'll dance with.

'They're respectful, they're my bredren,' she says. A sweet bwoy pulls Asase.

Testing, testing: one, two, three. Lights go on for a few seconds.

Only one type of man left for me.

A tall, light-skinned man, face the colour of wet sand, stalked green eyes, standing in his silence. Man pulls me with not so much as a 'What's up. Wanna dance?' Nuth'n.

Watchya: there're only three kinda man-pulls – usually from behind.

Pull 1: grip above elbow; pull-back-bend-ram-hard-rubbing.

Options: forget it!

Pull 2: hand-grip-spin-face-to-face-body-check-ram-rub.

Options: none. Best give up your body for one tune – at the very least.

Pull 3: soft bwoy tap on shoulder.

Options: nuff.

This man's trouble. I can tell by his use of Pull 1 and the size of his belt and the way he jooks himself into my centre of gravity. His body's not tuned for riddims; it's flexed for the war zones of history, the battles of the streets.

I tip my arse, inch my pubic bone away from his hard-on.

He puts his mouth to my ear, warm breath: 'Simmer down.' Flattens his palms against my batty, pulls me back in.

Version after B-side instrumental version, he grips me. Wordless. We're in a crypt in the thick of duppy dust; lost rivers, streams and sewers bubbling beneath us.

Smoke's taken over, thickening, choking me. And I wonder why I attract these kinda men, who are just like my father. Men who strike fear in people just by the way they stand. Skewering the silence with their stares.

Four dances in before I make my soft-gyal excuse, mouth 'Gotta go. Toilet.'

Man nods. I exhale. One floor up, I sit in the toilet cubicle. Smell candles and incense and old wood from the church. Light my spliff, suck more smoke into my lungs, feel Muma shoot into my veins.

I hear her song, her voice, treble, reed and flute. She cuts inna me with soundwaves, singing: 'Daughter, I-and-I is tune.'

Spirit or not, Muma's all I've got. The only one I trust.

'Stay,' I whisper. But she's gone.

I imagine my ganja smoke snaking around my dance partner, dragging him into the afterworld beneath the Crypt. But the man's waiting for me downstairs, to raas. One hand clipped on his belt like he's toting a gun.

'Inna it, baby,' he says, and pulls me into the dance hall, positions me against the wall, wedges himself into my body.

I hold my breath, and pray for a rootsy liberation track to put him off his slow-winding moves. But I'm locked in. Tune after tune after tune.

Three o'clock in the morning. We're ten feet below and the town's weighing down on us. Stench of sweat, stale gases and lead.

'Soon come,' man shouts in my ear. 'Need a light.' He takes a cigarette out.

I mek my move quick-time, slip into the mass of closed-eyed skankers, sucked into the slipstream of rippling spines. Try to get as close as I can to the decks, watch the MC, see how he handles the mic and the controls. We're dancing in darkness, skinning up with the dead. I feel them twisting around me, round and round, rattles on their wrists and ankles, broken-beat bodies of sound. The Dub Master spinning versions of delayed time. Slack-jawed, slicking-up words from tongue root. I wanna take the mic from his hand, blaze fire on Babylon. In my head, I'm chatting lyrics:

set it
set it
come mek we hear it from the uptown posse
get down
get down
every posse drive forward
fire!

Bodies rippling like seagrass. Synthesising air and bass.

Inna caves of sound, we skank low, spirits high. Drop moves as offerings to the soundboxes, wooden deities full of fading voices.

The regulars are scattered around the square, pillared vault. Rocked by storm sounds, swaying under the shelter of arches, some pressed tight against the walls. Others bubbling in the epicentre, below low-hovering smoke clouds. Strangers pass through, hold position on the edges. There's Eustace, the owner of Dub Steppaz Records, skanking next to the decks, one hand behind his back, the other steering the air. There's Cynthia, the lovers-rock queen with a bronze-sprayed Afro, who cradles her sagging womb when she sings, rocking from side to side to reggae love songs. And Lego in the middle of the dance floor, two-stepping best he can with his artificial leg. Skanking hard-hard, using his walking stick like a spear, firing it inna the air, shouting, 'Mash down Babylon.' Nobody knows if he's lost his mind or found a higher consciousness, like our men who lead the marches and rallies, chanting 'Black Power' over the heads of the sistren.

Lovers-rock time and our bodies are ships rolling through smoke and heat, under pressure from treble and bass. I sway in the broiling centre, far from the walls where men move with mute biological urgency, stabilising themselves with the weight of women.

The MC calls out over the mic, a voice in the darkness, shouting above the waves of sound. The deck's where I've always wanted to be. Changing the sonic direction. I'd fling down a rootsy dub track of the ancients chanting stories about the divinity of our emperors. Tek it to the outtasphere.

Someone takes my hand. Eases me around.

I wipe sweat from my eyes, look up. Dim lights from the decks flash on and off and I make out a face that's a smile resting on rocks. He's looking down at me as if he's known me from beyond time, cables of blue smoke twisting above his head.

He puts his mouth to my ear, says his name is Moose.

'OK for this dance?' he asks.

I see a wide-bridged nose, thick lips scrunched like he's chewing his thoughts. Yeah, he's one of dem men whose beauty is a throwback from the past.

'I'm Yamaye,' I say and give him the nod.

He positions a thigh between my legs. Puts his arms on my shoulders, keeps his crotch a polite distance away from my pubic bone. Electric guitars riffing. Groaning vocals. We dance, rub-a-dub-squatting, and his cheek grazes mine. Drifting scents of vanilla, cocoa beans and pine trees waft off his neck. I tremble as we sway under the limewashed roof.

With my body pressed against his, I feel the ancient songs vibrating beneath his ribs: Tambu, Sa Leone, Jawbone. This man's different. From the electricity running through me, I feel like my ending is gonna be charged inna his fate.

Everyone's in their power. The room's a furnace, sweating bodies. Moose takes my hand, pushes his way out of the Crypt.

'Let's get air,' he says.

We go up the metal stairway and the man's still holding my hand. When was the last time anybody held my hand besides Rumer or Asase? I slip my fingers out of his fist; pull myself together.

Out the side door into the churchyard where the paved walkway leads on to the high street. Into the cold November air.

Norwood is one of those small industrial towns on the western edge of London. Part village, part suburb, an overgrowth of the city. It's 1978, but the town feels outside of time, trapped somewhere in its past. The history books say it was built in the clearing of a forest of thorn trees that was once the site of pagan rituals, not far from the marshy banks of a prehistoric river. Mammoth bones and teeth are sometimes found by workmen ploughing deep inna the earth.

I blink my stinging eyes, take long, slow breaths of oxygen and exhale into the deep-blue night. Micro-bubbles of sound float in the air. The smell of rotting weeds from the old graveyard and the feeling that the dead might rise with the sensimilla smoke and supra-watt riddims.

Lighting from the side windows of the church backglows us. I take a better look at Moose: bronze-brown skin, irises patterned like the grain of trees. He's smiling at me from some shaded internal space.

Heat in my veins and a stabbing feeling in my groin.

'I came for the Dub Master,' he says, his voice the sing-song-bling of Caribbean islands. Says he's been in the country eight years.

'Nothing else round here,' I say. 'Unless you count the Wolf Pub or the cattle market.'

He looks me up and down, smiling. 'Looks like plenty going on.'

We walk to the front of the church, cotch on the wall, check the people on the other side of the main road: youth quabs with dead-route eyes and back-pocket knives, heading north towards the railway line that cuts through the heart of the town; an old man wiping down the tables in Delhi Wala cafe, preparing for the morning shift, the lights flickering above him.

'You're shivering,' Moose says. He takes off his suede Gabicci and drapes it over me.

I pull it around my shoulders.

'It's intense down there,' I say.

The man I was dancing with earlier skulks past with another man. They're talking on the down-low; they both seem vex.

Moose sees the way I look at him and asks if I know who he is.

'Never met him before tonight,' I say. 'Man pulled me to dance and wouldn't let me go.'

'Mind yuhself. Name's Crab Man, check the way he walks. Feet go one way, eyes the other. Watch his eyes. Never worry 'bout the legs.'

''Nough man like that round here.' I look at Moose in his black silk shirt, shimmering like dark water, and wonder what kinda man he is.

'No, this man holds women down inna his yard. Does what he wants.' He throws his arms outwards. 'Dashes them out like trash. Stabbed a few brothers. Never does time. Finds another hiding hole – like this town.'

I cross my arms, holding on to the empty sleeves of his jacket. 'How do *you* know him?'

'I rave all over. Don't check me so. That ain't my style.'

'Man dem carrying on a-ways.'

He puts an arm across my shoulder, rests his head against mine, and points to the purple universe braided with beads and sequins.

'Look,' he says, and I feel his breath against my face, soft and sweet and warm. 'Planets, stars,' he says.

'My ears and guts are ringing from the bassline, can't focus on anything else.'

'Hard-hitting down there. Voltage strong enough for a nosebleed.'

We laugh and he presses his body closer, takes my hand.

I look at the side of his face. Profile like mountain ridges; wanna trace my finger from his forehead to nose to lips to chin back to lips so I can push my finger in.

'We're all travelling,' Moose says. 'Like stars.'

There are shouts nearby. Crab Man and the other man are arguing at the entrance to the church. Crab Man's deep, rasping voice makes me shudder.

'It's cold,' I say. 'Let's go inside. I need to link with my friends.'

We go into the dance hall. Lovers rock is still playing. Moose presses his face into my hair and we dance, winding low, our thigh muscles trembling against each other. Bassline coming through his heart into mine, jooking us together. There's no oxygen now. We're high on duppy gas, more spirits than earthly bodies.

I rest my face against his chest, lean against the raft of his ribs. Close my eyes, wonder how long this feeling can last.

When the lights go on, the MC announces next week's dance and an upcoming Misty in Roots concert. Asase and Rumer wind back through the crowd. They stand on either side of me, checking Moose. I introduce them.

Moose nods, but I check the way he looks at Asase – how all men do, like everything has blurred and she's the only thing they can see.

Rumer is coughing and wheezing. The damp Crypt sometimes sets off her asthma. I lay my arm across her back.

Asase stands in front of Moose, arms folded, head cocked, lips curled like red fuse wire. 'Which parts you from?'

'East,' he says.

'Where's your crew?'

'Man can go solo now and then, can't he?'

At five foot ten, Asase's eyes are only a few inches below Moose's.

The Dub Master is calling, 'Last dance, last dance. Tek your partners.'

Asase sways her hips to the lovers rock cry, tipping forward. Next thing her arms are around Moose's neck and they're dancing. Close rub-a-dub style.

Moose looks at me over Asase's shoulder, raises his eyebrows into a question. I cut my eyes on him. A dread weight drops inna my belly. I look at the back of Asase's head. Never know how far she'll go. But it's gonna go the way it always does; Asase will get whatever the raas she wants.

Lights flash on and off. On again.

Six in the morning.

The MC calling out, 'Dis yah dance is done!'

I link arms with Rumer and she leans on me as we walk out. Asase walks in front, stepping the language of the streets, a bounce in her feet that says dis gyal's got things under control. Moose hangs back a little. We follow a slow line of linked lovers, groups and lone ravers up the stairs to the ground floor. And I swear two hundred people pile into the Crypt each night and five hundred leave, ancient spirits reanimated by sensimilla and body heat.

Bongo Natty is talking to people as they leave. He runs the sessions at the Crypt. He takes money at the door, preaches to people as they come in, preaches to them on the way out.

'Conscious vibrations, sistren,' he says.

His real name is Nathaniel Bailey, but everyone knows him as Bongo Natty because he organises marches where he drums and calls for Black revolution. He gives us red flyers about a new march against the sus law that says a policeman can just arrest a bredda on the street for riddim walking, skin-up talking, nose-hole breathing. Black being.

'Sound the revolution, iyah,' he says. 'See oonuh next week – if life spare.' His voice is almost a whisper, womanly soft.

He plays it cool, but he's like all the other men – rebels, rude bwoys, my poopa – super-sensitised to danger, set on survival mode, stepping on the streets, torsos swinging from their waists like obeah men, with panoramic views of a world that's out to get them.

Outside, the early-morning air is damp and grey, a strange apocalyptic silence; receding songs inside my head.

Hard-backed, hungry men pull women aside, plant dry-mouthed suggestions in their ears. Women, their hot-iron curls collapsed against boom-boom skulls, use their lungs like abeng horns to blow smoke outta their bodies.

We walk the concrete path that cuts through the front graveyard. My body is radioactive with sound and ganja, struggling to understand the game Asase is playing. Maybe she's sweeting-up Moose to get us a ride. Maybe she wants him for herself.

Moose's black Rover is parked with all the other cars further down the street, on the other side of the road near the Manor House, a decaying, timber-framed building that has gone through many incarnations; currently, it's some kind of business centre.

Men cotch against the bonnets of cars, clicking teeth, scanning women as they go by.

'You tekking us home?' Asase asks Moose. 'Everyone back to my yard? There's yellow yam and stewed peas.' She runs the tip of her tongue across her lips.

'Why not,' he says.

Asase slides into the front seat. Rumer climbs into the back behind Asase. I sit behind Moose, lean against the leather headrest.

'Girl, you're fast,' Rumer tells Asase. Her asthmatic voice is husky, as if she's running out of air.

'Don't start,' Asase says, her tone light, playful.

The car smells of him, blue river skimmed with musk. 'Lonely Nights' is playing on the cassette. The reverb fades and I'm back from the outtasphere. Inna my body. Back on the lonely streets of town. The isolated offbeat keys of a piano.

Asase directs Moose through the town, a town of Sikh temples, churches, mosques, tower blocks, five streams, two brooks and one river. Resurrection Cemetery, a rectangular piece of land that is full and accepting no more bodies. More bones than living flesh in our town.

Thin arrows of rain pelt the car windows. Hunched-hooded souls on the streets of duppy wandering. We drive past Dub Steppaz where the rude bwoys from the Crypt are now packed inside, taking refuge from the approaching daylight, pinned to the walls like myal men, their eyes rolling rocksteady. Into the Dead Water area, the car floating alongside the still-as-death canal. Across the hump bridge into the Tombstone Estate, a housing complex shaped like a tongue, surrounded by a dry ditch. An ancient well in the centre of the estate, in a dip surrounded by earthen banks, a metal cover. The old people say it's a sacred well of red iron water that used to run bright with crystals. The white concrete tower blocks where we live look out over the cemetery and the surrounding wastelands, and are connected by low, narrow buildings like railway carriages, a super-structure packed with people who light candles, smoke, drink, pound herbs – anything to dispel the scattered energy of ghosts that rise from the cemetery wanting the sounds of life. Skull and cross-bones graffiti on the walls.

Moose pulls up at Asase's block and everyone gets out.

'I'm charged. Gonna head home,' I say.

'You're not eating with us?' says Asase.

Rumer takes my arm. 'Count me out too.' Her scratchy-scratchy voice sounds like a stranger is trapped in her chest. She sucks on her inhaler.

Moose says he'll drop me home, but I point to the high-rise tower in front of us, tell him I'm already in my manor, I'll be fine. I take off his Gabicci and give it to him. He tells me to keep it till next time. I insist on returning it now.

Asase says she'll give Moose something to eat before his drive home. She smiles inna my eyes. 'Check me tomorrow, ladies.'

Rumer and I walk towards her flat, say goodbye, hug. I make my way to my tower block, where grey-white curtains billow like spirits at dark windows and metal coffin lifts shuttle between heaven and hell.

Options: none.

I ride the lift to our flat on the seventeenth floor. It opens into the dim hallway that leads to my door and straight inna Muma's front room. Everything's the way she left it twenty years ago, or so my poopa says. Yellow doilies wilting on the sofas like orchids. A silver ribbon microphone and a case of jazz records. Paintings of blue mountains, green sea, white ships in the distance – a portal to her world.

It's a small, one-level flat. A living room, two bedrooms, a concrete balcony strung with green plastic washing lines, a galley kitchen with a fold-down red Formica table, black root cracks on the walls.

I smell Irving's roll-up, the mush of loamy tropical earth. He's in the kitchen, sitting at the table reading the *Caribbean News*, scratching his metal-shavings-picky-picky hair. Irving, my poopa, is a panel beater. He resurrects broken cars, soldering, welding, spewing sparks. A red-skinned bush man from Falmouth, the capital of Trelawny, Jamaica. He says he's got Taino and Maroon blood; says he survived extinction. Once he told me that his father's father traced their bloodline by drawing circles of ganja smoke above the soil. That's as much as he'll say about our family history.

I don't resemble my poopa, though there's a look on his face sometimes that I recognise in my own. It's the way his mouth changes with his mood, a drawstring knotting flesh over bone like a stubborn root.

I call him by his first name to maintain the distance he's carved out between us, same as the distance between Mother Earth and space.

Me and that man are atoms, exploded out of the same haze. Ablaze in different zones.

Most days, he suffocates the atmosphere with his silence. Only speaking to ask, 'Who you is, fe true? Your mother's child more than mine, that's who.' Yet, when I'm sick, he makes ginger tea and fish soup, spicy-hot with red bells of Scotch bonnet peppers. And he'll soak tissues in Bay Rum which he puts on my pillow so that I can breathe. God, it feels good to be ill dem days. He can be caring, but more often he's cruel. What do I make of a man who carries on dem ways, his heart locked in a cage?

Irving's belt used to be his tongue. He's sixty-six, and the older he gets, the less he talks, only going out to see his friends at the Wolf Pub on the other side of town. Claims his memory is no good.

'Dancing with the dead again?' he asks, rolling his paper. 'Every week ah de Crypt, de Crypt.'

'And?'

'You too follow-fashion.' He lashes the air with the newspaper like a baton. 'Me tell you not to go where everybody go. Not to think like everybody outta street.'

He takes his roll-up from the edge of the ashtray, inhales. His face is eaten out, the flesh of his cheeks hanging in the hollows of his cheekbones.

'Skinning up wid bad-breed man!' he says.

I fill a glass with water and gulp it down.

I wanna ask him what the raas he knows 'bout anything apart from his work as a mechanic, tuning cars and bustin' handbrake spins, but the memory of the whip-sting beatings from my childhood always shuts me down. Yuh too outta order! Come in late from school, disturb the neighbours with loud music. Whatever I did that bothered him, he'd tell me – sentences punctuated with lashes – that Muma would be ashamed.

I hardly remember Muma in this house. She was an orphan, born in Portland, Jamaica, raised by missionaries somewhere in Kingston. After she married Irving, she became a midwife in Norwood, but she left when I was three or four to work in Guyana, and died there too young. That's all I know.

I remember one of the two or three memorials for her at the Pentecostal church. I must have been five or six. Afterwards, the flat full of people dressed in black; Oraca, Asase's mother, squeezing my hand, crying; Irving shaking his head as if he still couldn't believe what had happened.

It's one of the reasons I stay here – wanna be close to what's left of her. Waiting for Irving to tell me more about her; waiting for him to love me the way he must've once loved her.

'Going to bed,' I say.

'Gwaan, sleep all day like the dead.' He puts his roll-up between his lips, puffs, dips the beams of his eyes.

In my room I play a dubplate mixtape on the down-low, chat freestyle on my mic, let my anger out.

I send myself up in smoke. Wait for overstanding, looking at the picture of Muma on my bedside table. Dark brown skin. Black-pepper freckles. Plaits woven around her head like a basket. Lips apart, ready to sing-song some snake outta her hair.

Through the window, light from the fading moon, silvery as Muma's taffeta dress. I close my eyes, smell khus khus, earth and rainforest. My face burns at the thought of Asase sweeting-up Moose, taking something away from me, because she's good at that. Even when we were children, she would push me out of the scene if I stood between her and the attention she wanted. Magnetic as she is, sometimes I wonder if my fear of her outweighs my love.

I turn on some old, favourite dub tracks. I grew up listening to Irving play his Trojan records. Ska into rocksteady into reggae. The offbeats and rhythmic patterns of my growth synced to the emerging sound of dub.

The dead come to us through familiar sound waves. I chant, call Muma inna fire-rush tongue: 'Weh you deh?'

Muma's in the pit of my belly, like one of the pickney she used to birth. She's pushing me the way she always does, trying to get inna the world.

I breathe fast.

Her voice spins up outta my belly, like it does when I feel alone. I hear her in the air around me, a crying falsetto with living heat. Maybe she's keeping watch over me. Or I'm imagining her because I'm still a mystery to myself.

She's singing as she always does and I hear her:

'sending my dream
always be seen
daughter
let me tek you to the sea'

Thunder and lightning in my heart; sound and beat together, making fire. I set the levels on my mic to get my deep vocals right. But there's static, a loose connection somewhere. Muma's voice fades. I push the amp in. The microphone is humming.

'Muma?' I whisper.

The room's silent.

I hold my breath.

Nothing but thin wisps of smoke.

I've lost her again.

2

Abeng Horns

Nine thirty in the morning on a cold, bright Saturday. Asase, Rumer and me huddle at the bus stop near Dub Steppaz, waiting for the 207 into London. The record shop is one of our few places of refuge in dis yah town. Riddim is the foundation for all of them: dance hall; Pentecostal church where people sway and stomp, waiting for the white smoke of the Holy Ghost to enter their bodies; and Dub Steppaz, a fortress of black vinyl.

All of them governed by men.

I like to go to Dub Steppaz on my way home from the night shift, eight in the morning when the shop has the CLOSED sign in the window, before it's full of men jostling for dubplates in the small-island oasis. The walls plastered with glossy vinyl sleeves of Caribbean beaches and rainforests, musical revolutionaries in Kente print robes, their dreadlocks trailing into the earth, becoming the roots of trees. The ceiling painted with hummingbirds.

Eustace lets me in and locks the door, gives me a mug of coffee while he wipes down the counters and polishes the vinyl, a rare-groove track playing, something about silver shadows.

Eustace is a square-jawed man in his early forties; not exactly old, but with enough experience and wisdom to keep the youth on solid ground. Mothers and grandmothers drop in on their way from the market to get advice from him about a son or grandson running wild.

Asase loves nothing better than pushing herself into the crowded record shop late on Saturday afternoons when we return from the city. By that time it's ram-up with men, their arses pressed against the window, criss-crossing smoke above them. Rumer always tries to drag her past the shop, but it's pointless. Asase opens the door and eases herself in and – yeah, we follow.

She'll work her way to the back of the room where the records are stacked in tiered wooden cabinets. Me and Rumer go to the far side and pile our bags on the narrow counter that's littered with empty cans of beer. The place smells of body odour, stale rum and roll-up tobacco.

Asase likes to flick slowly through the vinyl, undulating her spine to the music as if it's a divining rod and she's seeking the water's flow. She sucks up the attention as men sidle up to her, asking 'What's up, baby-love?' If it gets too ram and rude bwoys get agitated, Eustace will raise the counter and let us stand with him.

Now I knock on the shop window and wave to Eustace. He waves back and then returns to sorting vinyl.

We board the half-empty bus for the hour-long ride into London, still dub-travelling on the undertow of ghostly basslines from the Crypt where we were dancing with Moose until dawn. He picked us up from Asase's place like he has done more or less every weekend since that first night a few weeks ago.

We've done danced Friday into the stratosphere, skanking as if our lives depended on it, scooping the air with our hands, back-kicking like we were treading water. We grabbed a fresh – a cat-wash and change of clothes – at Asase's yard. Mopped up stewed fish with breadfruit, dozed, smoked ourselves awake – or kinda. From rave to street, no sleep. That's the way we run it half the time.

I stare out the window, feeling Asase's weight shift into me as the bus turns.

Sometimes Asase goes home with a man after a blues party to get her tings. Other times, I spend the night with her, waking up Sunday afternoon, dozing on the maroon velvet sofa in the back room of her yard, watching black-and-white films with the curtains drawn while Oraca's in the kitchen. Oraca cooks nuth'n but fish: stewed, fried, boiled, but mostly stuffed with herbs. The house always smells of fish and the sea.

After dinner, when we're half-crazed from the fallout of ganja high and sound-system nosebleeds, Oraca lights candles and puts a jazz record on, the volume humming on the low-down like a distant sea.

We get on the floor, eat escovitch red snapper from big glass bowls, push our plates away and lie on our sides, Asase on Oraca's right, me on her left, and Oraca telling us about Queen Nanny of Jamaica, a Maroon leader. She tells us this with sound hissing through the tunnels of her clenched teeth.

'People call them runaway slaves. No! They fought the British and won. Nobody could put Queen Nanny and her warriors under manners. She was a supernatural leader. Her tactic was sound – long-range communication, the abeng horn.'

Maybe the way Muma sings to me is the same. She's transmitting memories. Like dub and reggae, communicating our history.

In London, Asase, Rumer and me float down side streets of boutiques starlit for Christmas, wading through the light, trailing smoke. Yes, iyah! We're high. Puss-eyed sunshades on, cooling our bodies in the glass-city.

We push through the swelling morning crowds of crutchers, shoppers, boasty in pavement bars pecking breakfast food like they don't know how to nyaam.

'I'm mash-up,' Rumer says. She rummages in her green-beaded clutch bag, finds her inhaler, sucks in whatever magic is in the blue tube.

'Gimme some a dat,' Asase says. She grabs it, breathes in. Coughs.

'Yuh crazy raas,' Rumer says.

'Stuff's good,' Asase says. 'Let's tek the city. Shop by shop till we drop.'

Rumer leans on Asase, holds her arm, eases her right foot out of her gold-tipped shoe. Stubby toes swollen and grey as slugs. She looks up at Asase and says, 'My feet are sore.' And there's that strange look in her eyes that she gets sometimes when she's close to Asase. Red flushing her face like she's blooming and bleeding at the same time.

'You're saaaft. Twisting up yuh foot wid skanking,' Asase says. She pulls away and marches ahead.

Street vendors toss peanuts in spinning copper plates that hum caramel notes like the flipside of a 45.

Tuuune in.

Tuune in till a morning.

People stare at us. We don't dress pop. We spin our garments different, wear our music on our bodies. Whipcrack pleats, spliced textures, rewind old-time swing skirts, turned-up bling.

I look at Asase. What-a-way she brucks style. There's Rumer in her men's grey Farah trousers and suede waistcoat, and me in my stitched-seam jeans, gold-tipped patent shoes. But Asase? My girl has customised a pair of cream high heels with diamond-encrusted toecaps – Stix-Gyal style – matched with an A-line georgette skirt, big-arse ducket on a rope chain doubled around her throat.

She stops and eyes a sashay dress with transparent bodice and rainbow pleats through a shop window. Bad'n'raas stylish. Cut to kill.

'That garment's gonna be the price of a second-hand Spitfire,' Rumer says. 'Probably get you inna jus' as much trouble.'

'Watchyah, nuh!' Asase says.

She presses the buzzer. Waits. Rings again. Two saleswomen, folding shirts, look up, assess and dismiss us with rigor mortis smiles. A blonde with fire-bombed rouged cheeks looks at the clock on the wall and shakes her head.

Asase takes out her snakeskin purse, holds it up and points to the outfit. Mouths, 'Five minutes,' filling the narrow doorway with her broad-shouldered stance.

They buzz us in. The blonde woman folds the dress and wraps it in bright pink tissue paper.

'I want a top-notch carrier bag for my garment, nothing plastic,' Asase says to the assistant as she writes a cheque.

I look at the signatory's name printed on the chequebook: Lucy Blewitt. I wonder who the hell this Lucy is, and I can't believe that Asase is hustling again.

Me and Rumer work nights at Bonemedica on the production line, operating machines and inspecting components – bolts and screws that fix the broken parts of people's bodies. A sprawling grey-brick building in the industrial area south of the railway, full of factories making canned meat, bread, pottery. We sleep in the daytime, come alive at night.

Asase works part-time for a company in the city that makes perfumes. Dressed in silk wrap dresses, sniffing and mixing. 'Like mekking music,' she says. 'Every scent's a note.'

She doesn't need to hustle. She earns enough to rent her own flat, but she's saving to buy a double-fronted house in the fancy town where she went to school. On her days off, she goes to the city with other crutchers, stealing clothes from designer shops, shoving them between their legs.

When me and Rumer are at Bonemedica in the dead of night with the other late-shift workers, Rumer's like a ghost, her thin frame hunched over the desk, inspecting the parts and updating the maintenance logs, her pale freckled face covered in tan foundation. She's quieter when it's just the two of us, as if she needs Asase's energy to fire her up. I wonder why she comes to the Crypt, the only white woman, getting bounced by Stix-Gyals, tuff'n'raas women like Asase, who hustle and fight to survive. They wanna know why she's there, where she's from. 'You mixed or what?' they ask her. 'Irish,' she'll tell them.

Rumer's family are Travellers. They move from town to town, country to country, in their caravans. She left them five years ago to get away from a man they wanted her to marry. The council gave her a studio flat.

Rumer's like me, trying to find where she fits. If she believes in ghosts or spirits, she won't say. When I try to talk to her about Muma or the things I hear, she tells me: 'Girl, that's just vibrations.'

The blonde shop assistant looks at the signature on the chequebook and compares it with the chequecard. She stares at Asase and Asase smiles inna her face. Not a real smile, a hard-faced show of teeth. The woman puts the dress into a silver cardboard bag and hands it to Asase.

'Sweet,' Asase says, except her tone might as well be saying 'Fuck you'.

Once we're back on the street I ask Asase where she got the chequebook. She doesn't answer.

'You can do serious time for stolen chequebooks,' I say. 'Who gave it to you? Do you know what they could have done to that woman?'

I almost never raise my voice with Asase, but there's been a sick feeling in my stomach since I watched her dance with Moose that night we first met, and a glow in my fists when I think of the risk she's exposing us to.

A fat vein twitches on Asase's temple.

'Chip, if you don't like it!' She's in my face, her eyes popping. Then she links arms with Rumer. 'You won't go soft on me,' she says to her.

'Gyal, you're outta order,' Rumer tells her. But she doesn't resist; she always gives in to Asase's touch.

What made Asase such a force? Maybe it's her family being from Alligator Pond, a fishing village in a valley between the Santa Cruz and Don Figuerero Mountains. The first people to navigate the sea and set foot on the island over a thousand years ago. Or maybe she's different because her father, Hezekiah, is a man who does what he wants and raised Asase to do the same. Like the time Asase's mother, Oraca, realised she was sneaking out to the Crypt when she was only thirteen. Hezekiah said to leave her be; the sooner she learned how to handle men, the better. She learned how to handle men, for sure. And now that Hezekiah no longer lives with them, she back-chats him in ways that even Oraca never could.

Or maybe Asase is different because she didn't go to the same run-down school as me and Rumer. Father Mullaney wrote a letter for Oraca and got Asase into a quality Catholic school.

Babylon school is where I learned not to do my thing. Redstone Secondary seems such a long time ago. Rumer came to my school when she was fifteen. We both left when we were sixteen. I used to sing in the choir. They were happy for us to entertain them in return for us receiving their stories of history. Teachers with bullwhip tongues, faster than the speed of sound, talking about their conquests, plagues and fires.

I learned plenty about *their* history, but I had to go to the library to educate myself. Read up on some of the things Oraca told me about the Black Atlantic, the abeng horn, the revolution of sound.

Asase went to a school fifteen miles away, in a sleepy town with a cricket green, hanging flower baskets, gardens with treehouses. She liked the uniform: a blue blazer with brass buttons, pleated skirt, and black tie with gold stripes that made her look like she was in the navy. She always carried on extra. I suspected she was trying to climb the ladder out of Norwood, seeking friends in higher places.

The lights in the shops go out. Asase and Rumer march ahead on the darkening streets. Best shut me mouth: the sistren need each other on the streets, in the dance hall. Together we are a three-pin plug, charging ourselves to dub riddim. Connecting through each other to the underground.

I look at their backs; they're almost the same height. Rumer's tall, slim body dressed like a Stix-Man, a hard-man-criminal, arms linked with Asase, slightly taller, who is sashaying her arse as if to tell me I can kiss it.

I think of the many nights I've spent in Asase's bed. It was some time after Hezekiah ran off with that young woman, when Asase was sixteen, that she developed a night-time ritual of stripping naked, dropping her clothes and underwear in a pool around her ankles. The first time she did it, I looked at the web of her black pubic roots, then her face.

What the fuck was she carrying on with?

She was nothing like Oraca and everything like Hezekiah, the father she says her spirit can't tek. Same flared huffing nostrils, cedar-coloured skin, and irises that flickered brown and green like shaken leaves.

She took her blue silk headwrap from under her pillow and covered her hair, all the time her eyes on me, her mouth set in a deep-cut line. I was wearing what I always wore, her oversized T-shirt with 'Sweet Pussy!' printed on the front. I pulled it down below my crotch.

She was supposed to light the ready-made spliff that was in the ashtray on the brass drinks trolley that she used as a bedside table. Then switch off the lamp, take a deep drag of ganja and pass it to me, like she always did. We would then blow smoke above our heads and watch it form ideas that we'd try to articulate before they dispersed into silver particles of sound. Then wake the following Sunday around lunchtime, our legs wrapped around each other, face to face, lips almost touching. We always woke that way, no matter how we set our bodies and intentions before we went to sleep.

Only that night she whispered, 'Yuh best wash your feet.'

'What?'

Silence, then zinging in my ears, like I'd been boxed in the head.

She screamed at me, 'Your feet! They're dirty! You think you can just walk across the bare floor and get into my bed?'

I didn't move for a few seconds. She was breathing hard. I went to the bathroom and washed my feet, although there was nothing to wash. The wooden floor was polished and spotless. Was she listening for the sound of running water? Would she want to inspect my heels? Poke her fingers between my toes? I walked across the floor and stepped on to the orange sheepskin rug and got into the bed. I turned my back on her and curled into a ball.

I feel the same stress now, watching her and Rumer walk away.

It always takes me time to realise someone's hurting me. A few minutes, a day, a year. Twenty-four years. Four hundred years. But at some point there's the familiar feeling as my blood picks up speed, tracks and traces some evolutionary chemical inside my gut.

Rage.

In front of me city loners appear as if they've bubbled up from underground streams. Steam winds out from basement bars. Shop lights are searchlights. Sirens blare in the distance. I think of our people who'll be snatched from the streets, swallowed by Black

Marias, where they'll curl up like bass clefs. Making breath marks inside the hold of those vans, knowing they may never be seen again.

My heart thuds. I wait for the screech of police cars coming to pick us up because of Asase's skank with the chequebook.

Them put death on our people, Muma moans. Sea spells, daughter, sea spells.

The sirens fade.

The light's gone and Asase's shadow looms behind her, a dark mass. I'm disconnected from her and Rumer, locked outta my feelings again, zoned out. But this is my entry into the chirring afterworld where Muma is singing. I see her in the winding smoke. Her tissue-twisted curls matted with seaweed. Her sparkling, salt-encrusted bones.

3

Terra Incognita

It's a week into the new year and winter storms are raging; seaside towns are flooded. Politicians say the country is being swamped by migrants. A Bangladeshi man in Moose's town is murdered because of the colour of his skin.

War with Babylon.

Daytime belongs to them, but we have zones of sanctity: Dub Steppaz; Resurrection Cemetery.

Nobody knows the rules of this yah battle. All we can do is rock on through.

Moose's car shakes with top-range sound effects from a dub track: windows breaking, explosions, the *whooszzzh-pap-pap-papp* of bullets.

Asase slides into the passenger seat, white rabbit fur slung over her shoulders, barely covering a low-cut, jade satin dress flecked with gold – Christmas presents from one of her admirers. Me and Rumer are in the back dressed in Farah trousers, camisole tops, sheepskin jackets. Asase likes to be the last person to leave the house, have everyone waiting for her. But she's gotta be first inna the rave. She always rides up front, steering with her mouth. Moose checks her as she buckles up, his lips slack as a noose, the blow-heater churning her sandalwood and oakmoss scent. Me and Rumer huddle together in the back for warmth.

'Why oonuh women don't cover yourselves up in this cold?' Moose asks. He looks at me in the rear mirror.

Just seeing his face messes with my heart in a way I didn't think was possible. Still not sure if it's me or Asase he's interested in. I pull on the spliff that Rumer passes to me; stare out the window into darkness. Wait for overstanding.

Terra incognita. That's me.

We drive out of the Tombstone Estate along the road of terraced houses, mud-pathed alleyways and gated shops. The Sikh temple comes into view, its gold dome a soundless gong pinned against the sky. Past the unlit stretch of canal, blinking phosphorescent glow of the minicab office and off-licence.

Asase swigs black rum from her hip flask. Offers it to Moose but he shakes his head. 'Uh-uh, co-pee,' he says.

With the tip of her scarlet varnished nail, she turns up the volume on the car stereo. Red frequency lights likk top range.

'Tek us outta town,' she says to Moose. 'We'll hunt the bassline. Whoever finds the rave . . .' She fires an imaginary pistol at a passing house.

Moose clicks his teeth – in agreement or irritation, it's difficult to tell. He drives past the Crypt where people are queuing from the side door of the church, past the graveyard garden and up to the street.

Rumer waves at them. 'Laters, everybody.'

Over the railway bridge, picking up speed, we fire on to the motorway. On the move now. We smoke and drink and laugh. Bend-up grooving in our seats. Come alive.

I crack the window open, suck in black breeze. Damn, this yah night feels good.

We drive through towns, bass-hunting networks of underground raves, listening for the call of drums and horns that signal where our people are gathered, back-bending and sidewinding themselves outta Babylon blues.

Fast-moving specks of rain fall against the darkness. The car is shooting through what looks like radio static. Vibrations hum in my head.

Asase licks the edges of a Rizla, rolls a spliff thin as the point of a knife.

'Open!' she says to Moose. She leans across, blows sensimilla in his face.

'I'm driving!' he says.

'Asase, stop handling him dem ways,' Rumer says. 'Man's got our lives in his hands.'

'We're safe,' Asase says. 'I've got nine lives. Ain't lost one yet.' She reverses the tape, plays a heavy dubplate version.

Soon there are trenches of black rain along the motorway, water spurting from the wheels of vehicles ahead of us.

Asase blows more smoke in Moose's direction and he tells her to stop.

I feel static on my skin and seconds later the car spins out of control. I hear Muma's voice, a one-note scream hanging in the air. My body slams against the side window as the tyres slough through a pool of rainwater and we skid fast towards the edge of the road.

Rumer is leaning forward and gripping Asase's shoulders with both hands. I close my eyes and brace for impact.

Moose brakes hard and the car screeches to a halt inches from the guard rail. The cassette tape stops. Nuth'n but the sound of the wipers swishing side to side. Headlights whoosh past like shooting stars.

Moose wipes his hands across his chest. 'Everybody all right?'

Asase turns to the back of the car, shakes off Rumer's grip, her expression more vulnerable than I've seen it in years.

'Speak to me, people,' Moose says. 'Everybody all right?'

Shards of rain beat against the windscreen, like glass hitting glass. The windows fog up.

I want to reach out to Moose, put my hand on his shoulder and thank him, but the close call already has me feeling exposed.

I don't remember Irving ever holding my hand. But I do recall his insistence that I learn to drive. Though I never officially got my licence, he taught me all his tricks – J-turns, Y-turns, handbrake spins, slalom – the steering wheel rotating between his weathered hands. At some point, I realised that these were lessons our people had been passing on to their children for hundreds of years.

First, teach them to shut dem mouth.

Second, teach them how to run.

And if somehow learning not to love was the unspoken third lesson from my poopa, then his teaching was done.

I think again about reaching out to touch Moose, but right then he turns sideways on, looking at Asase, me and Rumer. 'Saw rainforest light,' he says. He shudders and makes a sound at the back of his throat like he's clearing his mind.

'Enough drama for one night. Let's make a move,' he says.

And the moment's gone.

We take off again and light up another spliff. The car becomes a ghost ship sailing over motorway bridges.

The windows begin to shudder under a thudding beat. We follow it, picking up vibrations, then sound, until we're outside a grey estate of housing blocks rising into the brooding sky.

Moose parks near one of the buildings.. It's bitterly cold and there are puddles of rain, piss and God knows what else on the concrete stairs that wind upwards. We step over crumpled beer cans and sodden white takeaway boxes filled with gnawed chicken bones.

The lift comes down with two men and they tell us where the blues party is. We ride the lift to the twenty-fourth floor. Moose pays the tall Rasta with bead-tipped dreadlocks, his red trousers as tight and pinched as his nose.

We go inna the heat, slide through people in the hallway, into the front room. Dancers springing in and out of darkness like Jonkunnu masqueraders, faces masked with sweat. A record with scattergun drumming. MC calling out, 'Catch a fire.' The crowd pulling to the centre where two Rastas are blowing smoke out of pipes that are big as horns.

We line up against the wall, a firing squad of revolutionary roots riddims blasting us.

Drop inna our dance moves.

Die.

Rise up.

Sanctified.

Skank until we feel fire.

Moose dances with each of us in turn, content to go home with three shades of lipstick smudged on his shirt. He goes to the galley kitchen, comes back with his thick fingers splayed around three transparent plastic cups.

'Bubbly for the ladies,' he says.

'Sweet wine?' Asase says.

'Stop screwing up your face,' he says.

'I only drink rum. Black for life force. White for dashing out the dead,' she says, waving her hand through the air like she's banishing a ghost.

'They've got white rum,' he says.

'I'll tek it. Never know when somebody's gonna drop dead.'

Moose goes back to the kitchen. I track him, shouldering his way through the crowd, nodding here and there at people he recognises. By the time he returns with the drinks, Asase's pressed up against a red-skinned man in a turquoise satin suit. They're dancing by the wide window, their bodies smoky contortions; her arms criss-crossing his shoulders, hips dropping like scales, left to right on the off-beat, then hanging in the centre of the man's gyrating groin.

Low.

Lower.

Lowest.

Rude-rocksteady.

She raises a hand, beckons for her drink, takes it from Moose without glancing at him.

Me and Moose find a corner and dance by ourselves, orbiting each other, spiralling, our bodies pinwheels of sound. Rumer is skanking in the centre with some men.

Just before daylight, Asase finds us again, blueish shadows under her eyes, lipstick bleeding into the fine lines around her lips, curls flattened against her head like fossils. Rumer joins us and asks if we're moving to another party.

'I'm checking out,' Asase says and nods in the direction of a brown-skinned man who's standing in the doorway talking with a group of men, pulling leaflets from his jacket pockets and handing them out. An old man in a militant black leather bomber and skullcap takes a flyer.

'Careful is not some bad-breed man,' Moose warns her.

Asase raises her eyebrows. 'Herbert is a solicitor representing our people. He's giving out leaflets. Raising awareness. Says I can ride with him.'

'Safe,' Moose says. 'I've heard of the brother. Gonna check him.' He goes and shakes Herbert's hand and they say a few words to each other.

Asase stands there, smiling with the force of a bassline bustin' out of eighteen-inch woofers.

'Don't go,' Rumer says. She puts her arm through Asase's. 'Ain't the same without you.'

I say nuth'n.

Asase says she'll check us tomorrow at Dub Steppaz, then calls out, 'Me gaawn!'

The DJ is shouting, 'Repatriation through the bassline, mi bredrin.'

Rumer dances with a man, her headwrap and his stove-pipe hat knocking together in rub-a-dub style.

Fading vocals, muted horns, choked strings. Only hard-back ravers are left.

I skank, push down, buoyed, I float up again. My body feels looser now Asase's gone. I pluck imaginary notes out of the air. Scatter them around Moose's body. Move closer.

He takes my hand, pulls me to him. 'This is our dancing time.'

We melt into the sounds of a woman sing-crying, pleading with her man to save his best moves for her, and we dance between the white plastic cups bejewelled with lipstick marks, crumpled on the floor.

The selector puts on a scratchy old spiritual. We leave.

Moose drops Rumer at her yard before driving to my block. He keeps the engine running, ejects the mixtape. He's looking at me and it's a question or a statement and there's something that could be a smile, like his mouth doesn't know what it wants to do. He leans across and takes another tape out of the glove compartment and his arm brushes my knees.

My eyes are still in the smoke, and I'm feeling desire so strong I can't move.

'Special mix,' he says. He's looking inna my face and now he's smiling big-time as the song plays. Something about the goodness of country living.

I don't get out of the car.

'Take me with you,' I say. But that can't be my voice, me making the first move. It's more of a long-time feeling working its way outta me.

'Thought you'd never ask,' he says.

Half an hour of driving and we're in another urban town of tower blocks and small shops. Then across the River Thames into east London. We drive through towns that skirt a forest. Light morning rain. Flashbulb raindrops dotting the windscreen. Moose slows the car and points out a double-arch studio in a terrace of six identical buildings under an old railway bridge. The sign above the door reads MOOSE AND MAJOR, CABINET MAKERS.

'Me and my business partner, Nile,' he says. 'We set it up a while back. Doing a little t'ing, you know dem ways.'

He says they make furniture and sculptures out of reclaimed wood. 'Been training in Jamaica since I was eleven. Working with mahogany, blue mahoe, yuh know.' He strokes the side of the steering wheel. 'We don't cut trees. Keep nature sweet. Ah so it go!'

He drives for ten more minutes and everything turns green and we're on the edge of Epping Forest.

He parks outside a row of four-storey Victorian houses. Arched windows on all the floors. The rain has stopped and the sun's risen over the red roofs, slipstreams of white running through blue sky.

'Don't like cities,' he says. 'Never feel safe. Greener the better for me.' He opens the door and leads the way up the staircase to the third floor, the top of the house.

Inside Moose's flat, the early-morning light is like an otherworldly sunset. Polished parquet floor. Corduroy beanbags. The scent of pine and Bay Rum. Wooden sculptures of African women line the edge of the walls.

'Yours?'

He nods, crouches down, presses weed into the stomach well of one of the figurines. Lights it. Inhales like an obeah man.

Then he pulls me down on to the cushions. Our tongues coil, probe darkness. From the first touch his loving haunts my body, floods it with a desire that is both poison and antidote. Yellow-green smoke floats out of his carvings, sidewinding spirits with ringed empty faces, watching us.

He leads me into the bedroom. 'I'm all yours,' he says.

I tie my legs around his body, rock, roll on top of him, put my hands over his mouth, breathe against the dark interior of my body until my lungs open up and bottled-up feelings spill out.

Fuck us to sleep.

We wake mid-morning. Make love. Drift into lucid dreams, sound waves and down-low bruck-up voices.

No mek dem tek him, child.

Lunchtime and we're in the kitchen at the back of the flat. A pan of plantain and dumplings sizzling on the stove, Moose singing as he grates cocoa pods and nutmeg. I sit on a chair by a large wooden table. An arched window looks on to the edge of the forest.

'Don't get this kinda view on the Tombstone Estate,' I say.

He gives me a mug of syrupy cocoa. 'Yard-style,' he says.

'Who taught you?' I ask.

'Granny Itiba.'

'Granny who?'

He laughs. 'Grown men have grannies, don't they?' He sits opposite me, puts his feet against mine under the table.

'Cocoa tea is my ritual,' he says. 'For protection, energy. After last night, something tells me I'm gonna need nuff vitality to handle you!'

Heat spreads across my face. 'I . . . the weed—'

'Don't apologise. That kinda surprise I check for.'

He pours more cocoa into my mug. 'First thing in the morning, last thing at night,' he says. 'Boiled for eleven minutes, not a second more. Granny's a magician. She can mek food outta flour, water, air. Her dumplings are as light as sugar clouds.' He tells me that Granny Itiba spins cloth as fine as mist from lace-bark trees. I wonder about the texture of his heart, if it's as delicate. I ask where she lives.

'Maggotty,' he says. 'Small town at the head of Black River. Cockpit Country.' He sprinkles cinnamon and brown sugar on the plantains. 'Your people told you 'bout Cockpit Country, right? The Maroons?'

'Yeah, Queen Nanny, but not Cockpit Country.'

He does it Caribbean style, standing like he's got an audience of hundreds. He tells me about the runaway rebels buried there. 'Nuth'n but jungle humps and sinkholes with drops thousands of feet into the belly of the earth,' he says. 'Granny Itiba took me there, close to dread-drop zones that can tek yuh to death while you're singing for your soul.

'Man can find his way outta the bush. Nah so with the concrete city we live in. Too easy to get locked in, trapped. Don't wanna live with chains.'

The story moves like a trail of smoke, winding its way into my body.

'Granny knows Cockpit Country like nobody else,' he says. 'Took me there with me bend-up legs soon as I could walk. Vine round my waist, clenched in her hand, leading, tied me to her, connecting us to the bush.' He looks at me. 'Man needs connections, nah true?'

'Even to those who're gone?'

'Dead or alive, bonds are tight. Have to get back to our people, our land,' he says.

I think about Muma, replaying my faint memories of her singing, her voice syrupy, her eyes bright. In my visions, she takes me to a sugar-coated village of floating castles high on a mountain where abeng horns are blowing, the sound soaring over the ocean.

'I'm going back to Jamaica next year – Maggotty, my hometown,' he says. 'For good this time. Granny's the last of my family; don't wanna leave it too late. Don't feel free in the city. You know how it is. Having to stick to the places my Black face is known. Moving careful everywhere else. Time is eaten up by those places. The rainforest is calling me.'

I imagine the sounds of that place entering my body, cooling it.

Later, Moose drives me home, one of his mixtapes playing, a dub track of stripped-down drums and bass, duppy feedback. We turn into the Tombstone Estate. He parks and ejects the cassette, gives it to me.

'I made this the night I met you.'

I take the tape, it reads: *Cockpit Country Dreaming*. He's leaning forward as if he's going to kiss me. I don't know how to say goodbye, so I open the car door, take my bag and say, 'I'll play it tonight.' I get out of the car and watch him drive away. A new track playing, lovers rock, a woman's voice hitting a high C.

4

Resonance

I was living on empty before Moose, working the night shift Mondays to Thursdays, taking overtime at the weekends whenever I could. Now we spend all our Sundays together. Sometimes I go to his place after a Saturday rave. Or he calls from his workshop on Sunday afternoon to tell me he's finishing up and he'll head home, hold a fresh, then get me. But on those occasions I say no, we'll be losing time. Instead I get a cab, let myself in with the spare key he gave me.

His apartment is always quiet when I arrive. No music. Ganja burning in his wooden sculptures, a mug of cocoa and rum. His eyes half-shut.

I go to his bed and wait. Leave him reclining on the floor cushions, lost in his thoughts about the strength of the beams, whether to keep the notches and irregular cuts, how to slice into the inner parts of the wood.

The waiting is never wasted. My body's alight beneath the cool sheets.

We make love when he comes to bed. No talking. His large hands smooth out my body, like he's calculating the capacity of each limb, weighing up how much I can take.

Seven o'clock one Monday morning, me and Moose are in bed. It's dark, raining heavily outside. We'd spent all afternoon walking in the forest yesterday and I'm mash-up.

I roll over and whisper in his ear, 'What do I tell work?'

He turns on his side to face me and whispers back, 'I'll call. "This is Yamaye's partner. She won't be in for her shift tonight, she's been making love all night and she can't move." ' He's laughing hard.

I light-punch him on his arm.

'Stay a few days,' he says. 'Have the place to yourself. I wanna come home from work and find you here.'

'What's in it for me?'

'Cocoa tea, fried dumpling, ackee and saltfish.'

'I think Asase and Rumer know about us,' I say. 'Rumer looks at me funny whenever I mention you.'

'Look at your face. It can't lie.'

I stroke his cheek. 'Same as you,' I say, wondering whether he would lie.

He gets out of bed, puts on a rare-groove mixtape with songs about silver shadows, islands within islands and everlasting love.

He leaves for work and I stay in bed, re-dreaming the night, chasing his voice through the morning gloom. I'll live on this until I see him later.

March. Flecks of light-filled raindrops on the window. We're at Moose's flat, the day after a riddim-rocking Saturday night at the Crypt.

I'm sitting at the dining table in my knickers and camisole top, my legs tucked under my chin, chanting lyrics inside my head to the dub music that goes on and on. Reggae with the vocals replaced by exploding-planet instrumentals.

Moose is stirring a pot of red peas on the stove, dropping in sprigs of fresh thyme, swaying as he hums some old-time tune, his arse shifting left to right in his black boxers. His tightly packed back muscles are like undercurrents beneath his deep-blue T-shirt.

'Lunch in a hour,' he says.

'Not gonna last,' I say.

'The lower the flame, the stronger the taste,' he says. But he opens the oven door, spears two breadcrumb-coated chicken wings, sprinkles little dots of red chilli sauce on them and presents them to me on a side plate, running his hand through my plaits that are beaded with small gold seashells. Waterfall hair, that's what he calls it.

He goes back to the pot on the stove. 'Been thinking,' he says.

I bite into the crispy skin. 'Nice.'

'We should head out somewhere for a weekend. Next Friday.'

My chest is an echo-box, snippets of confused sound-feelings running through. I look past him at the hundreds of raindrops sliding down the window.

'Say something,' he says.

'I just wasn't expecting . . .'

'Found a lockdown cabin in Scotland. Mountains, walks, open fires.'

'Won't it be cold?'

'Yamaye, I'm asking you to come to Scotland, not Siberia.' He crouches by my chair and holds on to my arms. 'Everything all right?'

Red liquid bubbles up and threatens to spill over the edge of the pot.

'I've never been away with a man before,' I say.

'We'll be together on another level. A new scene,' he says. 'Thought you'd be happy.' He stands up, raises his arms, palms upturned, then drops them by his side.

I feel to tell him that I love him bad, but I'm afraid of songs with upbeat words and downbeat music and up to now that's all I've known of love. I wonder if this is how Irving courted Muma – gave her the world and then, once he had her, turned her world upside down.

Moose says if I'm not up for it, he'll go alone. After lunch, he's at the sink washing up, humming a song. Everything seems so familiar, easy. I say yes, yes, I want to go more than anything. Of course I do. If he notices the glint of terror in my voice, he doesn't say anything.

When Friday finally comes, we leave close to midnight, and the roads are clear.

Moose says he's more than up for driving this late. He's made four 120-minute mixtapes; it's deep-consciousness dub-listening time. I feel safe in his car; the smell of his river-water musk aftershave, old leather, petrol. The hypnotic swishing of the wipers. Light from oncoming headlamps flood the windscreen. The streets are deserted, the shops and historic buildings covered in sleet. It feels strange going so far from Norwood, outside the city. Uncharted waters.

It's snowing heavily by the time we get to Edinburgh, and we stop for coffee and a fry-up at a greasy spoon. We set off with snow spinning in the air, ghost notes, brittle, soundless. Moose steers in silent concentration through mutating roads and yellow mist. We arrive in Aviemore at nine in the morning.

Snow's even heavier now. After a few wrong turns we pull up outside Cedar Lodge, a two-storey cabin made of honey-coloured logs, set on a slope that goes down to a river. The agent is inside, and he opens the door as we park. We get out. Snow's whirring in front of my eyes; the wind's stinging. We plod towards him. He shakes our hands. We must look odd to him in our moon boots and neon ski jackets. He gives us a tour of the house, which smells as if we're in a forest. The lounge has a table and tartan sofa; the main bedroom has a small balcony and views of the river. He tells us the best places to go for meals and hikes.

Before he goes, he asks if we want a hand lighting the fire. Moose says he's a country boy, fires are his thing, and the wood burner is roaring in minutes.

We get our luggage from the car – two bags and the icebox of marinaded mutton and fish, fresh thyme, dasheen, yellow yam and ripe plantain that Moose has prepared. I look up at the mountains across the valley where scattered clouds are merging.

Moose scatters herbs into the fire.

'You can forget how a place looks, but smell and sound stay in your memory box,' he says.

'Shall I?' I ask and he bows and says, 'Go ahead.'

I put on a mixtape, one that I've made of myself singing and chatting lyrics to a rootsy dub track of spiritual drumming and chanting.

We skank around the fire like a returning tribe of warriors.

When the house is warm, we go out and walk up the slope out back. The snow-covered earth reminds me of the drop-out void in a dub track.

'Sing for me,' Moose says.

I sing:

'in the still of the night
a calm that inspires loving
I call out your name again and again'

Snow, valley, mountains and wind make my voice sound like a mutation of earthly and unearthly sounds.

'You inspire loving,' Moose says. 'Too saaaf?'

'You can't take it back,' I say. We laugh and I hold his hand and we walk down the slope to get a better view of the mountain behind the cabin, now in the distance.

Moose takes a Polaroid of us, our backs to the mountain. The slimy image slides out. I hold the photo; it's sticky as a newborn. I picture what a child of our own might look like. His brown eyes and noble wide nose; Muma's square-cut cheekbones.

'Careful, it's not developed,' he says.

Undeveloped, I think. That's what I've been up until now. With Moose, I feel myself changing.

I flap the photo and hold it up in the air. It begins to reveal his black-rimmed eyes squinting against snow light, his face like something projected from the past; I'm blinking, a cautious smile on my face.

We go back to the cabin and sleep. In the evening, he puts on the silly frilly apron that's hanging on the oven door. He stews the mutton and boils and grills the dasheen and yam until they're crispy and golden.

At the dinner table, as we're eating, he says, 'Still don't understand why you won't tell Asase and Rumer about us. They must suspect.'

'Don't want people up in our business.'

He puts down his knife and fork in the middle of his plate and pushes it away. 'I'm into openness, Yamaye.'

'When we're tight, we can tell them.'

'If this isn't tight, what is!'

'You're shouting.'

He breathes out, long and slow. 'Where do we go from here if everything's secret?'

'I just need—'

'Where did you tell Asase and Rumer you'd be this weekend?'

'Overtime.'

'See deh. Nothing good comes outta secrets.'

Can't tell him I'm afraid that Asase might make a move on him if she finds out how big his furniture business is getting. Don't know if my thinking is off. Maybe I've got Irving's secretive tendencies.

'I'm going for a walk!' he says.

'It's pitch-black.'

He takes a torch from the dresser and goes out.

I go to bed. The door bangs shut as he returns a short while later. Faint sound of a trombone blowing distant, lonely notes. He wakes me in the middle of the night with strokes up and down my back. Says he's sorry, though he hasn't done anything wrong.

I climb on top of him and he moans.

'Feel my love,' he says.

'I do,' is all I can say. 'No more secrets. I promise.'

Afterwards, he curls his body behind me and throws his arm over my shoulder. I drift off, floating across snowy mountains. Weightless.

April. One a dem nights. Bongo Natty's sound system is dropping macca tunes in the Crypt. Shimmering lines of electric bass; clouds of white noise. The regulars rocking and swinging, a body of people protected by dub force field.

Lego emerges, head bobbing in the centre of the massive, firing his hands and walking stick in the air. He makes his way towards us, nods at Asase and Rumer. Asks if I'm OK. We shout a few words into each other's ears, pretend we can hear what the other is saying. I give him the pack of cigarettes I buy for him every week.

We grew up together on the Tombstone Estate, same tower block. Undercover police trailed him for weeks before busting inna his flat two years ago. They were looking for his brother, Carlos, who was always up to no good. Lego knew he was in for a kicking or worse, so he jumped over the balcony, four storeys up, broke his leg, and crawled and hid in the rubbish chute till Babylon stopped looking. By the time he got to a hospital it was days later, and gangrene had eaten away most of his foot. His leg was amputated. Now he hides out somewhere in the Crypt. Father Mullaney gives him sanctuary. He never goes out in daylight. His black skin is ashy; he's more or less smoke. His real name's Grover Clarke, but Bongo Natty gave him the name Lego after he lost his leg, and that's all people call him now.

He doesn't deserve to be living like this. He used to go shopping with Ms Grace, his mother. Pulled the tartan trolley for her; carried bags of yam and cassava with no shame. He never ran the streets like his brother Carlos. He was usually in his room, fine-tuning sets for the sound-system men, adjusting acoustics between speakers, fiddling with faders and echo units. Listening to frequencies that no one else could hear.

Lego says he owes everything to Bongo Natty, who persuaded Father Mullaney to give him shelter by quoting verses from the Bible: *A refuge from the storm, a shade from the heat.*

I stay close to Lego so no one will pull me for a dance. Moose couldn't come tonight. He and Nile are working on a big project for a client.

The feedback sounds of the music come from a strange landscape. Reminds me of our weekend in Scotland, the way random animal sounds loomed out of the white silence at intervals; reminds me of my promise to tell Asase and Rumer about our relationship. I tried to when we were dressing in Asase's bedroom, but I couldn't get the words out.

Lego shouts in my ear; whatever he says is swallowed by syncopated snare drums and a clavinet bassline. Horns extend into vanishing points. Lego disappears.

I regroup with Asase and Rumer and we dance to a revival track before leaving.

It's fresh outside, a bright spring morning. We slip our satin bombers off our shoulders and hold our bare arms up to the sunlight. Our underground bodies fade away.

The streets are littered with cans and cigarette stubs. The air smells of urine and the bleach that a shop owner has thrown on to the pavement; incense from a newspaper stand swirls and fades. A man unloading crates of food from a lorry looks at us in our slip dresses and whistles.

'Don't bother with that,' Asase growls, and he spits on the pavement as we walk past.

There's a light on in Dup Steppaz and Asase knocks on the window. Eustace comes out from the back room. He smiles at us, raises the counter, opens the door.

'Good session?' he asks.

'Dub never lets you down,' Asase says.

He beckons us in and guides us to the rear room.

A tan leather and chrome sofa, a black desk with letters and wallet files, a bottle and a half-full glass. He shoves the papers into the files.

'Nice,' Rumer says.

'Not been here before?' Eustace asks.

'Never had the privilege,' Asase says.

We sit on the sofa and he pours shots of gold-coloured rum into coffee mugs.

He goes through to the shop and puts on a bass-heavy instrumental, the vocals stripped away to a ghostly resonance.

'He's not a bad-looking bredda,' Asase says.

'Married – out of bounds,' Rumer says.

'Just saying!' Asase says.

Music drifts in, a man's voice growing faint. Bassline isolated, suspended. A pulse fades and comes back again, stronger.

'Got news,' I say.

Asase squints at me.

'Me and Moose—' Cold excitement slides down my throat to my gut. 'We're—'

Rumer shouts, 'I knew it!'

I laugh with relief, giggle awkwardly.

There's silence as Asase tips the mug of rum to her lips before leaning forward, the gold ducket around her neck swinging like a pendulum. Then she puts the cup on the table, sliding it deliberately between the other two mugs as if she's playing a game of chess.

Her mouth opens like she's struggling to find the right words. 'Gyal, you been holding out on us,' she says. She irons out her face, straightens her back. 'Thought it was you and Lego that had a little thing going on.'

'Lego! He's like a brother,' I say. 'And he's—' I stop myself.

'Hiding inna the Crypt,' she says.

'No, he's not. I didn't—' I don't know whether Asase has somehow found out about Lego or has worked it out. No one else knows he's there.

She swats the air. 'Anyways. Good for you,' Asase says. 'Moose isn't everybody's type. But he ain't from Norwood. That's something, at least.'

'Bet he's got some moooves?' Rumer says. She gets up and starts gyrating, laughing.

'Fe mi business,' I say.

Me and Rumer are laughing. It feels real now it's out in the open, I feel the excitement of sharing this with my sistren.

'Where's your man tonight, anyway?' Asase asks. 'Sure he ain't got some baby-mother somewhere?'

'Asase!' I say, but I'm laughing.

'Just looking out for my gyal,' she says. 'Don't want no man messing with you. You know what men are like – raving every week while their woman's home with the pickney and nuth'n to look forward to but another repeat of *Colombo* and a slice of bullah cake.'

Rumer asks if Herbert is the same and Asase says he's always running off in the middle of the night to some police station to bail a youth.

I say that he's doing something worthwhile, and she can't be vex with Herbert for that. I tell them that I've been to Moose's place and there's no woman there. No children.

Music drifts in from the shop, slow roots drumming.

Rumer takes a big gulp of rum, closes her eyes. 'Tiredness is gonna catch us here,' she says.

'We sleep where we drop,' Asase says.

I wake up on the sofa. My face squelched into Rumer's armpit. A moth flits around the glass globe ceiling lightshade. Two more blackened bodies unmoving inside.

I hear Asase and Eustace talking and laughing. The volume of the music goes up. Their laughter fades into a taut push-pull riddim tension.

5

Psychic-Sonic Shay Shay

We're at Asase's house, lounging in the front room, killing time before we rave. It's spring and the trees are raining white and pink blossoms. Asase is lying on the sofa, her feet on Rumer's lap as Rumer varnishes Asase's toenails with Midnight Purple. I sit on the floor, my back against the wall, the window above. Blue Lady is on the TV outside Downing Street, ready to go in and take charge. She's standing there, stoosh with her white-powdered face, pearl earrings, long-arsed vowels. Police and journalists around her. A crowd cheering and booing. She's quoting St Francis of Assisi.

'Harmony and truth, my arse!' Rumer says. Her pale blue eyes are wide and bright. Her dyed-black hair is hanging down her back, static, sparking. 'All she's done is stir things up. National Front in pussy-bow blouses.'

'Things ah gwaaan,' Asase says, whiplashing forefinger against thumb. 'The first woman at the control tower of the country. Bad Blue Bitch! Show the man dem.' She jumps off the sofa, all muscle and outta-da-way breasts.

'She's a terror,' I say. 'Disconnect her.'

'Yamaye, you're too fraidy-fraidy,' Asase says.

I wanna snap back that there's more to me than that. Yeah, I'm quiet, watchful, like Irving. Safe in my cocoon, I keep my mouth shut. But still.

She finger-slaps with her right hand, says, 'Yuh batty's gotta likk the ground from time to time, Yamaye. But I'm inna you all the same.' She's laughing, the way she does when she's inside her yard, because this hard-back town won't let her wear anything but a screw-face. At home, she unclenches her jawbone, her eyes, her held-in breath. Takes off her mask.

Oraca comes out of the kitchen and stands in the archway that separates the back and front rooms. She's drying her hands on a dishcloth, the smell of fish and the ocean on her. She's a tall woman with wet, dark brown eyes and skin. At fifty, she still has a narrow waist, broad shoulders and sleek, muscled biceps. Always wears a hairnet, pulled tight around her face, hanging down her neck, her black hair trapped inside it. As soft as she's strong, Oraca is the one who cries for us, bawling at sad films, at the thought of Asase in pain or at the mention of Muma's name. Oraca's told me often enough that her village is where she learned to stare in the just-dead eyes of a fish, gut it head to tail with one twist of a knife. Must be in the blood, because Asase keeps a small ivory-handled blade in the zipped pocket of her raving bag. Oraca tells everyone that her ancestry can be traced to Ashantis from the Gold Coast, who were feared by the Spanish, French and English who enslaved them. Feared because of their rebellions, dances, drums and spells. Ashanti women who carried songs in their bellies. She says Muma musta been Ashanti too, because of the bandu-drum pitch of her voice.

'Woman must run things,' Oraca says. 'But dat Blue Lady ah trouble.' Her watery black eyes glint.

'Tell it, Mrs O,' Rumer says.

'Man preach revolution, but woman carry its sound,' Oraca says.

She says she feels the ocean in her belly when something bad is going to happen. Tells us again about the time she was pregnant with Asase and her husband, Hezekiah, took in a young woman lodger and put her in the back room with only a screen to separate her. 'Said we needed money for de baby,' Oraca says. 'From that day me start to feel sick to me stomach. Him tek himself to that dry-bone woman every night when my belly was big.' She brushes down her breasts with the dishcloth, twists her mouth. 'When Asase was born I didn't give her me breast. Couldn't give de child anything. That man bruck me spirit! Doctor wanted to tek Asase away.'

'As if!' Asase says.

'Hear me out,' Oraca says. 'One night me dream me dead mooma, singing instructions to me. Next day me steam black tilapia with peacock-flower seeds and saltwater. Me serve the food to dat man who still calls himself my husband. I fed him until he was black and blue. That fish twisted his insides for weeks. Him couldn't put him foot 'pon the ground. It sweet me, I have to say.'

Rumer says, 'My ma would love that recipe. Shut my pa up.'

Oraca twirls, her indigo skirt spinning around her legs, lashing the air of the back room with the dishcloth as if the tenant is still there. We bust out laughing.

'Two-two's and that beaded-head woman was gone,' she says. 'I wasn't ramping. There are ways and ways to do things.'

Oraca loves holding court in her yard, day or night. She works all hours at the bread factory. She lives vicariously through our talk of raves, the latest dance moves, men, sex. Hezekiah's long gone. He left nine years ago to live with a young woman on the other side of town. His clothes are still in the house, his slippers under the stairs. He darkens the doorstep once a month, lets his maaga self in with his key, hands shaking. All he says to Oraca is, 'Is the kettle boiling?' And she gives him a plate of fried fish and a mug of bush tea. Asase sometimes runs to make the drink so she can spit in it.

Oraca cotches on the arm of the sofa. 'Spirits know I gave birth to

Asase, wailing and singing, busting my heart strings to push her through. I teach her not to let no man put her down. Ever.'

She speaks in scalding undertones, and I realise that Oraca suppresses her anger, like me. Because nowhere's safe – not the streets, governed by police with barbed-wire veins; not our homes, ruled by men with power fists as misshapen as their wounds. The only place to live and rage from is our hearts.

A week later, it's a Sunday, but Moose insists on picking me up from home that evening. He doesn't want me to take trains or a taxi, says we're going somewhere special. After the long cold winter, the May sun feels hot on my face. The evenings are warm and musky with the smell of pollen, earth, cut grass and the scent of goats from yesterday's cattle market. It's one of those nights where everything sparkles: the air, trees, people's faces. The narrow windows of the tower blocks are wide open and old people are shaking rugs and cushions; youth are sitting on the stairwells drinking beer from cans, talking and laughing.

I get into the car and he whistles. 'Yuh gone outtanational with that dress!'

I'm wearing a black top and midi skirt spun in gauzy raw silk. Two weeks' wages and a small loan from Irving. It looks like it's been spliced from the moon and stars.

I haven't seen Moose in three weeks. He's been preparing a load of warped and twisted reclaimed oak, working out the cracks and loose knots to make the hull and planking for a model slave ship that a Guyanese artist, Kalihna, is creating. I've never seen him so excited by a project.

I bought the outfit so he would do to me what he's been doing to that wood.

The car smells like a forest pine with hints of flower-scented dew.

'Where are we heading?'

'I missed you too,' he says.

I laugh and he says we're going to the river.

I can see he's tired from work, so I don't ask any more questions. We drive through Norwood, past fields, scrub and wastelands where groups of people are camping in the fading light with food and drink, playing pop music about messages in bottles, hearts of glass and tragedy. Further ahead, red-and-green barges drift along the canals. I imagine a day like this, hundreds of years ago, pagans dancing around the beech trees, leaves braided in their hair, making offerings of seeds and song.

We drive through the heart of London, a steady flow of traffic, diners going in and out of restaurants and pubs. Black metal cranes loom over cathedrals and office tower blocks. We park on a side street near the pier and walk along the Embankment. People are clustered outside riverside taverns, laughing, singing football anthems and old ballads, shouting. We go down steps on to a pontoon where boats are moored. Brightly lit floating discos. Silhouettes of passengers on lower decks ripple to soft music. Black water lapping at the boats like the sound of hands clamouring against wet wood.

'This is us,' Moose says when we come to a large, two-tiered riverboat packed with people. We join the queue on the ramp and he gives the man in the booth our tickets.

On board, classical music streams – violins, cellos, organs, trumpets, horns – triumphant sounding.

'It's one of them dine-and-dance things,' Moose says. He sounds unsure, as if this isn't what he was expecting.

'It's different,' I say.

'I didn't think it was gonna be this kind of dance.'

'First time for everything.'

He holds my hand as we walk to the top deck. It's full of white-haired couples and tourists taking photos.

'Thought we'd have a serious date. Now that everyone knows about us.'

'It's perfect,' I say.

There are tables set for dinner at the bow. I stand at the stern, lean over the railings. He stands behind me, wraps his arms around my waist. The boat begins to sail through a deepening purple night, dotted with lights from boats in the distance. Past the old sugar warehouses of the West India Docks where abandoned flat-bottomed barges are moored. The music sounds less triumphant now, fragile, haunting.

'I wanted us to have a better look at the river,' Moose says.

'In the dark?'

'Feel seh you and me are searching.'

He points to warehouses with cast-iron doors and shutters, tells me that hundreds of years ago they were used to store mahogany from the Caribbean. There was a fire and thousands of mahogany logs were burned. I imagine burning black ash washed out to sea, drifting into the Atlantic, back to where they came from.

We stare into the depths of the river.

'A lot more of our past still hidden in that water,' Moose says. 'Kalihna could tell us all about it.'

'How would he know?'

He says Kalihna dives with marine archaeologists who document slave-ship wrecks. It feeds his art. He's always on the move between the Gold Coast, the Caribbean, Guyana.

He squeezes me. 'Where you and me belong, Yamaye? Jamaica? Some other place?' Maybe we could live like Kalihna. London to Jamaica to Africa.

I turn to face him. 'I'm not used to this.'

'This – what? Closeness? Talk about the future?'

The word closeness makes the heat in my heart rise to my cheeks and I feel shame for the way I make love to him. Wild and demanding because I love him bad-bad.

We go to a table near the bow.

Moose orders champagne; we clink glasses and I take big mouthfuls, feel my throat fill with bubbles. I tell him that I've never made plans with anyone before. Certainly not with the three so-so boyfriends that lasted a year or two each. Men I met at the Crypt and danced with in the corners of blacked-out blues parties for weeks before ending up in their beds, then their kitchens. When I started to burn the food, the dancing dried up, and the music stopped.

'The closest thing to intimacy I've known is with Asase and Rumer,' I say.

'Your poopa?'

'True seh, I don't wanna think 'bout Asase, Rumer, Irving or the Tombstone Estate tonight.' I imagine me and Moose sailing across the Atlantic, following those trails of molten sugar and ash, heading for a home far away.

'You're different without your friends,' he says.

'Good? Bad?' I ask.

'At ease.'

It's more than that. I feel Moose in the way I feel dub when the supra-watt bass enters my body. Deconstructing, rebuilding, firing strength. Hope.

Couples are dancing, their bodies moving like the stars above, a floating stillness.

'Let's dance,' I say.

'To this music?'

I pull him to his feet. 'Any excuse to get my arms around you.' He puts up his hands in fake surrender.

I rest my head on his shoulder, and as I look into the water I realise that what I want from Moose on the Sunday nights that I go to him is not his body. It's his peace.

The following Saturday, I'm at the Crypt with Asase and Rumer. Moose has finally finished the project and has taken the wood to the studio in Bristol where Kalihna is working, said he'll join us later if he's back in time.

Bongo Natty is handing out red leaflets by the door, as usual, shouting, 'Dis yah is the sound revolution. Tek it to the streets.'

Asase takes money out of her silk purse and pays for us. 'Man dem think the revolution is theirs. Fuckeries!' she says.

'You vex with Herbert?' Rumer asks. 'He skanked you?'

'He's too full of himself. Boasty!' Asase says. She says he's more inna his campaigns than her. 'I'm gonna drop him, he ain't bucking up his ideas.'

'He's representing,' I say. 'Respect to the man. You gonna dash him?'

Rumer places her arms on Asase's shoulders and pulls her towards the side of her body. 'Stick with the sistren,' she says.

'I'm not fixing myself round any man's schedule,' Asase says, and she shrugs Rumer off, pushes her way down the stairs where people are standing on either side, talking and smoking.

At the large wooden door to the Crypt, she pats the waves of her hair into place and says she's gonna find herself a sweet bwoy tonight.

We go into the dance hall and I close the door behind me, shutting off the slim beam of light. Lego dances with us in a small circle, squatting low, our arms pulling the air slow-mo, dragging ourselves outta the deep.

MC at the decks freestyling to the riddims.

Rumer's getting bounced by a stony-faced Stix-Gyal on the edge of our little scene. Rumer's pale face stands out in the darkness; she holds her ground, and Asase steps in, skanking in a wide arc, arms in front, like a minesweeper.

'Forward with yuh fuckeries,' Asase shouts at her.

The woman turns her back on us, shakes her batty and sways away. Rumer links her arm through Asase's, looking up at her, and Asase slows to a serious two-step, nodding her head like a hardened Stix-Man. She controls it like dat.

I dance the psychic-sonic-shuffle, rolling my shoulders to dub drums and analogue delay.

Moose's voice, a rubbery bassline from far away: *Always, Baby. Always.*

The lights in the Crypt flash. Off. On. Off.

Asase and Rumer squat as low as they can, gyrating to imaginary ropes. Rumer staying close to Asase, shaping her moves around Asase's body, a call-and-response sway as she smiles across at her.

Lego pulls me for a dance, a slow two-step shuffle, one arm around my waist, the other holding on to his walking stick. He dips with his right leg and slides to the left on his artificial leg. His neck smells of ash and the faintest whiff of mould.

In the limbo hours of morning, Asase starts to insist we all leave the Crypt to find one of the rare-groove parties in the Dead Water area on the southern side of town.

Moose still hasn't shown, so we take a taxi. As we pass by Dub Steppaz, Asase asks the driver to stop. There's a dim light. Asase says she's going to ask Eustace for a spliff, won't be long. She's not going to bed without a draw. Fifteen minutes later and she's still not back, the driver is getting impatient, blows his horn. When she returns to the car Rumer asks why the hold-up and she laughs and says Eustace took some persuading. Asase has been spending a lot more time hanging out in Dub Steppaz and I wonder if it's because I'm with Moose and not with her.

From the back of the car, I try to catch her face in the side-mirror on her side but she's looking straight ahead.

Pale grey light. Across the hump bridge, the road on the left takes you to Devil's Tunnel and Woodlands Place. The minicab turns right on to Shuffy Row, a narrow lane running alongside the towpath and the canal that cuts through the Dead Water area.

I don't want to party any more. Feeling just to head home and tune in to the mixtapes Moose makes for me. One a month since that first night together. Dubplate, roots, lovers rock, rare grooves. Each cassette has a title:

Going Back in Time
No Rhyme, No Reason
Mother Earth
Hear Me When I Call

But Irving will be awake soon, brewing coffee, smoking up the kitchen with his roll-ups, clearing his throat like he's got something to say.

We get out the cab and Rumer steps ahead of us inside the front garden, swaying to the music. 'Crucial scene, this,' she says.

Asase puts her arm through mine. 'Come on, babes. Still time for you to catch a sweet bwoy.'

'Thought it was you who was looking.'

She laughs. 'I don't need one after all.'

Inside, the bare room is almost empty – a few women bubbling in liquid dresses, shay-shaying. Men with philosopher's triangular beards and pine-tree cologne. Dancers strung around like an orchestra, playing their bodies. The Rare Groovers are there as usual, three shades of Black: cornmeal-yellow, conker-brown and blueberry-black. Three octaves rocking the revolution in their own way. After the raves they give out books about ancient Egyptians, filled with stories of secret trade routes and life-giving potions.

They're lined up side by side, stepping in the old ways: Shay Shay, Quadrille, Gerreh and Ettu. Backs arched so far back their heads hang behind them like duppies. Black duster coats flowing as they dance the Gumbay, their bodies wheeling.

Asase stands to the right of them, swaying in their slipstream. Rumer's winding up near the window seat, violet morning light streaming into her blue eyes, staring at Asase as if she's seeing her for the first time.

I dance behind the Rare Groovers. Their arms move like tentacles. A waxy dubplate likking slow-mo.

The cornmeal-coloured groover in the middle spins and faces me, looking inna my eyes like he knows everything about me. He turns again, picks up the flow of his bredrin.

And their backs arch further. They're dancing the Zella, the death ritual. A stirring in my gut, but I don't know what it means.

Two days later, Moose still hasn't returned the two messages I left on his answering machine the morning after the party. I wait a day before calling his workshop. I've never contacted him at work before and I feel like I'm crossing a boundary, fussing, cramping his style.

A man answers, says he's Nile. I say I want to speak to Moose and he asks my name.

'Oh, Yamaye. Where you calling from?' Nile asks.

'My yard.'

'You alone?'

'Why, what's going on?'

'I didn't have your number. Sit down, please,' Nile says.

'You're scaring me.'

'Moose was arrested on Sunday. He was in police cells—'

'Where? I'll mek a move, he'll need—'

'No, Yamaye. Listen, please!' Then softly: 'Please . . .'

There's pressure in my ears, broken images of Moose that flit like fireflies.

'They say he started fighting. They restrained him. My bredrin is dead.'

My heart's a single wailing note rising outta my ribcage, dragging my guts through my mouth. I coil the telephone cable round and round my wrists.

Pull tighter and tighter. Can't breathe.

'Yamaye, Yamaye, please. I'm so sorry to tell you like this.'

I drop the phone. Scream. My voice travelling. I'm looking down from the roof of the Tombstone tower block, seeing Black people getting sucked inna sinkholes of siren sounds, the yellow outline of a body on the ground. Fragments of Moose pulsing sound waves of red, green, gold.

6

Bluesing

A week of early summer rain floods the streets and Resurrection Cemetery. Grave flowers float in red clay water that flows like blood. Sandstone bubbles up to the surface carrying the thin, sharp bones of ancient fish.

Shutdown: I sleep and cry in the days. Take two weeks off work.

Asase and Rumer come every night. We stay up late, piled on to my bed, our backs against the wall, the large window above us. Sit in darkness except for the bleed-out light of a red sky. Lovers rock notes high inna one-way loneliness, Asase and Rumer either side of me, their arms linked through mine. They check my mood by how I look instead of listening to my body like I want them to.

At the end of the week, I see the way they check each other, as if they've tried everything and now what? I say thanks for the support but I'm gonna lay low for a while, cry this thing out.

I stop answering the door or the telephone. One thought going round and round in my head like a kete-repeater drumbeat: Why? Why? Why? I get up in the night, my legs are weighed down, my joints on fire. I rummage through the kitchen cupboards, tear open a packet of chocolate-covered biscuits, drink white rum from the bottle. Sugar.

It built Babylon.

Destroyed us.

I go to bed, pull the candlewick blanket over me. No control over my trembling body. My ribs are cold, chattering teeth. I shake into exhaustion, then sleep. Dream I'm deep-diving in the ocean with Black women. They look like Muma. And me. Same solar-plexus eyes. They've been floating there for hundreds of years carrying the weight of water on their heads.

Moose is underwater too, but he's further down, I can't reach him. His name erupts from my gut, a wild animal wailing. The voice isn't mine, but it must be.

At the end of the week, Irving comes home at six like he does most days. The old pipes in the bathroom clank and rattle as he turns on the rusty taps. Hawking, gargling, clearing his throat.

Grief has drawn out feelings I never knew I had. Sometimes I want to put my arms around Irving's neck and cling. Other times, I feel to circle his throat with my hands and squeeze and squeeze the silence outta him.

He's sitting at the kitchen table, stirring sorrel tea in the green enamel teapot, drinking it to clear his throat of the fumes of the garage.

I've been avoiding him, staying in my room, only leaving to grab water biscuits and slabs of cheese at night. Still refusing to take calls from Asase or Rumer.

'Sorry 'bout your man,' he says.

I don't say anything.

'Ah so life go.' He presses the back of the teaspoon against the red hibiscus leaves in the strainer. Pours the tea.

I hold the mug between my palms and let the fire soak into my skin. Go to the rain-speckled window. Within each raindrop I see memories, images flashing from Moose's photo albums: Granny Itiba on her land with an armful of cocoa beans; Moose and me in the woods sitting by a tree; Asase, Rumer and Moose posing by his car. Beyond the window, in the distance, I see the glinting criss-crossing train tracks that run into London, Cardiff, Bristol. And the green canal, twisting through fields and scrub like a serpent, one hundred and thirty-seven miles, through towns, cities, villages, going as far as Birmingham.

But in dreams I find myself in Moose's rainforest, following paths into long-gone times. Running from something or someone; my breath locked down in my chest. Moose has been captured; men are shackling his feet. Two of them hold his throat as they put a chain around his neck. Another one puts a scalding iron on his heart.

I see us the last time we were together, after the riverboat dance, in bed, fucking hard below the bassline, me on top, my hands pushing down on his chest. It's the only time, moments before he comes, that his face takes on anything like fury as he erupts. A second or two, then he's at peace. I lay my head on his ribcage. His skin smells of wet earth, heart hammering against ribs.

The sound of a train rattling against tracks brings me back. How long have I been looking out the window, seeing Moose, thinking that we should have planned our escape? Because history is never far enough away.

'Why yuh breathing so hard?' Irving asks. 'Yuh must get back to work. Keep the body moving.'

I want to say brucking your batty bone isn't the answer for everything, but instead I ask: 'Does it still hurt? When you think about Muma?'

He downs the hot drink. Makes a sound like he's dredging up sandstone rocks and fish bones from the bottom of his throat. 'Yuh muma dead and gone from time. What you stirring-up?'

'Need to know how long this pain is gonna last.'

'She was a nurse, working with life and death. "Burn me with song when me dead," so she seh. So me do. Cremation. A choir. In Guyana.'

'Why didn't you bring her home?' I ask, my voice rising.

'The heat. Bodies turn bad . . .'

He gets up, pushes past me. 'Let the dead rest. I've suffered enough!'

Don't know what feelings are buried beneath his hooded eyes but I see grief in the lines on his forehead, pulling into the centre like a whirlpool. Water fighting against itself. He's going to cry.

I stand up, move towards him.

'Badderation!' he says and walks away.

I go to my room, lay on my bed by the window, build a spliff, inhale hard. Hands shaking.

Radio on down-low. Static. Digitalised voices coming from FM Sub Zero.

I'm in the spirit, mattress sagging with dreams. Can't understand why Muma would leave me to help other children and mothers. Her cells are inside me. If I don't know Muma, how do I know myself?

I drop inna the dreams, see Muma, shrunken, a Vodou doll with a plait-head of spells, she's singing:

Send me your dream
I'll one day be seen.
Let me tek yuh to the sea.

Silver taffeta air molecules dissolving. She fades.

'No, no, no,' I call out.

I won't think of Moose in the police cell.

Won't think of the pressure on his heart. The sounds his body would have made as they broke it. I'll think of him on that burning red river, turning to ash, floating across the Atlantic. Heading home.

No, I can't bear to think of him at all. Can't bear the dislocation of more grief.

I put the spliff on my wrist. Fire enters me. The glow in my gut expanding. I hold the cigarette there, let it burn.

I can only sleep with music on the down-low. Version. No vocals. Space for Moose to speak. I wake up in the middle of the night with my head full of voices. None are his.

I use the bedside phone to call Nile. He picks up on the first ring.

'It's late. You OK?' he says.

I roll on to my back and look through the window at the sky. 'It's as if he's still here,' I say.

'It's gonna feel that way. Believe. Yamaye? Yuh there?'

Riddim of the rain on the windowpane relaxes my hearing. Moose's voice echoing after Nile's words.

'Moose was like family,' Nile says.

Peace, my brother.

'He told me 'bout you, Yamaye. I know man was planning his life with you,' says Nile.

Me and Yamaye, living sweet back-a-yard.

'Moose was gonna do good things,' I say. 'He's left me, bluesing in Babylon.'

'Live for him,' Nile says.

'I can barely put my feet on the ground,' I say.

'Stay strong for his grandmother. She may need you. Her bloodline's gone. She's bringing his body back to Jamaica soon as she can,' he says.

Connect to me.

'I'll try,' I say.

I exhale smoke and Moose's line goes dead.

'Can you hear me?' says Nile.

'Yeah, yeah, the line's crackling. It's raining, gusting outside.'

I imagine Granny Itiba, a knobbled walking stick of a woman, stepping a-ways outta mist and rain. Wailing, tearing at her stomach as Moose's body is lowered into blood-red soil.

'Moose had no family here. Some good friends and me. We went to Rights On,' Nile says.

'Who are they?'

'They're always in the papers, justice fighters. Solicitors, barristers.'

'You trust them?'

'They're pushing for an inquest.'

'Babylon's systems. We know how that's gonna go down.'

'We need answers.'

'I need more than that. I need . . . bombo-claat control!' I lose it, crying.

'Hold tight, Yamaye. I feel it too.'

'So tired. Body doesn't feel right.'

'Rights On are on top of this.'

Rain's battering the window now, a trance-like rhythm.

'What's Babylon's story?' I ask.

'You up for this?' he says.

I draw on the spliff and hold the smoke in my mouth, its uprising power in my head. 'Yeah.'

'They stopped him outside our workshop, said he looked suspicious. Sus law. Said he assaulted one of their officers when they tried to question him. Next thing he's in a police cell. My bredrin was dead ninety minutes later.'

'Moose wasn't an aggressor. Nature-wild and peaceful, that's who he was.'

'Rights On are trying to find out if there is any CCTV footage from the shops and businesses near the police station.'

'I need to speak to them.'

'One of their criminal-justice solicitors is on it. Here, take their number.'

I scribble the digits on the cigarette box and Nile invites me to stay with his family for a while. I say I appreciate the offer but gotta be in my own space. He says he'll check me next week and I hang up.

The next day I call Rights On and they tell me that Herbert Peters is dealing with the case. They put me through to him. Asase broke up with him a few weeks ago and I'm worried that the call is going to be awkward, but he doesn't mention Asase. He asks how I am, says there's a lot to go through and we should link.

I meet him a week later on a barge cafe in the Dead Water area, on a quiet stretch of the canal. It's run by Siobhan who used to live on the Tombstone Estate. It's a hot afternoon. I've only been outside a few times since Moose's death. The narrow windows of the tower-block flats feel like the glass eyes of surveillance. Like I'm being watched. I'm breathing different, faster. My body tensed. The drowsy swirl of warm air is disorientating. I sense someone behind me. I turn around. No one. Just the triggering beat of my heart.

I take the shortcut across the wastelands, walk along the towpath. Wreaths of leaves and twigs float on the green-black water and it smells of drain sludge, blue cornflowers and cut grass. The air is thick with pepper-spray pollen.

Herbert is sitting on the deck at a small wooden table with a green parasol. He's wearing a tan linen suit and white shirt, open at the collar, looking like he doesn't give a damn about anyone's approval.

He stands and shakes my hand. 'Sorry to be meeting under these circumstances. How are you bearing up?'

'So-so.' I smooth down my denim shirt-dress and sit opposite him. My hair is packed inside an emerald-green turban, sunlight prickling the back of my neck.

The waiter brings navy enamel pots and pours black coffee for Herbert and nettle tea for me.

At the table next to us a woman and her daughter, with a sleeping baby on her lap, coo over photos. There's a couple sitting on the other table, behind Herbert.

He stirs three sugars into his coffee and drinks it like his life depends on it. His perfectly round Afro, freckles and eyes are all the same amber-brown colour, giving him the look of a cheetah, focused and brooding.

'Nile filled you in?' he asks.

'Haven't spoken to him this week.'

'No one's taken statements from the officers, so we're still not clear what happened on the way to or inside that station. I do know he was . . . held in a caged area at some point.'

'A cage?'

'Yamaye, it could get worse than that – I truly hope not.'

'Do you know how they killed him?'

'They've done the autopsy. I've got the pathology report. Restraint-related death. A chokehold.'

I look across at the towpath. Gold pollen floats into the tunnels of shadowy light between shrubs, bits of it trapped in my swollen throat. My eyes are watering. Herbert gives me his crisp, white handkerchief.

The couple sitting behind Herbert are wearing lean-down heels and conscious frowns. Their eyes, clear as water drawn from a private well, tell me they're not from here. Something odd about their ragamuffin uptown clothes. They look like people who come tek the styles we're brucking underground, then cut and paste them inna fashion magazines, staking their rights to our trends and sound.

'Moose can speak through us.'

'I'll push to bring a case against the police.'

'How long would that take?'

'They'll drag it out to the bitter end.'

'Six months? A year?'

He leans forward, palms flat on the table. 'Think of outcomes, not the distance.'

I check him: mid-forties, concave cheeks, lines on his brown face, like cracking clay. This man doesn't waste time with smiles or sleep.

'Nothing changes,' I say.

'Be the change. Our people shouldn't live like troglobites, partying underground. Losing our sight.'

I look into his eyes. The irises are a strange yellow, pinwheels of gold.

I wanna know what lies at the core of a man like Herbert. He goes to dances to give out leaflets about solicitors, donations, campaigns. He works at the heart of Babylon, learned its rules. How does he operate in two worlds without getting the blues?

The baby starts crying, and the woman sways from side to side, shushing her. I glance at the couple behind Herbert. They're pretending to talk, but I can tell they're tuned into us.

Then it clicks. I've seen enough of them outside the record shop, the Crypt, the Tombstone Estate. Always following our people, tracking us.

'Bull,' I say. 'Undercover.'

'They're always in my shadow,' Herbert says. 'Can't afford to get angry. It's what they want.'

I'm afraid. I know how they can destroy lives.

Siobhan comes from the kitchen below deck, carrying a bamboo tray of sandwiches in her hands, black tattoos of serpents and dragons coiling around her thick arms. She looks at me and subtly tilts her head towards the couple.

'Let's go,' I say.

He taps his head. 'No fear here.'

'We don't know who we're messing with.'

'Complex cellular networks of power,' he says.

'Who's gonna take that on?'

'White limestone covers yellow limestone. Jamaica slid below sea level forty-five million years ago. Re-emerged millions of years later, tectonic uplift. An uprising.' He takes a breath. 'Change is slow. You ready to see Moose?'

'When?' I look at the couple, cut my eyes on them. They look away, hold hands across the table.

'It's arranged, whenever you like,' Herbert says. 'They won't let me see the police surgeon's medical notes, but I'm working on it. I'm trying to get an independent autopsy. They'll probably block it. This is what we're up against – corrupt systems investigating themselves.' He asks me if I want to go to the mortuary with him, but I say that Nile will take me.

The vertical frown line between his eyebrows deepens as he tells me to be careful who I trust. He stands up and holds his hand out to me. I place my hand in his and he squeezes it hard. The couple watch him walk away.

The black canal water is sparkling. Yellow butterflies flutter around the parasol and one settles on its green fabric. There's more pollen in my eyes; my throat is hot and dry.

The baby stops crying; she's gurgling. I look into her blue eyes and she stares back at me, unblinking.

Three days later, me and Nile take a minicab to the police station in the city where the morgue is. The driver drops us near a three-storey, red-brick building close to the Tower of London. Iron railings around a semicircular forecourt; a triangular pediment – symbol of power – above the entrance, flanked by two columns. Black-and-white faces look out from posters trapped inside glass cabinets on the wall outside. People lost in the vaults of the city. If this isn't the heart of Babylon, it's one of the control towers, for sure. As long as his body is still here, Moose isn't free.

Nile and I report to a policewoman at the desk. The reception area smells of coffee and sweat. We sit on orange plastic chairs. Men on bail come and go, signing into the ghetto, dragging their feet, the riddim-bounce gone from their souls. Uniformed police with thick sideburns and moustaches, some in suits with kipper ties, walk up and down the corridors.

A policeman takes us downstairs into a centralised mortuary in the large basement area. We go into a small room. Nile's arm is around my shoulders, shaking. The place smells of disinfectant, rotting fruit.

There, heavy on the table, is Moose: a mahogany sculpture; white mist cloth laid over his body. I lift the sheet, step beneath the beams of fluorescent light.

His eyes, nose and mouth are floating on the darkened dead tissue of his face. An almost smile that says, *Emancipate*.

I touch the tip of his nose.

I'm breathing too fast.

Too late to warn him about the risks of a successful Black man walking the streets, springing up on his toes, swinging his arms to show he's free. Too late to warn him about the risks of dry-season riots. Batons. Beatings. Police vans crawling like bugs, metallic, iridescent, sucking the sap out of night-time trees. Too late to sing him my roots-rock-rebellion songs. All I know of rainforests, he's told me; everything about his earth-riddim ancestry.

Abeng horn blaring inside my head, on and on and on. Heat inna my chest and gut. A repossession. A howl that can't be human. Blackout.

Suddenly I'm back in Moose's car as he drives us to the forest near his flat. It's the weekend after Valentine's Day. We're surrounded by woodland, 500-year-old trees, Iron Age earthworks and an ancient hill fort. We walk for hours without seeing anyone. We sit in his favourite spot near a copse of beech trees. Flares of red orchids half-hidden in the grassy banks. This far in, there's no one but us. The only sound is the soft rattle of dragonflies and the steady croaking of frogs in the long yellowing grass. The sun squats low in the sky, a gong surrounded by fiery vibrations. Moose sets up a small coal fire and grills chicken and corn with thyme and pimento on a metal rack.

'Got somet'ing for you,' he says.

'Show me.'

'Hold up.' He gives me a bottle of champagne and two plastic cups. I pour.

He's wearing black tracksuit bottoms, grey T-shirt stretched tight across his shoulders and chest muscles, white trainers and mahogany beads that he carved on a leather cord around his throat. His hair is shaped into a compacted Afro that's squared off at the top.

He makes a toast to the forest. To us. Says Granny Itiba sees our lifelines in the red sky, joined together.

'What do you see in your future, Yamaye?' he says.

'Left it late, but maybe university. Music,' I say.

'You're always singing; never too late for passion.'

'Not sure if universities are places of unlearning, and denial. Like school.'

'One way to find out.'

'There's always wild learning: travelling.'

'With anyone I know?'

'Mmmm. Need to think 'bout this.' Trying not to, but laughter explodes out of me.

'Come yah!' He grabs me. 'You're all mine. The trees are my witness.' He takes a tiny velvet box out of his pocket. 'Made this for you.'

Inside is a wooden ring inlaid with mother-of-pearl.

'Mahogany from an old chair.'

I put the ring on my middle finger.

'I'm a conscious brother. I'm feeling you, Yamaye. In a big way.'

'Hold me,' I say.

His mixtape is playing lovers rock, 'Lady of Magic'.

He takes a photo of us with his Polaroid. We're laughing.

The tape gets tangled in the cassette player and the song becomes garbled, spooling backwards.

'Hold me!' I shout. Desperate now. I'm in a below-ground dance hall of inter-rocking, squatting, winding bodies. I'm dancing with Moose, but his legs don't move. His arms chop the air like a hummingbird singing with its wings. He's floating away from me, into Cockpit Country haze.

'Moose!'

'Easy, sister, hold tight.'

It's Nile's voice I hear as I emerge from the black hole.

I don't remember how I get out of that mortuary room. Next thing I know, I'm hunched over one of the orange plastic chairs in the corridor, dust motes hanging in the air. Effigies. A woman police officer brings me a glass of water. A plain-clothed policeman comes out to us.

'Watchyah, nuh. We know what you did. Rights On are gonna get to the bottom of this,' Nile says to the policeman.

The policeman brings his face close to Nile and says, 'Watch your step on the way out. Don't want you to end up in the cage like your friend, do we?'

Nile doesn't move. His eyes are wide, the veins at his temples pulsing.

'Come on, Yamaye. It's time for us to go.'

And the abeng horn is blowing pressure in my skull. I clench my fists. See myself swinging and punching the policeman. Landing a blow on a sweet-spot that could be his brain.

But I'm leaning on Nile's shoulder and we're walking through the door.

Back on the street, tears streaming down my face. I turn to Nile and apologise for making a scene, tell him I was outta my mind.

'Let's get the hell out of here.'

Nile drives me home, knuckles white against the wheel. I can tell he's still thinking about the policeman's threat, that word, *cage*.

'Be careful, Yamaye,' he says, pulling up to Tombstone Estate. 'Don't know what they're up to, but Babylon is following me. Watch yourself.'

7

Mystic Roots Gold light disintegrates into fiery red. Hardens into grey.

Days of frost, then sleet, then snow. New Year's Eve. I set off early in the morning, walking down the cemetery road towards the high street in the cold, grey light, scanning every movement, every sound. Blackened slum houses, built out of time, slapped on to each other like mineshafts. The frosted branches of old lime trees are white as long-bones and ribs. Ice everywhere. I don't wanna slip.

Two weeks' bereavement leave from work turned into a month, turned into unemployment. Sometimes Asase and Rumer come round at weekends and take me out for lunch. At night, they rave without me; I'm not ready to dance.

When I couldn't get hold of Herbert on the phone, I started going to his office, hanging around, waiting for him to come out of meetings so I could get updates on the case. Herbert said I was spending so much time there I might as well make myself useful and join their volunteers. So I go three times a week, photocopying flyers, organising marches. The offices are in the basement of a large community centre in east London, on a high street bordering marshes, twenty miles from Moose's town. I take a train and two buses to get there. When I leave the centre late in the afternoons there's always a man hanging around – clean-cut, sharp-eyed, deliberately casual. Walking to the bus stop, the vertebrae in my back become my eyes, my shoulders are radars.

I tell Herbert I'm being followed now and he asks me to keep a note of everything – dates, times, what they look like. Says he thinks they might be trying to pin something on me so they can discredit Moose's case.

Snowflakes spin against my face. I hold my breath and listen to it. A soft, raspy sound.

The hushed tread of someone behind me. I turn to see a squat man in a puffer jacket and jeans. His scarf is concealing most of his face, but it looks like the plain-clothes policeman who was at the barge cafe. I cross the road and step quick in the slushy-slippy snow.

I get to the high street, deserted except for a few people walking dream-time slow. An old woman in a woollen hat and tweed coat is standing outside the butcher's where pink-skinned slabs of pork back hang on hooks; crates of blackened root vegetables stacked against shopfronts; red lights draped across the streets; two men, their voices muffled behind balaclavas.

The policeman follows me to Dub Steppaz. There are posters with red arrows pasted all over the window about Misty in Roots playing live at the Crypt later that night. I step inside the shop and the man walks past.

The place is empty, except for Eustace. It's too early for the men who'll later crowd the shop.

'How's my best customer?' Eustace says. He's polishing a record. An Upsetter track on the deck, a dread-slow mass scraping against cavernous sounds.

'Bull are following me,' I say. I look through the glass door. 'Babylon doing what it's always done – tracking, intimidating.'

Eustace raises the counter and goes outside and shouts, 'Mister Undercover, we see yuh!' Cold air rushes in as he closes the door. 'Man didn't turn around,' he says.

I put my hat and sheepskin gloves on the counter and unbutton my coat.

Eustace pours coffee into a blue enamel mug and pushes it towards me. 'You're an easy target in this weather. No one else to mess with.'

'Think they've been following me since Moose was killed,' I say.

He turns the music down, drops his voice to a whisper. 'Yuh sure?'

Don't know how to describe the feeling of being watched: my heart beating in my ears, drum language, a coastal-lowland sound that only my gut understands.

Eustace listens as I tell him that the man who just went past was on the barge when I was with Herbert Peters talking about Moose's case.

'Pressure the women to pressure the men,' Eustace says. 'War tactics.'

'I'll take the pressure if it means Herbert can push on with the campaign.'

Eustace puts his drink down, says, 'Mind yuself. The police can make your life hell, Yamaye.' He puts on 'I'm a Revolutionist,' ramps up the volume.

We bust our necks back and forth, channelling the vibe.

Maybe it's the vibes of revolution songs, a feeling that something powerful has been invoked, but it's sinking in: Moose is gone and there's nothing to lose.

The music stops and Eustace has a strange look on his face, like he's drifted some place else. 'Drink your coffee,' he tells me. 'Blue Mountain brew is the remedy when the soul is cold.' He plays a one-drop rockers-riddim. I nod my head and wind my waist as he polishes the next track.

I check for Eustace. Something comforting about his fleshy face, his sturdy body and square jaw. He puts on a dubplate, gives me his Shure SM58 mic. 'You've been talking about doing this for ages.'

I go behind the counter, set the treble on the mic, put the mid dial to two. My face is burning but there's nothing I can do with desire for the dead except curl the tip of my tongue, chat headtop lyrics, singing:

'Burn. Burn. Babylon burn.
Set it off:
We fe stay in the riddim and swing
Safe from de devil within
Fire-rush-rocking riddim
Babylon! Ah we carry the swing.
Fling it down, my selector!'

The track stops and I stop.

'How yuh mean! Ah yuh dat, Yamaye?' Eustace says. 'You should be on the mic at the Crypt.'

'What would the rude bwoys say? Let alone Asase.' I twist up my face.

Eustace sucks in his lips at the mention of her name. Seems like he's about to say something, but he looks up at the painted hummingbirds on the ceiling instead. As if he's found out something unexpected about them. Or maybe he's thinking about flying away.

'Everything OK with you and Asase?' I ask.

'Life's a time-limited offer, Yamaye. Tek it. Asase has her own fears to fight.'

I change the subject, telling Eustace about Rights On and the investigation instead.

Eustace promises to ask Misty in Roots to play a fundraising concert to support the campaign. 'I'm not inna knives and guns,' he says. 'Sound is the best weapon we've got.'

He gives me the bag of records that he's set aside for me and points to the window. Flakes of snow flutter in all directions, like ash from a firestorm.

'Troubles me when the world's white-up like that,' he says. 'Makes my blood run cold.' He zips his leather jacket up to his throat. 'We need truth for your man – for all of us,' he says.

'It'll be New Year's slush in a few days,' I say.

'Time is the master,' he says.

The riddim slows to fifty-eight beats per minute, key drops to A minor.

I look outside and watch the snowfall thicken into darkness.

At home, I pack my garments. It will be the first time I've raved since Moose died. It's time for a dose of supra-watt dub medicine.

Irving is in the front room, a lit cigarette dangling from his bottom lip, the radio gramophone tuned into some faraway station playing an old Trojan tune. His eyes are almost closed, just a sliver of white showing. He's in a trance, travelling between worlds.

I leave without saying goodbye.

Outside, I take small steps in baby-powder snow. Rock, pop, reggae, dub, all kinds of music beating against the glass windows of the towers. New Year parties in mid-swing. Disco lights flashing. I walk alongside the connected tunnels to Asase's block, looking behind every now and again to see if I'm being followed, but the estate roads are empty, no one else around.

Oraca's on the armchair; Asase's sitting on the carpeted floor between Oraca's open legs, her eyes half-shut. The gas fire's on and two green paraffin lamps on either side of the bay window are churning smoke. A bottle of golden rum, champagne glasses, fried garra rufa fish on a large plate. I stretch out on the purple-cushioned sofa. One of Oraca's old scratchy jazz records is on the stereo. The trumpeter's notes are a whirring feedback of sadness. I should feel comfortable, but the familiar things seem entangled in the past and I'm drifting in a fever dream where nothing is real.

Oraca rubs the pink setting lotion between her hands, heating it before massaging it into Asase's scalp and rhythmically combing stretches of hair.

I talk about Rights On, the marches I'm organising, and all the work that Herbert is doing. Asase says he may be good at his job, but he should have done better with her.

'He was too fenkeh-fenkeh,' she says. 'All the man wanted to do was talk about human rights. What about my rights to my t'ings? Somebody best drop some mannish water in his coffee.' She's laughing. 'We're heading into the new year. Time to move on – from Herbert and from Moose, may he rest in peace.'

I stiffen. 'Didn't Moose mean anything to you?' I ask her.

'Can't bring him back to life,' she says.

'Asase!' Oraca says. 'Respect for the dead.' She conks the comb against Asase's head.

Asase slaps Oraca's arm away. 'Muma, you can light a candle for him, send his spirit on its way. You check for that kinda thing.'

'Music will do,' Oraca says. She twists sections of hair and runs the hot irons through them, winding them into tight curls. The slow, aching notes of the trumpeter's horn goes inna me. Vibrations pulsing my cells.

'Bwoy can blow, yuh see,' Oraca says of the music. 'Tekking himself back to where we all came from.'

And we're quiet, feeling the music.

Images of me and Moose together flicker, sending sparks of electricity along my spine.

I shiver.

Asase's face relaxes and her eyes begin to close as Oraca parts her hair, like she's selecting pathways, dragging on the kinks and knots.

'Easy!' Asase shouts.

'Our music is language,' Oraca says. 'When Ashanti sent drum messages across the Atlantic to their people. See it deh!'

Asase twists around, looks at Oraca. 'Ah so?'

'Music connects the living with the dead.'

I slide into the sofa, wanting to connect to Moose, have him lead me on a vine through Cockpit Country trails. Deep into the rainforest of Water Withe, fireflies, mahogany and mosswood. A guitar likk disappearing mid bar, falling into an abyss.

Much later, after Oraca has gone to her room with her glass of rum and grated ginger, the smell of the sea trailing her, me and Asase go to her bedroom to get ready. Rumer called earlier to say she wasn't raving because the cold weather and damp in her flat were making her wheeze. Time at the Crypt and she would end up in hospital, sucking oxygen from a tank instead of rum from a bottle.

I'm sitting on Asase's bed and she's at the dressing table, lining her lips in red. A pile of dresses at the end of the bed.

'Wanna know the latest?' she says.

'New job?' I say.

'Guess again.'

'Man?'

She nods, presses her lips together.

'Someone from Norwood?'

She stands, picks up a white flared midi dress with tassels and holds it against her body. 'Eustace,' she says.

'Dub Steppaz Eustace! What about Loreen?' I say.

'Early days yet,' she says. She throws the dress on my lap and picks up a navy jumpsuit with cap sleeves and a gold waistband. 'Loreen's only interested in the kids. He's a businessman. He likes my ideas. Maybe he'll invest.'

Asase sometimes talks about creating her own range of beauty products for Black women, but it's always just been talk. I toss the dress on the bed, stare at the red lamp on her drinks-trolley bedside table. Asase's used to getting whatever – whoever – she wants, but I've seen the way Eustace talks to her. Like the kind of father we both wish we'd had. Thinking back to the look on his face when I mentioned Asase's name at the shop last week. No shame, no desire. More like – no, couldn't be. Pity?

'Anyways, like I said, it's a new year. Time to make moves,' she winks.

My stomach churns. For a moment, I feel trapped in her red-lit room. Don't wanna think of Asase like this, making a fool of herself.

She throws the jumpsuit on the bed and puts on a pair of leather trousers and a purple top with a draped neckline that shows her cleavage. Admiring herself in the mirror, she catches a glimpse of my expression. 'Nuh fret 'bout me,' she says. 'I know what I'm doing.'

'Do you?'

She sits on the chair in front of her dressing table and combs out her curls into waves that she sweeps behind her shoulders like she's closing curtains.

She's hard ears, not listening to anyone, hearing what she wants to hear. I've seen her like this before, an amplification of energy that makes me afraid of what she might do.

'Maybe skip tonight,' I say. It's always the three of us on New Year's Eve and I'm not feeling it without Rumer.

'Party season and you wanna miss it!?' Asase says. Her eyes go booom! And then she switches, just like that, softens her voice and says, 'Girrrrl, come nuh, let's make it a night to remember. We'll walk. I'll deck you out in style. Forget your clothes. I've styled some garments. Tek one.'

We leave a little before ten wearing rabbit furs, knee-high pigskin boots, and black suede fedoras with gold-stitched musical notes around the rims – all Asase's. Her clothes don't hang right on me. Feels like she's stitched tight on to my body and I can't move the way I want to.

Arms linked, we walk across the bombed-out whiteness of the estate.

Mish-mash sounds of rock-pop-country-reggae fight it out on the airwaves. Christmas lights flashing in people's yards. Shadowy figures trudge through the snow shouting, 'Happy New Year.' Snow-static-hum.

A cackle of electric, like those first few seconds when the needle drops on vinyl.

The wastelands, like everything else, is snowed over. It's a short-cut to the Crypt, but it'll be impossible now to follow the track and avoid the things that are dumped there, like the old fridge that was found in the summer, a bin bag with a rotting arm stuffed inside, or the TV with smashed-in screen, a small revolver cotched on a glass valve like a trophy.

We head west. Holding on to the splintered wooden rail, we tek our time down the stone steps and puss-foot along the canal towpath. Not as quick, and the lighting is nuth'n more than a pitchy-patchy glow from street lights on the road above. At least the gravel path is salted, not as slippery as the pavements.

My eyes shut down in the blackness of supra-watt bass night. Listening takes over: the crick-cracking of the canal, the surface an ice-breathing shell. Clanking noises way below, like a vessel underwater.

We flick our lighters on, hold them close to our faces. We go through the tunnel below the bridge. The temperature drops, the icy air nips at my cheeks and nose. I push my hearing beyond the weight of silence.

'If duppies exist, this is the night for them!' Asase says.

'Shhhh!'

'Who yuh shushing!'

'I heard something.'

We stop, look around.

'Miss Fraidy-Fraidy,' she says.

'And you're not?'

'Of darkness?'

'Snow. It's a gag over the world,' I say.

'It's fresh. Like grinding, makes me feel alive,' she says.

We put our gloved hands in our pockets; our other hands hold on to our lighters.

'My tongue's gonna freeze at the root,' I say.

'Suck it up,' Asase says. 'Once we're inside the Crypt, it's pure fire-riddims heat.'

She bends backwards, busts a move, rippling her spine, arms pushing away from her body, parting invisible waves.

'The Water Flex,' she says. 'Next big thing in the dance hall. Like me and Eustace. The big-time couple running things. Making serious money so we can get outta this town.'

I don't say anything and she goes quiet.

I'm walking on the side closest to the thick bushes of ivy and bramble growing against the sloping wall. Asase is near the bank of the canal. The fast-flowing water beneath the ice must be cold as death.

'Mind the edge,' I say. I point my lighter in her direction.

Her shadow flickers on the ice, spreads, and I suddenly remember last night's dream. *Me in a dark-green ocean, watching as a naked Black woman crouches on the rails of a ship, her tied hands pointing as she dives, a spear firing into the depths. A sailor runs to the rail, shouts for help, jumps in after her. Lights from a lantern on the deck beam on to the sea. I follow their paths through the murky water. I'm underwater, diving alongside her. She can't see me. Her breath bustin' out of her eyes.*

The sailor grabs her feet; she kicks him away, red algae swirling around her body like wings. He grabs again, and this time catches the ankle of her left foot. She undulates and twists, spinning them into a death roll, dragging him into the depths; the downwelling light from the ship becomes a distant tunnel. I feel her anger in the two-beat kick of her feet. It's my rage in my ribcage, trying to break out, rage for the policeman who was following me and all the others, their eyes and power everywhere; for the men like them who hold on to our bodies in the dance hall; for Irving controlling what I know about Muma, his secrets. The secrets of men.

The sailor kicks away to the light. There's fire in my clenched fists. I unfurl them and put my hand out to the woman. But she can't see me.

There's a sound behind us and I look back through the tunnel we've just come through. I raise my lighter and the shadow's upon us. Crab Man, belted into a trench coat, a scarf snaking around his throat.

'Miss Thing, yuh-one carrying the swing,' he says to Asase.

He pushes between us and puts his arm across her shoulder. He's laughing, a crusty hawking sound.

'Tek yuh blood-claat hands offa me!' Asase shouts.

He drags her towards his body. 'Nuh chat to me so. Yuh hear!' he says.

Asase pushes his hands off, tells him to kiss her batty-hole. Her voice spins across the acoustic emptiness of the frozen canal.

Silence.

Crab Man grabs her arms and shakes her. Her head snaps back and forth and she drops her clutch bag.

I point the lighter towards him. 'Leave her alone,' I shout.

I pull at his arm and he turns, bats me away with his free hand and looks at me as if he's unsure about something. He won't remember me. In the blackout dance hall I was just another body to drag and grind against.

What is it that stops me from pushing my fingers in his eye sockets and drawing his eyeballs out like two corks? I think of the policeman who threatened Nile at the mortuary, the fury I felt then. What stopped me from slamming my fist into his nose and shunting his nose bone up into his brain and waiting . . . one, two, three, lights out? Only the fact that I don't have the strength to take on a man, and not knowing where the violence would end.

I clench my fists.

Crab Man shoves Asase and she staggers and slips on to the frozen canal.

'Think you're too nice, eh? Gwaan,' he shouts as he walks on, disappearing into the darkness.

I shine my lighter on Asase. She's on all fours, her feet sliding on the ice as she tries to get up.

'Slowly,' I say. 'The ice—'

I don't know where to look. Watching her and looking around, afraid Crab Man might come back.

'Fuck the ice,' she says. She slips and sprawls.

'Tek time!' I say.

I hold my arm out to her. She stands up and walks forward, her hands wide, one small step at a time.

A light beams on to us from further ahead and we're in a tunnel of white. The canal, the holly, the gritted path, everything sparkling raw, metallic cold.

'What's going on?' It's Siobhan from the barge cafe. She's standing on the deck in her dressing gown, waving a torch, her vessel entombed in the ice.

I grab Asase's hand and she steps back on to the towpath.

'Where's my bag? No blood-claat man's gonna mess with me,' she says.

'Are you OK? Let me see,' I say.

Torchlight widens around us. Siobhan is running our way.

'Let's head home,' I say. 'You're hurt.'

'Nah, nah. He's not messing up my night,' Asase says.

'Your coat is damp. You'll catch pneumonia.'

'I said I'm OK!' Her eyes look odd, unfocused. She's rubbing her neck and moving her head from side to side.

'He's probably going to the Crypt,' I say.

The feel of Crab Man's body pressed against mine is still under my skin. Yes, I'm still afraid of him, but I'm just as afraid of what might happen if my imagination grows wings and my rage flies out.

'Mek him. Eustace will deal with him,' Asase says.

Of course she's set on going. Eustace will be there.

Siobhan is next to us. I tell her what happened, and she shines the torch around the bush, searching. She picks up Asase's bag.

'He must have got back onto the road,' she says. 'I didn't see him as I came up.' She says we should come on board; she'll warm us up with tea.

I say yes. But Asase insists she's OK.

'Mind yerselves. That one's trouble,' Siobhan says. 'Always hanging around here. He knows it's a shortcut lots of women take.'

We walk with her to her boat and she gives us her torch to take with us. The wind picks up. Dead sounds of Oraca's trumpeter blowing sea chills into my body.

When we finally make it to the Crypt, Bongo Natty is on the upper floor behind the table, collecting the money. Box Bwoys are eating rice and peas and stewed chicken from plastic containers. Sweet gyals in silk pleated skirts, suede bombers, velvet turbans and gold-tipped shoes are swaying next to them.

Asase asks Bongo Natty if he's seen Crab Man.

'Sisters, sisters,' he says, 'you come again bringing your riddim. Sound always comes full circle. Like the revolution. Crab Man isn't here.'

She begs a puff from one of the Box Bwoys and pulls hard on the spliff. Her hand is shaking. Her pupils are dilated, her eyeballs are cross-firing notes. I'm angry with Crab Man too, but it's her mood that's worrying me.

We go downstairs into the Crypt. There are only a few groups of people, it's still early. A light is on around the decks. The maintenance crew are still messing with cables, the engineer's tuning the system, the MC's warming up the mic: 'One – two – three. Irie. Irie.' The dance won't get going for another hour or so.

Watchya nuh: man dem decide when the dance starts.

Man dem decide who's gonna dance with who.

Man dem decide when the dance is done.

I see Lego in a corner of the room, near a locked doorway. Bongo Natty told us that it leads to a northern chamber, down into vaults, some filled with coffins. Lego makes his way towards us. I tell him what happened with Crab Man. He says he'll stay close to us through the night. He builds a spliff and I drag hard on the sensimilla. Fill myself up with spirit. Go down into worlds where there's nothing but sound.

As we head towards midnight, the Crypt fills up with gold-drenched dancers and silver whistle-blowers. Double-speed drum kick-kick-kicking. Reverbs and delays haunted with spirituals.

Misty in Roots are on the makeshift stage – eight serious-looking men dressed in black leather jackets, berets and African print shirts. Small spotlights on them.

'Welcome to a rootical live session. History is destiny,' the lead singer calls out. 'We ah go throw down some sound bombs tonight!'

Percussion and piano likks and we're calling out to Jah Jah. Flailing our heads like whips. Musical drones and everyone knows when the first bomb's gonna drop.

Silence. I buckle. One, two, three: drums and bass explode. Feel my lungs fill with bubbles of sound.

Misty in Roots are chanting and scatting, marching as they play. Soldiers on the front line firing their weapons.

A backwash of treble. My backbone curving, an ancient movement from that first landing from sea to land. The first gasp for air.

Eustace is on the other side of the Crypt, moving between different groups, talking. He stops inside an archway with a group of women. I don't know them. They're dressed in wafty, halter-neck midis. Short, sleek hairstyles. Eustace nods in our direction and looks away.

'New year, new year,' the singer calls out again. 'Time is the master.' And I remember that's the last thing Eustace said to me before I left his shop last week.

One of the women says something to Eustace. He laughs. They're close-dancing.

A granular buzz in the air that reminds me of falling snow. Chills in my bones as the massive sway and flow.

I look at Asase. Her neck is thrust up like she don't business. She's sipping white rum from her hip flask, side-stepping in her leather trousers, the seams stitched like scars; foundation a little lighter than her skin colour; lipstick as dark as her mood.

Lights flashing, whistles blowing, the singer counting down to midnight. A wailing siren track and a cymbal clash. Black soundbox is shaking. I see Koromantyn women inside, busting old-time moves, their wombs wired for sound, ovaries – left side, right side – filled with red-seed echoes, two million voices.

The lights go off just before a big-bang explosion of dub kick drums.

I close my eyes and buckle under sonic compression of strings and reeds and brass. The DJ toasting lyrics.

'New Year Version right about now
live and direct from Jamdown.
riddimmmm maccaaaaa!'

'I'm going over there,' Asase shouts in my ear.

Her eyes still don't look right. She's buzzing, pure energy. I put my hand on her arm. She shrugs me off and I watch her push through the crowd, smoke trailing her.

Asase steps between the woman and Eustace and wags her finger in Eustace's face. He's shaking his head and tries to turn away, but Asase sidesteps in front of him. He takes hold of her arm and leads her towards the arched door.

I wind my waist faster, try to get the cold feeling outta my body.

Dubplate's laced with gunfire popping, a soft waxy track that warps on the deck. The crowd roars, slash-and-burn skanking. Eight-bar drums with reverb, phaser and slurred ghost vocals. Four, five, six riddims and Asase ain't come back.

Suddenly the lights are flashing and the record scratches to a halt. Dancers sway, unsteady, pulled from the outtasphere before time. Men run up the stairway. I shade my eyes from the light.

There are shouts from the floor above. Someone yells: 'Call an ambulance!' People push towards the stairs. I follow them, running out the main door and upstairs to the small entrance on the side of the church. Outside to the churchyard where church lights and moonlight are bearing down on a group circling a woman, one of the regular Crypt dancers. She's kneeling on a fur jacket in the snow. Eustace is lying on the ground, his eyes open like two flat stones in stagnant water. The woman puts her jacket on his chest. His eyes droop and his head rolls to one side. Blood blossoms into the snow near his left shoulder. I gag and swallow bile, my legs give way and I'm on my knees rocking back and forth, crying. I feel the cold go into my bones as the smoke from people's breath rises. Cars stream past, making a noise like the sea rolling away from the shore. The circle of people press inwards.

'Get back,' Bongo Natty shouts. 'Let the woman do her t'ing.'

No one moves.

Sirens are blueing up the air.

I can't see Asase in the crowd.

The ambulance crew is on the floor beside Eustace within minutes. The woman stands up, the hem of her skirt wet. Blood on her hands. Bongo Natty puts his jacket around her shoulders and pulls her face into his chest. They're shaking. Eustace stares up at the stars. Says something, then his eyes close.

More sirens. Indigo lights scanning the sky.

They put Eustace on a stretcher and drive away. Sirens blaring. Everyone stands there, dazed. Lego is jabbing his stick in the air like a spear.

'Have you seen Asase?' I ask him.

He pushes me away and starts skanking, jabbing his stick-spear, singing: 'Fire rush inna me bredrin.'

I grab his stick. 'Where is she?'

'Fire rush inna me, sistren,' he says.

8

Dissonance

A helicopter is outside the window. A jarring noise, breaking up the sporadic winter birdsong. Me and Irving are on the small terrace, seventeen floors high. He's wearing his navy shirt, camel jacket, baggy wool trousers and a tweed flat cap. Smouldering cigarette stuck on his bottom lip. His pockmarked, olive-skinned face and black moustache slicked with coconut oil.

'Look deh,' he says, pointing to the police helicopter flying in circles, flashing red lights in the winter sky. 'Peenie-wally – firefly.'

The aircraft bobs on acoustic blue streams and bubbling white clouds. Pressure-wave winds burn my cheeks. I've been calling Asase's house for two days, but no one answers. Won't know what to believe until I see her, but Eustace is still in the hospital in a critical condition. The rumour going around is that he was stabbed in the back. I shudder.

'Dem is bugs,' Irving says of the crawling Black Maria police vans on the streets below.

The neighbours are bug-like too. I went to the corner shop earlier, and they were creeping through the dim hallways, scuttling away. Voices behind closed doors, low-frequency loops.

I look at the tiny figures below, old women dragging trolleys, young children running around the swings and the rusty slide.

The helicopter floats upwards and I imagine what the pilot can see looking down. Tower blocks, neat columns in straight rows, orderly as a slave-ship mortality list.

Why are the towers built so close to the sky? Segregation by airspace.

'I going to Hezekiah. Man-and-man fe talk about this,' Irving says. 'Eustace was hard-working. Is a bad-bad business.'

He will go find his bredrin Hezekiah, Asase's father, at the Wolf Pub, where they usually meet with other men in the first week of the new year, putting the world to rights. There's a dread feeling in my gut that things are shifting further out of their control.

He comes back an hour later. I hear the front door slam and he calls me out of my room. We stand in the hallway under the dingy light of the red, tasselled lampshade.

'Asase stab Eustace!' Irving says. 'Look now! Trouble fe everybody.'

'What are you talking about?'

'Bongo Natty heard cussing in the churchyard. Him see Asase with Eustace, carrying on bad. Police hunting her.'

I squat on to my haunches to stop myself falling. 'Uh-uh, can't be.'

'Hope you nuh mixed up in this.'

My heartbeat's in my ears on a loop, loud-loud.

'That family finish,' Irving says. 'Retribution now. Stay away from them.' He walks towards the front door.

'Where are you going?' I ask.

'Fe mind me business. Stay in de yard until them find her.'

'I'm not a child!'

He goes out and slams the door. I go back to the balcony, scanning the sky and streets below.

The helicopter hovers close to a terrace in the next block and a man leans over the wall, waving his arms. I think of the people who've jumped from the Tombstone towers over the years, their bodies hanging in blue air like dissonant chords.

The red light of the helicopter flashes through the window.

I don't know what to feel. All I'm aware of is a dread feeling, like cold water running down my spine.

The lights flash, the helicopter disappears into clouds. Police with sniffer dogs are running across the estate, the animals barking and growling. The clanging sound of black metal bins being dragged out of the rubbish rooms. I lean over the railing, my body full of electricity.

The doorbell's ringing. Someone's holding their finger on the buzzer.

I go to the hallway, fling the door open. 'What?'

A man with cropped red hair, sideburns. He's wearing an unbuttoned black raincoat, shifting from side to side, trying to look friendly. I know he's police – that patented power smile; the measured, cold-blooded movements of his hands.

'Detective Simeon Grey.' He holds out his ID. 'May I?' He steps forward.

Watchya, there're only three kinda ways Babylon come inna yuh yard:

Entry One: knock on the door, smiley-smiley, twist up facts, wheedling and whining for intel.

Options: nuff.

Entry Two: to arrest someone, flinging open dis and dat, nuff bangarang to blood-claat.

Options: none. Best let them mash-up yuh place.

Entry Three: bruck-down-door dawn raid inna. Kick-down anyone in sight.

Options: forget it!

Don't know if this one's got backup somewhere outta sight. I block him.

He shakes his head and makes a sound that could be a laugh or a grunt of disgust.

'Your people don't talk much, do they?' he says.

'As if anyone's blood-claat listening!' I shout. I hear doors opening, neighbours whispering in the corridor.

'Asase Shand,' he says, and he slides his foot over the edge of the doorway. 'An incident two nights ago.'

I pull the door closer to my body.

'A seriously wounded man. Friend of yours?'

'Eustace is gonna be OK?' My tone softer now.

He puts his hand on the door and pushes it. I kiss my teeth and stand aside. He follows me into the front room, sits in Irving's hard-backed one-seater. I perch on the armrest of the sofa opposite him. He's got a broad, square head. Droopy, red eyelids, like tongues, conceal the top of his eyes.

'Asase was seen with Mr Frankson,' he says. 'She had a knife. She's your best mate, I hear. Know where she is?'

'No.'

'You were with her at the Crypt. See anything?'

'She went outside. I stayed downstairs.'

'What did she say before she left you?'

'She was going up for air. She needed to breathe. All our people do.'

He stands up, looks down at me, clears his throat. 'Mr Frankson was her fella, was he?' His voice is deeper.

'No,' I say.

He goes outside to the balcony, looks down on to the street and across towards the wastelands. 'Where would you go if you were on the run?'

I think about it. With Moose gone, there's nowhere I could go.

I say the place I hide from Babylon is inside dub riddims. Drum. Bass.

He comes back into the living room. 'That so?' He says something under his breath, then goes and looks at one of Muma's paintings on the wall. 'Why do you lot dance in a crypt? That's for dead people.'

I stand in front of the painting, block his view. 'It's a refuge from Babylon,' I say.

He raises his eyebrows. The droopy eyelids lift and I see the full shape of his eyes, alert, suddenly bright.

He walks to the front door and pushes it wide. As I'm pushing it shut he says that if I see Asase I should tell her to hand herself in – it's too cold to be on the run.

I say we don't need nobody telling us how cold it is on the outside and slam the door.

It's headline news three days later. Asase was found hiding in the chambers below the Crypt. Lego must have helped her. But the article says nothing about him being captured or turning her in.

I look at the morning paper: DEVIL WOMAN'S SAINTLY HIDEOUT. I can't imagine Asase crouched down in the darkness among the brown dust of the dead.

I call Bongo Natty, the newspaper still spread out on the floor.

'Who *is* this?' he says.

'Yamaye,' I say. I don't know why he's acting as if he doesn't recognise my voice. His young daughter is shouting in the background. He tells me to hold on, he's going somewhere private to speak.

I ask if Eustace is OK.

'Your friend jook him in his back. Right on the man's artery.' His voice is cold, accusatory. 'He was walking away.'

'He's going to be OK, isn't he?'

'No joke what she did.' Every word unmodulated: Bleng. Bleng. Bleng.

I want to say, *Bongo Natty, it's me, Yamaye. Don't do me like this.* But I just ask, 'Which hospital? Can I visit?'

An explosion of breath. 'Yamaye, check yourself! His people don't wanna catch sight of Asase's friends. Man nearly bled to death. He's lucky to be alive.'

'But I—'

'Loreen is moving the family to Brighton.'

'But the shop.'

'Locked-off. FOR SALE sign going up any time soon.'

'That's Eustace's life,' I say. But I want to scream out that it's my life too. The last place of refuge in Norwood.

'If I were you, Yamaye, I'd keep my batty quiet for now. People ain't happy about Dub Steppaz closing.'

I ask how the police knew where to find Asase.

'Informer, who else,' he says.

'One of us?' I ask.

'Jah know,' he says.

I try to keep him talking, hoping he'll change his tone. I say that it's a good thing they didn't find Lego; he must have a dread hiding place in the Crypt.

'Listen nuh, best not to chat these things on Babylon's phone,' he says and he hangs up.

I put the handset in its cradle and place my hand on top of it. Wait for it to ring, Bongo Natty on the other end of the line saying he's sorry, he was too harsh; me and him are still friends. The silence cuts into me. I pace my room, but the strength goes out of my legs. I double up, cross my arms over my stomach, rock back and forth.

At lunchtime, I call Rumer and she says she's well enough for visitors. She had a bad asthma attack on New Year's Day that turned into flu. The dry, cold air of winter always gets to her. I haven't seen her since everything happened. We spoke twice on the phone, but not long enough to get inna it.

Rumer's wearing a navy dressing gown, the cord hanging by her sides. Her blonde roots are showing through the black. Her face is thinner and waxy grey.

I follow her into the living room. We're on the third floor and from the window, looking down, I can see the black-wet streets and people walking around.

She makes mugs of coffee and stirs in brandy. We sit on the floor like we always do. The threadbare carpet stinks of cigarette ash and beer.

'This is all we need,' Rumer says.

I tell her Eustace is in hospital and Bongo Natty said we should lay low.

'We're gonna feel the heat from everyone,' she says. She pours more brandy into her mug and puts the bottle on the floor between us.

'We don't know everything yet,' I say.

'You sure you didn't see nuth'n?' she asks.

I tell her about Crab Man shaking and pushing Asase earlier that night and how she seemed to be hurt, but insisted on going to the Crypt.

'Hurt bad?' Rumer asks.

I nod. 'She didn't look good.'

'Then why was she brucking her neck to get to the Crypt?' She pulls coils of hair from her eyes. 'You holding out on me?'

I bring the mug to my face and stare at the stray coffee granules bobbing on the surface. I don't want to be separated from Rumer by secrets. Need to talk about what this means for us.

I tell her about Asase and Eustace. She looks at me, red blotches burbling and spreading across her neck. She picks up her inhaler and breathes out, then presses down on the canister.

'You OK?' I ask her.

She takes the inhaler out of her mouth and puts her hand on my shoulder and waits before sucking in more medication. 'Asase is trouble,' she says. Her voice is strained.

I link my arm through hers and she pulls me to her, says she's OK.

'The police came to my yard,' I say. 'Questioned me.'

'You know her better than anyone. You're as good as family.'

I sip the coffee and the brandy leaves a trail of fire in my throat. A thin layer of condensation spreads across the windows.

'We've let her get away with plenty,' Rumer says. 'Asase's hard. Asase's brave. Asase's got that . . . that energy. Cha, don't know what to say.' She bursts out crying. Her chest is still tight, and she starts coughing and gasping. She puts her hands over her face. 'I love her,' she says. 'I love that woman so bad it burns.'

I pull her hands away and look into her eyes. 'It's OK, Rumer, I think I've always known.'

She stops crying, heaving dry, racking breaths.

We hold each other and I go limp in her arms, feel the weight of secrets dropping away.

It is Bongo Natty who calls me the week after to say that Rumer has left town. His tone is still hard. He says he saw her at the station early Wednesday morning carrying a brown patent-leather suitcase, wearing her long military-style coat and red, gold and green knitted hat. She told him she was going to Ireland for some country air. Back to a mother and father who dote on their five sons. Maybe to marry the cousin her parents want her to. Try to be something she can never be. She told Bongo Natty the smoke was gonna kill her if she didn't leave. His voice an electromagnetic hiss, as he says I should think about checking out of the area too.

And I understand why Rumer doesn't want to be the first in this ancient town. And why she didn't want to say goodbye. But it's too much, this expanding isolation feels like a compression against my chest.

I'm afraid of ending up like the other solitary people on the estate. Caught in contractions of the past, trying to find their futures.

Riots in Bristol take us into spring. Black people kicking off against harassment by the police. Poor people wanting more food and heat.

And we burn ourselves, night into day, on dub riddims in the Crypt, praying Babylon won't take our world away. Father Mullaney says the police are trying to close down the dub parties in the Crypt, but Bongo Natty and his lawyers are fighting to keep it open. I'm constantly uneasy, carrying the feeling that I'm still being followed, although I haven't seen the man for a while.

We organise silent demonstrations for Moose outside police stations across London in the evenings, holding red church candles, swaying, humming like an oncoming storm.

His murder follows me wherever I go. At night, I dream of him in yellow limestone caves, his voice reverbing dread, and I think this is when Asase could have done good with her energy and fearlessness. But maybe in all revolutions there are rebels who turn on each other and themselves.

Asase's case goes to court in the middle of summer. I sit two rows from the back of the public gallery. Dark, wood-panelled walls, grain-patterned stories of our uprooted past. Dead air. The kinda place that makes it difficult to believe in an afterlife. Black people walk into the gallery with rigid, immobile features. They've switched faces, like vinyl flipped to B-side, voiceless.

The gallery is on one side of the room, looking across to the jury on the other. Asase is at the back with a prison officer. She's staring straight ahead in the direction of the barristers and judge in front of her. I'm looking at her, wanting to connect, but she won't look at me. The hollow acoustics of the room match the emptiness inside me.

The white-haired barristers are MCs preparing for a sound-system clash, polishing their records until they gleam, sharpening their needles before they let their versions spin. The judge chatting about how things are gonna run. There's a bored, impatient expression on Asase's face. She's sitting upright in the dock, her body still powerful. Nature must have built her that way, knowing she'd have to fight and run. Oraca, who is near the front of the public gallery, turns and stares at me. We smile. That's when Asase finally looks at me, her eyes wavelengths of silence.

I nod. And I can see now that Asase was my friend because I didn't want her as an enemy. I'd been in a prison of my own making.

Love her. Hate her. Love her. Hate her.

Right now, I hate her for what she did to Eustace. And yet. The nerves in my body twisting and turning like mistuned notes.

Eustace's parents and Loreen are sitting in the front row. His mother is leaning against her husband's shoulder. Eustace isn't with them, can't see him anywhere. I pray they don't turn to look at me.

The barrister for the prosecution, Mr Lyons, stands up.

'Your Honour, I would like to call the prosecution's first witness, Mr Eustace Frankson.'

There's whispering at the front of the public gallery and the usher takes a note from Loreen and gives it to Mr Lyons.

Mr Lyons speaks to the judge, says that he has a doctor's note, Mr

Frankson is unwell. They talk for a while and the Judge says the case will continue. 'I'd like to call Mr Nathaniel Bailey to the witness stand,' Mr Lyons says. People up front whispering. Probably wondering the same thing as me; whether Eustace is still recovering or just doesn't want to testify against Asase.

The judge asks for silence.

Bongo Natty walks up to the stand wearing an African print shirt and matching tie, his locks piled into a red, gold and green knitted hat. He takes the Bible from the usher. Inhales a large breath, like a trumpeter about to blow his horn.

'I swear by Jah Rastafari, Conquering Lion of Judah, that the evidence I give shall be the truth, the whole truth and nuth'n but the truth.'

The judge glances up from his papers, looks at the barrister and blinks several times.

Mr Lyons asks Bongo Natty to tell the court where he was on the night of 31 December 1979 and what he saw.

Bongo Natty looks around at the people in the public gallery, his jaw muscles flexed for fight or flight.

'Mr Bailey, if you please,' Mr Lyons says.

Bongo Natty clears his throat a couple of times. 'It was snowing,' he says. 'The people was inside. I was at the table, with my crew. We were, yuh know, smoking, drinking, niceing up the place.'

'Can you describe the layout for the court?' Mr Lyons asks.

'Yuh step inna the door at the side of the church on to a landing, a gallery where the set-up was. The table and everything. Metal stairs went down inna the Crypt. Asase and Eustace came up from the Crypt. They went past me, outside. She looked vehexx.'

'Vehexx?' Mr Lyons asks.

Someone in the gallery laughs.

'Yes, angry,' Bongo Natty says.

'Do you mean vexed?' Mr Lyons asks.

'Yes. Swell up. Plenty people were upstairs. She had to shuub to get out. They didn't shut the door behind them. Cold air was blowing in. I went to close it. Heard cussing and things. Looked out. My man – Eustace – was on the floor. Asase was holding a knife.' Bongo Natty turns to the judge and raises his empty hands.

Cross-fading whispers from the front and back of the courtroom.

The palms of my hands are hot, sweaty. I wonder if it coulda been me. If Asase could have turned on me one day. I look at her but she's looking down at her hands.

'What did you do then?' Mr Lyons asks.

'I ran towards them,' Bongo Natty says. 'She likked concrete.'

'I'm sorry? Licked concrete?'

Someone in the gallery shouts, 'Running, iyah, running.'

The judge orders the man to be taken out.

Bongo Natty continues: 'Yes, running fast. Hitting the pavement.'

'Yes, yes, I see,' Mr Lyons says. 'Were there other people nearby?'

'Yes, stepping 'pon the street, going towards the station.'

Mr Lyons asks Bongo Natty a few more questions about his relationship with Asase and Eustace. Then he calls Loreen, Eustace's wife.

It's stuffy with the smell of people's warm bodies and breath. Mr Lyons blows his nose. His selector rummages in files, pulling out papers and giving them to him.

Loreen takes the Bible and makes an oath to God Almighty. She's older than Eustace, in her late forties, tall, glow-dark coppery skin. Wearing a navy dress with a white collar, a short silver Ethiopian cross necklace. She stands with her chin out. Mr Lyons takes off his glasses, holds the silence like an MC. Puts his glasses back on, turns and looks at the jury while addressing Loreen.

'This will be difficult. We'll go at your pace. Can you tell us about your husband, Eustace Frankson?'

Loreen faces the jury. Their eyes flicker. She places her right hand on the cross at her throat. 'He is a good father,' she says. 'Too soft with the children.' Her voice is deep, slow and heavy. 'He put so much into the record shop.' She stops, tugs at the cross. 'I won't let him run that place any more.'

'This is obviously upsetting for you,' Mr Lyons says.

'Is all right. I mus' do this,' she says. 'Eustace gave too much time. Helping any and anybody who came off the street.'

'Loreen, please tell the court what kind of help,' Mr Lyons says.

'The youth don't have anything. Eustace let them stay in the shop. Gave them food. Money.'

Eustace's mother lets out a muted wail. Her husband pulls her head to his chest and quietens her.

'He always told the youth to walk away from trouble,' Loreen says.

'Were you aware of any relationship between your husband and the defendant?' Mr Lyons asks.

'Relationship?' Loreen takes her hand off the cross. 'Eustace doesn't run up and down with other women. He's a good husband. That woman was chasing him. She is *slack*!'

I stare at Asase. Her expression hardens, a below-surface burning.

Loreen slow-mo cuts her eyes in Asase's direction. 'Eustace is too trusting.'

Asase stares ahead. Her jaw twitches. Silence except for the rustling of the barristers' gowns. And the sound of the defence barrister going through his files, like someone flicking through history's dusty papers. Lost truths. Radioactive decay.

'But he did go to late-night clubs like the Crypt?' Mr Lyons asks.

'Music is his business, his life,' she says. She turns to the judge as if she's speaking to him personally. Arms folded across her chest. 'It nearly killed him!'

Wood-darkness closes in. Guilt, rage, grief and love explode inside me and I'm thinking of Moose and how Eustace almost died. I'm crying, and someone's arm is around, the other arm covering my mouth with their hand, telling me to keep it down. It's Junior, the young man who worked at Dub Steppaz.

He gives me a tissue and I'm wiping my eyes as Mr Lyons says he has no further questions.

Loreen is leaving the witness stand as someone starts shouting from the back of the courtroom, just behind me.

'Tek me, Your Honour!'

I turn and see Hezekiah holding up his arms, his wrists locked together as if he's cuffed.

'This yah is my crime as a father. Me daughter innocent.'

He starts to run, darting between the bench where Asase is sitting, past the jury, the barristers' and the solicitors. Asase is looking at him with disgust and turns her head away. The usher and clerk run towards him as he heads for the judge. They try to hold him back, but he's pushing and shoving. They manage to wrestle him to the ground and a policeman cuffs him.

People in the gallery are calling out. Some are saying leave the old man alone; some are saying throw him in the dock with his daughter.

'Order, order!' shouts the judge.

The policeman takes Hezekiah out of court and the judge calls for a recess.

There are cracks in the air now; people poised like springs. Whatever Hezekiah was trying to do has backfired. Eustace's friends are staring at me, kissing their teeth. There's heat in my face and my throat is tightening. People in the gallery are huddling into groups, talking in loud voices. I leave the courtroom quick-time. Run down the corridors and out into daylight. Wanting to likk concrete, get as far away as I can from this place. From everyone.

I catch a taxi to the Dead Water area. Searching for sound imprints of Moose. Samples from the past, alive with the now. Entanglement. I'll be OK if I can hear again that one gospel-swaying note that brings something of him back.

There are lights inside the old cottages, grey clouds rising from factories in the distance. I remember the rare-groove women in their floaty dresses swaying, Moose's favourite song in my head. I sit on a bench on the towpath. I take his mahogany ring off my finger, hold it up to the light and look through it like a portal.

I stay that way for hours, watching the last of the summer light skimming the water, slipping further and further away into the tunnel.

Coulda pushed myself up with other people. Maybe Cynthia, who runs the community centre – a hall with a snooker table, some battered chairs and ripped cushions with foam spilling out. Or Georgia, a young mother with a two-year-old girl who lives in the flat next door. She's always begging my company because she's trapped in her yard day in, day out, no money to do anything. But I keep myself to myself. When Irving's gone to work, I light up the flat with fiyah dub. Leave my body. Speak to the dead. Hover in their world. Try not to think about Asase and what I know. Afraid I might be called to the witness stand and break down under questioning.

Herbert calls on Saturday morning, says he's coming round. Irving's at the garage. It's the day after the inquest into Moose's death. Nile had tried to persuade me to go with him, but I didn't.

Couldn't bear the thought of looking at the policemen flipping through notebooks, spinning their version of truth.

'I need coffee,' Herbert says as he walks in.

He's wearing a black T-shirt and grey Farah trousers, his khaki messenger bag hanging on one shoulder. For once, his Afro isn't shaped; it's like an explosion of electrodes. The muscles round his jaw are tensed.

He follows me into the kitchen and sits down at the table, facing the small window where light and a late-summer breeze blows in, disturbing the stale smell of Irving's tobacco smoke. I mix milk and coffee granules, pour water and stir anti-clockwise. Backwards spinning time.

'Sit down, Yamaye,' Herbert says. His voice is remote, restrained.

I put the mugs on the table, sit opposite him.

He clears his throat. The murmur of the radio comes from the front room.

'Eight to two majority,' he says. 'Lawful killing by the police.' His eyes are steady, rooted.

I look down at my hands. Jangled heartbeat. Compression around my throat. Can't breathe. Moose's fear inna my blood.

Herbert puts his hand on mine. I shake him off, flop on to the table, my head in my hands. Moose's pain is a toneless weight in my body.

'This is just the start, Yamaye,' Herbert says.

He gets up and pulls me into a sitting position, keeps his hand on my back.

'They're not going to be prosecuted,' I say. 'How the fuck can that be! Tek a life and walk free? Asase didn't kill anyone so how come she's locked up right now, guilty before the verdict, but police are innocent whatever we prove.'

'We'll push for an independent inquiry,' he says. 'This is just the start.'

'Chances?'

'The jurors at the inquest wrote a letter criticising the police. Now we need public sympathy.'

'Babylon is under pressure for once.'

'They may try and take the spotlight off themselves – put question marks over the campaign, make it look like someone close to him is the threat. You're not involved in anything?'

'A puff now and again. Nuth'n else.'

He sits down, relights his cigarette. 'You need a clear head. They may ramp up the surveillance.' He blows smoke. Lips puckered, eyes puckered, nostrils puckered. 'You were Moose's woman. You're Asase's friend. Easy target. Guilty by association.'

'Dancing partner, not partner in crime. And you knew her too . . . for a while.'

'Asase,' he says. 'Beautiful professional woman stabs a man for no apparent reason. But there's always more to it. I did offer my help.'

'And?'

'She doesn't handle rejection well, does she?' His tawny irises and yellow pupils spin, and his face recedes into a gravitational centre of knowing.

'Pride,' I say.

'You know her better than me.'

'Thought I did.'

He extinguishes his cigarette; gulps coffee, both hands around the mug like he's strangling it. He takes something out of his bag and places it on the table. A photo of Moose. It's in black and white, but there's a blue background. Moose's shoulders are turned slightly away from the camera, leather jacket, white T-shirt, oiled, clean-shaven face, buzz cut, join-the-dots pods of hair. He's looking straight at me. I put my fingers on his lips.

'Our photographer added some touches to this. It's for the marches. See you at the office next week?'

I nod.

'Switch up your routes. Be careful,' Herbert says.

'What good did careful do for Moose?' I say.

When he's gone, I open the windows in the front room and the cool voices of ghosts call: 'Lonely, lonely.' Grey clouds, big as islands, float by, and it feels like the tower block is moving, caught in a slipstream.

Herbert phones me a few days later to tell me that Asase's been found guilty of assault with a deadly weapon and sentenced to five years. I had told Herbert about Crab Man assaulting Asase earlier that night. He says the defence made no mention of that.

I remember the way Crab Man shook Asase. How her eyes rolled back in her head. How it left her wired. Flexed to fight. Herbert says that maybe Asase saw the headlines, the way the press were describing her. Maybe she knew it was pointless trying to show herself as a woman who was afraid after she saw her grainy mugshot in the paper – uncombed hair spiky as barbed wire, white duppy dust from the vaults powdering her face. Another Black suspect trapped inside the prison of black-and-white print. I feel pain at the thought of not seeing her on the outside again for a long time. Like a central bone in my body has collapsed, my nerves raw and exposed.

'It's the end of our dancing time,' I say to Herbert, then hang up without saying goodbye. I wonder if one day I'll write a song, a sound memorial for the times we had. Those winter nights of music and heat, Asase, Rumer, Moose and me.

Now I've been thrown overboard into a dark sea. My soft-body is coral, taking root on the ocean floor, nothing to hold on to but coldness and darkness for centuries to come.

9

Echolocation

Late summer is dry as tinder. Then it rains. Heaviest September rainfall in hundreds of years, the papers say. River and streams flooded. A giant sinkhole opens up on the wastelands near the Tombstone Estate; it fills with muddy rain, creating a brown watery eye. The pit swallows trees, bushes, burnt-out cars and tyres, just missing the community shops on the northern periphery.

The Residents' Association decides the towers are built on unsafe land, limestone that's dissolving under rainfall. They say it's surely a matter of time before the flats collapse. They start a campaign to tear the estate down and rehouse the residents in the modern blocks that are being constructed across London.

Mr Everleigh, who runs the Residents' Association, has lived in Norwood all his life, and can remember when there were more farms here than houses. Wheat, barley, grazing sheep, cows, and brickfields where clay was dug up from the ground and mixed with chalk and ash to make bricks. He said that hundreds of years ago, a local architect made bricks that were used to build palaces and castles all around the world. Never built a palace here, he says. From all that digging, they found hidden trenches, defensive walls, and the grave of an ancient Viking with lead weights and gold rings. Mr Everleigh said tearing up the land for bricks must have disturbed the earth. People had no business churning up the past.

Bongo Natty is telling everyone that the sinkhole is an underground cave. *Echolocation, iyah, the ancestors trying to reach us from hideouts below ground.*

People get heated up about whose version is right. There are meetings and talks even as the temperature rises and the rain stops.

I think of Asase locked in a cell while summer, her favourite time of year, fades into autumn. All her beautiful dresses hanging in the darkness of her wardrobe. I consider going to see her in prison, but there are surges of electric voltage in my gut when I think about facing her. She'll be vex fe true. Yeah, she'll accuse me of breaking the sistren rules. Dropping your sistah when she needs you. Don't want to look inna her face, knowing that she jooked Eustace in his back. I'm probing and measuring the circuits of our relationship from afar. Don't want her current running through my heart.

Herbert calls to say he's got hold of CCTV film from a bank. It shows that the police had Moose on the floor, cuffed, face down. There's more, but it's sensitive to the case and he doesn't want me or anyone else to see the footage at this stage.

We talk about the silent march that we're planning outside the police station in Moose's town. I ask if we should say anything about the CCTV footage at the march. His voice goes all tight. For now, he wants to power the case without any smoke.

I want to tell him to bring the fiyah and the smoke. But I'm worried he's checking me as if I'm the same as Asase. Expecting overspill.

I wait for him to say something reassuring, personal. Anything outside his metronomic handling of the case.

There's an awkward silence. I say, 'Laters,' and hang up. I'm on my own. Someone to be organised, filed away, retrieved when there's more photocopying to be done.

Hundreds of people show up at the silent march. The heat is likking twenty-two degrees. Dub dancers, bovver boys, punks, soulheads, Sikhs in leather jackets and turbans. By early evening there's a wave of placards facing the station, some with Moose's face smiling down, some with the faces of other men who've been killed by Babylon. The police are a barrier of blue guarding their station, glinting behind transparent shields.

Herbert is addressing the protestors, standing on a small wooden block. I'm three lines from the front with Nile and a group of Moose's friends and clients, our arms linked. It's strange being in a crowd without Asase and Rumer. Now they're gone, I only think of the good times. Dancing in the dark; wet, salty bodies sliding in and out of bleeps and horns and haze; transformed by bassline, a better version of ourselves in the grey light before dawn.

I look to see if anyone else from the Crypt is there and notice Crab Man further along, puffing on a thick cigar. He nods at me, moves towards us, pushing people aside.

Heat in my face and hands. 'What the fuck is he doing here?' I say to Nile.

'Who?' Nile asks.

Before I can say anything more, Crab Man has squeezed in on the other side of Nile and linked arms with him.

'The massive dem reach,' Crab Man says to Nile.

'Yes, my bredrin, thanks for supporting,' Nile says.

I pull on Nile's arm to get his attention, warn him about Crab Man, but the police advance, shouting, 'Move back.' We push against them, a wave of bodies and placards as if we're one heaving breath.

The police move towards us again and we lean into their force, sea breaking against rocks. The wind blows and bright red leaves fall off maple trees in the station courtyard, the air raining blood.

Crab Man is gone.

Herbert puts a large black loudspeaker to his face, calls out the names of men who died in custody:

'Gloria Simons 1975
Prem Singh 1976
Julian Ferreira 1977
Barry Floyd 1979
Moose – Marlon Bohiti 1979'

Rights On are on the front line, wearing T-shirts emblazoned with the organisation's name. One of them, an older white woman with a scarf knotted under her chin, blows a horn as each name is called. The names go on and on. We stamp our feet until the names become acoustic shadows. I follow them beyond the range of hearing.

It's the Friday after the silent march. There was a debrief at Rights On yesterday. Herbert said the far right are planning a march in Norwood in ten days' time and the Anti-Nazi League are organising a counter-demonstration. He says a riot is brewing and warns me to stay off the street.

The day of the far-right march arrives; unseasonal heat is likking thirty degrees and rising. I spend the afternoon watching TV. There's a news report about a riot in another city. People kicking-off about the same thing. Police brutality. Racism. Hardship. Ghost-shaped yellow flames clash with darkness; flames big as balloons expand in a bank before a loud bang as the building explodes; rows of police walk backwards as the air ruptures with bricks, a crowd of men running at them. There are shouts and the camera is knocked to one side. The film clip stops and switches to a journalist asking a Black man why people are rioting.

'Harassment,' the man says. 'We're Black people, defending ourselves to live free lives, free from the torture chambers of the police.'

I hear music blasting from one of the flats nearby and I go on to the balcony. The windows in the tower blocks are open, the air is still. Groups of people walking across the wastelands, stopping and picking things up from the ground.

Billowing clouds merge and grow. Borderline strangeness this far up. I'm hiding out in the sky. Fraidy-fraidy, like Asase says. Drumbeats in the distance, a thunder-bass heartbeat calling me. I put on tracksuit and trainers and walk to the high street. Young and old are hanging out in shop doorways, cotching on walls; roadblocks of people stand firm in the middle of the road. Shadowy sinewaves from the Crypt seep into daytime.

Norwood has come alive.

Everybody ready to claim the light.

Mothers pushing prams, old people arm in arm, children ramping. Youth dressed in khaki jackets, parachute trousers, silk tracksuits, gold chaps and belchers. Floating on the surface, shades and caps on, waiting for the call of the abeng horn.

In the other direction, heading south towards the fields, there are stalls selling flimsy handmade political books and cassettes with speeches. A Black man wearing a long, indigo agbada robe shouts, 'Pound a prayer. Let me pray for you. Your dreams will come true.' A woman in a sari is laying out logs of quartz and chunks of blue rock on a table with signs saying CRYSTALS FOR PROTECTION. Journalists are speaking to people, asking them how they feel about the far right marching through their town, what they think about police stop and search. A camera crew is filming. Police cars and vans are parked on side roads. A helicopter circling overhead like a giant moth.

I walk towards Lionel's Liquor Mart, past Delhi Wala Foods. I want to stand with some of the Crypt posse who are outside Dub Steppaz, but they're cutting their eyes on me. Vex about the closure of the shop. The door is padlocked, but men lean against the windows that are covered in Bongo Natty's posters of red arrows firing into a dark universe. I cross to the middle of the road where people are circled around Misty in Roots. The band is decked out in Kente robes, guitars hanging over their shoulders like machine guns. Indian drummers in flowing white cotton play with them, tearing up goatskin drums, mekking hypnotic sounds. Youth, elders, families, everyone clapping, swaying, as if today is the one day to break a curse, start again.

White bwoys in a punk band further along shout, 'People unite! Babylon's burning.' In their black boots and braces, they strut and twist their guitars across their bodies, left to right, as if they're rowing for their lives. Electric guitar and drums kick in and they're singing.

Somebody blows a horn and the massive raises their fists, shouting, 'Forward! Forward!' And people join the crowd on the road. Pepper-spray dust in the air. The shining dome of the temple radiating a strange, red-gold light. I catch my reflection in the shop window. I've cut my hair, razed it close to my skull. My eye sockets are holes in the ground, sunken cheekbones are craters. My backup crew is gone, my armour's on.

The drums slow and the crowd quietens as the far-right group march towards us, coming from the direction of the train station. Police with batons and shields on either side of them.

The lead singer of Misty in Roots shouts over the mic, 'Don't let them in our community. Stand strong!' One of them blows the abeng horn. The Indians play their tablas in response.

Faster and faster. Women drop down, gyrate and ululate. Shopkeepers pull down metal grilles, drag in crates of fruit and root vegetables that look like the hooves of prehistoric animals.

I imagine myself walking up the street, away from the chanting throng, turning the corner, heading home, taking the lift to the empty flat, lighting a spliff, falling asleep to Muma's lullaby.

Cha! I ain't going nowhere! The dry layers of loss and loneliness in my body have been lit. I'm ready to walk through smoke; come out the other side.

I chant with the crowd.

Fire rush. Fire bu'n.

Men lean in doorways, balanced on one leg, heads cocked like guns, waiting for the call to kick-off.

Bongo Natty is standing outside Dub Steppaz with the Crypt posse. He shakes his dreadlocks as I walk towards him. I try to speak, but he looks at me hard, two lines between his eyes.

'Go a yuh yard,' he says. 'September's gonna bu'n.' He marches off to the centre of the crowd, springing from his toes.

The abeng blows three times as the police and the far-right group come to the edge of the crowd. Babylon push through, and suddenly there's the hot-breath *whoozzzh-whoozzzh* as a Molotov cocktail flies through the air towards them. Synth splashes and molten spurts, the smell of palm oil and petrol. The crowd charge the police, surging off the black tarmac road with heroic badness – peel-head bwoys, Rastas, shaven-haired punks, women with cane rows and rebel hoop earrings – dropping all kinds of moves with supernatural war cries, whistles and wailing. Some of them bust through, fist-fighting with men inside the barricade. Grunts and shouts. The sound of truncheons likking shields and skulls and backbones. Someone over a loudspeaker shouting, 'Riot squad!' And then the sound of horse hooves as caped police on horseback ride towards us, waving long white truncheons.

People run in all directions. The explosive noise of glass brucking-up. Fires popping. Shop alarms clanging. The far-right group is fighting with our rebels in small groups. A tall, wiry man running at them, shouting, 'Bruck dem up. Bruck dem.' His navy balaclava dominated by the burning red O of his mouth.

Two men with slingshot, pellet eyes are standing on top of an upturned car, pounding it like a steel drum. Police on horseback fly at them like bats.

The church bell is ringing and ringing and smoke pours out of a shop on to the street; a pile of crates in the road burns, flames lapping the air.

I see Bongo Natty and men from the Crypt running towards a group who are waiting for them on the edges of the police barricade with open arms, fists clenching metal rods and bats.

Our rebels are chanting as they run in all directions, sonic expressions of pain, exaltation and destruction that shake the ground. It's as if heaven and earth are shifting against each other like tectonic plates. I'm raised up by the rhythmic roaring and I run with the massive down side streets, shouting, 'Mash down Babylon!'

We follow percussive trails of drumbeats, up and down narrow alleyways. Caught in infinite loops. I'm running and dancing all at the same time. My body sweating out stars and the dark universe that's inside me. This is where I need to be, unified with my people through rhythm and tone.

People break off here and there like flakes of skin from a shedding snake. Drum and bass thump from powerful speakers as a car drives down the side street, half on the pavement, swerving between people, leaving menacing vocal bites.

We're brucking out against the aimless afternoons on street corners.

Brucking out against loss and fear.

The sun is sinking low. Sky rippling red. Everyone in a heightened state. One consciousness. One intention. To bust outta our bodies. I sanctify my tongue with the dub lash and cry out with everyone else, 'Mash down Babylon!'

Police on foot are dragging people off to waiting vans.

I'm afraid of being thrown into a van and caged like Moose. I break away. Crouch down in the doorway of a corner shop, breathing hard, a sharp pain in my side.

The sound of police batons beating against shields, a dense dread pulsing. I run away from the sound, through a series of dark alleyways, until I'm at a side road near the Crypt. The light is fading as I run up the road. Father Mullaney is on the forecourt at the front of the church. He's on his knees praying for peace, people kneeling around him holding candles, their eyes closed.

I go to the side of the church and beat on the door to the Crypt. Footsteps stop on the other side. I say it's me and Lego opens the door. He pulls me inside. I stop at the top of the stairs, double over, trying to catch my breath.

'You OK, sis?' Lego asks.

I stand up. 'Feeling the heat,' I say.

'What you doing on the streets?' Lego asks. 'Father Mullaney says he's never seen so many police in one place.'

The long table where Bongo Natty used to stand is still there, a red chair pushed underneath. I lean against it. Tell him what's going down outside.

'Wish I could be out there throwing down some likks on Babylon.' He aims his walking stick in the air like a spear and jabs it several times. 'Come, rest up,' he says. 'Wait till Babylon gone.'

I follow him downstairs into the Crypt. He walks quick, despite his artificial left leg, holding the rail with his left hand, his black metal walking stick in his right, tap-tap-tapping on the steps.

Dim lights in the arches leave shadows on the ground. Strange to see the Crypt without the cave-like speaker boxes, the wires hanging like vines, dancers blowing whistles, waving lighters in the air. Stranger still to see it without smoke.

'No more dances here,' Lego says. 'Babylon put a stop to that.'

He says Bongo Natty is checking out new places. He stops outside the bolted doorway, looks at me. 'True seh Bongo Natty is vex with Asase.'

'And you?'

'Asase did wrong,' Lego says. 'But I let her in. Not throwing anyone in the lion's den of Babylon.'

We sit on a wooden bench in one of the alcoves, dust floating like small stars. The emptiness is filled with the low rumble of long-ago drum and bass, warped sounds that have never escaped.

I tell him I heard that Eustace is moving away and ask if he thinks I should write to Eustace and Loreen and say sorry for what's happened. Lego says best leave it. Eustace needs to sort his head out. He's shaken up. Bad. Loreen is at the control tower now. Got herself a job. Eustace is gonna stay home for a while. They're cotching with Loreen's mother in one of them big yards in Brixton until they go to Brighton. They're not coming back.

Lego stops talking and the sound waves overwhelm me with memories of dancing with Moose, Asase, and Rumer; the air overflows with droning sonics that dissolve into nothingness. I swallow the heaviness in my throat.

'I-and-I still here for you, Yamaye,' he says.

'Bongo Natty has always been the one who lets me know you're OK down here. Now what?'

'Give the man time. He can't get to Asase, so he's throwing it all at you.' He taps his artificial leg with the stick. 'Heightened feeling in this foot now it's gone,' he says. 'I learn about people inna the dark, their shapes.' He looks inna my eyes. 'Don't worry 'bout me.'

But how can I not worry. His face is dry; there are grey patches in his deep brown skin, ashy rings under his eyes. He's mummified by the dark.

I ask how come the police didn't find him when they were looking for Asase. 'Someone told the police where to find Asase,' I say.

He starts coughing.

'You need light,' I say.

'Fuck light. Man needs freedom,' he says.

'Who do you think the informer is?' I ask.

'Nah fret 'bout that,' he says.

I follow him down steps and through a wooden door; he switches on the light in a small, arched vault with four black marble sarcophagi. Floating, brown dust, the earthy smell of lead, charcoal and quicklime.

'Asase was in here,' he says.

'You?'

'I know every inch of this place, more than Father Mullaney. He's out most of the time, checking on the sick and dying.'

He leads me through an archway and down more stairs into a room with benches. He pushes one of the benches aside. Underneath is a wooden trapdoor cut into the paved stones. He opens it. We go down steps into a small, stone vault.

'This is the place I hide when I need to,' he says. 'The rest of the time I have a room upstairs by the office. That's where I spend my days and nights.'

Hard to say whether Lego's free or not. He says if the police ever catch him, they won't be taking him alive. He won't go down without a fight. He starts skanking, his arms raised, holding his imagined machine gun, firing into the air, 'Mash down Babylon!' He throws his head back, laughing and coughing.

'You took a risk hiding her,' I say.

'Father Mullaney was vex. Warned me from doing it again,' he says.

'Everybody is vex with somebody in this town right now,' I say. 'Like it's my fault Dub Steppaz is shut down.'

He asks if I need to stay until the morning when hopefully the riot will have died down. Only, Father Mullaney is worried the police may come looking for him tonight, so I'd have to stay with him locked in the stone vault. I say I'd rather try to get home.

We go upstairs and he's singing about whipping Babylon and making a whipping sound with air trapped between tongue and teeth.

He stands behind the vault door as he opens it. Says it's best I don't come again. Father Mullaney and Bongo Natty can coordinate visits. Father Mullaney won't want anyone else coming and going.

I kiss his cheek and he shuts the door behind me.

I don't know how long I've been with Lego. Time in the Crypt isn't linear. It's dub time. Refractions. It's dark when I get outside. The priest and the people praying have gone. I can see that their prayers did no good. There's smoke in the air and an upturned car is in flames acoss the street, outside the old Manor House.

I sprint through the grounds of the Manor House on to the waste-lands until I come to Resurrection Cemetery, a shortcut to the Tombstone Estate. But the back gates are chained.

I've cut through here plenty of times with Asase and Rumer. Never at night. Never alone.

Yuh can do this, I tell myself. Gwaan!

So I climb the gates, putting my feet inna the spokes, pulling myself on to the wall. I jump into the cemetery.

The dead are livin' better than us, in their fancy tree-lined avenues.

The office's porch light is dim, but the path is dark with shadows. Not sure if I should sprint. I tread slow, checking every step. Heat rising from the midnight zone. A vast expanse of land; a plantation sucking Black bodies into the earth.

The thought spooks me and I start to run, almost crashing into a big nah-fuck mausoleum. There are tombs with statues of angels with age-blackened faces.

A figure on a grave rises.

I scream.

'Dread hideout, baby,' it says, coming towards me. Matted, spiky, Afro hair, a crown of thorns. Thick-lipped goatee smile. Black-blue skin. It's not a ghost, it's a man.

'What yuh doing?' I shout.

'Gunfire back there,' he says. 'Lovin' dis graveyard silence.' He circles, checks me, waist to face.

'Look, I gotta step,' I say. My voice is shaky. 'Get inna my yard before the town burns down.' I try to walk past but he takes my arm, holds my wrist.

'Please, please don't—' I drop to the floor, whimpering. I'm scared, working hard for mercy.

'Stop mek noise!' he says. 'I ain't troubling yuh. Bull has sealed off the road ahead. No way out, baby. S'all I'm trying to show you.'

I look back at the cemetery wall and the chained gate. He pulls me up to standing. Brushes down a black marble tomb, sits on it. Sings: 'Riot time, and the pickings are easy.' Laughs.

'You're scaring the fuck outta me, dread,' I say.

'Feel no way, baby.' He leans against the angel at the head of the tomb, the wings on either side of him. 'I'd drop you home. From my wheels stra-a-ight to yuh yard. That's how I run things. Seen? Right-about now my car is sealed off, tyres flat. Cities are burning. World's on fire. Dis is the place to be.' He slaps the tomb. 'Come nuh?'

I step back.

'Cotch, babe. Spirits won't skank yuh,' he says.

'It's not the spirits that are troubling me,' I say.

'Give me some overstanding, babe. Trust me.'

'Nevah trust no man who asks for trust.'

He laughs. 'Monassa's my name,' he says. 'Now sit.'

I sit on the edge of the tomb at the far end. Smell mould and rotting flowers.

He makes a clicking sound at the back of his throat, then throttles his earhole with his index finger. Relights a spliff. Inhales. Exhales a declaration of peace.

'Ganja grew on Solomon's grave, overstand?' He likks a beat on the gravestone with his left hand, toasting, 'Burn, Babylon a bu'n. Wicked have fe learn.' He's wearing blue seam-stitched jeans, a white capped-sleeve T-shirt with six red arrows on his chest, like the arrows on the posters that are plastered everywhere.

'You one of the revolutionaries?' I ask.

'Revolutionary? I like that,' he says.

He says one of his bredrin is doing time in some offshore prison for something he didn't do and that's he happy to darken any area where people are rising up against racists and the police. He asks me why I was there and I tell him about Moose.

'Didn't know the brother,' he says. He asks me if I know Asase. Says he heard about the stabbing. 'You must have known her,' he says. 'Everyone knows everyone in this town.'

I admit she was my friend. We talk about it for a while, and he says a woman like that should have been put under manners before now.

'Think it's safe to go yet?' I ask.

'Go if you want. Bull ain't catching my raas tonight,' he says.

There's the sound in the distance of a loud explosion and popping, like guns going off.

'I'll wait with the duppies,' I say.

He laughs. 'Sister, sister, you're one a dem, huh? A woman who fears not the dead.' He leans towards me, takes my face in his hands, squeezes until my lips push out. 'Ashes or bone? What are you?'

I jerk out of his grip.

'Don't turn away from me. I don't like it when a woman does that.'

I go to another tomb and sit on it. Flip my lighter on. The inscription reads:

THERE SHALL BE NO DARKNESS
NO DAZZLING
BUT ONE EQUAL LIGHT
NO NOISE
NOR SILENCE
BUT ONE EQUAL MUSIC.

Smoke-fall. Black soundbox sky perforated by stars.

Moose is everywhere, I hear his voice: 'Stay cool, baby, you ain't nobody's fool.'

'I'm just buzzing,' Monassa says. 'Apologies.'

He quiets his arse. Keeps to his grave. Tells me he lives with his crew, Dungle and Racer, in a lock-tight safe house in Bristol not far from a slave port. 'Racer's a white Caribbean. Dutch ancestors. His people were abandoned on some volcanic island hundreds of years ago. White tribe. Rootless, like me. And you.'

I turn my back on him.

'It's in the eyes. You don't fit nowhere, do ya?' He gets up, pulls me on to his grave, stretches his feet out. Tells me to sleep.

I look at him. Black skin with the volcanic shimmer of reds and gold, like he's fresh from the core of the earth. He looks right back at me – hard, like he can see everything. My pain, loneliness, fear.

He pushes my head on to his chest. He smells of ganja, perfume, sex-musk. I exhale, grateful for human touch.

He presses his hand against the back of my head, directing it towards his crotch. 'While you're down there, baby.'

'Yuh raas.' I try to pull away, but he holds me like a hug.

'Jokes!' he says.

The man's messing with me, trying to lighten things up. I laugh, uncertain.

'I'm gonna catch some sleep,' he says. 'I'm bleached. Shut yuh eye.' His breathing slows.

I keep my eyes open, watch the graves. Black-note sounds of souls rising and fading into darkness. Lights in the distance go out.

The sky churning clouds from the burning town; pressure in my ear, an underwater head spin. I hear the stars, each one a name.

Gloria Simons 1975
Prem Singh 1976
Julian Ferreira 1977
Barry Floyd 1979
Moose – Marlon Bohiti 1979

Birdsong wake us at first light. We walk to the other side of the cemetery, climb the wall, and head to the Tombstone Estate. Burnt-out cars and tyres, broken glass and blood on the ground, a trainer, a sock. A lone milk cart rattling along the road. A boy on his bicycle, hands in his pockets, cycling as if travelling through a dream.

Monassa walks with a boasty right-foot slide and bounce, like he's not afraid of anything. I move closer to him.

We stop outside the doors to the lift.

'I'll call you a taxi somewhere so you can sort your car,' I say.

We ride the coffin-lift, rising together. Dried vomit in a corner, a puddle of piss, the jagged end of a green bottle. I put my hand over my nose and mouth.

Irving's bedroom door is shut; he must be asleep. I make Monassa wait in the front while I call a taxi.

I see him to the door. He leans in as if he's gonna kiss me. I put my hand on his chest and push him away. He laughs, takes something out of his back pocket and hands me a glossy black card with his number printed in gold. No name. Strokes my cheek. 'Nah let the duppies skank you, baby.'

Then he's gone.

10

Earth Riddim

Autumn bleeding into winter. Awake with spirituals inna my head. The after-effects of the stabbing and the riot spread like bacteria through town. People watching each other with suspicion, staying in their own micro-bubbles. Herbert says it's not a good idea to hold any more marches for a while. And he's focusing on the casework and investigation into Moose's death, gathering documents to show that the police destroyed and contaminated evidence. Some law students are assisting him. There's nothing more I can do for now. I sign up with an agency and start temping all over London, partitioned in a cubicle, typing, feeding white tapes of coded messages into clattering telex machines.

Evenings, I hold it down in my room, writing lyrics, singing, sometimes walking through the narrow alleyways to Devil's Tunnel, searching the Dead Water area for the old cottages where I once danced with Asase and Rumer. The houses are set back from the streetline, boundaried by ancient walls; dark timber sash windows. I never find the places we raved in.

Waiting for the phone to ring. I look down at the empty streets below. My world is my room now. A double bed by the window; a high-tech Promised Land stereo; teak dressing table with cassette tapes in the four drawers.

Monassa and I speak on the phone most weeks. He asks about my day, wants to know I'm OK, whether Babylon is following me. Once every couple of weeks he comes to Norwood to see a man in the Manor House business centre who is running an investment company. Strictly offshore, Caribbean islands, Monassa says. If he's not rushing back to Bristol, we meet for a bowl of stewed peas in Dutch Pot, a small cafe off the high street. He says he cares about my welfare, with all the uprisings everywhere. He tells me about the riot in his city and how he and his men coordinated part of it. He doesn't seem afraid of Babylon.

If he doesn't call for a few days, I feel bent out of shape, cast-off, like those mangled scraps found on the wastelands. Not because I feel anything like what I had with Asase and Rumer. Nowhere near the comfort I got from Moose. More like an explosion of yearning for something unfamiliar that can change me in some way. Like the clay that used to be dug up from the old brickfields, the mixing of chalk and ash.

The phone doesn't ring and I feel an aching loneliness. I put on my coat and ankle boots and walk across the estate to Oraca's block. I haven't seen Oraca since the trial four months ago. Irving cut her off and warned me that as long as I was under his roof I wasn't to business with them. Everyone in town is avoiding Oraca, and I was too.

Oraca flings the door open like she's expecting trouble and is damn well ready fe it, dressed like a sorceress in a long, black woollen skirt and oversized red cardigan. Her face is hollow; an empty net of skin where flesh used to be now hangs below her chin.

She tilts her head to one side and arches an eyebrow. 'Look yah,' she says. 'I live to fight another day.'

Doesn't look like she's living to me. All the weight gone from her body and a frothy ring of white hair around her temples like the tide's come in.

She doesn't hug me.

I follow her into the back room, the space that was for visitors, hardly used, always in shadow. She stands in front of the paraffin heater, sways against the heat.

'Irving know yuh here?' she asks.

'No,' I say.

'What him saying?'

'You know him.'

'Same as everybody else? Madness inna we blood?'

'I should have come before. There's been so much—'

'Yuh standing like stranger. Sit. This is your home.'

I take off my sheepskin coat. It's heavy as armour and I feel exposed without it. I sit on the small, velvet two-seater and she squeezes in beside me. Almost a year since I've been here.

Word is she hardly leaves her home, and Hezekiah doesn't swing by any more. The house is the same as it ever was, steam drifting from the kitchen, the smell of fried fish and herbs. Nothing's changed, except a large, framed photo of Asase hanging in the adjoining front room above the fireplace where a picture of Jesus used to be, her neckline and gold medallion submerged in shadow.

Oraca takes my hand, squeezes it and holds it in her lap, but it feels more for her benefit than mine.

'How's Asase?' I ask.

'You should find out for yuhself. She say yuh dash her away. Ah so?'

'She hasn't sent a VO.'

'Yuh must mek the first move. She needs our protection!'

'Asase?'

'When your muma died, I protected you,' she says.

'I know. Weekends, holidays, I was here,' I say.

'Your muma and me came to this yah country with nuth'n.' I know where she's going with this; it's a story she's told many times. 'Me and your muma met on the steam ship, *Reina del Pacifico*, sailing to England. We were on deck one morning. She was leaning against the railing, the sea spread out behind her like empty airmail paper. Your poopa clapped eyes on her in that coral dress and candy-box hat. Man couldn't see nuth'n else after that. We came with our grips and polished shoes. What little we had we held on to. He was possessive.'

'Why won't he say more about Muma?'

'Yuh poor, poor muma. Straining dat weak body of hers to birth yuh. Calling out that the devil did lash her face as you came outta her belly. I was with her. It wasn't Satan did her harm!'

'Our people don't talk straight. Too damned secretive.'

'We had to talk with our feet, not hang ourselves with our tongues.' She gets up. 'I have fish and bammie.'

'Not for me.'

She pulls the paraffin heater closer to us and sits down again.

Oraca tells me what she's told me many times before, how after their arrival in England, the two couples – Muma and Irving, Oraca and Hezekiah – lived in an underground air-raid shelter for six weeks before finding rooms at a shared house on Alexandra Road, on the other side of the railway line.

Oraca says what she never gets tired of saying: 'Me will never, as long as me live, understand why somebody who could sing like Muma would give it up.' She talks about the two years in the shared house and how good it was, a honeymoon period for everyone. Asase was born there. A woman from St Lucia rented another room and they all lived there with the older Jamaican couple who owned the house. Parties every weekend, amped-up, condensed bodies shuffling and twisting, working their way into their new world. Muma was the star attraction, singing for everyone at the parties, until Irving accused her of flirting with other men.

I stop her. It's the first time she's said anything like this about

Muma. I can taste the smoke in the back of my throat. 'Flirting?' I say. 'What kind of flirting?'

'All that singing about love and passion, yuh know. When she step offa that stage, them feelings, them longings musta been inside her. The men came running, grinning dem teeth. She enjoyed attention. More and more.'

She says they were good days, Muma began singing in smoky clubs in Soho. But I interrupt her, I want to go back to what she just said.

'Was Muma just flirting or was she seeing other men?' I ask.

Oraca leans forward, opens the small glass vent of the paraffin heater and adjusts the wick. Dark shapes float out. Tight heat spreading across my chest.

'There was a musician, around her age. Played the trumpet. Could sing too. His top notes were right behind your muma's. Man was always sniffing around her. Handsome bad-bad-bad, skin like varnished wood, puppy-dog eyes always full of saltwater. Irving suspected everyone, but this man was different. Close as we was, your muma didn't tell me everything. She grew up alone, kept things to herself. All I knew was that he played in a band that she sang with sometimes. Can't say if anything happened between them.'

Oraca says she doesn't remember his name or anything more about him, although she can remember his face good-good. She goes on to tell me that when the two couples were housed on the Tombstone Estate a year later, Irving told Muma she couldn't sing at the clubs any more. She was pregnant with me and he said mothers had no business in them kind of places. So Muma picked herself up, went back to her maternity work. Three or four years later, she was gone.

'That was 1958. Never saw her again,' she says.

'Why Guyana?' I ask.

'Me tell you plenty times: to nurse mothers and babies. Some missionary people.'

'Why didn't she take me?'

'Malaria and fevers in those places. They were paying her good money. Said she had plans.'

'Like?'

Oraca looks towards Asase's framed photo on the wall. 'Your poopa judging us. Let him who is without sin cast the first stone,' she mutters.

'What yuh saying?' I ask.

'Your muma was running.' Her voice is bassy, breathy.

'From?'

'Guilt plays out in mysterious ways. People live life, but act like dem dead.'

'From Irving?'

'Your muma was too soft. You tek after her.' She gets up and goes to the stereo, puts a jazz record on low. Another trumpeter blowing storms in the air. 'Irving was slapping her around,' she says.

I lean away from her. 'Hitting her?'

She moves closer, whispers, 'Beating. Bad-bad.'

I rub my hand along my thigh, remember the shock I felt every time Irving hit me when I was a child. The hurt and shame of being made to cry. The fear that things might go out of control. Those feelings always worse than the sting of leather on my skin. I feel the heat of rage for myself and for Muma.

'Should have known he could take it that far,' I say. 'He loved raising his hand.'

'Yuh won't remember. You were too young.'

'I remember . . . they're memories, or . . .' The images are just below the waterline. The shouting, me squeezing my eyes shut, tightening my fists, the silence before the sea pours in and absorbs everything.

'You can't remember her. And him can't look at you without remembering her.'

You can't remember her. Those words so final they burn.

'And your poopa has the cheek to judge us?' she says. 'Huh! Him is the last person should be throwing stones.'

'The man's gutless,' I say. 'No wonder he can't look me in the eyes.' I wish he were here right now so I could lash his eyes and mouth until they're bruised and closed and he can't use them to lie any more.

Black coils of smoke come from the top of the paraffin heater. I inhale it, draw the heat down my throat and it's Muma's voice, singing:

sending my dream
let me tek yuh to the sea

The burning stops. I was singing along with her.

'How you know that song?' Oraca asks.

I shrug.

She looks at me and her pure-black eyes narrow like spear tips. 'That was your muma's favourite song. She always closed her performance with it.'

I think of Muma on a small stage in a dark, airless club, unable to make out faces in the audience through the haze of cigarette smoke. Bringing her act to a close, her final scalding note.

I ask Oraca, 'Did Muma speak to you before she left?'

'Her spirit wasn't strong then. She was too quiet. Told me she would send a ticket for you as soon as she'd found a house. She never had a house of her own. She wanted that for you. Never heard from her again. Your father was mash-up when she died. Lord, the crying.' She stands up, shakes her legs. 'We should play music for Asase, your muma, Moose. Call down the spirits inna dis yah house.'

She puts another record on, drops the gold needle into the black pool of magic. It's an old, blistered jazz vinyl, a man singing in a sulphurous tone about Vodou. Oraca holds out her arms to me.

'Me pickney.' Her voice is powerful, rattling like a speaker box.

She leans on my shoulder. I take her weight, feel us sinking under the pressure of submerged memories.

'Nuth'n I won't do for you and Asase.' She pulls my face into her breast.

She hums, dredging her voice up from her gut, and spins me round and round in circles. I feel the vibrations of other feet from long ago, oiled with red copper earth, encircled by fire. Asase looks at us from her picture on the wall, looks across time, bloodlines. My face is burning, my tongue dry.

The record stops and Oraca drops to the floor, gasping, 'Asase, my daughter, Asase.'

'Easy, easy,' I say.

She heaves several times and catches her breath.

'Your muma loved the ocean and the mountains. There was a day we went to the seaside together when she was pregnant with you. She carried you to the coast in her belly. We took a train. Spread a blanket on the sand. It was autumn. The beach wasn't full, but it was warm enough. Your muma said water soothed her soul. She wanted peace for herself – and you. Heaven help her. The man was hitting her when she was carrying you. The sound of the sea was her gift to you.'

She stands up and picks up the record sleeve, takes the vinyl off the turntable, puts it inside and places it face down.

'Asase has no peace,' she says. 'Them messing with her mind in that prison. Telling her she'll have fe change her identity when dem let her out. Move far from here because Eustace family not going to let it go. We not living with fear. I doing what I can. Yuh understand?' She grips my arm. 'Yuh Asase's true friend. She needs you. Yuh think you any different?'

'I don't know—'

I'm spinning away from her, this house, caught in another force of gravity that's dark, liberating, frightening, arousing. I pull my arm away. I want to tell her I *am* different. But maybe she's right. I've killed people a thousand times in my head – men who bounced me on the streets or in dances, Irving when he used to hit me. The police who killed Moose. Maybe the past is in our bodies. In our hands, our minds. Maybe there's fire in me to stab or kill.

Oraca and I look at each other in silence. Her stomach is bloated and pulsing strange noises, like the bass-speaker bins, birthing sound. I'm connected to Oraca, same as those plaited cables of sound systems. I can switch my feelings on and off. They'll always come on again.

I smile at her.

She smiles back, lifts up her jumper. A thick scar runs from her clavicle to the top of her navel. Her body is the strange, black-grey-purple of stagnant water, and her breasts hang like two knotted ropes.

'My heart is failing,' she says. 'They cut me two weeks after the trial. Don't know why me bother.'

Her face shines with a layer of gold. I remember what Moose said one night when we were stopped by the police on our way back from a blues party, that if Babylon only looked beneath the colour of our skins, they'd see the gold that's there.

I bring my face close to Oraca's and look inna her eyes, something you never do with your elders.

I see that familiar expression of hers: observant compassion. She's done all the things mumas of our community do for motherless children – fed me soursop juice, told ofolk stories about Ol' Higue, showed me how to dance Koromanti. Turning my head, I see her from another angle, and remember how carefully she watched whatever Asase said or did to me. Never intervening. Wanting Asase to come out on top.

I feel the air around me full of spirits and sound. My body is light. Spinning away, I'm caught in another force of gravity that's liberating and frightening. Neither good nor bad. Just necessary.

I stand up to go.

'Stay with me. Long as you want.'

I shake my head.

'Running, like your muma, eh?'

I walk out the door.

I go to the high street, look for people I know. But all I see are unfamiliar faces. Half-running-half-walking, the streets seem endless. On to the towpath. The canal is flat, unmoving, silted with wintry darkness. I feel the emptiness of Norwood. Babylon and the town watching me with black-bolt eyes.

11

Remixing

I bu'n weed, sitting on my bed, watching from the window of my room. The signs are all there in the darkness of this November night, the Vodou-drift black clouds, electronic loops of planetary sound.

I think of everything Oraca said about Irving beating Muma. Muma singing in clubs. Irving shutting her up with likks. Telling her she couldn't perform any more.

Muma's voice, loud and clear: *I want to sing.*

'We will,' I say. 'We will.'

On the window ledge, black roses with gold stems sent by Monassa.

'You've lost your man and your friends,' he said the last time we saw each other. 'Step up a gear. Life's not here.'

He wants to make sure I'm never alone in a tight spot again. Doesn't think I belong here. Nuth'n but corner shops and ashy-skinned men. What he says makes sense, and I feel it too. With Moose, Asase and Rumer gone, I feel a pressure, like a dark tide, pulling me in, then pushing me out, further and further each time.

Sometimes Monassa is high, intense, talking about how he's always two steps ahead of the police, who have been after him and his crew for years. He says Norwood is small enough to be discreet for his kind of business. Other times he's quieter, watchful, on edge. He can remind me of Moose – the generosity, the attention – but he's also distant like Moose never was, like he's locked inna his own world; the shadow of a tune, the B-side whirring in and out of voids.

But more and more, I look forward to seeing him. The black freckles, danger marks, on high cheekbones. That, and there's no one else right now. This full-of-it man my only ally.

The phone rings. I pick up. It's Nile.

'This too late for you?'

I turn on the bedside light. The radio is on in Irving's room. I can hear him snoring.

'Everything OK?' I ask.

'Keeping body and mind together. You?'

Too much treble in his tone.

'What's going on?' I ask.

'True seh I don't wanna scare you.' His voice low now; I can hardly hear.

I rest my spliff on the rim of the ashtray, get up and turn on the main light, trailing the telephone cable behind me.

'It's just . . . I've been getting warnings to back off the campaign. Phone calls.'

The line crackles.

'The police?' I ask.

'Whoever it is, they know everything about my family. And you. Phones must be bugged.'

He asks if undercover are still following me. I say yeah, even though I haven't seen them for a while. I sense they're watching from the backwards-droning ruptures in the air.

'Could be some far-right group,' I say. 'You told Herbert?'

'Yamaye, I'm heading out. Accra. Fresh start with my family. It's not the same without my bredrin. I have to live free.'

'You're chipping?'

'My woman, my youth. If it was just me . . .'

'Yuh leaving me to catch fire?'

'Chip, Yamaye. You can do better. Moose always said—'

'Don't tell me what the fuck Moose said.'

'Don't gwaan dem ways, Yamaye. I'm trying to help.'

'By dropping the campaign? Me.'

'You and Herbert are on it. I'll do what I can from Accra. Can't be looking over my shoulder, waiting to be dragged off the street.'

Another one down. Only this time, there's nobody left to lose. The walls of my room are closing in on me.

'Do what you gotta do. I'll sort myself,' I say.

'We're good?'

'It's just me now, you know that?' The line crackles again and there are garbled voices in a distant crossfire of static. 'Someone's on the line,' I say.

'Find a safe place, Yamaye,' he says and hangs up.

I put the smouldering spliff on my wrist. This town's on fire and I'm the one that's burning.

I turn off the light. Turn down the music. Whisper, 'Muma, me and you are getting out.'

I call Monassa and one of his bredrin answers the phone. There's a muffled conversation before he comes on the line.

'Rhatid, baby, yuh inna the midnight mood, eh?' He's buzzing on something, his voice jeggy-jeggy.

'Need to cotch somewhere for a while,' I say.

'Just say it, baby. You miss me.' He laughs.

'Babylon's putting on the pressure and I've got nothing here any more.'

He makes that dutty clearing noise at the back of his throat.

'It'll just be for a month or two.'

'Hey-hey-hey, no limits, baby. That's not how I run t'ings. Pack your t'ings. I'll swing by.'

I pack jeans, Gabicci sweater, trainers, gold-tip shoes. Leave the dance-hall dresses hanging in the wardrobe, each outfit a reminder of dancing with Moose. I put my nose to the black knitted skirt-suit stitched with stars, his scent smudged into the cloth: blue-river musk, pine, earth.

I take his mixtapes, my vinyl and my mic. Scribble a note for Irving. He won't understand why I have to leave. He'll put doubt in my mind. Try to stop me. 'What out there for you?' he'll say. 'Stay safe. Stay small.' And despite everything I now know about him and Muma, I feel guilty for leaving him, because I know the drip-drip-drip effect of loneliness. But I'm done waiting for him to love me.

I fold the letter, put it on Muma's dressing table, imagine it's her reflection in the mirror, telling me: *gwaan*.

Monassa arrives at six in the morning. I see his car from the window. I take the lift down. The light's broken and I descend in darkness.

When I get into the car, his hair is braided in fresh tight cane rows, the ends twisted like little fish tails. His oiled face is shiny as a river. He looks at me in my purple velvet tracksuit with red satin down the sides, navy suede trainers, black rabbit-skin jacket, cropped hair and gold pirate hoop earrings.

'Baby, you're carrying the swing rightabout now. Something different 'bout your face.'

'Yuh full of it this morning. Sweet.' I want to say, *It's called pain*.

I catch a glimpse of Oraca's flat as we pass. There's a light on in her bedroom window. I turn back as we drive further away. Maybe I should have stayed with her, for a while at least. Paid my dues. But something tells me that Oraca will always be there, immortal in the stronghold of her kitchen, waiting for Asase to come home.

One last look at the ghost-white tower blocks, squat three-storey buildings, terraced houses – dissonant chords playing the morning darkness. Sadness welling up in my throat for Irving, Oraca, Lego – the ones left behind. Bitter-sweet sadness for the only home I've known.

12

Version Excursion: Reverb and Delay

B-SIDE/DUBPLATE, 45 RPM

Slack Time

Listen hard, gyal: this place is a version excursion. A dubplate special. The B-side of your spinning world.

Keep working the controls. A little more balance! Rise on the air treble. Tek time with the subterranean bass.

Are those your bruck-up vocals? Or memories played out to eight-bar reggae beats?

Simmer down, gyal. Nuh bother asking yourself: how the raas yuh get here? Inna this world of sonic dust and analogue delay. No buildings. Some place sparked into life from acoustic storms and oceanic spray.

Yamaye, you're far from tombstone estates, blackout dance halls and false trails.

This world of ghost-ridden sounds is familiar-strange.

Check it, gyal: you once danced in an underground world of Echoplex screams, rimshot thunder, sirens reverberating voices of the dead. Sound rebels dropping moves: bucking, flexing and cotching. Driving themselves backwards and forwards. Skanking until that grinding exhalation, when the spark in all of you was ignited.

You're charged on sonic intelligence.

The ravers are busting moves to your Sonix Dominatrix sound system. They're likking drums cut from driftwood, shaking sand calabashes. Sounds are discordant space. Those midnights of long ago when you danced yourself into other worlds, trying to find your voice.

But you got lost inna smoke.

Gwaan: try and forget Moose. See if you can. All the things he told you about the rebels of his rainforest, their skeletons six hundred feet below ground. Maroon and Taino voices in Cockpit Country sinkholes. Their warrior dance moves frozen in time. Petrified in coral, mollusc and red mud.

This place is no safe house. No hideaway. Listen, nuh! Your ancestors are here. Bustin' tunes inside crypts of swirling mists that roll in from the sea.

Check it, gyal: those mountain peaks in the distance are wavebands of time.

Only, time don't exist on the B-side.

BOOK TWO

Safe House
November 1980–November 1981

Dub draws the listener into a labyrinth, where there are false signposts and 'mercurial' trails that can lead to the future, the past . . . or to nowhere at all.

Paul Sullivan, *Remixology: Tracing the Dub Diaspora*

13

Slipstream

We drive for an hour before Monassa stops at an old market town. It's cold but the sun's shining. A medieval-like bazaar, shops and stalls selling everything from blue shimmering Chinese silk to yellow yams and orange kumquats. It's eight in the morning and there are hunched elderly women leaning on tartan shopping trolleys, drowsy, sweaty men coming off late shifts. We go to a Turkish cafe and Monassa orders black coffee, lamb and onion sandwiches. We sit at a small wooden table. His eyes are red, puffy. He unzips his brown leather bomber and leans against the wall. A jiggy-jiggy pop song's playing. He shakes his head as if he can shake the sound outta it, says, 'Baby, those songs are full of linguistics I can't fucking decode.'

'It's people that are hard to work out,' I say. 'Music doesn't lie.'

Two large, bearded men nod at Monassa as they walk by and he raises his hand to them before leaning across and taking my hands in his. 'Do your thing from the Safe House. No one will trouble you,' he says.

'Your crew?' I ask. Worried his friends won't want a woman on their scene.

'No one enters or leaves unless I say,' he says.

'What do you mean?'

'Lockdown. That's how the place must run.' He lets go of my

hands and cuts his eye on me, and I'm afraid he's going to say he's changed his mind.

'I can pay my way,' I say.

He laughs. 'Lie low on some dark tracks for a while, baby. I don't need your donzai. Didn't we have fun in the boneyard? Eat your food.' He bites down on his sandwich, knocks back the tiny glass of coffee in one gulp.

After breakfast, we're on the road for half an hour before it starts to snow, a light slushy downpour that gets heavier. We drive through towns of patchy white. He winds down the window and sniffs the chalky air.

'Rising revelations, snow's dropping hard. Me and you in a storm, baby. Just the two of us.' He says this like he does sometimes, switching between song and speech. Like American bluesologists who sing-talk about the coming revolution.

I tell him about Cockpit Country and say I hope to go one day and find Moose's grandmother. He says he didn't grow up with his father, but he heard that his father's people were descendants of Maroons who lived and fought in Cockpit Country hundreds of years ago. Says they're buried in the sinkholes, and that's probably where he would have ended up if he were back in that time, because he's never taken shit from anyone, least of all the police. Rebellion is in his blood. This is the kinda protection I need.

An hour later we drive into Bristol, cruise by the Floating Harbour where the water doesn't ebb and flow and ships are always afloat. He shows me the caves, Georgian squares, cathedrals, bombed-out churches, castles and sugar houses. He parks by a small lane of Georgian houses with red and blue doors. We go down a ramp and walk along the river. A green bridge connects to the other side. Barges and boats moored on both banks.

He talks in detail about the slave-trade ships that left from this port. The kinds of chains they made to shackle slaves. 'They didn't just uproot our bodies,' he says. 'They uprooted our forests, our rivers, our seas and seeds. Reparation is needed so we can replant ourselves.'

Translucent snow falls in the grey air like stars. I look into the dark river, a melted universe of star leaves, froth clouds and black waves. Hear the gasping breath of multitudes caught between sea and sky.

'Come, the temperature's dropping and we ain't dressed right,' he says.

We get in the car and drive down side streets, where men with cigarette-thin legs and scarred faces stand in shady corners, striking matches like flints. Fifteen minutes beyond the city, surrounded by fields, a ghost town of deserted industrial estates and scrub. He stops outside an abandoned estate that's fenced by barbed wire and has a padlocked gate with long, heavy chains. A network of ugly glass and concrete buildings and corrugated-iron sheds. Bricked-up doors and windows, pipework and cables snaking on the walls.

I tell myself that a refuge is a refuge, no matter how dark it is.

We go through the black cantilever gate and he locks it. I follow him to a five-storey, brownstone tobacco warehouse with faded signage. Wide-arched entrances, steel-framed windows – four up and four across; grime and dust blur the windows that aren't broken. On the far right of the building is a blue metal shutter. Monassa presses a bell on the side and after a few minutes the shutter rises and we step into cave darkness. The door is on a timer and it closes. A low light comes on.

'Racer is my co-pee,' Monassa says. 'Man's tongue can be sharp, but he's on a level.'

'That a warning?'

He sings the reggae song 'There Are More Questions Than Answers'. I leave it at that.

We're on the first floor of the warehouse, in a large echoing space with cathedral-high ceilings, rusting metal beams crossing from one side to the other. Smoke-blackened walls. The bones of old train tracks piled in the corners, sawn-off railway sleepers. The woody smell of musty tobacco. A shaft of grey-white snow light beaming from an arched skylight. Graffiti and scrawls on the wall like prehistoric cave paintings. A tremor in my ribs, a strange feeling pushing against my chest. I follow Monassa through a small rusting door and down two floors of a black-bricked stairwell. In the basement, there are no windows, no natural light. We walk through rambling wings laid out in a staggered formation. Pipes as big as logs run along the walls; green, vine-like cables hang from the ceiling and trail on the floor. He points out dimly lit corridors. Identical rows, each with one large storage room and three small adjoining office spaces. Dusty upturned desks, broken-down chairs, a battered filing cabinet in one of them. Toilet cubicles and a doorless room with stained urinals at the end of each one.

The men have their own corridor, with their bedroom in one of the offices. Old strip lights in the corridors give off more shadow than light. At the far end are passageways that slope downwards into darkness. I try not to breathe in the smell of mould and sulphur. Try not to let the shadows in.

'Off limits,' Monassa says of the men's areas. He points out the kitchen and bathroom. He says Dungle is an electrician – used to be a stringer for a sound system – and he's rewired the basement, so it has everything they need. There's a workout room with bars and weights, a tan leather punchbag hanging from the ceiling on a chain, two rusty training benches.

I follow him down the corridors clogged with dust and time. We come to a pale-grey-painted room that is one of the office spaces. This is where the men are. They're sitting at opposite ends of a great hulk of a table made of metal railway lines stacked on wooden sleepers, toughened glass on top, everything secured with sling-shot-sized bolts. They're playing dominoes and don't look up straight away. Railway-signal light shining above them, pulsing red, yellow, green. Monassa says who's who.

Dungle, a bulletproof hulk of a man in his late forties. Plump, cushiony lips, pouchy eyes. He's wearing narrow-legged, black jogging pants, purple silk T, Jerry Curl hair hanging just so. Racer, a short, maaga fidget; smoke-ring eyes, nose thin as a crack. Carved, wooden pipe-snake coming outta his mouth.

Black sheepskin rugs on the concrete floor; two wrinkled burgundy leather sofas; framed drawings of futuristic buildings on the walls, which Monassa says are his. A silver stereo. Electric heaters with twisting rods of red heat and light plugged into the four corners. Roots riddims on the down-low.

'Welcome,' Dungle says. 'I'll make souse. What the body needs in weather like this. Yard's cold enough to freeze bassline mid-air.'

'W'happen,' Racer says.

I'm not sure if it's him or the snake talking.

Monassa sits at the table that's piled with Rizlas, dominoes, beer cans. Air thick with black hashish.

I smile at them, say, 'Respect.' I get a sense of who they are by their hair and teeth. Dungle with his curly-perm and one solid gold tooth seems to be the friendly one. Racer's blond hair is razored to within a millimetre of his scalp; two front teeth framed in gold. Looks like this man don't skin-up with no one. Monassa has cane rows, a small ruby in the centre of his front tooth. True seh, I'm still working him out.

'Babes, sit you raas down,' Monassa says. 'No rewinds here. Seen?'

God knows I'm tired as hell and cold. I drop on to the sofa and cover myself with a grey cashmere blanket that smells of perfume.

Racer leans back in the swivel chair, eyes me with a poker face, his legs twitching faster.

We eat the souse, smoke hash that's as potent as volcanic dust and makes my head spin. Slowed-down dub saturated with wet reverb fills up the cave room. Sound effects whirl like bats. The red bars of the heater twist. I drift inside my body.

Muma's in the underworld of my belly. In a sac of blood-drums. An acoustic ghost. I dream that the Dead Water canal is seeping into Dub Steppaz record shop, into the sinkhole and the Tombstone Estate. Into my mouth. Suffocating me.

I wake in the middle of the night, disorientated. My jaw clenched, I'm twisting my mahogany ring round and round my finger. For a second, I think I'm in Moose's bedroom and he's in the kitchen making cocoa. Then I remember. I switch on a lamp on the floor. I'm in a strange room on a double mattress on the grey office carpet. A desk, and on top of it my bag, case of vinyl and cassettes. A small blow-heater fans dusty warmth into the freezing room. It's ten past midnight. I get up and open a large grey metal locker; my clothes are inside on a rail with someone's navy Farahs, navy duffel coat with gold buttons, dresses, leather skirts and shoes. There's a side shelf with quilts, pillows. I wonder who the garments belonged to, but it's too soon to start asking questions.

I hear the muffled voices of the men from further along one of the corridors, smell the moss and sage scents of their cologne. Their footsteps going up the stairway. I leave and wander up and down the corridors before I find the kitchen, a small airless room with a cooker, a fridge, a worktop made from railway sleepers, a rusting stainless-steel sink and a green-painted mahogany cupboard. A tin of condensed milk, a litter of sodden teabags and takeaway boxes with yellow grease stains on the draining board. I bite down on a cold rib, razor my teeth against a layer of fat. Tip the contents of the can into my mouth. When I put the empty can down, red cockroaches scuttle towards it, their feelers out. I retch into the sink. I go back to the freezing room and take three quilts out of the cupboard, get into bed. Push down thoughts of Moose; can't handle the low-toned vibrations of grief in my chest.

Muma's somewhere in the shadows now. She's not singing. Gotta be as gentle with ghosts as with newborns. Sing them songs in return for their truths.

I try to sing, but my voice is dry. 'Stay,' I say.

Nothing.

I'm remembering her voice, the outline of a face in the slow, white drift of memory.

'Sing,' I say.

The cold air stirs; she's close to my face. Singing about children killed in their dancing time.

14

Static

The next day I get up and put on the duffel coat, pull on the hood. I want to go to the river, but none of the men are about and they've explained that for now they'll let me in and out. I understand that the house has to be secure but there are no windows, no air. I feel locked in. I walk up and down the freezing corridors. The walls seem to be moving, small tremors. I place my hands on the peeling paint and realise it's me that's shaking.

I hurry back to the main room. The electric heaters are on full blast. The concrete walls are wet with condensation; rust drips hang from the ceiling like stalactites.

I play tunes with the volume low. Scribble lyrics. Sing until the tremor in my ribs stops. Something like a heavy liquid draining off my chest. I've made it out of Norwood. I've got backup. A chance to get inna music.

The men appear at midday dressed in sweats, red-eyed, loose-jawed, sour-skinned. They grab cold leftovers from the kitchen and bring the food to the table: meat patties, spare ribs, fried chicken. They stuff whatever they can between wedges of hard-dough bread; chase everything down with pint glasses of rum mixed with tomato juice and chilli sauce.

I don't say a word because their minds are still wherever they've been in the strange hours after midnight.

'Baby, this is man time. You best check out,' Racer says to me. His smoke-ring eyes are half-closed; his wooden pipe-snake seems more alert.

I look at Monassa and he laughs, tells me I should explore the area, get to know my way around. He'll introduce me to some clubs and music people soon enough. Won't be long before everyone knows I'm with him. No one will trouble me. Dungle walks me out of the building, says I best be back at six – he'll be waiting by the gate to let me in.

I walk through the time-capsule brownstone city and the hyper-tuned tremors in my legs slow down. I need to dance, let off moves. I go inside the fourteenth-century church built into the city walls and listen to the waves of silence. It's been a sanctuary for hundreds of years. It reminds me of the Crypt, and I think about Asase and Rumer. If they were here now, Rumer would be cracking jokes about Bongo Natty and man dem. Asase would be screwing up her face at someone. We'd be tight. Here, on my own, it feels like I'm moving outta sync. I want to go back to the dry days before Moose, before love and pain.

I step-bounce-swing in the crisp cold November day, bare beech trees swaying like dancers in the shrouded vocals of the wind. I check out museums and castles, visit the Floating Harbour. I find Foot-prints Record Shop on a side street off one of the leafy squares where paths cut through rows of trees. The shop has a blue door with a bell that jangles as I go in; a small corridor leads into two large rooms. Rows of wooden cases of tightly packed records and cas-settes. Dub, reggae, jazz, pop, classical. Two young men with long, stringy hair at the two counters, one in each room. Packets of vinyl polishers and styluses hanging on wall racks behind them. I try not to think of Eustace, but I see him at the counter, the sharp edge of a black vinyl balanced between finger and thumb, basslines pumping his chest up and down. I buy four records and go back to the Safe House.

It's six o'clock and Monassa and Racer are at the table playing cards. Black hashish smoke floats above their heads. Racer is dipping salty plantain chips into a can of condensed milk and chucking handfuls into his mouth.

Monassa shouts out to me, 'Time is silent, baby. Mek some noise in the place. DJ for us. Tek us to the outtasphere, we need to gain some blood-claat hours.'

I go to my room and get my mic. Back in the main room, I put on one of the dubplates, a ghostly track with fading voices and horns and strings. I set my voice level, reduce the bass, add reverb to the mic.

> *'power to the sistren!*
> *I am the MC controller*
> *dialling digits to the number-one power*
> *elevating lyrics*
> *this is a gyal takeover'*

'Hey, selector,' Racer calls to me. He's wearing pale blue tracksuit bottoms with yellow lightning strikes on the sides. He flings down a card on the table, smiles at me with fake tenderness. His words come outta twisted lips: 'Can't you do betta dan dat!'

Monassa and Dungle lean back and watch.

I tune inna Muma, her voice now in my chest. I pull myself up taller. Put on a heavy bassline dub, pick up the mic, stand in front of Racer. He cuts his eyes with exaggerated indifference.

I drop some headtop counteraction lyrics:

'special request to the Monassa posse. Listen good. Seen!
right yah now people
Obeah Woman at the control tower
every style you can think of
NO other man can chat-a-like-a-me
cos me flex wid Koromantyn vibe
everything me chat you know-a-is true
me no like it when man dem full a dust. Trust!
me no like when man fight and fuss
cos me ah Obeah Woman
me no ramp and cuss
when me play dub riddim 'nough t'ing me a sus
check it:
switch back from time
dig down, dig deep, inna primitive time
switch back inna sound space style.
easy skanking my bredrin'

'Go deh, baby,' Monassa shouts. 'Didn't know you could chat lyrics like dat.'

'What other tricks you got up your sleeve?' Racer asks.

'Nuff,' I say.

'Yeah?' Racer is eyeballing me.

I don't move. Dub force inside me. I feel 'trang. 'When you mess with the afterworld, you best be tuned,' I tell him.

Monassa laughs. 'That's it, baby, nah let that fucker skank you.' He slaps Racer on the shoulder. 'The woman's just like you – silent but deadly. She can flex with us.'

Racer sucks his teeth and I'm not sure if he's vex fe true or enjoying the sparring. Probably something in between.

Monassa pushes the cards away and gets up from the table. He stands in front of the red-hot electric heaters, stretches out his legs.

'Listen up,' he says, 'let's hold a session tonight. Introduce Yamaye to our tribe. She deserves an audience.'

The men say why not, and Dungle and Racer go out to get liquor and box food. Monassa makes the call. I empty the ashtrays, put out plates and cups, get my case of vinyl and select the tunes.

They arrive just after one in the morning. A man with perforated skin that looks like woodworm, with one ginger- and one black-haired woman on either arm. The women's lips are wet with red lipstick. They're wearing matching white furs and see-through, black nylon dresses with nothing underneath; silver cowboy boots with the toes studded with diamanté stars.

'Yes, my bredrin. This is Yamaye,' Monassa says to the man. 'Rising revelations, how to introduce a dread bredda like you?'

'My man, just call me the Heartist. That is what I am. And these are my works of heart.' He squeezes the women's waists. They pout their red lips, their skulls hanging like limp flower-heads on their maaga bodies.

His voice is a subterranean baritone. He's wearing an orange satin shirt, green velvet trousers and pigskin ankle boots. His greasy hair is receding. He takes the arm of each woman and turns them like spinning tops into the centre of the room, where they thrash their heads from side to side.

Dungle and Racer reach for them, Dungle dancing with the dark-haired woman, who looks Asian, and Racer with the red-haired woman. I put on a lovers-rock track, but it doesn't seem right for the rough out-of-step way they're moving.

The Heartist sprawls on the sofa, his feet dangling off the seat. He tips his tan leather cowboy hat off his eyes and stares at me.

I wonder what the hell Asase and Rumer would make of this scene. Asase's lips would be flying. She'd be telling me: 'Eh-eh, popping style with man dem! Think you can do better without me? You can't handle our small-town men. How you gonna deal with these roughneck people?'

I push down any thoughts of what Moose would think as I wind down the lovers rock, raise the volume on a dub version. Standing in front of the deck, tapping my feet like I'm playing kick drum. Balance the bass and top range; turn the equaliser up and down, my voice coming in and out. I'm safe in the white space sound of spirit.

The women dance faster, their breasts shaking under their gauzy dresses. Racer's hands are on the ginger woman's waist and he's twisting her left to right like he wants to drive her body into the earth.

Monassa's the off-beat, sitting at the table, a drink in one hand, stroking his goatee with the other, nodding to the music. His glassy eyes stare through the room.

The Heartist calls me over to him.

'Gwaan, baby,' Monassa says. 'He only bites in daylight.'

I don't want to, but I sit beside him like I'm told. I feel like I need to please Monassa because he's doing so much for me. The Heartist leans towards me, tells me that he gets anything he wants by working on people's hearts.

'What yuh doing in this place?' he asks.

'Fresh start,' I say.

'Sound Woman, if you're tight with Monassa, you're sweet with me.' He raises his glass of white rum in a toast, puts it to my mouth, and holds the back of my head. I swallow a small amount, then push the glass away, harder than I intended, and the drink splashes on to his crisp shirt.

Monassa stands up, but the Heartist raises his hands in surrender.

'You should play some tunes at one of my parties,' he says to me. 'Earn a few shekels. Monassa says that's what you want.' He looks up at Monassa, smiles and nods.

The two women are curled up on the floor giggling, playful as newborn kittens without full use of their eyes or bodies. Dungle and Racer pick them up and carry them away.

The Heartist and Monassa go outside into the passageway and I hear them talking, but can't make out what they're saying. Monassa comes back into the room.

'Is he vex with me?' I ask.

'Simmer down, baby, you'd know if he was. He's scanning you. Man's got connections in high places. Judges, politicians, diplomats. His women get to them. Busting heart strings until they talk.'

'Where is he?'

'Gone to join the party. Everyone's in Racer's room.' Monassa sucks in his cheeks and raises his eyebrows at me. 'Coming?'

I step back. 'Uh-uh! Not my scene.' Whatever is going on, I want nothing to do with it.

He walks me to my room, stands outside the door.

'Small-town vibes limit vision, baby. The Heartist is a good contact for you. Trust me. Rivers and cities are what you need,' he says. He leans forward as if he's going to kiss me. He pulls away and says, 'Don't worry, I got you.' I watch him walk down the corridor towards Racer's wing.

Like Moose, he wants to protect me. Only he's a dub version of Moose; not enough vocals to know who or what he really is.

I relax into the riddims of the Safe House. Everything is smooth for the first few weeks into the new year. The men go out at midnight two or three times a week. They return just before the sun comes up. We spend late afternoons in the main room where the men play cards, drink, while I drop tunes, sing. They nod from time to time if they like my lyrics. Poopa taught me silence; Muma taught me sound. It's easy to sense the men's vibrations, work them out. I know more about them now.

Dungle's the grounded one. He has a mother, a father, siblings. He visits his elderly parents every couple of weeks. He's the peacemaker. Racer's quick to get vex, skittering arms and legs. Monassa chats about himself. On those days when he seems manic, I've learned to listen, say 'Wow!' and 'Seriously?' And not interrupt, because if I do, he'll repeat his last few words with a pointed look that says fuck you. He claims he can smell music, taste noise, feel thought through a wall of steel. Other days, he barely speaks. It's a side of him I never saw when he used to come to Norwood, picking me up in his car, speeding past Resurrection Cemetery, the windows wound down, saying, 'Irie, Irie. Life is good.'

Sometimes the Heartist comes round, always with different women. He asks me to DJ at his parties. I say I'm still practising. Monassa stays close to me, reclining on the floor by the stereo, propped on his elbows. Him and the Heartist smiling at each other, nodding as if they're playing a secret game.

On Saturdays, Monassa takes me to an old inn where we eat bloody steaks and chips and drink black stout. Four-beats-to-the-measure is how he moves. He says I'm different. Sensitive. Need looking after. Leaning in. Listening hard to everything I say. In the gloom of the salon, the smoky closeness of the air, I'm moving nearer to something that feels dark and unknowable. Attraction-repulsion-attraction-repulsion. I'm on four beats too. Dub-stepping on a tightrope, shaking midline.

Every so often, I think about calling Irving. But apart from an awkward conversation at Christmas, I don't. Too much confusion about who he is and what I feel. Part of me needs to hear his voice;

part of me is still waiting for him to open up. Thinking about him makes my heart ache, but I'm not sure if it's for any love that existed between us, or for something I've wanted for so long that I've imagined it.

In March, Monassa buys me a 36-inch belcher gold chain. Don't know if it's a gift or a collar. As he puts it round my neck, he says he's thought of a way I can earn my stay in the Safe House.

'The police been on our arses for years. We weren't killing or robbing. Stopping and searching us, trying to pin crimes on us so they can lock us up. So we busted inna the Safe House and went underground, where Black people have fe go when Babylon puts the pressure on. If we're here, we gotta have something to live on. This is a revolution.'

'I'm ready,' I say. I want to please him, want him to feed me more attention. More darkness, whatever it is he's doing to me.

'Inna it, baby,' he says. 'Dim the light, hold tight, you're coming with us tonight.'

I wash and put on the Farah trousers and duffel coat that were in the cupboard when I first arrived. They're on the big side but the look's crisp: trousers hanging on my hips; hemline swinging on my gold trainers; shoulder pads of the duffel are wide, like something out of a black-and-white film where women skank the men.

The crew are waiting upstairs on ground level. Dressed in black jackets and jeans, Russian hunting hats. Monassa has leather gloves on.

'You sure about this?' Racer asks Monassa.

'Easy, Star, she won't blow us out,' Monassa says. 'A white brother and a soft-faced woman up front – the bull ain't gonna look too hard.'

Monassa and Dungle get in the back of the dark brown Dolomite Sprint. Racer at the wheel, I sit next to him. It's just past twelve; cold, thin, dewy air.

'Yeah, yeah, midnight moves with Yamaye,' Monassa shouts. 'Hold tight, world, we're gonna pluck the stars from the sky tonight. One by one. Put them in our back pockets.'

Dungle says the car is moving good and Monassa says it should because Racer upgrades his wheels more times than his women.

'She's my baby,' Racer says.

'Racer is the best,' Monassa says. 'Keeps the car tuuuned. Large carburettors, competition camshafts. No one can beat my man on the roads.'

We cruise along the deserted streets, past alleys, courtyards. No one around except a few rent boys with broomstick-thin bodies sweeping up and down the streets. Racer slows along a road of antique shops, but something doesn't look right and Monassa tells him to move on. We drive past old warehouses at the front of the Floating Harbour. Barges and small boats bob in the black river; large buildings with slit-window eyes.

The men are quiet. I hear the different riddims of their breathing. I imagine the ships that sailed from this harbour; sailing to Africa, taking its people to the Caribbean; the women sitting on deck, rubbing salt into their sores, singing air and fire alchemy. I smell the ocean in the distance, salty, bitter. Muma's voice: *Let me carry you across the sea*.

We pull up on the south side of a crescent lined with three-storey limestone and slate buildings that look like galleries or museums. Monassa gets out of the car, slipstreams into darkness. Blood rushes to my heart, my legs, my eyes.

'He going alone?' I ask.

'He's the Shadow Skanker,' Dungle says. He laughs. 'Man been skanking shadows since he was ten.'

Racer strikes a match, a small flare in the dark, lights a spliff and gives it to me; tells me to simmer down, skanking is survival.

Two hours later, Monassa is back. He slips into the car as easily as he left, and Racer speeds off. My heart's beating faster and there's sweat under my arms, between my legs, on the top of my lips. I'm shivering. We stop at an all-night bagel shop, eat steaming fresh bagels and drink black coffee. I hold the cup just to bring warmth back to my shaking body.

'Yamaye, you're my lucky talisman,' Monassa says. 'I got plenty stars tonight.' He puts his arm around me and kisses me on the lips.

Adrenaline is in my blood. A burning frequency I don't want to turn off.

Dungle is eating quickly, focused on his food. Racer has on his vex face, his legs twitching. He tells us to mek a move and stop the sweeting-up so early in the day.

We drive out of the city as the sun comes up, go into the countryside. The leaves on towering oak trees are red, gold and green. Cows in meadows blowing morning steam outta their noses.

Racer parks in front of a large, timber-framed house. It's two storeys, made of red brick, and has triangular-shaped windows in the roof. A black sports car and a white jeep are parked in the driveway. Racer knocks on the side door and a blonde woman opens it. We enter the open-plan kitchen and the woman steps around me, checking me out.

'This is our Sound Woman,' Dungle says of me.

The blonde woman's name is Christina. She looks at me with something like scepticism.

We sit at an oak table that's as big as a boat.

Dungle asks, 'How's things? Kids all right? Husband still skanking in banking?'

'So-so.'

Christina's about thirty, maaga, leggy with a blunt bob. She's wearing a white jumpsuit with a silver chain belt. A diamond necklace hangs close to her throat.

'Hope you're not taking advantage of her,' she says to Racer. She smiles at me and the lines around her mouth deepen into split seams.

'Life's putting on the pressure, but she's safe,' Monassa says. He turns to me. 'Isn't that true, babes?'

I smile and nod.

Christina makes Irish coffee and lays out croissants and cold, spiced sausages on the table.

'What the fuck kind of prison breakfast is this?' Racer asks.

'It's continental,' Christina says, each word clear as crystal.

'Give me some musical intensity,' Racer says.

She plays jazz.

'That's cry-cry music,' Racer says.

'Don't you have enough drama in your life?' Christina says. She joins us at the table.

'Good night at the museums?' she asks.

'Rising revelations,' Monassa says, 'we're just taking back what was ours.' He pulls a small black pouch from his pocket and gives it to her.

Dungle slaps him on the back.

Now I know exactly what I'm helping them do.

Christina opens the bag and empties jewels into her hand. A yellow diamond the size of a domino, set in a gold ring.

'It certainly was a good night,' she says. She lays an arm around Racer's shoulders as he's ramming a folded croissant stuffed with sausage into his mouth. He shrugs her off and she smiles, her eyes brighter.

Christina is someone Asase would have described as having 'good blood' – genetic glamour. She slices into her sausage with a silver knife and places tiny slivers between her teeth. She isn't the kind of woman to nyam anything. Her skin is as shiny as the pots hanging on the walls in her fancy kitchen, but her eyes have dark shadows.

She takes Racer's hand and leads him away. He comes back half an hour later, dishevelled and alone, and then we head home.

Dungle tells me that Christina has two young sons in boarding school and her husband works all the hours in a bank in the City, staying in hotels in London during the week, flying to islands where there are offshore banks. He knows nothing about her hustling, selling on the goods for the men. 'She's a good mother,' he says. 'She's helped me out plenty of times.'

'Her man don't satisfy her,' Racer says. 'She gets her highs with us. Even mothers need a little something on the side.'

'They need respect too,' says Dungle, and he sucks in his cheeks, gives Racer a look that could be disapproval or warning.

It rains all the way back; the windscreen wipers make a hypnotic noise. I fall asleep in the car, dreaming of Moose.

We're in his Rover. He's driving over an aquamarine river, palm trees. A firecracker sunshine day; a home far away. He speaks to me:

Feel no way, I've come to wake you, baby.

I reach out my hands to him, but it's Monassa who takes hold of them. Pulling me into a soundscape of heavy-breathing vocals and alarm-bell drone.

It's late afternoon by the time we get home and everyone goes to their rooms. I kick back in my room. My body is lifeless, drained of sound. Deflated after all the excitement.

I wake up shivering in the dark. I walk down the dusty corridors, follow the music coming from the main room, four rows away. There's Monassa, sitting cross-legged on the floor and rocking from side to side. He's at the music deck playing a spell-casting, slowed-down riddim.

'Come yah, baby, keep me company.' He pats the black sheepskin rug next to him. His voice is soft, calm, controlled.

I've been here all this time, and he's asked for nothing but my attention and my tunes. I can grant him this.

'We're duppies come back from the dead to take control,' he says. He's laughing. I kiss my teeth.

Static on his fingertips when he puts them to my lips. The stench of his pheromones under my nose. Drop my face and he tips it up, pushes the chillum pipe to the back of my throat.

'Pull,' he says.

I inhale a black storm. Separation of positive and negative.

I become supernatural.

He twists my nipples. Tuning me.

'What are you doing? No. I ain't ready for this,' I say.

He drowns me out, spits lyrics: 'Let's get inna this, baby. No time to play.'

Fight, flight or freeze. I freeze, like I always do. Unsure.

Then he's on top of me, thrusting inside me, grunting, heating his blade. Whenever I pull away, he pulls me back.

'Wind you waist, gyal! Smooth me in.'

I become supernatural: shock-out-shock-out. Leave my body. Float. Inna the cave of my gut, a split-faced god watching me with snake-coiled eyes, its vex-line mouth chanting: fight! But I'm frozen stiff.

Monassa ain't done. He's stroking my hair. 'Baby, you need to let loose.'

Static in his hands as he pulls me outta my roots.

I become supernatural. Pray to the god in my gut, its hollow face silent.

Jumping needle record on repeat.

There's static in his eyes as he comes.

My body stays in lockdown. I'm outside myself, hanging with spirits until it's safe to return.

Afterwards, he gets up and leaves without a word.

I stumble to my room, hashish smoke winding through my veins.

Don't feel anything except a heaviness under my ribs.

This feeling won't go away. There's no release from grief.

I'm too far inna shadow. The light nowhere in sight. I finally realise there may be no escape from the Safe House.

15

Bad Blood

The next morning, Monassa comes into the kitchen where I'm making coffee. First time he's been up this early. I keep my back to him but he steps behind me, whispers in my ear: 'Black and sweet for me.'

I pour coffee into a mug, stir in brown sugar, still not turning to look at him. Everything I do is mechanical. He's acting cool and breezy, like it's just another day.

I turn and look straight inna his eyes. 'Last night, you didn't—'

'Last night, last night,' he says. 'Putting them moves on me. Seductress.'

'I never—'

'Winding your body like that!'

'You're the one—'

I flip between feelings of shame and fear. Try to tell myself, *Gyal, this is what you want.* But it's not. I'm trying to spin revulsion into desire. Mek my own beat. Keep my mind from dropping inna the bassy emptiness of a fathomless sea.

'Baby, simmer down. Know that I ain't checking you like no slack woman. You wanted me. Nothing wrong with that. At-all-at-all-at-all.'

High E strings in my stomach, pulling on my guts, but I can't seem to dredge the siren sound to my throat. Have I mixed things up? The notes in my belly twang so I try a haul-and-pull, lifting the needle off memory, dragging it back to the first bar again and again. Feel the foreboding and dread of truth. What happened was real. I press against the worktop.

He leans forward as if he's gonna kiss me, but he places his right hand on the top of my head the way a pastor does when they believe they're healing you. That guitar-twang dragging on my insides again. I want to double over, howl, but I hear myself asking if he's ready for breakfast.

On a Thursday night, we head out to Shackles Shebeen. A dutty little club where they go most nights after their midnight moves. Monassa has been coming to my room ever since that first night, over a week ago. His blood pumps against my spine, filling me with his shadows; his bones curve around me like the skeleton of a ship that's run aground.

We drive into the old part of the city, over the bridge across the river. Monassa takes the road tight around the edge of Queen's Square. White marble statues of slave traders loom out of the darkness. Abandoned rum taverns and sugar warehouses, medieval-style churches, elegant terraced houses and squares lined with wild cherry trees. Truth is somewhere in my body, lost in undercurrents. I'll go to my deep, dark place, if that's the only way to drown it out.

Racer pulls up under a railway arch of grilled garages. Halfway down, a neon sign is flashing SS and the image of a chain. We go down a metal stairway at the end of the passage and come to a black security door. A boulder-shouldered bouncer blocks the doorway. When he sees the men he opens up and moves aside. Two more flights of scarlet-painted hallways and steps and we go through a low, narrow arch into a cavern of burgundy walls, red Chesterfield booths on the left, a long wooden bar on the right. Hundreds of bare bulbs hang on rusting chains from the ceiling. People dancing on a raised platform in the centre. DJ lined up against the back wall. The bassline likks my body, stops the shaking. A crusty-throated MC is toasting:

> *'me a go flash down some original style!*
> *likk off operator!*
> *playing from the top to the very last drop*
> *meditate these lyrics, people!'*

The session is ram-up. Bull-necked men and peeny-wally boys riding the beat like jockeys. Young women with faces like the ones you see in missing-people posters, ashen, shadows under their eyes. A grey-haired white man wearing jeans belted too far above his waist is grinding up against an olive-skinned woman with a wilting wig and leather bondage cuffs on her wrists linked to one on his.

'Check it, yah,' Racer says. 'That's a two-faced judge sweeting himself up on that gyal. Man like him can't get enough of the nasty scene.' Mr Chen, the owner of Shackles Shebeen, is Chinese-Guyanese. Black hair pulled into a knot behind his head, a long plaited beard, nostrils the shape of a double-barrel gun. He slaps the men on their backs and shows us to a reserved booth. The men order drinks. I wade through the dance floor and stand with the mic sharks by the deck, watching as the operator cuts the music in and out while the DJ chats. The controller drops a dubplate with reverberating water effects. I imagine taking the mic from him and bubbling inna lyrics, spontaneous:

> *me deh pon the mic*
> *rebel inna de night*
> *me come fe show you*
> *the light*

I go to the bar, order a double shot of overproof white rum, down it. The holy liquid ignites the rage in my throat.

Mr Chen is sitting at a scarred table just outside the kitchen, past the booths. Chicken bone in his hand, bowl of wings and breasts solidified in orange grease in front of him.

I tell him what I want. Say it's my remedy for pain.

He laughs, wipes his greasy lips. 'Allyuh woman always talking 'bout pain. Woman bring trouble. Always do.'

'Don't pay me until I block up the dance floor,' I say.

'Yuh does mad! Yuh own night in my place? Know how much man want the same? Want it bad.'

He holds the bone like a blowpipe in his mouth, aims it at me, sucks the marrow. Maybe he's trying to show me who's boss, but I've got nothing to lose.

I go to the deck, tell the maaga selector not to pull up the tune until I say; ask the operator not to mix me up as I wanna stay in the flow of the riddim. They ain't listening good, so I say 'Excuse me' before taking over the decks, likk back the same version – a dubplate track of trumpets, drums, rattles, synth bass waves. Mix myself in. Freestyle.

The dead wash in through the music, sea-glazed eyes, tongues red as torches.

The fire's in me, the swell of loss and rage. I channel it from my hands to my heart, to my throat, to my empty belly. Coil the black pearls around my neck, squat, shake my arse, rattle my tongue. Take back control of my body. Chant fury like I've never chanted before.

'Sonix Dominatrix at the control tower
flexing with fire
skanking beneath bassline
sucking ganja smoke between my teeth

disrupting the man dem beat
Sonix Dominatrix at the control tower
bleeding the massive
night after night
stringing yuh up on the mystical oneness
of sound
Sonix Dominatrix at the control tower
drawing life outta the living with
treble, bass, reed, flute
cutting inna yuh with fire
soundwaves
I-and-I skank with the dead
I-and-I is tune'

I'm dragged under reverberations, the spinning wheels of time. Dancers wave their arms, air horns blow, a ship lost at sea.

Go deh, the massive shout. Electrified jerks of their heads. Clockwork arms. They come alive on the dance floor. Pull-back motion of spines. Juddering-stalking-rotating. All the stored-up, winding energy of the old times.

I come up for air fifteen minutes later. Go back to Mr Chen. He buries what's left of the chicken bone under a serviette. Rubs the grease into his plaited beard, looks me up and down.

'Fiyah raas! Somebody trouble you?' He laughs. 'Tuesday night is dry,' he says. 'Monassa said yuh was looking for some sessions. Take it if you want it so bad. Remember, if you get into bother, don't come to me.'

I go back to the table. Dungle is the only one there.

'Dem lyrics are deep.' He looks at me with questioning eyes. I shrug quickly. Avoid his face.

A woman is waving to him from the bar on the other side of the room.

'That's Charmaine,' he says. 'Woman's lived a lifetime or two. Looks like she's having one of her good days.'

Charmaine pushes through the dance floor and comes over and sits next to him. She could be one of the women in Muma's paintings – women who slip between the fissures in blue mountains, 400-year-old braids hanging down her back, black as whip marks. She drapes an arm across Dungle's shoulders. He introduces us, asks her what she thought of my lyrics.

'Nuth'n special,' she says.

'Hey, hey, manners,' Dungle says.

'I'm just messing,' she says. 'No fret yuhself.'

I'm just glad to be talking to another woman, so I tell her she's right, I've got a-ways to go.

Dungle gets us drinks and goes to the bar where Monassa and Racer are chatting to the Heartist. Charmaine points out the regulars, the DJs and MCs.

She pulls me up to the dance floor and dances close to me, knocking her hips into me as she winds, like she's trying to find a way of hooking on to me without leaving a mark.

The club serves mutton and rice at five and Charmaine pushes to the front of the queue, holding my hand and pulling me with her. In the kitchen a woman is at the stove, wearing a white headcloth, overalls and plimsolls. Big doughy neck sprinkled with black warts, arms solid as rolling pins. Singing spirituals over the large steaming Dutch pots.

'Two plates, chef,' Charmaine says.

'Y'all right?' the woman says and then she piles rice on to a plate, ladles gold-coloured curried mutton on top and the mound collapses.

We sit at one of the scarred tables outside the kitchen and eat.

When we finish, Charmaine pushes her plate away and says, 'Usually eat alone. I check for you.'

'Same,' I say.

She gets a pen from a man in the queue and writes her number on the lip of a cigarette box, tears it off and gives it to me.

'You remind me of myself when I came on this scene. Looking out for you will be like minding young me.' We're laughing when Dungle comes and says the men are ready to leave.

She shakes her head at me and nods to my hand where the cigarette lid is folded up. It's obvious what she means. Whatever is happening between us best be kept under wraps.

Back at the Safe House, Monassa tells me to meet him in the bathroom.

If we're not in the Safe House, we're on the streets at night. No light. I'm afraid of how life can change so quickly. Afraid what these changes can do to someone who has nothing except dub music to ground them.

The bathroom is at the far end of the corridor, two doors along from the main room, just beyond the kitchen. It's a small shadowy room, clay-coloured walls, rusting zinc bathtub, corner basin, a cast-iron radiator piled with towels. A large, silver railway-signal light hangs from the ceiling, glowing red. So far down I can smell the dampness of earth. He's already there, naked, sitting on the edge of the bath which is full of steaming water. He takes off my clothes and we get inside it. A rush of numbing heat from the boiling water and I exhale.

Protector and predator. Mind-fuck. My body says no. Fear says: stay.

He pours Bay Rum, coconut oil and black salt into the bath from glass bottles on a shelf. The water's too hot. I shift around, light-headed. He's still as a snake. I'm at the end near the taps.

He leans back. 'We must burn out the bad,' he says.

My heart's thudding and I'm wondering what he's gonna do next.

He lights a spliff and sends out the smoke.

'Bush bath to clean the soul,' he says.

'You have a soul?' I say.

'Baby, don't gwaan dem ways. Me and you are gonna get rid of some demons right about now.'

His hair is in cane rows, tightly woven, zips to different parts of his mind. What goes on in that head of his when he comes to my room and breaks into me? Bass-speaker frequencies, like the force of grief, hitting my solar plexus.

Monassa's body is the weight of shame, another burden to carry. Along with the feeling that I'm being watched. He always leaves the bedroom door open when he's fucking me as if someone's outside in the corridor looking through the door. Racer? Have the two of them made some kind of dutty agreement that Racer can get off on watching us?

'Mr Chen says you're starting next week. I gave my approval.'

'Approval?'

'It'll keep you out of trouble,' he says.

I get out of the bath, shut the door and get back in.

'You're inside my power, baby,' he says. 'A superstructure. Like my drawings on the wall in the main room.'

'They look like plans. You want to build them?' I ask.

'Our people need homes that face the sun. Not prisons.'

'Afro-futuristic, huh.'

'Our musicians are revolutionaries, showing us we gotta improvise.'

'That what you're doing?'

Golden discs of oil float on the surface of the water like plankton. I break them up with my fingers and they bloom into clusters.

He leans forward, grabs my legs, which are inside his, and spreads them.

'I throw everything in: obeah, the Sixth and Seventh Book of Moses, overstanding from the weed. Im-pro-vise.'

I pull my feet together and press my toes against his cock, put pressure on his balls.

He laughs and the shadows under his eyes widen. He never sleeps. He's always at the table, sketching, making notes. He falls asleep on the sofa in the afternoons for an hour. Jumps up like he's been reborn.

'The stone, the sap, the fire, the earth – the blood that makes homes,' he says. 'I'm gonna build something indestructible. So nothing can ever likk it down. No hurricane, earthquake. Everlasting. Rooted. To rhatid.'

'Is that what the midnight moves are about?' I ask.

'A man that ain't schooled makes his own rules. True thing. We're still on them slave ships. Overcrowded, kept below. We can go overboard, underground or soundbound,' he says.

I shiver when he says soundbound.

'Check my body,' he says. 'Touch it, I'm all yours.' He says it like he's giving me the gift of life.

I look at the lean muscles of his molten black-blue legs. I slide deeper into the water, submerge my face, hold my breath, sea words babbling in my head. I surface and look at him again. Trying to make him out. Getting tangled in doubt.

'Bad blood runs through some people,' he says. 'Not you.' He strokes his chin, raises his top lip from his teeth. 'What were you and Charmaine talking about the other night?'

'Getting to know each other.'

'Had my fill of bad gyal.' He leans forward, takes a short curl, coils it between his fingers and pulls me towards him. 'Yeah, safe,' he says. 'I wouldn't touch a woman like Charmaine. Worse, a woman like Asase. Fit but dange-er-ous.'

'You didn't know her. You think you know me.'

'Give me some overstanding, baby. Asase had rep. I saw the three of you at the Crypt couple times. She was the one cutting her eyes, skanking, spreading out like a man. Trouble was always heading her way.'

'Sure her style didn't come-over for you?'

He grabs my hand and whispers, 'Bad blood in that family, probably the mother.' Then shouts, 'It's always the mother.'

There's more smoke than blood in me. It's me walking with the dead, not him.

'Asase's mother is a good woman,' I say. 'The father gave them a hard time.'

'Ah so it go,' he says.

'And your mother?'

'The mask of mothers is a skank.'

It makes me think of Muma. I'm afraid that I'll never get to be who she wanted me to be. Not in a place like this. In my mind, I call her. But her voice is carbonating inside my ribs.

Monassa slips under the water and stays there unmoving for one, two, three minutes. He rises like a sea monster, tributaries running through his cane rows, sliding into his open mouth.

'It was just me and my mother in that cramped council house,' he says. 'Damp, dutty, haunted. Rising revelations. That woman was the blueprint for beauty. Most nights I came down to find the front door swinging on its hinges, wide open on to the fucking streets. I was six! Anybody coulda come breezing in. She was hustling men.

Fools bought into her looks. I won't make that mistake. I check for the quiet ones. Like you.'

The water is cooling now, the smoke and steam gone; the stone walls are damp as a cave. He pulls a cord hanging from the ceiling and the light goes out.

'How old were you when you started skanking people?' I ask.

'Nine, maybe ten. There were plenty like me on the streets. Bruck-up homes, shit like that. Only education I had was from hustlers. Swim or sink.'

'And now?'

'Babylon is no joke. Superstructure slave ship. I ain't jumping inna the sea. Best to start a mutiny.'

I'm fired up when he talks like this. We're fighting the same war. But the bath's turned cold; my skin wrinkles and I know what's to come.

We put on black towelling bathrobes with hoods, shove our feet into our trainers, our heels hanging off the back. We shuffle like monks along the winding corridors. Arched ceilings, lights dangling on rotting cables, mangled as seaweed. Ochre-coloured walls with large pores, sea sponges.

'You're safe from Babylon,' he says. 'There are tunnels beneath Racer's apartment. An escape route from the police if they ever come. Links to old passageways used by enslaved runaways and pirates. One of them goes to the sea. We'll go as deep as we need for freedom.'

'Can I see where they are? In case—'

'Nah, nah. Only we know the way to those.' He walks faster.

I pull the robe tighter around my body as the air penetrates.

I think of the sea flowing past the tunnels. Upturned world of kelp forests, dragnets of coloured fish, trapping the smoke of disturbed silt.

We walk back a different way, cutting through a door in one of the storage areas, going into narrow passageways that go under. Repeat like harmonic patterns. Scratching sounds of rats and who knows what else. Falling plaster, waterfalls of white dust.

'Wouldn't know how to get to the main room from here,' I say, thinking *but I'd find my way to the sea somehow.*

'That's how it's supposed to be,' he says and strides ahead.

At the end of a passageway, I hear the monomaniacal growling of the generator, a peeling, red iron carcass that Racer restored; the monster that keeps us off-grid. We get back to the row of corridors and go back to my room.

'Come, let me dry you.' He pulls the robe off me and rubs my back, chest and legs, moving from ankles to the tops of my inner thigh.

We lie on the mattress; he straddles me. Darkness in his eyes and a small gap of light, the glow of obeah men who make people drift into dead-flesh sleeps.

'I want your obsession,' he says. 'Nuth'n less.'

It's not gonna be me, not after what he's done to me, but I can see why a woman would be obsessed with him, possessed by him. Eyes dark-rimmed, remote. I recognise the hard set of the mouth, a clamp holding in soundless pain from the long-gone past. Seen the same thing in Irving and Crab Man. The pain's in me too, but in a different way.

'Maybe I was afraid of Asase,' I say. 'Jealous. I thought every man bought into her beauty and power.'

'Darkness is power. Let's see how Asase moves in prison. She'll be up against some hard-backed women.'

'Don't want that image in my head,' I say. I want to forget Asase, because thinking of her has a pull-push effect on me. Missing her, wanting her protection, hating her ways. This isn't the time for confusion. I need to tune in to riddims to stay focused on what I'm gonna do to handle this man.

'You're with me now,' he says. 'Women leave when we say. Best remember that.'

He pushes himself into me and I sink into the midnight zone where Black sea-slimed bodies float slow-mo in surge and sludge.

16

Channels

By the end of April, I'm running things at Shackles Shebeen. My weekly session, 'Sonix Dominatrix', is fiyah. I'm the controller, selector, toaster. On the decks all night. No mic sharks. Hip cocked, in my gold snakeskin shoes with six-inch heels, skin-tight black leather trousers, silver-sequinned butterfly top. Charmaine two-stepping by my side, blowing her whistle when the dutty bassline rips through her nervy body.

True seh, this is when I come alive. Blown out of my thoughts by high-frequency vibe. Outside the music, I feel wrong in this yah time. Monassa's words all over my body. Here in the outtasphere is the only place where death of the body is the birth of voice. The only place I feel no shame.

After the session, we're in the car and Racer's driving by the Floating Harbour, a psychic wasteland, low-frequency horns on the back end of the wind.

Eight in the morning and I'm still under the influence of the sacraments of dub music, fader-controlled distortion of my mind. My nerves and cells aroused. I'm flexing on this yah dread routine: three nights a week hustling the duppy-hour streets, Tuesday my Sonix Dominatrix night. Two hours' disturbed sleep most nights with Monassa putting on a performance of ganja blow-backs, drinking black rum from my pum-pum before fucking me.

Here in the daylight, in the car with the men, I've got no voltage to draw on. Sunlight casts strange shapes on the river where barges and rusting ships are moored. White shrouds hang from the cross-trees of masts, flapping. I'm bleached, high, manic, hyper-vigilant, my heartbeat pounding in my ears. I don't tell Monassa that I live for my Sonix Dominatrix nights when I'm on the mic, blazing fire. Raising hope.

The men talk about reparation, why they only steal from galleries, museums, antique shops, places they say have been built on the wealth of Africa. They talk about their visions for the future. Racer wants a boat to live lawlessly on the seas. Dungle wants to do right by his two boys. Monassa wants to save his people and for them to love-him-off. After each night on the streets, when he's slipped alone into the shadows of museums filled with our stolen past, a little more of him is missing.

Racer and Monassa are communicating with glances, nods, a kind of telepathy like me and Muma. I wonder which one of them is the ghost.

'We're dropping you at Christina's,' Monassa says. 'Give her the goods, stay with her.'

'Don't wanna skin-up with her,' I say. 'Drop me at the Safe House.'

Racer says, 'Go chat women's business.'

We drive with the windows down, the air is cool and smells of spring flowers and earth and leaves. Along winding riverside roads, through a forest under green canopy and then out into open countryside. Racer pulls on to the gravel forecourt of Christina's place and Monassa gets out the car and I walk with him to the back of the house. He gives me a small, red velvet pouch to hand over to Christina.

'Go chill with her. Keep her sweet.' He slaps my arse. 'You'll get your reward later.'

I hear them laughing as they drive off.

*

I sit on a stool around a bar in Christina's conservatory of wicker furniture, floral print coverings and flowers. She stands next to me. The place smells like a dried-out summer. She pours champagne and orange juice into long black glasses. She's decked out in coffee-coloured silk shorts and matching low-cut waistcoat, cream sling-backs. Vine-like veins all over her legs. She says her husband is in the Cayman Islands for a week, the children at boarding school. She's vex that the men didn't come in, but she sprinkles sugared rose petals on top of the drink like she don't business. Raises her glass, 'To the men and their midnight moves. Long may they rule the shadows, if not the waves.'

'You been with the men a long time?' I ask.

'Sweetheart, don't pussyfoot around me. You want to know about Monassa. We all do.'

She's gotta be charged on something more than champagne. Coke, maybe. There's a light in her eyes, like she's seeing God or paradise. She opens the red velvet pouch, empties it on to the bar.

A gold ring with a sapphire the size of an eye and the colour of the sea.

'African, antique, fifty K,' she says. She leans towards me, strokes my hair. Her hand moves near my breast. 'Nice body,' she says.

I put my hand on hers, move it away.

Her lips are on mine. I turn my face and her mouth is on my ear.

'Yeah, make me work for it,' she says.

'Nah.' I push her aside.

'Let me taste you. Feel what I can do,' she says.

'I said no!'

She inches back, cocks her head. 'Let me know if you change your mind. A year or two with those guys and your type are off men for good.' She laughs.

'And you?' I ask.

'I'm not doing this because I need to,' she says. 'I'm doing it because I can.' She picks up the glass bowl of sugared petals and throws it on the ground. 'Fucking flowers!' She looks at the broken glass on the floor, her nose flaring.

I down the champagne, refill her glass and hand it to her. She kicks the glass splinters aside.

'Don't let Monassa in your head,' she says. She shakes glass off her shoe. 'You've lasted longer than the others. Must be gold in your fanny.'

'Or poison,' I say.

She laughs.

'Who is he?' I ask.

'Monassa? Last year he said he grew up in a care home. Three years back he said he lived with his psychotic mother and her boyfriend.'

'And the others?'

She tells me that Monassa and Racer go way back, went to school together. They used to fight older boys on the estates where they grew up. Other pupils paid them to protect them from gangs. They've always had each other's backs. And years later, Monassa skanked his way into a private club where Dungle sometimes worked as a bouncer. Time and time again, he found a way into the screw-tight building until Dungle just waved him in.

Christina uncorks a bottle of wine and drinks a large glass of it. She throws open the French doors to the garden – a massive lawn with a raised, polished deck at the rear, more wicker chairs and tables.

She strips off her clothes, pads across the grass and lies down on the decking.

'Get naked,' she shouts. 'Sun therapy. It'll be gone soon. Nothing lasts.'

I stand at the threshold of the doorway looking at her white-blue skin, the green bruises on her shins and arms, her small triangle of pubic hair, and I wonder what would happen if I went into the garden and lay under sedative sunlight with her, put my head to her darkness. Would I be trapped and choked in the hold of her body?

She falls asleep. I go inside and sweep up the broken glass.

The men pick me up early in the evening. They've been gone for ten hours. Christina slept through most of it. They're charged on hash and the smell of perfume and different body odours.

Back at the Safe House I go to my room. It's freezing underground despite the spring sunshine outside. There's a story Oraca often told me about Queen Nanny, how she jumped ship just off the coast of Jamaica and with the help of spirits made it to a Maroon settlement, safe from British soldiers. I'm dreaming it's me in the ocean, voices calling out to me:

Swim, don't go under. Swim!

Hours later, the door opens and Monassa slips in. He strips, gets into bed. He smells of earth, freshly sprayed cologne and ganja, but he looks exhausted.

'Dungle's brother, Jammy, is locked up for a robbery he didn't do,' he says. 'Cock-eyed witnesses. Every Black man looks the same to them.'

He puts his arms around me and falls into a fitful sleep.

I move my ear close to his half-open mouth, listen to his breath. If I'm gonna understand this man, it won't be from the words that come outta his lips.

17

Midnight Moves

Summer nights and our living is easy.

Too easy.

We all have our roles.

Racer goes out by himself on foot, scouting the city and beyond for antique jewellery shops, colonial museums with anything from Africa or the Caribbean. The men spend weeks scouring maps, planning and plotting before making their midnight moves.

We all go out two or three times a week, middle of the night. Sometimes Monassa does a break-in alone. Most times they go together and leave me in the car for hours as lookout. I'm in too deep but the frequencies of pain and pleasure are reverb and delay, mixed up, disorientating me. Three seasons in the Safe House and I'm not sure what I've become.

A hot Friday night in August and we're parked outside a street of gilded houses, chandeliers in gleaming windows strung together like charms. We dropped Monassa inna darkness two hours ago.

Dungle is in the back seat leaning forward, his face between me and Racer up front. He paws his goatee. 'Man's been gone way too long. Something's wrong.'

Racer's hands are on the steering wheel, turning it left and right. His grey skull looks as misshapen as the stones that get washed up on beaches. He lights another cigarette, drops ash out the open window.

I know enough about how they move, the things they steal, to imagine Monassa now. He's gliding through the grave-dust darkness like the obeah men who leave their bodies and travel across oceans at night. He's got a sixth sense for vulnerable people and buildings, ribcages that can be prised apart, hearts and minds snatched out. His shadow flits and pools outside an ochre-bricked antique jewellery shop. He deactivates the alarm. Slides the lock with his device. Three minutes and he's in. Welcomed by faces from centuries ago, smiling out from gold frames. Rifles slung over their shoulders, their feet on the neck of a lion they've just shot. Monassa picks the lock of the safe. A cluster of blood-red gems.

'He's never been this long,' Dungle says. 'I'm going in.'

'Stick to the plan,' Racer says.

'He should go,' I say.

Racer looks at me. The muscle in his throat contracts. 'Monassa's put a gold necklace on you and you think you're Queen Nefertiti, huh?'

'And you're Aten, the sun god!'

Dungle is laughing, but a blue light tints the darkness behind us and Racer is shouting, 'The bull.'

Racer starts the car.

'Spin round,' Dungle says. 'We don't leave him.'

Racer cracks inna first, turning the wheel in short, sharp bursts like a hill-and-gully rider, his arms straight as drumsticks. Speedometer lickin' fifty as he turns a corner, the car almost on its side.

'There he is,' Dungle shouts.

Racer pulls alongside a Georgian-house museum, slows. Monassa jumps in. Racer takes off, speeding along the river. Waves of blue lights behind us, a tide coming in.

'Fuckers are on our backsides,' says Dungle.

Racer switches off the headlights and we explode into deep darkness. Wet air streaming through the open windows. Trees, benches, bollards flash into sight and drop away as Racer steers the car clear at the last second each time.

Lights off. Speed hypnosis. White road markings spin off the road, fly at the windscreen like arrows.

'You're gonna kill us!' Dungle shouts.

Police sirens blaring somewhere in the distance now.

'Can you drive?' Racer asks me.

'My poopa taught me—'

'Take the wheel. We're bailing.'

'I don't—'

'Tek the wheel! No headlights or they'll see you.'

'Meet us in Shackles, baby,' Monassa says. He's calm, almost serene.

Racer leaves the engine running and they jump out. I slide across to the driver's seat and crack it into first, second. Stall. Skid-start. Accelerate.

I force myself to breathe deep. I'm at the control tower. I spin the wheel. And it comes back, everything Irving taught me on those country roads. J-turns; Y-turns. Blood pumping, I feel the whiteness of my bones, my heart a flashing alarm.

I speed through the Floating Harbour with only dim street lights here and there. For the first time since Moose's death, I'm alive. For the first time in my life, I'm in full control.

Thick white smoke pours out of the bonnet, spreads out in the darkness, blows backwards inna my face.

I do a handbrake spin, spin-turn, drive into what seems to be a side road. The car goes over a humpback and floats in the air, hovers for a few seconds in the ether, and crash-lands into blackness. The top of a steep stairway with narrow railings on either side. No turning back. I steer the car down. Going too fast.

Feels like I'm sinking.

Naked Black women are swinging from nets around a ship, jumping into the sea. They're on their backs, drifting spirituals on the ocean. *Float*, they sing to me.

I switch to first gear and the engine stalls, but the car rattles downward. I restart it, move my body with the car, taking it from hum and purr to growling speed as I get to the end of the stairway and spin left on to the main road. I become the car. I race into darkness. Backwards inna time. Abeng, kiake, gombay, merrywang.

No sirens now. No blue lights. I'm alone.

I park on a side street. Light a cigarette, inhale to stop my body shaking. Exhale long, deep breaths until my heart stops thumping. Then I drive to Shackles Shebeen.

The bar is lined with men jostling for space, some laughing, others flexing as if they were born with flat-lining mouths. Charmaine is on the dance floor with two twig-thin women, moving their heads and arms like trees. The air smells of body odour, stale beer and breath. The crew are sitting at one of the metal tables against the wall.

Dungle gets up, hugs me. 'Safe, Yamaye?'

'I'm OK, but the car's taken a battering.'

'That's nuth'n,' he says. 'Racer'll fix her up.'

I look at Racer. 'Safe,' is all he says, only this time he ain't cutting his eyes on me.

Monassa pulls me into the seat next to him and puts the flat of his hand against the back of my head. 'This woman's dread! Look at her. Not even bustin' a sweat.'

Dungle pours me rum from a bottle, tops up the other glasses and raises his glass in a toast to me. Monassa rolls a spliff on the table, slides it to Racer.

'Light the fuse,' he shouts and Racer obliges.

We smoke, drink. Get on to the dance floor, jammin' with the small crowd, Monassa balancing on one leg, squat-skanking.

Charmaine dances towards me. I'm still buzzing from the car chase, the weed, the rum. Right about now, feeling like a revolutionary with the men, like they're the antidote to Babylon.

'Am I missing something?' Charmaine asks. 'A celebration?'

'Kinda,' I say. I start singing:

'I'm a mic chanter
the original banter
woman tekking over'

Charmaine blows her whistle, pivoting and twisting on alternate legs. We dance together until the music switches, then we go to freshen up.

Inside the toilets, I tell her about the car chase. She laughs and says, 'Moves, gyal!'

She flings open the doors to each of the white-tiled cubicles. Strip lights flickering overhead. They're empty. Satisfied, she raises herself up on to the sink unit and crosses her legs. She tells me she used to be the Heartist's woman. 'He has another woman now,' she says, 'but no way he's gonna let me go. He pays the rent on my council flat.'

I think of Monassa coming to my room every night, inside my mind and body. Unlike Moose and Muma, Monassa always returns from the pitch-bending darkness of history, the vaulted buildings with stolen marbles and masks of the dead.

The Heartist doesn't want her body any more, Charmaine says, but no one else can have her either. She has to be here at Shackles Shebeen every night, skinning up with people, getting information for him.

She asks what I do in the daytime. I tell her I'm usually in my room writing lyrics. Late afternoon I stew big pots of chicken, mutton and brisket and serve it to the men in the evenings before we take the leftovers to the bandstand in the park where homeless people sleep. Monassa says he's been on the streets before and can't bear to think of people going hungry.

I'm afraid that Monassa is going to hold on to me the way the Heartist has Charmaine under manners. Maybe those homeless people we feed are better off than me. Better to be alone in the cold, committed only to yourself and the darkness.

Charmaine says we should link every now and then. 'You still got my number?'

I nod.

She ruffles her plaits, puts lip salve on her lips and we go back to the dance floor, stooping, shunting, rowing the air. Bouncing into Racer and Dungle.

Sweat, smoke, stars leaking out of my skin.

A record is playing, a song about searching for a lost lover. It's one of the tracks on Moose's mixtapes.

I run out, climb up the metal stairway and go on to the street. Strange amber and violet light.

I close my eyes and hear the glass-blown waves of the ocean far away, roaring seabed secrets. An uprising of sound inside me.

18

Echo Chamber

Monassa still comes every night, staying longer through the night now as we slide into autumn. Checking me out when he thinks I'm sleeping. Maybe it's the way I took control of the car that night. Or maybe he's noticed something in my sleeping face. My mouth curving around a dream that he's not in. I feel his grinding breath on the side of my face in the darkness. I wait until he's murmuring in his sleep, then watch him. His jaw slackens, his face releases its mysteries – bottom lip hanging down, sucking his tongue like a teething child.

Maybe I'm stronger than him.

I've become his obsession. It's the way men are when they sense a woman doesn't want them.

He's just come to my room. We're lying together in bed. I ask him to tell me more about the Safe House. Other exits. Where they lead.

He sniffs my neck, under my arms, between my legs, hunting for my soul. Says that's a restricted privilege and I've got more to do to prove myself. He does tell me that he found underground plans for the Safe House building in the university's library six years ago, when he was studying architecture as a mature student. He got thrown off the course. Wouldn't say why. Hung on to his library card and went back to the library every day to teach himself. He found an old book, *Bristol Archaeological Evaluation and Planning*, printed in

1835. Inside was a map of the tunnels and their connections to the red sandstone caves that had been mines hundreds of years ago, mines that made ice-blue glass to trade for slaves. He broke into the Safe House building a month later.

'Think our families' troubles go back to slavery?' I say. 'Your mother, my father.'

'They're duppies,' he says. 'Forget them.'

He lights up, sucks on hashish. Tells me ghost stories about River Mumma, a spirit that haunts rivers and draws you to the water so it can drown you. 'I wanna scare you, baby. Scream for me,' he says. 'I keep you safe. You need me. Nah true?'

'Ain't afraid of water. Nor you,' I say.

'Nuh gwaan so,' he says. He turns on his side.

Rejection is his weak spot. I get it now. Hard-back people like him, Asase, Crab Man, they're all just fronting. Beneath the ice is watery emotion, feelings they don't want anyone to see.

'Don't even think about leaving me, baby,' he whispers.

I clench my fists, keep my body as relaxed as I can.

He rolls back to face me. 'Check this – dem clothes in your room, the duffel coat, the Farahs. That Stix-Gyal woman thought she could just leave. I gave her top-notch protection from a gang. There's no getting away from this yah scene. It's a one-way ticket, baby. Seen?'

'What did you do to her?'

He presses the side of my face into his chest, his hand on the back of my head.

I hear the sea in his body, oscillating, glugging. His heartbeat underwater, slow.

'Shhhhhh.' He presses down on my head. 'Ask no questions. I'll tell no lies.'

Strange, but there's no fear. Just a shiver knowing I'm gonna have to skank this man in his own dark way to get myself outta here.

He releases his hand and sits up, rests his back against the wall. 'My muma was a dread skanker,' he says. 'Fucked off to Miami with some bwoy. Love me some slackness, but not when it's your own mooma. You're not one of dem woman.'

He thinks we're the same because we haven't grown with love. The difference is Muma is around me, soft-pitched, her voice caught in the suspension point between dead and alive.

'Did you love her?' I ask.

'Who?'

'Your muma.'

'Love?' He sounds confused.

'Must have been some good times,' I say.

'Nuth'n. Never held my hand when I was small, shit like that.'

I press my lips against his chest. I gotta play it cool, because the love of a man like this can be more dangerous than his hate.

'We treat each other right, don't we?' he asks.

'Like history taught us,' I say.

'You always going deep,' he says.

I watch him fall asleep.

The next evening I'm getting ready to go out with the men. Monassa is calling me: 'Yamaye, what the raas you doing? Move your batty bone, gyal, we're ready.'

They're waiting in the passageway outside the main room, wearing Italian silk suits. It's the Heartist's birthday party at Shackles Shebeen.

Racer raises his eyes at my outfit. My hair's slicked back and studded with gold butterfly pins.

Monassa runs his hand through his goatee, pops his lips. 'Yuh are looking foine, lady!' He pulls me into his body and hugs me.

'Enough of that,' Dungle says, but he's smiling, looking at Monassa as if he can't believe what he's just seen.

I pull away, twirl as if it's all for him.

We drive through the Floating Harbour beneath a limestone moon. Vehicles jammed in tight on the road running by the railway arches. Cars drive by in slow-mo. We park forty yards or so away from the entrance to the club on the other side of the road.

'Yo,' a man calls to us. He's big and slabba-slabba, with a cutlass-curved moustache dominating his face. He's standing next to a maroon Stag with three sullen men, all wearing long, black leather coats. The whites of their eyes are strung with red veins. The man with the moustache, who seems to be the gang leader, steps to us.

Monassa leans against the Dolomite, smiles in a tender, exultant way. 'Yeah, my man, what's up?'

The man's posse step around their leader in one loose-jointed movement.

'Seen. Seen,' they say.

The leader asks Monassa, 'How's things?' In other words: What's happening? Any bull around? Which side of the street has the best likks and tricks? Come on, give it up, nuh!

Monassa says, 'Easy.' Meaning: The runnings are sweet, rude bwoy. We're cleaning up out here and we ain't tellin' you shit!

The leader looks at me, works his way up and down my body with an attitude of scornful attention. When he gets to my face, he closes his eyes with exaggerated indifference.

Muma's wrapping herself around me, part of the humming texture of air. A protective layer of sound waves. Drumbeat in my ears, a warning. Make moves: quick step, quick step.

'Respect is due to the woman, rude bwoy!' Racer shouts. His body's twitching, his eyes quick-fire blinking.

The acoustics change; a crisp, bright silence. Raindrops pelt the air, glassy baubles tinged with darkness.

The leader strokes his moustache and leans closer to Racer. They're fighting-distance apart. Racer is a couple of inches shorter than the man, but he pulls himself up and pushes his nostrils into the other man's airspace, the tips of their noses flaring in hard-core harmony.

'This woman moves with us,' Racer says, and he drags me forward, waiting for the leader to give me a respectful nod.

They face off in silence, their eyes locked on each other's, one of them a short way away from undisputed peace.

The rain is heavier, flowing in all directions. Yellow lamplight throwing shapes in the air.

Dungle drags me backwards and steps in front of me. 'Get inside,' he says, 'and stay there.'

I step across the road, look back. Monassa has pushed himself between Racer and the leader. It's just the men, their cars, the deadly quiet street and the summer rain.

I go through the front of Shackles Shebeen. The inner doorway to the stairs leading down is closed and the squat, bearded bouncer is standing there.

'Trouble,' I say.

'Monassa?'

'Some gang looking for fiyah,' I say.

He opens the inner door and tells me to go down. Then he goes outside.

I stay by the main door. He can't have been gone more than five minutes when I hear noises outside. Tyres screeching, dogs barking, whistles, other voices shouting.

The bouncer comes back. 'By the skin of my teeth. Bull have cordoned off the area,' he says. 'If you step foot outta here you're on your own.'

I open the door, look out. The air is hissing with rain. Two police cars on either end of the street, a roadblock. A Black Maria in the middle. Policemen are springing back and forth on their toes, waving their batons at the gang leader who's lashing at them with a studded chain.

'Come if yuh bad!' he shouts.

Two of his men are cuffed, spreadeagled against the police van, two policemen pushing against their heads.

Racer and Dungle are back to back, flinging punches at the policemen that surround them. Three police are on top of Monassa, trying to cuff him. He crouches down with their weight, secures his power, then erupts, roaring. The police go flying, skidding on the wet road.

Dungle throws a punch to the temple of a policeman and the man drops, but Dungle slips as he turns and lands on his back. Two policemen pile on top of him; one of them hooks an arm around his neck.

Racer springs forward and lands a flying kick on a policeman's stomach; other police topple forward across Dungle's body. They're on top of Racer now. All I can see are his white trainers kicking.

Dungle is not moving.

A policeman is beating Monassa in the back of his head with a baton, but Monassa's throwing punches left and right at the two policemen in front of him as if he can't feel the blows. On and on Monassa's punching, pummelling as if he's one of his superstructures of steel facing the sun god, the one that will never fall.

I go closer to the roadblock, crouch behind a car. One of the gang members is dragged along the ground, lifted by his arms and legs and thrown into the hole of the Black Maria. Sounds, like mallets striking metal. Grunts. Then wailing. The man calling for his mooma.

A vision of Moose in the police cell, face down, cuffed. Choking. His skin breathing in white-noise sound. I double over, vomit black bile.

I watch as all the men are cuffed and thrown into the Black Maria before its doors slam shut; the van rocks from side to side as it drives off. The police cars follow.

I run into the street. Upending silence. Flecks of blood mingled with rain. A ripped leather coat, a trainer. A gold ring.

I run back to Shackles Shebeen.

Mr Chen, the bouncer and two other men are inside the main entrance. I tell them the police didn't follow us here, we're always looking out. The bouncer says the police were probably on the tail of the other men. He didn't recognise them; they weren't from the area.

'Police get lucky,' Mr Chen says. 'Me sorry for dem bwoys tonight.'

He says I should come inside. They're going to shut the security door downstairs. Lock-off. No one coming in or out until they're sure the police aren't heading back.

Inside the club, Charmaine, sitting with her back against the bar facing the dance floor, is nodding her head to the music. The Heartist is at the other end of the bar, a woman on each arm as usual. Mr Chen buys us brandy and goes off with the men who had been standing at the door.

I tell Charmaine what happened. She takes my hand and leads me through the club into the steamy kitchen. Cook is ladling food on to plates and handing them to a small line of people. I follow Charmaine through a door out into a cobblestoned area where bins and crates are stacked.

Just a few flecks of rain, electronic spit. We lean against the wall by the bins. The area smells of rotting food and stale beer.

She puts her glass on the bin, lights a cigarette and exhales as she asks, 'Where's your head at?', her voice a smoky chain of husky notes.

I take several sips of brandy.

'Your eyes are on the run, all over the place! Do better than that.' She squints at me. 'Don't let no man know what you're thinking.' She draws on her cigarette again and again as if she's the one having to make a plan.

I try to steady my gaze.

'Heel nevah go before toe,' she says. 'Don't do nuth'n yet. Wait.' She drains her glass. 'I should know.'

'You tried to leave the Heartist?' I say.

'A practice run,' she says. She laughs. Then she goes serious and she's inna my face. Her breath smells of smoke and brandy and dry-dry saliva.

'Monassa ain't a man you can leave just so. You need to know where to drop that stylus of yours.' She shakes her head. 'Even then. That man's baad.'

She passes me the cigarette and I inhale. Feel the smoke tuning my bloodstream as the rain starts to fall again.

Dungle calls me from prison two days later, says they're on remand. The courts are backed up with cases and their solicitor says they could be inside for just three weeks, or for a year. Monassa and Racer are in solitary. He tells me, in coded hard-core patois, to lie low and keep the Safe House locked.

I'm alone. I should be relieved. But Monassa's absence from the Safe House doesn't seem real. Like a voice stripped from a dub track, the space left is more powerful. Absence as intensity. Like he's watching my every move.

All the clothes that he's bought for me – snakeskin slingbacks, midnight-blue cashmere slip dresses – hanging in the cupboard like the shrunken bodies of women. Charmaine's right. I have to steady myself first. Make a plan before getting outta the house and stepping off the tightrope.

That first week, I clear their cards and dominoes off the table in the main room, spread out my papers and pen. I write lyrics in the mornings. Evenings I sing, trying to find the hidden pockets of sound in my body, the truth of what Monassa's been doing to me. My voice is weak as it connects to the low-end warps and wefts of fear and disgust that send my mind reeling. And I realise that it's not death that takes away a voice. It's fear.

The following week, I walk to the harbour to link with Charmaine. It's a bright day: lilac sky; slow, sweeping clouds. A small white boat is moored against the harbourside, so close I could jump into it and sail away. A red ferry with people at the front is cruising by, surf bubbling at the prow. I watch the movement of the river, the waves in my body slowing.

I hear Charmaine call my name, like someone calling out to a long-lost friend they haven't seen for years. She's coming towards me, walking past a row of leafless trees wearing a fuchsia ra-ra skirt, lean-down ankle boots, black leather jacket with oversized shoulders. She's a tall, thin flower among the stripped-back trees.

'Yes, sistren, another nice day in our spot,' she says.

She sits beside me on a bench, shakes her head, lashes her plaits over her shoulders. 'Heard anything from the men?'

'Nuth'n. You know how dem stay.'

'Feel it for my man Dungle, though.'

'Just Dungle?' I ask.

'Mind yuh business,' she says. She's serious for a few seconds, then she starts laughing. 'You know that's not how me and Dungle run things.'

I check her face to see where her mood's at. High. Low. Dark. Bright.

She peers into the water, looking into the white boat. 'I listen to your lyrics good-good. You talk truth on that mic.'

'Nuth'n's changed,' I say.

She jumps down into the boat and lands hard. She stays down, rolling and shouting, 'Bombo, that's busted me up.'

'You OK?' I ask.

She gets up, goes to the wheel and plays at steering the boat. 'Let's get the fuck outta here.'

She rummages around the back of the boat and after a while throws up a rope ladder. She asks me to secure it to the bench. I do that and she climbs back up to the harbour. She lifts her skirt and presses the grazed skin at the top of her thigh.

'Maybe I can be part of your plan,' she says. 'You give me some donzai to get myself a vessel, sail outta here. We'll help each other. They have a stash somewhere in that place.'

'Why would I take that risk?'

'A way out for both of us. Sistren must do it for themselves, for each other.'

'If I steal their money it's a one-way ticket to the other side.'

She takes my face in both her hands and squeezes my cheeks. 'You don't get it, do you?'

'No.'

'The Heartist. Now Monassa's off the scene . . .' Her hands drop to my shoulders and she shakes me. 'You need waking up, gyal.'

'What about the Heartist?'

'He's not steaming in yet,' she says. 'But if Monassa isn't out in six months, he'll make his move on you. Another woman to do his dutty work.'

I feel sick. More psychic footsteps stalking me in the dark. I tell her I need time to think about where to go. Somewhere Monassa won't find me.

We walk along the harbour to one of the cafes and drink sweet tea from white polystyrene cups. She crushes the empty cup in her hand and holds out its crumpled shape to me.

'Me,' she says. She takes my cup and crushes it. 'You, if you don't move your batty soon.'

I'm afraid to leave. Afraid to stay.

Charmaine says her mind's not her own any more. Not the Heartist's, not anyone's. It's free, does its own thing whenever it wants, and she's grateful for that. She has a little bit of money stashed away; all she needs is another grand – for the small Monark sailing boat she's got her eye on.

'How will you manage a boat?' I ask.

She says her father worked as a fisherman on the Bristol Channel. He told her a Black man was only safe on the sea if he was in his own boat, and that was the first thing he bought, not a house. He taught her how to sail and fish because he didn't have any sons.

'Easier to punch against those big tides than fight a man,' she says.

'What about the Heartist?'

She shrugs, says she can do a hundred miles in a long day's sail. Calculate secondary port tides, heights and times. 'My mind is a little messed up sometimes, but don't take me for no fool,' she says.

'Monassa's always talking about reparation,' I say. 'Maybe it's me and you that need it the most.'

'Sistah, you're on it.' She laughs.

'Let me think it through.'

She says I should get intel from Christine about when the men might be coming out, because when I run I'll need a head start. Women don't just up and leave.

I watch her walk away, her arse shaped like a heart – with all the life flattened out.

That evening, I search the abandoned corridors of the Safe House. Everything seems darker than I remembered it. There are inscriptions on the walls of some of the passageways, images of stars and fires and circles, dates from hundreds of years ago. Names. One of the corridors is blocked off by a one-way door. Like people from the past never went away, they're still in the darkness in this choked-black throat of a building.

The corridors go on and on, repeating in a zone of unknowing. I imagine Muma in Guyana, in rainforests, plunging into a void. I keep going until repetition is ritual and I open myself up. Muma's voice inside me, smoke rising from rebel fires, secrets stuffed inside snakewood. I see her in an abandoned village in the interior of Guyana, in a wooden hut on a prehistoric site, caught in a time warp of conjoined rivers.

I'm the only one can get her out.

I'm the only one can get myself outta this.

'Are you there?' I call out. My voice echoes.

I walk back towards the main room, head down one of the dark corridors to Monassa's apartment. It's locked as usual. He never let me inside, not once. I use one of the men's plastic shields to slide the lock the way I've seen them practise.

A large, square room with heavy strip lights. Stone-grey lino on the floor. Flickers of Monassa's shadow in the dim light. Sex-musk, sweat. My hands are shaking. I remind myself that he's over a hundred miles away inside a prison, in a coffin-tight cell, lying north to south, his face hidden from the sun.

A wooden table runs the length of the room. The walls are covered with his red sketches of towering buildings that look like spaceships.

Angular, irregular layering of apartments, three-dimensional spaces, an other-worldly form.

In the corner, a king-sized bed backed up against a row of six filing cabinets. Everything is locked. Monassa says he doesn't trust banks because they were built on the backbones of his ancestors. The money must be here.

I bend the metal nail file I've brought and pick the lock of the first filing cabinet, rifle through the green hanging files that are filled with photocopies from books, what look like his old university essays. In the bottom cabinet a large leather case with reinforced-steel corners takes up all the space. I unlock it. It's filled with banknotes, split into one-thousand-pound bundles separately bound in elastic bands. I count the money, putting it into piles on the floor. Every now and then I look in the mirror, afraid of seeing his reflection.

Sixty-five thousand pounds.

That will go a long way. Reparation for me. Thirty thousand pounds to Rights On. Aside from my testimony, that's the best I can do for Moose and others like him.

A line of heat spreads across my chest, a borderline between gut and heart.

I shouldn't have come to the Safe House.

I should have fought back against Monassa. Not given in to fear.

If I take his money, what will it make me?

I see my face reflected in the mirror and look away.

Put the money back.

I drive to Christina's. The house is in darkness. No one answers the door.

Back at the Safe House, I make myself a bowl of cornmeal porridge. Irving often made this for breakfast when I was a child. Never fed me sugar-loaded cereal from those cartoon-covered boxes filled with plastic toys. I try to picture Muma in our kitchen, singing as she cooked, but all I can see is a dark pool of emptiness floating in the flat, her voice rising and breaking up, a fractured aura.

I'm alone.

Irving is the only one in my bloodline left. Blood is fire. Fire burns. There's always smoke.

I phone him and he answers straight away, like he's been waiting for my call. I picture him sitting at the wooden telephone table, a bench with a large green cushion, Muma's orange doilies on the small, triangular table section, the red rotary phone in the middle.

'Eh-eh! Ah you dat,' he says. 'You still deh about.' He sounds out of breath, agitated.

'Is that all you can say?'

'You facety, ever since yuh was a pickney.'

I chance it and ask, 'Is it strange without me?'

'Strange how?'

'It's always been the two of us.'

His voice deepens to its normal bass. 'What is loneliness to a man like me?'

'Does it make you think of Muma?'

'Of her?' His voice vibrates at the back of his throat.

'After all this time.'

'Man wants peace when him old. The past can bruck you.'

'You always talk in riddles.'

'Look 'pon you! Gone just like that. Call me out of nowhere once a year. Not even a number me can call. Who's the riddle?'

I break the rules, give him the number of the Safe House.

I ask about Oraca and he says he can't remember seeing her or Hezekiah on the streets. But his memory is bad, he says, getting worse. I tell him I'll visit soon. He grunts and hangs up.

I stay on the phone, speak into the receiver, talking to a dead line: 'Is there anybody there?'

I hear the sound of the sea inside my head. Voices rushing together. I throw the handset on to the table and a long, large, black crack appears in the glass top. I drop on to the floor, holding my stomach, crying, crying for the mother and father I will probably never know. The loss of me in the shadows. My limbs feel shackled, chained to something that's drifting down and down.

I can't move.

I force myself to get up early the next morning. Drink a mug of black coffee before driving to Christina's house. Large, grey clouds like caravels fill the sky. A rough, relentless breeze bounces against the car.

There are lights in the windows upstairs and downstairs. The back door is locked. I knock and knock before going to the front door and ringing the bell. She flushes red when she sees me and pulls me through the hallway into the kitchen. She's wearing a black polo neck, riding trousers and boots. The only thing missing is a whip.

'What the fuck are you doing here?' she asks.

It's not the welcome I was expecting or need.

A man's voice from the first floor calls, 'Darling, who is it?'

'Won't be long,' she shouts back.

I want to tell her what happened to me, woman to woman. Get the information I need, maybe even some sympathy. I say the men are in prison.

'Think I don't know,' she says between clenched teeth. 'This scene is way too hot. House is on the market. Got a job with an American magazine. My husband's firm has offices in the States. Persuaded him we need to move for my career. Ain't that the truth! We'll be gone by the end of the week.'

'Do you know when the men—'

'Probably about six weeks. That's how long you've got.' She takes money out of a turquoise clutch on the kitchen table and presses a wad of notes into my hand. 'Don't come here again.' She marches me to the door without a word.

I get in the car and stare up at the window. Her husband's looking down at me. A tall, baby-faced man with thinning blond hair, green pinpoint eyes.

Monassa and the men won't grass her up. She'll land on her raas. A woman like that ain't gonna end up in jail. Next I hear of her, she'll probably have her own column in that glossy magazine. A divorcee guru writing about families and the threat of addiction and crime.

19

Sonix Dominatrix

Later that evening, I take all the money into the main room and spread it on the table. Think about Eustace, Rumer and Christina. Ask myself why I'm always the last to bail out. I push half the cash across the table towards Monassa's chair.

Don't know if my mind is steady enough to take their money. Need to fire myself up with dub riddims before I decide.

It's nine. My Sonix Dominatrix night doesn't start for another three hours, but I twist my hair into Chiney bumps studded with black pearls. Pull on a maroon silk jumpsuit, gold trainers; string an empty bullet belt diagonally across my body. Pack my vinyl in a silver case. Drive through the city, spinning the steering wheel like a 45 on a turntable. Floating, unburdening, time and space going round and round.

Deserted winter streets. Howling wind. Red light bulbs flow around the arch of Shackles Shebeen, a shrine in the swampy darkness. Inside the club, I'm enveloped by the familiar smog of smoke and rub-a-dub body heat. Music playing on a mixtape.

It's early for this place. A few men govern the wooden bar in gunmetal-shine suits; four women in diamanté dresses are shooting stars on the circular dance floor. The Heartist is sitting in one of the Chesterfield booths with two women either side, deep in conversation with a man sitting opposite.

I adjust the lights around the deck to understorey shade. Everything in position: two turntables, cross-fader mixer, mic, headphones. I set it off, playing dub riddims for resurrection of the dead from Black Marias. From the Atlantic, where sounds sweep from the Guinea Coast, on and on into time.

The club's filling up. People two-stepping on the dance floor.

'This one's dedicated to the man called Moose,' I call out over the mic.

The Heartist looks up at me. I flash the lights on the deck. Turn the volume up on a chanting, horn-blowing riddim from centuries ago. Chat my lyrics hard:

'Sonix Dominatrix at the control tower
drawing life outta the living with
treble, bass, reed, flute—'

The burgundy-coloured walls drip with condensation as dancers bruck out, winding and turning, tangled as String Algae. Mr Chen is alone at his table, twisting little knots in his beard. Watching. Two hours and the place is fiyah, the faces of the dancers blistered with sweat.

I think of Rumer and how she made her move quick. Soon as she was up on her feet after her illness, the woman was gone. Wonder where she is and what she'd say to me.

The countryside is beautiful, gyal. Clean air, everything open and clear. No smoke. No concrete. I loved Asase. You did too, in a different way. We were all living a lie. Get outta the city, gyal. Ain't no truth there.

I call out over the microphone: 'Yeah, this roots-rockers tune is dedicated to my friend, Rumer. In Ireland somewhere.'

I play one of Rumer's favourite tracks. Imagine her skanking, flashing her red hair. My voice is choked up with tears. I pass the mic to a youth who's hanging around the decks. Go to the bar, drink two shots of sorrel and white rum. Burn the tears back down.

Charmaine comes over. The bar area smells of syrupy brandy and rum, cedar and amber men's cologne, stale sweat.

'Same for me,' Charmaine says.

I buy her a double rum. The place is steaming, but she's wearing a brown sheepskin coat, ankle snow boots with lean-down heels. I still can't work out whether she's insane or wise or brave or just on the wrong side of time.

'I know things!' she says. 'Things that went on in this city way before we were born.'

'Things?'

'I've been burned enough times,' she says. Her eyes circles of fire; white froth at the corners of her mouth.

I lean back from her stale breath. She's having one of her bad days.

'Don't step from me!' she says.

'Charmaine, I was just—'

'Don't call me no Charmaine. She drowned centuries ago. Call me Princess.'

'I'm going back to the decks.'

'Kiss my batty,' she shouts.

I tell her to simmer down, and she takes hold of my arm as I turn away. She whispers into my ear, 'Don't you wanna know what happened to your man?'

'Monassa?' I say.

'Moose,' she whispers. 'The one Babylon killed.'

I put the flat of my hand on her shoulder blade and push her into the small cloakroom to the side of the kitchen, just beyond the booths. I give the ticket assistant some notes and tell her to go buy herself a drink and come back in ten. She looks from me to Charmaine, ducks under the counter and leaves.

'The fuck you going on with?' I ask. 'How do you know about Moose?'

Charmaine twirls a plait around her little finger and the 400-year-old child in her resurfaces with big, sad eyes.

'We're women,' I say. 'You help me. I help you. Seen?'

Just then one of the women who was sitting with the Heartist comes in looking for her coat. Charmaine tells her we're covering while the attendant gets herself a drink, but we're talking about heartbreak and losing men if she wants to join in. The woman looks at her, unsure, then leaves.

'Charmaine, is there something else I need to know?'

'There's always more,' she says. She tells me that one of the Heartist's contacts is a police informer who moves from place to place, changing identities. Infiltrating Black Power groups and campaigns for justice. Born in this city, the man comes back every few months to rest up. She describes him.

'Crab Man!' I say.

'No other.'

'What's that fucker got to do with Moose?' I ask.

'Crab Man was on your tail for the police. Trying to dig dirt on you so they could mess up the investigation of your man Moose. Your barrister man is on to something big. They're watching you both.'

I lean against the counter. The furs, suede and leather coats on the rail look inhabited. The arms in mid-motion. I close my eyes, trying to get rid of the images of Moose's body in the morgue.

'I know what went on in this city,' Charmaine says. 'Old-time things jangling in my head like glass eyes.'

She goes on to say that it was also Crab Man who told the police that Lego was hiding out in the Crypt, and that Asase might be there too.

'Crab Man was vex the police didn't find him. Made his intel look bad.'

I don't say anything about Lego's secret place. I ask, 'Why didn't Crab Man inform on Lego before then?'

'Lego was crab bait,' she says. 'Where one runaway finds safety, others follow.'

I think about the night Crab Man hassled me and Asase by the canal. He must have been following me.

'He's doing what he wants on the streets,' Charmaine says. 'Long as he's doing Babylon's dirty work, they let him get away with it. Power's gone to his head.' She says he grew up in a care home and he doesn't have an attachment to anyone or anything.

'Is he your friend?' I ask.

'There are friends you chat your business with and friends you do business with. Nuh so?'

She smiles, her startled child-eyes glistening. Something don't look right. I see what it is, the thing I recognise in myself in the too-bright pupils. The translucency that could be timelessness, or something out of its depth.

The cloakroom woman returns, her arms folded across her chest. She says she'll get in trouble with Mr Chen if she doesn't get back to work.

Charmaine pulls the thick coat tight and buttons the collar around her throat. We go out and stand in the passageway outside the kitchen. Cook is by herself, hunched over a steaming pot.

'You need to get your raas out.'

'I'm scared—'

'We need reparation for our minds and bodies,' she says. 'We won't get far without money. Now I done told you all this I gotta leave too.'

'I've got you,' I say. 'We're in the same fire. Just need to think how much to take and where to go.'

'Time's running out,' she says. She turns to go and then shouts, 'Don't call me no Charmaine Brown. I'm Princess. Daughter of an African Queen. Shhhhh.'

She's wired. Disconnected. Weak. Strong. Sad. Hopeful. On her way. Long gone. But she's live and direct with herself and me about the blues and blips that trouble her soul. And right now, this makes me trust her. We're inna this together. A fundamental frequency. Connected in a way I never could be to Asase because of that defensive wall around her feelings.

I feel something like the beginnings of love for Charmaine. Or maybe it's the first sign of softening towards myself.

I go back to the decks and watch as she dances. Flashing her braids. She's in the centre of the dance floor, a dim bulb swinging on the end of a long chain light fitting hanging just above her.

I want to join her, spill my guts, talk in tongues with her, claw at my bruises, bail out from my mind, let her and the water in. Sink. But the Heartist is watching me again.

I take my mic from the youth.

'shock-out, shock-out
become supernatural
tek over the control tower
push the chillum pipe
to the back of dem
throat
smoke them out
smoke them out'

And with each word that I fire out to the crowd, I feel sound growing in me. My future, the treble, below the rising bass of Moose, the alto of Muma. All of them becoming one voice, telling me to take the money and run.

Cold winter air rises like a low transmission. I sit on the bench by the Floating Harbour, waiting for Charmaine. After that night at Shackles Shebeen, we agreed to meet every week to coordinate our separate plans, check in on each other before we leave.

The sky is the tanzanite blue of lost, empty towns. White-haired, old people, stiff as statues, stare at the ground, walking as if the earth is about to swallow them up. Memories bubble up from trenches of sound in my belly. Moose, Asase, Rumer, Lego and me crushed in the dance hall, sweating, buoyed by the swell of floating bodies.

It's one o'clock and I've been waiting for an hour. I'm worried that the Heartist has found out that Charmaine passed information to me. Or that her mind has cut free again.

I drive back to the Safe House and call her at two, then at three. She doesn't pick up.

An hour later, the phone rings.

The strange dragging, cracking sound of someone trying to breathe.

'Charmaine?'

A few more breaths. Then a man's voice.

'Can't . . . can't catch me breath . . . can't see.' It's Irving.

'Easy, deep breaths,' I say. I try to stay calm, but I'm wondering if it's the thing I've been waiting for, his life-or-death moment to help me decide what I feel for this man, to get me beyond the misfired jolts that feel like love trying to take off, but grounded in fear.

'Hold tight,' I say. 'I'll call an ambulance.'

'No . . . no sah.' The sound of rasping as he tries to get his breath.

'Not going to no . . . no . . . hospital fe dead. Me going dead inna me yard.'

I tell him I'll drive, be with him by early evening.

Green and blue signs of towns and villages with ancient names whizz past, consumed by speed and fading light. Always more tarmac road ahead, a black horizon. I'm scared he'll die before I get there. I don't wanna see another dead body as long as I live. It's two and a half years since I had to look at Moose's and it feels like yesterday. Does life play out in sound or numbers? If Irving dies there'll be another kind of silence – all the things he knows about Muma, but holds on to for himself, maybe the things that will help me find myself.

It's the first time I've known him to be sick. The man's always been tough. Still working in his old age, manipulating spools of fire with his welding torch. His body has been shrinking and bending out of shape like a rusting coil spring from one of his cars, yet he was still walking with a crocodile's slow, dragging steps and heavy-eyed watchfulness. Still sitting at the dining table at weekends, wordless, polishing small car parts like sherds. Listening to the weather forecast, making notes about low-pressure systems as if he's waiting for a hurricane and the snakes that'll come crawling out of the earth. Maybe thinking his Taino blood will be an offering to any storm. Turning it from its path.

I reach Norwood just after seven. Mulchy darkness, silver frost on cars and trees. Men leaving Lionel's Liquor Mart holding large bottles of spirits like fire extinguishers.

I drive into the recurring dream of the Tombstone Estate and its morass of shadows. Look all around in case Babylon or Crab Man are following me. I should have asked Charmaine whether Crab Man was still in Norwood.

I let myself into the flat. The curtains in the front room are closed.

The bulb blows when I switch on the light. The furniture looks misshapen, unfamiliar in the darkness. What will happen to the flat and Muma's spirit if Irving dies?

I go into Irving's room. He's lying on his back in bed, his lips cracked and red.

'Irving?' I lean my ear to his face. A sweet, rancid smell coming from his open mouth. I touch his shoulder. He doesn't move. 'Wake up!' I shake him harder.

'Yamaye, is you?' He opens his eyes, stares up at the ceiling, attuned to something I can't see.

'Take it easy,' I say.

'Sugar in me eyes. I can't see properly.'

'I'll call the doctor.'

'Undertaker breeze,' he says. 'Throw rum in the room, I beg you!'

The window is wide open and the greyed net curtain billows outwards as if someone's just jumped. I shut it. Call Dr Shepherd. Give Irving tea and wipe his burning face with a flannel soaked in Bay Rum. My chest is burning, I'm choked with confusion and pain. I need to either love or hate.

'Doctor's on his way,' I say.

'When me eyes close I see your muma,' he says. 'She must be dead.'

My skin feels hot and sticky like magnetic tape, overloaded with data, peeling away from white bone.

'Must be dead?'

'See her there,' he says, looking at the ceiling above the bed. 'Woman is vex.'

I look at the empty space. Refracting basslines drag my thoughts where I don't want them to go.

'She's been dead for twenty years,' I say. I'm above him, looking down at him the way he used to tower over me before a beating. But there's no satisfaction, just a recoiling feeling of pity. 'Isn't she?' I ask.

'Can't feel my feet and hands,' he says. 'I'm dying. Retribution.' All the bass has gone from his voice; he's nothing but treble. A look on his face I've never seen before. Shame? Vulnerability?

He tries to sit up, but collapses back on to the pillow, moaning. 'All them clubs in London wanted her. Couldn't let no woman of mine go to dem places to be taken advantage of. I met her on the ship. The sea was rough. I thought I'd saved her. Then she slipped away like the tide.' He starts crying. The burning in my chest hardens.

'I'm not asking again,' I say in that tone he'd used on me when I was a child.

'Your muma . . . disappeared,' he says, his voice cracked and strained.

'She's not dead?' I ask again. 'No cremation?'

I'm pacing the room now, afraid to look at him, still not believing. And when he won't answer, I take the radio off the bedside table and crack it against the wall, throw the bottle of Bay Rum against the dressing-table mirror on the other side of the room, shattering the glass.

'Disappeared where? Did you report it to the police? Did you search for her?'

'She wasn't happy. God forgive me. I . . .' He looks at his hands as if he's afraid of them, as if they're prehistoric tools, lost to history. 'She went to Guyana to nurse women and pickney.' The slow drawl of his words sounds like dub spooling backwards on a cassette tape. 'Six months. That's all it was supposed to be. Some charity paid her danger money.'

'Why danger money? Where in Guyana?'

'In the bush, snakes and things all about. Some strange name. Can't remember.'

I slump into his armchair and look at the ceiling above him, anywhere but his face.

He tries to sit up again and slides back on to his pillow.

'She wrote and said she wasn't coming back to me,' he said. 'Said she would send for you. Three months, four months, five months, a year – nothing. The charity went bust. Them was stealing money, sending people to these places without the things they needed. No one answered my letters. It was shameful, my woman gone like that.' He says that Muma was a countrywoman at heart, born near the Blue Mountains, close to Maroons in that part of Jamaica. She liked the privacy of the countryside. He says she was put into a children's home in Kingston when her parents died. She was six. It's the most he's ever spoken about Muma. It's everything I've ever wanted, but I still don't trust what he's telling me.

'She might be alive?' I'm on my feet again, shaking his arm. His head rolls from side to side and he puts his hand on mine, tries to push me off. I let go.

'I used to think so. But now . . . all these years.' He moans. 'She never came back. I tried to find her. She would've come back for you – if she could. She loved you.'

I'm speechless.

'Me see her last night, in spirit. She must be dead.'

I replay what he's said in my mind. Hold my breath, withdraw inside myself, press my ear to the silence to hear truth. I come back for air. Look at him again.

'Fuckeries!' I shout. 'Lies! You've been lying my whole life.'

His eyes are misty lenses. I see nothing of myself in him. The limestone-pocked, olive-brown skin, the sloping eyes, slick-straight hair. Man's as distant as the echo at the bottom of a well.

'Yamaye, nuh look 'pon me like that. I was raised hard.'

'So was I!'

He's crying without tears, his chest rising, catching, falling.

'What kind of man are you?'

'I thought she musta gone back to Jamaica. But no one who returned my letters ever said they'd seen her. I didn't think she was coming back.' He heaves, his breath ragged. 'Me tell everyone she was dead.'

He says that he didn't go to the police because he was afraid they might take me, his child, away, put me in a home. Keeps saying he looked for her for years, wrote to the orphanage where she had grown up. Homes of Hope, it was called. Says he remembers because she always said the nuns gave her hope. But they gave him none. The nuns couldn't tell him anything.

I ask for their names, their letters. He says he threw them away.

I ask if there's anything he kept that might be important but he's mumbling, moaning, crying. The strangest noise I've heard. A burbling turbulence.

His words are footfalls leading nowhere.

I switch off the light and go to the balcony to wait for the doctor to come. I look out beyond the tower blocks at the wastelands and the brickfields where hidden trenches and defensive walls were dug up along with the graves of ancient people, weighed down with lead weights and gold.

You can't keep the past down, I say to myself. I turn and look at the front-room wall and Muma's paintings of blue-mist mountains in Jamaica, shaped like the sound waves of a song, calling me.

Now I know where I've got to go.

I say, 'Muma, we're going home.'

20

Understorey

The next morning, I call Charmaine and she answers. Says she's had some tuff n'raas days, heaviness in her head, she couldn't get out of bed for three days. I tell her where I am, say I've got a plan. We agree to meet when I get back.

I walk to the other side of the estate, on my way to get Irving's prescription. Dr Shepherd told me last night that Irving's sodium level is low. He said something about early signs of dementia and that Irving was crying a lot and showing signs of agitation. As he was leaving, told me that the sinkhole had gone; the council backfilled it with rubbish to stop everything collapsing. That's what Irving's done with my life, filled it with lies so his wouldn't fall apart.

I look up at the sky beyond the towers and imagine Muma looking up at the sky in a moment of need. All these years of sensing her, feeling her thoughts around me. Could a spirit be that strong? I think of all the things that could have happened: she was kidnapped, injured, had a breakdown, decided to stay with the villagers in Guyana, start a new life. Maybe there are things the women at the orphanage wouldn't tell Irving, but they might open up to me. My throat tightens and I cry.

On the high street people look at me twice, unsure if they recognise me. The last time I was here was the day of the riot. In a way, nothing has changed. Same shops. Same townspeople. The smell of cattle from the market in the air. The street shaking as trains go by.

Did Muma take one of those trains on her way to the airport? Did she walk where I'm walking now, wondering where to go?

Did she go into the church to pray? I stand outside the church and look at the stone saint at the front of the building. I'm afraid of Muma's physical presence, although it's the thing I've wanted the most. Her electro-acoustic spirit is all I've known. I'm afraid of the bottlenecked words that could come out of her alive mouth that might have nothing to do with wanting or missing me.

I've been listening so hard for her that I've disappeared into her songs. I've been missing, too. If I can find her, she could bring me back to life.

I think of all the soundscapes I've travelled through in my dancing nights at the Crypt. The spatial manipulation of dub music where I've been lost and then found. Muma has to be somewhere. Dead or alive. I've got to find her.

I get Irving's medicine. Then go to the bank and take out all my money, eight years' savings from Bonemedica and the sessions at Shackles Shebeen. Three thousand pounds. I put a thousand into a brown envelope and write the telephone number of the Safe House on the back.

I walk to the church and knock on the small wooden door at the side. I stay there, knocking on and off for fifteen minutes before the door opens a crack. A hand pulls me in and bolts the door. Lego's skin is grey and waxy; dark pools under his eyes. He's leaning on his stick.

'Yamaye, yuh forget 'bout me?' He squints. 'Yuh all right? You look . . . different.'

'I left after the riot. Had to get away.'

'Father Mullaney is at the hospital visiting Mr Everleigh, he's not doing so good. Come.'

He leads the way downstairs, holding on to the rail in the dim light.

I think of Asase and Rumer and all the times we walked down these stairs, following the smoke and bassline, wading through bodies.

We go through the Crypt door and Lego pulls back red velvet curtains that are draped around some arches. Small enclaves, booths set with cushioned benches and tables, gothic candle holders on the walls.

'What's all this?'

'The Crypt Restaurant.'

'You serious?'

'Babylon closed the dub-music dances. The church was using the income for its community work. Feeding the poor, paying deposits for rent. This is the new earner.'

'Who comes?'

'Out-of-towners. Wanting a piece of the past.'

I follow him to the back and he pulls open a new sliding wall to show me a shining, stainless-steel kitchen, a large central stove surrounded by workspaces, freezers, pots and pans.

'When does all this happen?'

'Weekends.'

We sit in one of the booths and he lights the red candle on the wall above.

'You're OK here?' I say. 'With this going on.'

'Livens up the place,' he says.

'That's not enough.'

'Been here too long.'

'I'm in Bristol now, going to Jamaica.'

'Outtanational, eh-eh!' He stops and puts his fingers to his lips. 'Thought I heard something.' He taps his head.

I listen, but there's nothing but our voices to hear this far down.

I tell him what Irving's told me about Muma and at first he doesn't comment. His mind seems to be somewhere else. I tap his shoulder and he says, 'Yeah, yeah, I hear you, go easy on the old man.'

'He's sick. I'll stay until he's better,' I say.

'Your old man is strong. I remember him working on cars, lifting parts. That man has a dread face. Used to scare me,' he says.

'Crab Man, that's a face. That's who you should be afraid of.'

'What yuh know 'bout him?'

'Informer. He told the police about Asase and you.'

'Bombo!' He fires his walking stick into the air and calls out, 'Mash down Babylon.' He lays the stick on the table and slides his finger along the tip of it. 'Bongo Natty says that Crab came out of nowhere. Wetting up our streets. Police never troubled him. Never been locked up. We shoulda blood-claat known.' He spears the air with his stick again.

'I came to warn you,' I say.

'Man's disturbed my peace,' he says. He looks at me and the shadows under his eyes swallow them up, black glass holding back the ocean. 'Is he disturbing you too?' he asks.

I shake my head.

'Not any more.'

'I've always looked out for you, Yamaye.'

I get up. 'You shouldn't have to live like this.'

We hold each other. There's nothing to him: no weight, no flesh, no bones. Man's disintegrating into dust.

He starts coughing and I take my hands away. 'Got to get back to Irving,' I say. If you need somewhere to stay. I've got a lock-tight place – for now.'

We climb back upstairs. When we're at the door, I give him the envelope, point to my number on the back. Say it's strictly confidential. Tell him the money will help if he decides to leave. He won't take it at first, insists I'll need it for my trip to Jamaica. I push the envelope into his hand. Say I've got more than enough. I'm tapping into rhatid reparation money.

I take one last look at the Crypt. As the door closes behind me, I feel the tremor of bassline at the base of my skull.

Outside, I cross over to the Manor House, where the business centre used to be. There are boards on the street window. A haunted hideout again. I imagine Crab Man at one of the darkened front windows, watching.

I remember the night at the Crypt when he pulled me to dance. A lifetime ago. Flattened his palms against my arse, wouldn't let me get away, four tunes in, his breath heaving in my ear. His hard-on is something I feel in my body to this day. I imagine meeting him on the street thirty years from now, bent forward, arched like a bow. I'll put my hand on the base of his spine, push him forwards on to soft, rotting bone.

Back in my block, I visit Georgia, who lives next door, ask her to look after Irving. Her little girl, Ruby, is at nursery now and she says she needs to earn some money, but jobs are hard to come by. I give her five hundred pounds and promise I'll send her the same every month.

For the next few days I stay inside the flat, watching from the balcony and the spyhole in the front door, looking out for signs of the police or Crab Man. I keep the chain on the door and bolt it top and bottom.

I haven't seen Herbert since the protest march over a year ago. I call him to tell him I'm in town and to find out how the case and his report are going. It's late, but he's still at his office. He says the investigation is progressing slowly because the police are holding back evidence. Rights On are running out of money, they're launching a fundraising campaign, holding a big event in the city. He asks if I'll come and say a few words about Moose. Months ago, I would've said no way, I'm not up to it. I think back to when I collapsed at the morgue, the horn blaring from my throat. I could barely tell Moose himself what he meant to me, much less tell thousands of strangers. But I realise the Safe House has changed me. I think about what my body and mind have been through. And, despite everything, remember there was fire in me that helped me to take control of the wheel of Racer's car that night. When I got on the decks at Shackles Shebeen, tuning the crowd to my psychoacoustics. I've been to hell and now I've risen. Less afraid to think about Moose and my love for him. Ready to take the money and go to Jamaica and start the search for Muma.

I'm running things. I say yes.

I make ginger tea for Irving. He's pretending to be asleep, and I leave it on the bedside table. I check the mail and there's a brown envelope with a black stamp addressed to me. It's a prison visiting order from Asase. Oraca must have seen me from her window.

Four days later, I leave for Rights On's fundraising event. Irving is moving about by himself in the mornings. The hallucinations seem to have stopped, but his eyes dart around the room, avoiding my gaze. He goes back to bed after breakfast, where he stays rolled over to one side, the blanket on his head. I go to his room, say I'm leaving and ask if there's anything he wants to say. He rolls around to face me, shakes his head, and starts to cry.

I say I'll phone in a day or so and he tells me to walk good.

It's a bright, dusty day, the smell of frying meat oil emanating from the cafes. I drive past shop owners dragging crates on to the pavements; packs of children in woollen bobble hats heading for the canal with fishing nets and jam jars. Once I'm over the railway bridge, I wind my window further down and let the breeze flow in. Glancing at the wood-panelled dashboard, I feel like I'm in the captain's quarters of a ship, steering out of choppy seas. I think about Muma; if she's alive, finding her is surely just a matter of fine-tuning the resonance of heart and gut and brain, fusing to source, third-ear call-and-response. Changing up a gear. Listening. Waiting.

I push in one of Moose's mixtapes, *Hear Me When I Call*. A lovers-rock tune, a woman singing about paradise. Her voice floating alone above other-worldly harmonies. I feel the aching loneliness.

'Coral Anderson – Muma – I'll find you,' I say out loud.

The roads into London are congested; end-to-end buses, cars and lorries. The river is a long stretch of silver on the right. Brutal needle-point skyscrapers claw the sky. The bronze statue of a slave merchant glinting in the winter sunlight, his right arm raised, holding distant buildings in the palm of his hand. I park a short distance from the pier where Moose and I embarked on the riverboat tour. The old sugar warehouses are set back in shadow. The river gleams red under the rising sun.

I go into the gilded reception area of a large conference centre and the man at the desk directs me to suites on the fourth floor. I take the lift and go through heavy fire doors into a wood-panelled auditorium with a built-in stage. The ceiling is studded with small LED lights that glint like stars.

Herbert is on the stage standing at the end of a long, glass table where two women sit in the centre poring over papers. He waves when he sees me.

'Yamaye. You came.'

He comes down the steps that lead from the stage and puts an arm around me. 'You're doing the right thing. It's time.'

He's not wearing a suit, he's in a T-shirt and jeans, his Afro is gone, his hair woven into thin cane rows. I nod in approval. Say I'm ready.

He introduces me to the women: Carolina, a trainee solicitor from Colombia, a petite young woman with hair shaved at the sides, blonde spikes running down the centre of her head. And Nompu, a South African barrister with a small round face and sharp kohl-shaped eyes. I go to shake their hands, but they embrace me. While Carolina gets up to set papers on side tables and greet people, I sit at the table with Nompu and she talks me through the programme, tells me there's no need to plan anything, just speak from the heart. She says I should start with the personal, then she'll join me and speak about the points of law of Moose's case as well as some of the other cases. She asks if I would be comfortable with Rights On recording my speech so they can show it at other fundraisers. 'That way, you won't have to go through this again if you don't want to,' she explains. I swallow and nod.

The rest of the morning is a blur. I drink cups of coffee and eat half a pack of malt biscuits while people drift in. By ten, the room is packed. My mouth is dry; there's a jabbing pain in my stomach, like a stylus snagging on my guts.

Herbert taps the mic at the podium and the voices of the audience die down. He makes a brief introduction and then gestures for me to come forward. I grip the sides of the lectern and stare into the crowd. There's a glitch in my throat, words not coming up. I picture Moose and Muma standing on either side of me, Moose on my left, Muma on my right. I hear their voices in unison: 'Let your mouth fly, Yamaye.'

I think of Moose's spirit leaving his body, soaring up out of the police cell, the acoustics of white light, a tunnel of rotating mystic humming.

I feel the feedback energy of the audience, expectant, like the dancers at my Sonix Dominatrix nights. I align myself with the vibrations of Muma, the beating wings that flutter from my gut to my heart. My body is the control tower now. I clear my throat, set the tone of my voice to bass-low, then play it at top range.

'I'm honoured to be here,' I say. It doesn't sound like my voice; more like that of an older woman, a voice on the undertow of the past. 'There were moments when I didn't think I would ever be able to do this. But life forces us to defend ourselves.' Something lodges in my throat and I pause for air.

Herbert comes to my side and squeezes my hand. 'You've got this, Yamaye,' he whispers. The crowd is silent, I clear my throat.

'Moose isn't here to tell you about his dreams,' I say. 'But I was lucky enough to hear some of them. He planned to return to Jamaica to care for his grandmother. He loved her bad-bad. She believed she'd see him again before she leaves this world.'

A woman in front is looking up at me, close to tears. I keep my eyes on her. 'He believed in art, beauty and transformation. He believed in protecting the earth and everything in it. He loved rainforests and trees. He believed he would walk in the rainforest again with his grandmother. With me. He believed he'd be around to protect the two of us. He believed in our love. My dream was to marry him and raise our children in Jamaica, in the countryside. When we choke the life out of a man like that, his spirit doesn't disappear. It haunts us. A reverberation.'

And I feel Moose passing through my body, shuddering electric waves. *Yamaye, I'm here. You're not alone.*

'Please, if you all can, just a few seconds' silence. Listen. Feel. Have faith. If you believe in Moose's spirit and all that he stood for, please help Rights On fight injustice.'

Time is suspended for a few moments. The audience is applauding, and it sounds like a roaring waterfall. As if I'm slipping into memories I'm not ready for. Herbert takes my hand and I lean against him, let him lead me away.

I drive back to Bristol and the Safe House with my heart warm but my head thudding. I think of how strange it is that the future I envisioned with Moose was cut short, while the life I never thought I'd have with Muma might be a possibility.

It's late, but I call Charmaine and she says she can meet at our spot by the Floating Harbour.

It's cold and dark and there's frost on the surface of everything. The stars look like icicles. She's there already and takes sips from a small bottle of brandy without offering me any.

I tell her that I'm going to Jamaica. She says no way she can tell me where she's heading. Only that there are a few places she wants to go. People she's hoping are still there. People who never expected much from her. Yet even if she turns up as her cracked and weathered self, as long as her body and soul are at last humming to their own tune, she'll be happy. And who knows, maybe she'll come check me in Jamaica one of dem years. She'll charter a boat and we'll sail round the islands for a few weeks or months. If life spares.

I slip her an envelope identical to the one I gave Lego in the Crypt. Her gloved hands shake as she stuffs it into the inside pocket of her sheepskin coat.

'For the boat,' I say. 'I'll wire the rest when I've banked it in Jamaica.'

'My sistren,' she says. 'You've come good.'

'When will you go?' I ask.

'Shhhhh,' she says. 'Cover your tracks. Nuh chat your business.'

We walk along the riverfront, past barges and boats. She says she's going across the bridge ahead, going back to her flat. We say goodbye and I go up the ramp to the lane where the car is parked. I watch her walk across the green bridge. Her tiny figure moving along the empty bridge strung out across the moving darkness of the river.

Two days later, I drive fifty miles outside the city to a small town just before closing. I buy plane tickets to Montego Bay. The flight is in three days' time.

Driving back into the city, through a thin line of rush-hour traffic.

Trance-like, yellow headlights, one behind the other in the darkness. I notice a black Beemer a few cars behind me that's been there for a while. I check the rear mirror, come eye to eye with the Heartist. Man looks vex. I know straight away that he knows I've been helping Charmaine. I shift into fourth, press hard on the accelerator.

The oil light is flashing. I clench the steering wheel. I'm only a mile or so from the Safe House, but there's no way I can get out of the car and unlock the padlock of the main gate before he gets to me. Just wanna shut myself in my room and tune into Muma and Moose before I get on that plane. But this blood-claat man is in my way. I'm fucked off with being tracked and followed by Babylon and man dem. Their eyes always on me.

Anger rises, slow at first, from gut to arms to clenched hands. And raaah-tid! It feels good to mek it take over. Every revved-up, rage-carrying cell lighting neurons in my brain with images of destruction. Ah me dat thinking 'bout driving across the train tracks, leading the Heartist towards old platforms and warehouses part-hidden in undergrowth. Ah me dat thinking 'bout steering away at the last second from a shunting yard, so that he crashes into it, flips his car. Ah me dat watching him and his black Beemer go up in flames.

Nah, nah, this is his terrain. Have to do better than that.

Time fucks with us women like nobody's business. I think of Crab Man's hard-on pressing into me. Monassa holding me down. That was then. This is now. After a year with Monassa and his crew, I've got moves too. I've watched their skanks, their ability to shape-shift, switch gears. Bruck in. Bruck out.

I listen to my breath going in and out. There's no turning down the volume. Not now.

A coal train is travelling along the harbour track in the opposite direction. They only run at high tide to take the stress off the river-bank. It's winter; the river deathly cold. There are three cars behind the Heartist. He can't do anything stupid. I'm in front; it's down to me to run things.

I speed past the station on to the roundabout. Turn on to Guinea Street. Parked cars are ram-up against the opposite side of the road. I take the keys for the Safe House and push them into the pockets of my jeans. I accelerate, swerve and cut across oncoming traffic into a tight parking space, hitting the headlights of one of the parked cars. Horns are blasting, people shouting, a blur of voices and rushing air as I jump out.

I sprint through cobbled streets, my breath singing in my chest. I get to Redcliffe Parade, high above the harbour. Georgian houses on the other side. I run down the steep steps of a small lane that leads to the riverside. I can hear the Heartist calling out, 'Blood-claat bitch!' He's a little way behind me. I run to the arch of Redcliffe Caves, pull at the rusty metal gate, but it's shut. There's nowhere else to go but the river. No street lights, pure darkness. A yellow ladder on the side of the wall going down into the water. The Heartist is closer now. I can hear his breath. Or is it mine? I climb down the ladder with one hand, gripping the keys to the car and the Safe House in the other.

'Biyatch!' He's right behind me.

Explosion inside my head, pressure binding my temples and jaw. The water is as cold as fire. My teeth chattering. Breath dragged outta my mouth. I swim in what I think is the right direction to the other side, but it's pitch-dark and so cold that it's hard to focus. Impossible to see anything except a semicircle of distant lights. My limbs are heavy, as if they're shackled. I turn on to my back to see if he's following me. I can't see anything except black water and sky. I kick, my arms floating at the side.

My right foot knocks into something and I feel tingling along my leg, a burning sensation. I'm terrified of anything in the water that can drag me down. Adrenaline floods my body.

I flip on to my front. Time to get into the business of sound and movement. I draw down a dub beat: riddim-riddim. Kick to it, swing side to side to it. Dread time, nuh so? The shore seems to be getting further and further away. Am I moving? My legs and arms are heavier and, worse, I can't breathe. Cold lodged in my throat and nose.

My face in black water, I see inside my head. A seabed. Murk. Kelp forests. Footsteps in the sediment. Pink jellyfish floating like hearts. Upwelling light, Muma's face floats up from the understorey of another world, her eyes hollowed and sparkling.

Daughter, don't go under.

I flip on to my back again, gasping for breath. I try to float, but my body is shaking so hard I sink.

I kick to the surface, fear pumping adrenaline into my body. My shoes are dragged off by the current. I crawl forwards towards a floating pontoon. I hold on to it for a few seconds before I can pull myself on to the platform. I roll on to my back, coughing and vomiting water. I'm shivering, my teeth clashing against each other. I crawl on to the bank. My clothes sodden with water. Lying down, too tired to stand, I strip off to my underwear. Get to my feet and run. A pub up ahead. Not sure where to go. It starts to rain. I think of Asase and Lego in the cramped vaults, crouched in the suffocating dark; Crab Man's body in the black sarcophagus. Entombed. Men's bodies chained in the holds of slave ships; women on the decks, jumping overboard into the unknown depths. Where would Lego hide? I remember when I asked him why he stayed in the Crypt, he said that the first territory that rebels claim is the night.

People outside the pub are smoking and drinking. They stare at me. Someone shouts, 'You all right, love?' I keep running. My heart pumping too fast in my chest. Down cobbled back streets and to the church. Arched windows and a spire like a dagger piercing the sky. I run down three steps and into the church's park. The rain heavier now.

There's nowhere deeper and darker in Bristol than the park's bandstand at night. A circular platform, columns supporting a blue dome roof. An acoustic shelter where people are camouflaged from the world in cardboard tents. Stained, strained and haunted; men and women curled up like frustrated fists on the face of the earth. This is where me and the men took leftover food packed into foil trays. Monassa and Dungle would hail them as if they were their bredrin. Shake their hands, say 'Respect'. Racer would give them bags of weed, but not get too close.

I push to the front of the queue where volunteers from the church are handing out containers of soup and paper bags of bread and cakes, warm clothes. A woman pulls me into her body and starts rubbing me down. She wraps me in a large quilt and gives me a cup of hot sweet tea and offers to take me into the church. I say no and she hands me a bag of men's clothes, a sleeping bag. Someone has tied plastic sheets around the bandstand to stop the rain coming in. There are fifteen people in sleeping bags, some talking to each other. I climb into the sleeping bag, strip off my underwear and change into the dry clothes. I keep watch all night.

At four in the morning, I walk back to the Safe House.

21

Lights Out

At the Safe House later that morning, I shower, but I can't get the stench of the bandstand off my body. I lie on the sofa and doze in fits and starts. Dream Monassa and the Heartist are lurking in the passageways. I wake at lunchtime with sleep gems in my eyes, silver smoke in my throat, funde drums ricocheting inside my head.

I phone Mr Chen to tell him I won't be able to play my Sonix Dominatrix nights for a while. I'm not surprised when he tells me he knows what's going down with the Heartist, so my sessions are over, whatever my intentions are. He says the Heartist left this morning to track down Charmaine. 'Birmingham. Wolverhampton. Manchester. She has contacts there. He'll check them places good. Four days at most. Take yourself off this scene. Otherwise you next. Remember, I don't help women in distress.'

I go to the kitchen and cut industrial-sized wedges of hard-dough bread, spread them with sliced banana, guava jam and brown sugar. I gorge on sweetness, but the emptiness is still there. Drink chilled milk and white rum from a mug and return to the main room. Sit at the table looking at my reflection in the heavy slab of glass atop the wooden sleepers.

I take Asase's visiting order out of my bag. Even from prison, she's capable of making demands. The date is set for Wednesday. Tomorrow.

*

With the Heartist off the scene – at least for now – and nowhere safe to stay until my flight, I take my chance to walk along one of the bridges by the Floating Harbour that criss-cross the waterways, going by the harbourside train track. Before I leave Bristol for good, there's something I need to see.

I hear jazz coming from an old rusting barge and think of Oraca, in that low vinyl-crackle voice of hers, telling me it was Muma who got her into that music. And I think about the trumpeter and wonder if Muma had an affair with him. I hope she found love with someone. Muma would have made it big, Oraca always said, but maybe that was what Irving was afraid of. She said, 'Our men in dem days couldn't get opportunities that matched their talents. They didn't just come with their grips. Those men had plans. In the end, their egos were all some of them could hold on to.'

Children's voices from a school playground on the other side of the park. Reminds me of childhood summers, me and Asase running wild on the wastelands and fields beyond the estate, Lego and his friends chasing us, and Asase chasing them back with switches that Oraca had shown her how to cut from birch trees. Our voices popping and crackling in the golden light.

I step into another past, the one I've come to see, the Sugar Museum, once the home of a slave owner. A collective of Black artists, ArtConscious, have done a takeover. The outside signage says the exhibition, *Reverberations from the Depths*, is the product of a three-year partnership with Everything to Dive For, a group of international underwater archaeologists documenting and archiving artefacts from slave shipwrecks.

Other voices roaming the four floors: dining room, study, drawing room, ladies' room, cold-water plunge pool, a hidden staircase. Polished wood doors and red silk curtains. Baubles of old dust hang in the air. The sound of a large grandfather clock, a wooden heart beating against time.

From the window on the first floor, I look down into the silty river. The owner must have looked out at his ships bringing mahogany, cocoa, rum, tobacco. Did he realise he got more than he bargained for when he stared into the eyes of ghosts, their voices fluid in his heart stump?

I go down the circular, winding staircase to the tiled ground floor where the exhibition is, in what used to be the drawing room. Brooding, thundery, underwater sound effects. Ceiling lights pouring on to a large blue notice on the wall:

It is hard to know at what depth these echoes will reverberate and die away.

Gaston Bachelard

Six transparent boxes filled with iron ballast. Shackles. Wooden pulley blocks. It says they were discovered by divers from Everything to Dive For. And the main feature, a wooden ship in the centre of the room, six feet long and three feet wide. Black flattened bodies painted on a blue sea floor around the ship, half-human, half-algae. By the ship a cream card on a glass stand names the artist as Kalihna Williams. It's the artist that Moose worked with before his death. I realise the ship must be made of the wood that Moose spent countless hours coaxing into shape. I twist the mahogany ring on my finger. Moose said trees were portals. But to what? The afterlife?

I listen for Muma, but she doesn't come. Is she dead or alive? Or somewhere in between, like the human–algae bodies?

A group of schoolchildren in navy uniforms are listening to the recordings. A silver-haired man in a tweed suit, probably their teacher, asks me what I think of it. His cologne smells of forests; his eyes are the same cool grey as the river.

I say water holds memories.

The following day, I arrive at the prison before lunchtime. Grey granite walls, thirty feet high – it's more a cliff than a building. I expect to walk in and fall off the edge of the world. The sun is blinding, beating down on the block. I haven't seen Asase since her trial. I'm surprised at how excited I feel. Despite everything, I want to know she's OK. And I'm hoping that the visiting order is a sign she's ready to tell me what really happened that night at the Crypt.

The security guards check my VO and let me into an interior courtyard where there are stone-and-steel dormitory buildings. Syncopated beats of clashing steel and jangling keys. Metal language, objects have voice. Humans ain't speaking.

I go through an administrative centre, follow red signs along limewashed corridors.

The visiting room is charged with drug-dust stillness. Green tables, grey plastic chairs. Posters of Dos and Don'ts and helplines plastered on the walls. The ceilings are high, long strip lights glow fluorescent white. Around a quarter of the prisoners are Black. Dazed captives, mystics who've spun their minds outside their bodies. Their husbands, mothers, friends and children on the other side of the tables.

Asase is sitting alone. I recognise the ramrod posture. Same way I've been holding myself in the Safe House. Toughing it out. But really wanting to bail.

'Wha'ppen, girl. You reach!' she says. She makes a rounded shape in the air with her hands. 'You look good in tight trousers. Never knew you could fling down style like that.'

I sit down, facing her. Her face is bloated. Her flesh heavy, hanging like a cloud. Seeing her like this brings up a cold ache in my chest. Like one of them blue streak notes from that jazz trumpeter whose records Oraca plays. Unsure how to ask how she's flexing in prison, 'Thanks for the VO,' is all I manage to say.

'Where's Rumer? I sent her one too,' she says.

'The gyal chipped. On the road with her people,' I say.

'Blown us out! Good luck to her.' She makes a *cho!* movement with her hands, then leans back in her chair. Specks of sweat above her lips.

I swallow, try to shape the words. 'You OK?'

She flinches.

I'm trying not to see the bronze-coloured lipstick that's melting off her lips. Chalky foundation, unsettled on dry skin. 'Need anything?'

She pulls away. 'I'm locked up, blocked up.' Her voice breaks, 'Where yuh *been*?'

'Couldn't come without a VO.'

'Been sending them from Day One.'

'I'm not in Norwood any more.'

'I heard.'

'Oraca?'

She nods.

'Irving never said there was mail for me,' I say. 'He must have seen the prison stamp on the envelope and kept it from me. I was at the flat when this one came.'

'Your poopa is dread.' She shakes her head and laughs with something that could be admiration or repulsion.

'I should have written,' I say.

She backslaps the air. 'A nuth'n.' But there's a chink in the glint of her cut-eyed look that says it's a big deal.

One of the children starts crying and a woman hushes her. Asase calls out to the prisoner whose visitors they are and the woman points with pride to the child, who must be hers.

'Reminds me of us when we were that age,' I say. 'Staying with you in the summer holidays. Sneaking down to the kitchen at night, drinking Hezekiah's white rum and Oraca's sherry. Topping up the bottles with water.'

'Ma knew. Woman ain't nobody's fool. She never got vex with you,' Asase says. 'Always making your favourite food, fussing over the poor motherless child.'

'I never—'

'Miss Nicey-Nicey, ain't yuh.'

'Because I'm not like you?'

'Because I had to be tuff for both of us. And when I need you, yuh blank me.'

'I didn't come to fight,' I say.

'Fighting? That all I'm good for?' She's breathing faster, her hands trembling. She leans forward, puts her clenched hands on the table. Her knuckles are two mountain ranges that seem insurmountable. All I can see is that she needs something from me. I reach out and cover her fists with my hands.

'I'm sorry.'

'Not for me!' She looks down at our hands. Turns her palms upwards and our palms touch and I feel the heat of her hands before she slides them away.

'Thought me and that man were tight,' she says.

'Eustace?'

She makes a throat-clicking sound of disgust. 'Yeah. Him.' She takes a deep breath and tells me how she used to check Eustace in his shop, late at night. How it felt good because she didn't have to act bad with him. He listened to everything – about Hezekiah and his man-ways, and when things with Herbert started to go wrong. They talked about him helping her set up her business, make-up for Black women. Her eyes are wide and she's looking up into a future that never materialised.

'I wanted a good man,' she says. 'Not like that poopa of mine.'

'Didn't know you were feeling Eustace that way.'

'Ain't I a woman too?' Her eyes are red and watering. I'm not sure if she's holding down tears or whether she's charged on drugs. When we were kids, she would style out her pain. Oraca always told her cry-cry pickney don't get anywhere in life.

She looks away from me, speaking quickly, as if she can't get the words out fast enough.

'Eustace said I got it wrong. He loved his wife. Thought of me like a daughter. I was beautiful and had moves and even if he had them kinda feelings, he wouldn't do anything. The man dem on the streets looked up to him.'

Her voice is softer than I've ever heard. A breathing, like air going in, not coming out. There's a scraping noise as she shifts her chair away from the table.

'He shouldn't have come to the Crypt,' she says. 'He saw me standing on the other side of the room, but he blanked me. Too busy dancing with that woman.'

'He always danced with women. Never disrespectful. Eustace only ever tried to help you, same as he did me. You shouldn't have been trying to make him leave his wife. Did you want a man like that? Like your poopa. Repeating history?'

'History? Like we got any.'

I'm surprised at the desolate tone of her voice. Not sure if it's just about Eustace or being locked up. She turns her head, looks at the guard at the door, leans towards me. 'We went outside the Crypt. I was crying.'

'*You?* Crying?'

'Eustace put his arm around me, said I should tek it easy. I could still feel Crab Man shaking me, trying to whipcrack my head off my neck.' Her breathing is all tangled up with her words.

'You're safe,' I say. But she's somewhere else, not hearing me. Her voice is displaced, tuned out of time and space.

'Eustace was trying to calm me. But everything in my head was blurred. Felt like I was on the frozen canal again, and it was cracking, or something inside my head was cracking, breaking up.'

'Crab Man hurt you bad,' I say. 'We should have gone home. Called Dr Shepherd to check you out.'

'Can't remember taking the knife out of my bag. Stabbing him like that.'

We're silent for a moment, reliving that time. Inmates and visitors are whispering, laughing. Vibrational smog, their voices are the cold, lo-fi crackling of that night.

She leans away and tilts the chair on to its back legs, eyeing me from another angle. She exhales a long breath and lets her chair drop back on all fours. She's crying.

'Did you tell your solicitor everything?' I ask. 'You didn't look right. Like you were in shock or something. You should appeal.'

'Babylon always wins. You know that.'

I want to tell her that I'm going to Jamaica, to Cockpit Country, land of the Maroons, and Babylon has no power there. But I can't tell her anything because Monassa can get to her through the underground communications of prisons, and maybe she'll speak. 'Make a fresh start when you get out. Leave Norwood,' I say.

'Like you? That what you're doing with that Stix-Gyal styling. Bouncing like yuh got sound inna your shoes?'

'I'm trying to help.'

She flings her arms out like she's thrown something at me. 'You're lucky your muma's dead.'

'You're tekking liberties!'

'Ah suh?' she asks.

A small child sitting on her father's lap is looking at Asase, her bottom lip trembling.

'Please, Asase . . .' I say. She ignores me.

'I grew up watching my poopa push Ma around,' she says. 'Huffing-puffing-cussing-swell-up-frustrated. Never put his hand on her, but he was always wanting his likkle piece of power under his roof because he couldn't get respect out in the big wide world. Because he's a Black man.'

A guard comes over to the table. She has silver cropped hair, head shaped like a bullet, thick leather belt pulled tight across two rolls of stomach fat; fleshy, smirking lips.

'Keep it down or your visit's over,' she says. 'Got it?'

Asase looks at her and makes a small movement with her head but doesn't answer.

'Last chance,' the guard says and walks away.

'Take it easy,' I say.

Asase wipes spit from the corners of her mouth.

The smell of women's bodies, salty, musky, their holy waters drying out in the overheated room. Hushed, desperate conversations, distant sounds of cells slamming shut. I feel trapped. One of the prisoners in the far corner of the room is crying, her hands over her mouth.

Asase's hands are still shaking. I ask her what she's on and she says anything she can get. Visitors crutch every kind of drug into the prison. 'When I'm high, these walls fall down like the walls of Jericho,' she says. 'No pressure. Bubbling, like I'm dancing in the Dead Water area. Music up inna my head.' Her eyes are half-closed, her pupils floating.

'And when it wears off?' I ask.

'I drown.' She's staring through me, her eyes the swirling brown-green of the Atlantic.

'I hear duppies at night,' she says.

'In a place like this, I'm not surprised,' I say.

And I can see now what she means by overflow. Different kinds of emotions bustin' out of her eyes. She's all over the place.

'I'll send you another VO. Smooth me in some drugs,' she says.

I tell her that I'll send her favourite chocolate, magazines, the pink hair treatment she likes. But I'm not hustling drugs. 'That why you sent me this VO?' I ask.

She's laughing and now I'm not sure if she ever did post the other VOs. Either she's lying or Irving has been holding out on me. The thought of the two of them and their ways digs into something deep within me, like a wound being scraped out.

She's still laughing, a mean, hollow sound. I look into her eyes, the whiteness of her teeth, the back of her throat, the dark opening into her soul.

My voice is calm, firm. 'Asase, the sisterhood is complex. Maybe we wanted to love each other. But we just didn't have the right start in life.'

Asase lunges at me, shouts at me to shut my mouth.

It feels like the explosion we both needed. I push her hands away. 'The sistren no longer exists,' I say as I stand up.

I feel energy running up and down my spine, power in my legs. The fire's inna me, same as her. But now it's me that feels like crying. If I'd confronted her before, maybe she wouldn't have been so hard and I wouldn't have been so saaf.

The guard is standing over Asase.

'Sorry, I upset her. She's OK now,' I say. I pick up my bag, swing it over my shoulder.

Asase slumps in her chair. 'Best not to miss the last train outta this place,' she says. Her body deflates and tears are running down her face. I give her a tissue and squeeze her hand as she takes it.

'Wipe yuh nose,' I tell her.

And she does.

I walk to the door and she calls out to me, 'Ma named me Asase, Ashanti soul-strength name so no man can bruck me down. Ever. That's what Muma said. No man.'

I feel like I'm already on my way, thousands of miles between Asase and me. Part of me wanting to turn back for one last look, another part of me wanting to run.

I walk along the winding limestone corridors, thinking we should have stayed underground in the Crypt, dancing through the hours, days, weeks and years, until blood and flesh and bones became water, light, sound.

On and on dancing until.

Lights out.

22

Black Sarcophagus

When I get back to Bristol, I go to the barber on Duke Street just before closing. A shoebox-sized shop with a red-and-white-striped awning, two silver hydraulic chairs, one ceramic basin and a wonky-toothed old-timer.

'Clean it off,' I tell him.

He shrugs, grunts, wipes his hands on his white starched apron and goes to work with scissors and razor. When he's finished, and not before, I look in the mirror. Pods of short curls, neat as if they've just been planted. Sharper features. A stronger mouth.

I go to the Safe House for the last time. Make up a bed on the sofa in the main room. The place is freezing and I'm shivering from adrenaline, fear and cold. The electric bars of the heaters look like twisting, red serpents. The phone rings at seven that evening. The only person who used to call was Charmaine. I'm afraid it might be the Heartist. I don't answer. But when it rings again at eight, I think it could be Irving and that he's ill. I pick up.

'Yamaye?'

I exhale. 'Lego.'

'You alone?' he says.

'What's going on?'

'Voices. My head.'

'Get out of there. Rights On will fight your case.'

'Too late,' he says.

'For what?' I ask.

'He came for me.'

'Who?'

'Crab Man.'

'You let him in?'

'The Crypt is for traitors now. Repurposed.'

'Is he still there? He'll bring the police.'

'Man's not bringing anybody anywhere.'

'Don't believe anything he says.'

He laughs, a strung-out hollow sound. 'Crabs come out at night,' he says. 'Ghost crabs on Atlantic beaches, their eyes standing out of their heads, watching people's business. Waaatching. Waaaiting. Camouflaginggg, burying themselves in sand.'

I try to interrupt, ask questions, but Lego talks over me; man's in a trance.

'Crab Man came,' he says. 'Wanted to catch me so he could get the glory with his police bredrin. I showed him the black sarcophagus, the one with "traitor" written on it. Told him it was empty, waiting for him. Traitorrrr.'

I focus on the vibrations of his voice, afraid of what he's going to say.

'Living with the dead all these years,' he says. 'They made me do it.'

'The voices aren't real. You need a doctor.'

'Babylon doctor kill Black man.'

He tells me there's a sword inside his walking stick. Crab Man rushed him and he pulled out the sword, pushed it into Crab Man's stomach. He says blood came out of his crab eyes and wide mouth.

'I put him where he belongs,' he says. 'Inside the black sarcophagus.'

My hands are shaking. I'm afraid to speak, as if I'd be disturbing a sleepwalker, jolting them into a reality that could kill them.

'I've confessed to you,' he says. 'I'm free.'

'Lego, is this real? Are the voices speaking now? Get Father Mullaney.'

'Walk good, Yamaye,' he says.

The line goes dead. The air hums and whirrs with everything he's said. And I know that no amount of firing imaginary spears at Babylon will free Lego even if he has killed Crab Man. He's as imprisoned as Asase.

Vibrations from his voice hang in the air, vapour compressing, decomposing, turning into fossils of sound. I'm entombed, like Lego. Locked up just like Asase. Have to make moves outta this place.

I go to the table. A pile of money near Monassa's chair; another near mine. I sit in Monassa's chair and pick up a handful of green fifty-pound notes. Spread them like cards, Queen side up.

I know Monassa's skanks. His nervous system scanning the night, finding ways to flex in and out. Haven't I watched him make the ghostly leap into grave-dust darkness and return again and again.

He's warned me that I can never leave. To him it's betrayal. Like an obeah man, he's got the power to do good or evil. His spirit is out there, in the outtasphere. Watching. Breathing slow, barely there, biding his time.

He knew just how far to go inna my head. Technological manipulation, spawning dread. How far should I go? Sixty-five thousand is nuth'n but loose change for him. Plenty more in his offshore accounts.

I pull the two piles of money into the centre of the table. Think of all the times I've played the wrong card. Shut my mouth. Played dead.

The squeal of tape reel in my gut. My patois voice rising up.

Bust a note that ain't smooth, gyal. Fractured sounds make the best healing.

I tell myself how far to go.

Tell myself to go further.

I push all the money towards my chair.

Yeah, they'll come. The Heartist. Monassa. Not straight away, but they'll come. They'll scan cities and towns. True seh, now I know how to play their game. I'll hide in the bandstand until my flight tomorrow. They'll search Shackles Shebeen, Mr Chen's house, the church built into the city walls that has been a sanctuary. Tombstone Estate.

The bandstand is the one place they won't look.

I'll bury myself with the homeless, cold stone bodies, saints with sepulchre eyes that see nothing but ghosts.

I pack a khaki bag, take a Walkman, torch, blanket, meat patties and rum, a small carry case of records, Moose's cassettes. Put some of the money inside the vinyl sleeves. I make slits inside the hood and sides of Dungle's duffel coat, feed the rest of the notes through before sewing them up. I put the coat on. A last look at everything, the table where the men played dominoes, the music deck where I busted tunes.

I leave the Safe House around eleven that night. The air is damp and cold. I walk through the barren landscape of industrial estates and fields. Coming into the centre, past the roundabout, the burial ground and caves. Then, crossing the Floating Harbour, with the church spire in the distance, I walk to the bandstand as it starts to rain. The transparent sheeting has come away from the railing in parts and it's flapping like a giant jellyfish. I hang cardboard from the railing down to the floor and secure it with my bags, making a small roof. I spread some of the plastic on the floor, switch the torch on, and put it on top of the record case. I keep the duffel coat on and cover myself with the blanket. Look around me at the other shelters. Some people are in sleeping bags. Others wrapped in white cotton quilts. Ghost orchids in black-sediment darkness.

Moose had been working towards a better life and here I am with the dispossessed.

'Stay with me and I promise I'll start again,' I whisper.

I switch on the Walkman, put in one of Moose's mixtapes, my favourite: *No Rhyme, No Reason*. The last song plays. Then . . . Moose's recorded voice:

'*Yamaye, it's me at the control tower, selecting tunes just for you. Ain't no rhyme or reason why I love you. I just do. Your voice, your quiet fire. There's no life without music, no life without you in it. Think about moving back to Jamaica with me. Country living. Enjoy the mix. I hear you in every song. Hope you're tuning inna me too.*'

I've listened to it so many times, but his voice sounds different every time.

Tears stick in my throat. I pummel my chest, trying to dislodge them. Nothing moves. I can't breathe. Unfeeling is the heaviest burden in the world.

I switch the Walkman off.

The dark is rising all around me. I'm drifting, trying to hold on to an image of a home far away. I think of a time with Moose. As if I can think him into vibration, into being. A triangulation of sound, desire and feeling.

Six on a cold February morning. Me and Moose naked in bed with a tray of bullah cake, mugs of cocoa tea mixed with brandy. We'd been to a ram-out rare-groove party with Asase and Rumer and, as usual, he'd dropped us off at Asase's block. It was getting harder and harder to keep our relationship secret. I walked with Rumer to her block, waited outside for Moose to spin back and pick me up.

We drive to his place. He puts snacks on a tray. Puts a tape in the stereo. We sit up in bed, the tray on his lap, my head on his shoulder.

'Tell me another story,' I say. 'I'm hyped, my ears are ringing with bass.'

'Yeah? Stories cost, I'll be taxing you for some TLC.'

'If the story's right, I'll pay.'

'Don't nyam all the bullah cake while I'm talking. I know what you're like.'

I take a thick slice of the rich brown bun and bite into it, laughing.

The music plays.

He clamps his thighs around my legs and strokes my hair as he begins.

'Granny took me walking in Cockpit Country every week or so. Said it was important to know our land. One day it was raining – it rained a lot in the bush – and true seh I didn't wanna go. Bwoy, did she shame me. She grabbed me up. I was about eight or ten, and we headed out. We walked along an old hunters' track; she'd never taken me there before. I could barely see the trail it was so faint. But Granny she said it was bright as stars. She knew where the sinkholes were, even though most of them were hidden by scratchbush. If we'd stepped inna one, that would have been it – a fall so deep our voices would have echoed for days and years afterwards, like the ancestors she said she could hear. Africans, Tainos, people who'd been seeking refuge and freedom. I asked her how she knew where to go and she said, she just kept in her mind that old-time saying: "Walk good."

'We were walking for a long time and the rain was coming down hard. It was cold, but Granny kept on going, her face set hard. I was vex at first, and then I got inna it. Thinking "Walk good, walk good" until I was in a trance and my blood was warm. Rivers rushing underground. Granny stopped near some rough limestone rocks.

'"Look ya, son. Ghost orchid."

'There were lots of them – light green flowers with creamy lips, no leaves, growing on the rock. I asked her if they were really ghosts.

'"This yah place full-up with spirits. Old-time runaways."

'I got scared then. Bawled like a baby, begged to go back to our yard. Granny just dragged me up by my arm and pulled me on. Everywhere I looked, I imagined duppies, slaves, Spanish pirates, Arawaks. I'll never forget that day. Walk good, that's my motto for life. Made me a man.'

'You believe in duppies?'

'Granny was telling me she believed. I trust her.'

His voice fades.

'I trust you, Moose,' I whisper into the dark.

The temperature drops in the night. Impossible to keep warm. It's not safe to sleep, I tell myself over and over.

An unearthly howl wakes me, like someone's pain being torn from their body and tossed, like meat, into darkness.

'You cunt. I'll cut you up. I'll . . .'

Two men fighting. Grunting. Rolling. Tearing each other into pieces in a drunken rage. Someone staggers to my shelter.

Don't move.

I see dirty white plimsolls, too-short trousers, bare skin, braided purple veins at the ankles. The stench of shit and vomit and sweat.

'A fucking light. Somebody gimme a fucking light.'

I pick up my bottle of rum, ready to slice veins if the feet come any closer.

Another voice call outs and the feet move away.

I look at the bottle in my shaking hand. I'm capable of drawing blood, same as Asase. But I won't have to, not tonight.

Next day I'm on the early-evening flight. The plane takes off and a roaring sound sucks us into cavernous ranges of magic, red fire unravelling behind, Muma's face stained in the haemorrhaging sky. Too much adrenaline in my body for sleep. I look out of the small oval window, stars strung like waterfalls. We cross from darkness into citrine light. Eighteen and a half degrees north of the equator, south of the Cayman Trough. Green jigsaw-piece islands below, the past floating on blue.

The Atlantic

23

Version Excursion: Trailing Infinity

B-SIDE/DUBPLATE, 45 RPM

Spatial Fug

Gyal, you've learned to flex wid fire. Suck ganja smoke between your teeth. Burn the massive night after night with dub dread beat.

You reach! On dis yah beach, on a cay looking across to the main island. Forts and dungeons spread along the headland. Whitewashed castles, their towers rising high in the air. Superstructures of white like the Tombstone Estate.

A ship in the distance, its sails are floating smoke. The ocean rippling around it is black as a crypt.

You're at the control tower, equalising treble and bass. The fractured voices of Monassa and Moose sliding off vinyl with gunshots, sirens and thunder. Mixed together. You don't know who's who.

Ravers from across time beat riddims with bone-tipped sugar-cane spears, their eyes fixed on the ocean.

This a sound-system clash. You, Sonix Dominatrix, versus the wind coming off the ocean with its 200,000-watt bassline.

The movements of the dancers become convulsions. As if they're taking bullets, or truncheons, or whiplashes.

A dancer moves towards the stage, blurred in sunlight.

Wearing an old-time black dress.

Her left eyeball sunken below the rim.

'My heart's flooded,' she says.

She's swaying, unsteady.

'You OK?' You move away from the controls, step off the stage towards her.

She circles her arms, as if she could scoop up the cay and island beyond. 'Our rebels were here hundreds of years ago,' she says.

You tell her your Tombstone Estate revolutionaries spent their nights dancing in crypts, blues dances in tower blocks and dead-water zones.

She goes inna it, telling you how her rebels criss-crossed rainforest rivers, launching guerrilla attacks on soldiers at night.

You tell her you're gonna make explosives on the mixing decks tonight. Launch them inna the air in honour of all the sound rebels.

'Sounds never die,' she says.

She takes a mouth bow, a curved piece of wood with a string made from a vine, places it on her hips, vibrates it.

An upwelling movement of the dancing massive, and she disappears into mixer-fading tension. Lost to the breaks in dub sound.

Gyal, you tell yourself, you well-and-know that ancestors like her have always been inside you, spewing spells, hymn-squalling, connecting you here.

It's midnight. The waves come in bursts.

Riffages and skirls of bassline.

Everyone entombed in the star-speckled darkness of the universe. Shooting stars are tail embers of spliffs burning out into nothingness. Lightning flashes like the on–off lights in the Crypt when the dance was done. And for a few seconds the ravers stop. In limbo. Disconnected.

Dismembered riffs, spooling backwards, strangled.

The dancers chant the name of their dead. Women, men, shot, hanged, choked, chained.

Black clouds float overhead.

A lo-fi howl in response that might be coming from you.

A tall, thin man on the beach is playing a trumpet, circled by dancers. He pushes them out of the way and stands in front of the decks. He's got the same downward-slanting eyes as you. Puts the trumpet to his lips. Each blowing breath sanctifying you with life force.

He reaches for you before disappearing into spectral resonance.

The ship crawls further away from the headland. The wind carries the voices of women on the boat, their songs mussing the sea, turning it red.

One of the ravers on your cay is singing, her voice floating above your dub riddims.

Red cables on your mixing deck connect to a mic that she's holding, pumping ancestral bass into your bloodstream. She has freckles; her thick-as-rope hair is hanging over her shoulder, loose and wild.

'Hey you,' she says. She's as familiar-strange as this place. Her face is watery reflection, a reverb bouncing back from another time. Like looking at yourself: the same heart-shaped brown face, square-cut cheekbones, inlaid brown eyes.

She puts the mic to her lips. Sings in falsetto, a microtonal song, like drops of water.

The last drops in an apocalyptic world.

If there are words to her song, you can't make them out; if there are other worlds, looks like she's just stepped outta one.

Her salt-glazed eyes widen as she lets out a star-bound note. You wait for it to fall and light the next revolution.

You turn down your 45. She comes closer to you. She's about twenty-seven, the same age Muma was when she disappeared. But that was ten, thirty, a hundred years ago.

She says she was a rebel and that rebels aren't born like everybody else. They explode into life. Hair, back, legs, voice, alight, eyes spinning wheels of flames.

'We should sing together,' you say.

'We always have,' she says. She fades into the elastic reverb of waves.

You turn up the volume. The ship is closer now. Light from the deck colouring the sea gold.

You're dreaming Moose. Remembering that he said Cockpit Country mist was part echo, its caverns filled with sound. But he's B-side voiceless. You clasp his waist as you drop through worlds luminant with ganja smoke. Landing hard on limestone rocks. The lights go outta his eyes; black notes crawl from his still nostrils.

The ship stops on the borderline of dark sea and aquamarine, its white sails flapping like wings.

BOOK THREE

Outtasphere: Cockpit Country November 1981–January 1982

Dub is the ghost in the machine, a voice coming through the Gates of Horn and Ivory.

Richard Skinner, *Dub: Red Hot vs Ice Cold*

24

Floating Points

I go down the stairs of the aeroplane into mango-scented morning heat, half-conscious from going so long without sleep. Tread on to the melting black tarmac with the other sluggish passengers. Montego Bay. Gold waves hanging in the air are music staves. I walk through the vibrations, stepping to the island's beat. Shade my eyes and look at green, triangular mountains in the distance lined up like gods. Red, coral and violet flowers strung across the landscape. I'm drifting into another time.

Inside the airport, the crowds are nomads, laden with crates, barrels and wicker bags. It takes two hours to get through customs.

Music everywhere, in the glass-lit souvenir shops and restaurants. People sing as they walk, musical testimonies to their past.

I go to the toilets and wash my face.

I stare at my reflection. Bare head, eyes narrowed and dark at the corners, Muma's full lips, their thick vermilion borders.

I lock myself into a cubicle, slit and rip the lining of the coat with a nail file and take the money out. I leave the notes in the record sleeves. I change the money at a foreign currency desk and wire ten thousand to Charmaine's account, hoping she's made it to her destination.

I go into one of the airport shops. Rocksteady music, slowed down, easy-living vibe, is playing. The cashier is talking and laughing with a tourist. I buy a tie-dye beach dress with a braided white rope threaded through the chest panel and neck, bikinis, sandals and shades – a map.

It's two in the afternoon when I step out of the air-conditioned building into a wall of heat and scents of cinnamon, cloves and cocoa crushed into glassy sunshine. Porters in red caps and brown shirts and trousers hustling tourists. My legs are shaking.

'Aie, missus, look yah, yuh want a taxi?' A short, puffed-up man in Cuban-heeled shoes is standing by the passenger door of a black-and-yellow taxi. He sing-talks: 'Come ya, missus! Come steppa with me! Me likkle taxi is well irie.'

He takes hold of my bags.

'Where yuh going, missus?'

'Maggotty.'

'Need a place? Me know a good lodging house. Come, missus.'

I get into the back of the car, too tired to think. My body smells bad. I'm leaking weariness. No sleep that night at the bandstand or on the plane. My head's thumping from tiredness and the heat.

The driver turns on the engine, wipes his brow with a white kerchief. 'Me name Carlton, missus.' He speaks in the lilting intonations of a preacher. Dark brown face with glints of blue, puffy as a cushion with a button nose and mouth. The polished, maroon leather interior of the car is the same colour and sheen as the Bible that Irving keeps by his bedside. He's never returned to Jamaica. He has an older brother, different mothers. They didn't grow up in the same household, but met at family gatherings. The brother moved to America many years before Irving left for London and they lost touch. He's never seemed bothered by it. All he says is, *Every man must make his own way in life*. I wonder whether he expresses himself in a different way from everybody else through those old cars that he welds into shape, alone in his garage with the build-up of heavy gases. Stray currents. Burning dust.

We're heading away from the coast into the country, an area of the Windward Maroons. Muma was born in Portland on the north-east side of the island, near the Blue Mountains, where Queen Nanny's Moore Town Maroons held strategic positions over Stony River via a 900-foot ridge.

Muma must have been acting strategically when she left for Guyana, knowing that Irving couldn't follow her into a remote village. Now I'm doing the same, putting an ocean between me and Monassa. Hoping that whatever went wrong with Muma's plans doesn't happen to me.

'Me grand-cousin has a likkle place in Balaclava, not far from Maggotty,' Carlton says. 'Me will tek you there. What you have, Missus Foreign, dollars or pounds?'

'Pounds.'

'Aie, aie, the pound stronger than the dollar. You in fe a good-good time on the island, missus.'

I feel air coming from the ground and I look down and see the road through rust patches in the floor of the car.

'We gonna make it?' I ask.

'Don't fret yuhself, Missus Foreign. We gonna have a nice run through some pretty-pretty place. Balaclava is a backwater village in Cockpit Country. You know 'bout that area? Caves, underground rivers. Beautiful – but dangerous.'

'I know about danger,' I say.

Rocksteady on the potholed hairpin roads, Carlton is a hill-and-gully driver, like Racer. One arm on the steering wheel, chatting, checking out the scene left-to-right-to-road. We drive along the coast, past mountains of inky whorls, harbours with white boats rocking on a silver-sheen sea. The medicinal smell of green vegetation. Ganja waiting to be lit. The motion of the car lulls me to sleep.

*

I wake when Carlton pulls up at a roadside shack. Tourists are sitting at tables made of electric cable spools. Two tall, slim women cooking chicken in upturned oil drums. A man roasting a pig on pimento wood, essential oils from the wood smoking the air like incense.

'Drink something, missus. If you dry out in this yah heat, you will drop.'

We sit at a spool and a man strikes the head of two coconuts with a machete and gives us the shells of sweet coconut water. I realise how hungry I am. The last thing I ate was some sandwiches ten hours ago. I order jerk chicken for me and Carlton and we eat with our hands, tearing off burnt skin, chewing the flesh, sucking the bones.

'This is rebel food,' he says. 'The runaways cooked hogs underground, no smoke. The Redcoats – British – couldn't find dem.'

I tell him about Muma and ask if he knows Homes of Hope. He says it's just outside Kingston, run by a French priest with nuns from Africa. Everyone knows it. He offers to take me there.

He talks about slave uprisings and settlements of Maroons – Africans and Tainos – who set up territories in Cockpit Country and other parts of the island.

'Dem mek up fires inna the wetlands, used vines of cacoon plants to camouflage themselves, walked backwards, setting false footprints to sinkholes. The British and Spanish must have thought they were fighting ghosts.'

'I know how that feels.'

'Ah, Missus Foreign, you coming from concrete jungle. That full of duppy. You home now. Mek the island clean you out.'

We set off again, driving inland. Carlton points to citrus groves and dairy pastures. He calls out, 'Look down, missus!' In the valley below is a red mud lake shaped like a snake.

In the warm dusk we drive up an avenue of motionless trees that

Carlton says are agaves and Spanish needle. He says we're in Maroon territory. People here are free.

'The British only knew 'bout face-to-face fighting in open spaces,' he says. 'When your enemy bigger than you, you must ambush, tek dem enemy by surprise. This is ambush territory.'

'Noted,' I say.

We pull up to a wide, two-storey colonial-style house painted white with a pale green roof, yellow shutters and a wrap-around veranda that's set back from the narrow country road.

'Aye, aye, Miss Ermeldine,' Carlton shouts from the car window before getting out.

I stand in the yard as Carlton gets my bags. There are trees and a flower garden filled with the smells of over-ripe fruit and dewy petals. Three smaller houses to the far side of the main building. The sound of clashing pots and pans and a voice calling out in response. A lantern with a bright light hangs above the outer door on the veranda. A brown-skinned woman wearing a white turban, black horn-rimmed glasses and a yellow housecoat comes out onto the porch. She tiptoes down the steps, all bosomy shape – hard to tell where bosom ends and waist, hips and thighs begin. She gives me her hand.

'Miss Ermeldine,' she says in a stoosh accent.

'I bring a little business for you,' Carlton says. 'A daughter returns. She tired o' them foreign places.'

'Welcome. First time on the island?'

'My father's from Trelawny, my mother's from Portland.'

'You are one of us. My lodging house is clean and quiet,' she says. 'No guests right now. It's low season.' She shifts her turban and sucks in her breath. 'Some people from Belize will be here in a few weeks.'

'Great,' is all I can say.

'Eight dollars a night.'

I'm beyond tired. She could be offering me a cave for all I care.

'How long will you be staying?'

'A few weeks, maybe more.'

'Business or holiday?'

'Looking for family.'

'Everyone on the island connected one way or another,' she says. 'But this island, this piece of rock, is bigger than it looks. Carlton will help you get around.'

Carlton says all I have to do is call, he lives in Mandeville, not too far away. He says he's going back to the airport for more tourists, gets in his car, toots his horn several times and drives away.

Miss Ermeldine calls out to someone in the house. 'Fern makes the meals. She has a good hand. Two dollars a day. If you don't want to spend off your money, you might as well eat here. I wouldn't bother with that little store up the road. Only healing oil and water crackers in that dried-out shack.' She calls out, 'Fern!'

Fern, bauxite-brown skin, tamarind eyes, moving like she's tuned into rare groove, glides out of the house. Miss Ermeldine introduces us. Fern squints at me, smiles, takes my bags and leads me into the house. We walk up the wooden stairway. Everywhere smells like Oraca's kitchen, the same potent scents of herbs and spices.

The yellow shutters in the room are closed.

'Miss Ermeldine likes it dark for coolness sake,' Fern says.

Slate-tiled floors, a mahogany dresser, wicker chairs and a table with guidebooks. A double bed covered in a gold crocheted spread. Fern switches on the ceiling fanlight in the centre of the room and it whirs and hums.

There's a vase of pink flowers on the bedside table.

'Oleanders,' Fern says. 'Miss Ermeldine wants them in every room, even if them empty.' She squints her green eyes at me like a cat that can sense oncoming spirits. She's wearing a simple cotton dress printed with red peacock flowers, blue plastic flip-flops, a maroon headscarf tied round her hair. She leaves me to unpack and comes back an hour later with a tray of limeade, sugar-cane pieces and gingery coconut drops.

'Only pickney and old-time people here,' she says.

'From where I'm coming, this is paradise. Believe!' I say.

'Tell me 'bout the parties in England. How the man dem stay?'

'Crypts, tombstone estates, cages. Underground darkness.'

She sits on the bed and watches me as I put my clothes in the dresser. 'I'll be here for a while,' I say. 'You can show me around.'

'You should stay a long time,' she says.

A bright yellow butterfly floats into the room and settles on the flowers.

'Been travelling . . . running, since . . . since, I don't know when.'

'Then is time for you to catch Doctor Breeze and sleep,' she says.

I sense the tranquillity of her spirit in the gauzy, beatless quality of her voice. Before she leaves she tells me her bedroom is downstairs at the back of the kitchen. If I need anything, I must call on her, day or night.

I drink the limeade and shower in a small bathroom on the landing, scrub myself with mimosa soap.

The bed is comfortable, the sheets smell of flowers. I leave the shutters open and watch the sky darken.

I exhale and let the bed take the weight of my clenched muscles. I know my body has made it outta the Safe House, but my senses are still catching up.

The sound of Nyabinghi drumming in the mountains and crackling cicadas. I call to Muma and feel her in the thick, warm air. A pressure pushing against my chest. I'm closer to her here on this island. Closer than I've ever been. Even if I never find her, there'll be something of her here.

I sleep in snatches, waking sweat-drenched, not knowing where I am. My body is in the bed, but my spirit is still somewhere in the red, burning sky.

I'm out of it for two days, dreaming that Monassa is in the room, a body of coiled smoke.

'You won't find me here,' I whimper. I dream of tempered-steel-vine trailing rainforests of concrete trees, birds squawking in metal cages with bleeding throats.

Fern brings jugs of coconut water, glass dishes of starchy yam and dasheen in pools of stewed meat. Labourers' food, even though I barely lift my head off the pillow from one day to the next.

On the third morning, Fern fills the vase with newly cut orchids and opens the shutters.

'You will rot if you don't get up,' she says.

I ask her to bring white rum and she comes back with a small tray, a bottle and glass.

I get out of bed, pour the rum in my hand, splash it in the corners of the room.

'Spirits chasing you,' she says.

'A shadow man,' I say.

'Ah so? Him on the island?'

'In England.'

'Husband?'

'No name for what I was to him and me to him.'

'Him nyaam you out.'

'Yeah, he took something of me. I took a little something back.'

'Tek time,' she says. 'Me will care for you.'

Her kindness chokes me up, but I don't know how to cry any more. I go to the window, my back to her, and say, 'Respect.'

Fern takes me for a walk in the afternoon after her chores. She puts her arm through mine, pulls me close, and we step down the yard on to the country road towards nearby Marlborough Hill. She points out the pitchy-patchy, whitewashed houses dotted in the mountains, tells me about the people who live in them. Villagers are washing cattle at roadside taps; mountain men and women in vests and cotton trousers sit on rocks, still, their eyes full of sympathy for the moving world.

'Easy, nuh,' says Fern. 'You foreigners step too quick. Nobody chasing you here.' She pulls me to a slow pace. 'Well all right!'

'Been going fast for a while,' I say, thinking to myself I've gone deep inna grief and fear and darkness, never knowing if I'd make it into the light again.

We walk past the abandoned railway station, a two-storey, wooden building with fishtail fretwork. It's padlocked and chained and reminds me of the Safe House and the underground tunnels.

The village is made up of veranda'd houses, some mounted on pillars, some built with limewashed wattle and daub. Fiery, red bougainvillea splashed against the walls. Calypso playing on a radio somewhere. People calling out to each other across yards and plots of land. Everything and nothing going on.

We sit outside on the steps of the village post office drinking purple iced syrup that darkens our lips. A woman humming a hymn waves to us as she walks by. I think of Muma and her life in the orphanage. There's no way of knowing whether she stayed in Guyana, or returned to London, or Jamaica. But there must be a reason she didn't return for me. And here, where the orphanage is, seems like the best place to start.

Low-lying clouds swell and Doctor Breeze blows. Leaves big as lanterns swing in and out the green light of trees. A lizard climbs off a cottonwood tree on to the ground.

'Anole lizard,' Fern says.

I watch as it changes from brown to the bright green colour of pimento grass as it slips into the bush.

Camouflaged. Like me.

Carlton collects me early the next morning to take me to Moose's grandma's place. Need to pay my respects to her before I do anything else. We drive past seventeenth-century ruins and abandoned sugar plantations. The Black River, with its dark layers of rotting sludge, runs alongside the road.

We arrive in Maggotty and Carlton asks a man walking by the road for directions to Granny Itiba's house. He points behind us to a narrow path hemmed in by bushes and Carlton turns the car around.

I see a house in the distance, isolated in a mangrove of hog-plum trees.

I'm worried that my arrival will be an aftershock for her. And I'm afraid of seeing Moose in her face. Afraid of not seeing him there. Carlton drives up the mule track and stops outside a small house of red clay and stones.

'Nobody living here,' he says. 'Not. A. Living. Soul.' He sniffs the air. 'Mebbe she passed away.'

Human dust and shadow float in the late-afternoon light. Copper-coloured crops shimmering.

'Ms Itiba?' I shout.

A bird cries out from a tree where over-ripe mangoes and coolie plums droop from hooked spines. Carlton stands by the open car door, his nostrils flaring.

'I smell something bad,' he says.

'I'm gonna check inside,' I say.

'Look yah, Missus Foreign, we can go back to the main road, check out the centre, ask about.'

'I'm going in.'

He shakes his head and mutters words that sound like 'Hard ears'.

I take off my shades and look at the house. Two wooden shutters at the front are open. I walk past a rotten tree-stump crawling with red ants on my way up the overgrown path. I push the rickety door. It moans and opens into a room with a waxed floor and Indian matting. It smells of oranges and thyme. Three cashew-nut dolls on a shelf on the wall, dressed in reed-grass dresses, mahogany-coloured faces with black seed eyes. Wooden beads and palmetto fans hang by a large window at the back.

Granny Itiba is slumped in a wicker chair by a table. Islands of white froth hair on her skull, eyeballs bobbing on watery eye rims. Nutmeg head toppled to one side. Her eyes float to the centre and she looks at me, then drifts off as if she thinks I'm a dream.

'Ms Itiba?'

She opens her eyes again. 'Thought you was a duppy,' she says.

'I'm Yamaye, Moose's—'

'Me bwoy, me beautiful bwoy.'

I crouch down and hold her hand.

'It woulda nevah cum to this if him did stay with me.'

'Let me help you.'

'Bring me little sugar water please, madam.'

I go to the kitchen at the back of the house. Through a window I see a stream threading between cocoa trees. I scoop two teaspoons of molasses sugar from a stone jar into a mug and pour water from a plastic jug.

I give her the drink and she takes some powder from one of three bowls on the table and sprinkles it in the water and drinks it.

‘The pain burns me,’ she says. Her voice is high, her eyes rolling. Her yellow, claw-like nails clutch her starched green dress.

‘Why did he want to go to England? What for? I nevah wanted nuth’n more than to be the country gyal that I was. Pounding gully roots.’ She pulls my head towards her chest. ‘Listen?’ she commands.

I hear a slow drum.

Drum.

Drum.

Her heart’s playing on the off-beat.

I tell her about the campaign, the silent marches. She says, ‘Cho! No rebellion without magic. Invisible smoke, false footprints. These.’ She points to small bottles on the shelf. I remember Moose saying that she was a magician. Now I think I know what he was trying to tell me.

I go outside and follow the tyre tracks to a spot under a tree where Carlton is waiting by his car.

‘I’ve upset her. It was a shock me turning up.’

‘These country people are hard, no worry yuhself.’

‘Can you buy some provisions for her? Meat, rice, butter, bread.’ I give him some money.

‘Look, Missus Foreign, we catch her at the wrong time, that’s all. She tired. Look yah, she have mango and yam in her kitchen. I tell you, that woman was up this yah morning digging up her food. Country woman dem strong.’

He sets off for the village and I go back to the house. Granny Itiba is in the doorway, patting her face with a white cloth.

‘That was not a proper welcome,’ she says.

‘I should have sent word,’ I say.

We sit at a wooden table inside, out of the sun.

‘My bwoy said you were his woman,’ she says. ‘He wrote every month, telling me everything, always sending likkle money. He is back where he belongs. On our land.'

She asks me to walk with her on the old paths. Moose will be with us. I ask her if she's strong enough and she puts her hand on her heart, laughs and says, 'Sounds like I am.'

'Can I see Moose's grave?'

She whimpers a little, and I put my arm around her shoulder.

'His muma and poopa there too. Fever tek them. Scarlet fever. His poopa used to mek his own whitewash, dig out white limestone from likkle outcrops, where it bruck the surface.' She holds up her yellow claws. 'I put me bwoy in the heart of the banana bush,' she says and she starts to bawl.

I follow her outside to the back of the house. She's as thin and papery as mango leaves, but she's still talawah – strong – walking with firm steps, her body steady and upright. The banana bush is close to the stream. I wade into it, pushing through dead leaves and red flowers and buds with new life bursting out. Six obsidian-black gravestones laying side by side. Moose's gravestone is at the end.

MOOSE MARLON BOHITI
THERE IS A GREEN HILL FAR AWAY.

The clicking and humming of tree frogs and cicadas skim the silence. It feels like the night I first danced with Moose, when I laid my head on his chest. Bitter-sweet pain that at the time felt like a homecoming that was too late.

Carlton returns with the provisions. I stew goat meat and boil green bananas for lunch and we all sit on rusting iron chairs on the tiny veranda, trays of food on our laps.

The air becomes saturated with the buzzing of grasshoppers, high ultrasonic. Purple orchid bees and green butterflies float in indigo.

We sit and talk about Moose. Later, we watch the stars come out. Perforations in the violet sky, draining light away.

Carlton says it's getting dark and we best leave. I clear the table and wash the plates and pots.

At the doorway she calls out to me, 'Daughter, me spirit tek to you. Come, kiss me on me jawbone.'

I go back and kiss her. She takes my face in her hands and looks into my eyes and says, 'I know why you come.'

When we drive away from the small house set back in time, I feel the acidic burn of grief in my gut and heart and throat. Wish I could stay longer on Granny Itiba's wild, overgrown land, tending Moose's grave, plucking mangoes from trees, digging yam from the earth. I want to walk the rebel paths that she walked with Moose and find my own freedom. Sit at her feet in the evenings, listening to stories of her and Moose in their Cockpit Country dreams. Her irregular heartbeat pounding like steady footsteps searching in the dark.

Carlton drops me at Miss Ermeldine's lodging house. I pay him and he tells me that this is how the old live out their days in the bush.

Fern has left a tray with fresh limeade and roasted cashew nuts in my room. There are moths clinging to the light. The sound of drumming in the mountains. I wonder how Irving will see out his days.

Oraca said our house was the centre of attention in the first year on the Tombstone Estate, filled with migrants from the Caribbean. Most Saturday nights Muma cooked food, Irving played records, organised card games. Muma set the scene, but she was an observer, Oraca said. People thought she was an extrovert because she was a singer, organised parties. But she always stood back, on the edge of it, watching, waiting. Oraca thought it was because she grew up in an orphanage. She said Muma found it hard to stay one place, it was hard for her to fit in.

I fall asleep and dream a red, pulsing heart dangling from the ceiling by a long nerve. Monassa's voice coming from the heart:

Me face in the shadow of the moon
Me footsteps close behind yuh.
Don't mek me come for you.

The heart turns black and falls from the ceiling, flying around the room, flying around my face. I scream, wake up. Something dark flapping near the window. I scream again. Miss Ermeldine's outside my door shouting, 'What happen?'

I get out of bed and open the door. Miss Ermeldine stands in a turquoise nightgown and turban. Her face crumpled on the right side, her right eye barely open.

'Something's in my room – a bat!'

'You city people!'

She rattles the jalousies, but whatever it was has flown away. Miss Ermeldine sucks her teeth and closes the shutters. 'You're in country now. Rats, bats, snakes, spiders. We're living side by side. They won't trouble you.'

I go back to bed. The drums are beating louder, chanting, a male-toned drum, carrying a low note that travels far into the night.

25

Acoustemology

Early on Sunday morning at the end of that week, Carlton drives me and Granny Itiba the six miles or so to Accompong, the Maroon village. She wants us to walk the routes she used to explore with Moose so we can feel close to him, sense his spirit. We drive along the Black River with the sound of singing and tambourines coming from small churches. She speaks of the people who believe that the river is not dark from dead vegetation, but death. She sings:

'What nega fe to do?
Tek force by force
Tek force by force.'

She tells me that this was sung by ten men from the area in 1816, just before they were executed for plotting a rebellion. 'Black River falls in the dry season,' she says.

At Accompong, Carlton drops us at the main road that runs up a hill surrounded by other hills. He says Accompong is Ashanti for the lone one, the warrior. He toots his horn three times and drives off, leaving a cloud of dust.

Granny Itiba is wearing a long, brown bandana skirt, a man's navy plaid shirt and scuffed leather boots. A small rucksack on her back. Skinny plaits like branches all around her head. She takes a flask and scatters white rum on the ground for the ancestors. We move into the star-shaped valleys of dub sirens, bleeps and space-echoes. One hundred per cent humidity, our bodies raining. We walk single file on the overgrown path, thick bush patterned with peepholes, red lizard eyes watching. At first, I think I hear her whispering to me or herself not to rush. Then I realise she is saying: *fire rush*.

'Me bwoy is tethered to me, always,' she says of Moose.

I feel him in the leeward curve of the bush, his limbs camouflaged with black genip, his shadow dissolving into flat-bottomed basins of sound.

'I'll fight for our dreams for a new life, country living,' I whisper to Moose, as if he can hear me.

'Step!' Granny Itiba shouts.

She's in front, swinging her sharpened machete right to left, conducting the rainforest orchestra: vibrato of Jamaican blackbirds; rhythm-section crickets and grasshoppers clapping their bodies like castanets; 20,000-watt underground bassline. She stops here and there, singing and shouting to the spirits to let us pass. She sings in a high pitch, her voice trembling and cracking. It's the rainy season, and the thundery sky is dub echo delay.

'Come, me bwoy,' she says.

I tell her about the other men who've died in prison cells.

'Mountains will always trap rain clouds,' she says. I think of Muma and wonder if she is trapped in the rainforest in Guyana somewhere.

Granny Itiba tells me that there are no police here in this region; their ancestors fought for that. She says Moose was free here. She points out Moco John, broadleaf, beefwood and bloodwood. I think of all the blood that's been spilt and wish that Moose had stayed on this land. That we'd met here in another lifetime.

She rests at the bottom of a hill, and I climb to the top with fire in my lungs. I see nothing but the tips of green mountains, pools of water that look like turquoise rocks. I can only imagine the karst, the sea of bones, where the Maroons are buried.

The air smells of old gunshot.

I call out to Muma and Moose, and their names bounce back and drop into caverns.

I feel alive, in my body, as if for the first time.

I climb down and we walk further into the thick bush until we're enclosed under a forty foot high canopy.

'Our foremothers used the rainforest in their fight, herbs and spirit,' Granny Itiba says. 'Not pen and paper and marching up and down.'

She tells me that women gathered peacock flowers so the seeds of their bodies, their babies, wouldn't be born to be thrown across the Black Atlantic to go down in history as slaves. Women with black-rice teeth singing in the rainforests, their voices travelling backwards in their throats so no one would understand their words, boiling the magic seeds of the peacock flower, drinking it as they pressed down on their bellies, pulling out the fruits from their wombs.

I wonder how Muma felt when I was in her belly. Maybe she thought about drinking herbs to flush me out into another world, like the women in my visions who jump off slave ships into the sea.

We stop again, at a litter of stillborn rocks that Granny Itiba says are five million years old. We drink soursop juice and eat cashew nuts wrapped in lace-bark cloth.

'Our women were focused on their mission, concentrated as three-pointed gods,' she says. 'They set fire to the Black Atlantic with seeds and song. That was their rebellion. Better to sing ourselves burning into the understorey of the rainforest than go across that black sea.'

She looks into my face as if she can see everything. 'Set your ghosts free if you want liberty,' she tells me.

She follows the vibrations of trees and underground water, taking us into cloudforest, the star-shaped valleys of runaways. Deep in the bush, alternating light and darkness, same as the lights in the Crypt. Mist floating around large, human-like cacti. The sound of thunder in the hidden sky. Red-earth streams running down from the mountains, percolating downwards, into the networks of caves and rivers beneath. Liquid-filled leaves dripping time. Mosquitoes sucking blood outta my body. Panting and sweating, swigging water.

Am I fooling myself? Is that Moose's voice rising from the fractured white karst calling, '*Lonely, lonely.*'

Granny Itiba moves further away, into sonic space. My body feels stronger than it ever has. The muscles on my thighs pumped and straining. I step up my pace, jump over a small rock and land in a thick padding of red vine. There's a raw, stinging sensation in my right foot, as if I've stepped into broken glass. I look down and see red ants crawling around my ankles. I brush them off, but my skin is blistering, my ankle swelling. I call out to Granny Itiba.

She hurries to me. 'Sit down. Eh-eh! Fire ants.'

The blisters spread up my leg and my ankle puffs out like an inflated bullfrog.

'I can't breathe.'

'Tek it easy. Slow de breath.'

'I'm gonna pass out.'

She gives me the small bottle of rum and I take a sip. My heart drops inna my stomach and I vomit.

'Stay here, child. Leaves and bark are inlaid with secrets.'

'Don't leave me—' But she slips off the narrow path and disappears.

A crack of thunder far away. I hope the rains come. I'm so hot. I hear the women rebels singing, or is it the acoustics of the rainforest, underground streams, the caves pushing upwards?

I imagine all the things that could go wrong: Granny Itiba's heart gives out and I can't find my way outta here alone; my foot turns black and has to be amputated; a wild animal attacks me; I fall into a bottomless sinkhole.

My leg is burning, and my whole body is hot. I take off my T-shirt, leaving on my bikini top, and roll my yellow jogging bottoms up above my knees. I step off the path in the direction that Granny Itiba went. It's shaded by a large cluster of tall mahogany trees. I sit under one, leaning against its trunk, and it takes the weight of my feet, the weight off my grief.

I smell Moose in the moss and roots and bark of the trees, see traces of him in the wood ants, the land crabs, the snails, the beetles – the small things that move along the earth, tracing pathways, round and round into vanishing points.

The rainforest closes in and I'm floating above warped shore-lines, hearing the boom-back voices of the dead, high above the cockpits.

Moose is standing in front of me, a thin membrane of light, his face and body blurred.

Tune in to me, Yamaye.

Every cell in my body buzzes in response. I'm lit up with sound, but no words come out of my open mouth. His voice is as distant as his image is weak. I want to turn up the volume, hear him loud and clear, beg him not to fade away, stay in whatever way he can.

He's just outta reach, his voice charging me with something like electricity.

'Moose? Don't leave.' Echoplexed sounds radiate across collapsed caves, disappear mid-bar.

I cry like I haven't cried before. A single-note bawl in the lowest of low registers, that feels like it's dragging all the stale, coiling smoke outta my guts.

I call for Granny Itiba and yellow birds fly out of the trees. She comes running, her arms full of bark and thick branches with leaves.

'I'm seeing . . . things,' I say.

'Everybody step foot yah is a ghost,' she says. 'Me feel me bwoy. Him all right.'

She grinds the bark with a stone, mixes it with water, and I drink it. She pounds the leaves and makes a poultice that she smears all over my leg.

'We fe go back,' she says. 'It going dark soon.'

She gives me one of the branches as a walking stick. We turn back on the path. The swelling goes down a little, but my leg is painful and every step is agony. The colour of the day changes from green to stone grey. We're chasing the last of the daylight. A cocoa farmer on the outskirts runs ahead to the nearest house and calls a taxi that takes us to Granny Itiba's place.

She lights candles and puts them in wooden bowls at the bare windows.

'I never sleep more than so,' she says. 'Two hours at the most. Is a vigil.'

She tells me she spends the mornings working on the land, sleeps in the afternoons, and in the evenings she rocks the night away in her chair on the veranda.

So I lie in her bed, watching a large, brown moth flitting around the candlelight. The pain in my ankle keeping me awake. Listening to her rocking chair moving backwards and forwards, creaking like the limestone caves as they push against the earth.

A few days later, I follow the route of the Black River again when, on an edgeless blue day, Carlton takes me to Homes of Hope orphanage. We track the river through to Santa Cruz and into Mandeville, where the air smells of oranges, red dirt and oleanders, slowing in the traffic as we pass a market ringing with the voices of vendors, reggae, revving engines of trucks packed with green bananas, breadfruit, yam. On into Spanish Town, going over Flat Bridge, where the liquid turquoise of the Rio Cobre fuses with the molten bronze sun.

Carlton drives up the steep incline, straight into spears of light coming from the horizon where two bright yellow buildings are set like mirages in the distance. Smaller white blocks are scattered around, in the thick of trees and ferns. Everything surrounded by a sea-blue concrete wall. White winding steps drop from different parts of the houses into the bush below, like piano keys waiting to be played. I imagine Muma singing, making her way down those stairways.

Carlton stops outside a wrought-iron gate with a large cross on top.

'Gwaan, Missus Foreign,' he says. 'Step good. Look hard 'pon the papers.' He switches off the engine, pulls out a newspaper and leans back in his seat.

I get out of the car, press the bell on the wall and the gate opens. I go up zigzag concrete steps to the yard of the biggest yellow house. Children are sitting cross-legged on the third-floor veranda as a teacher reads to them. A boy is watching me, his head poking through the railing. A floating, one-beat semibreve pulsing in the air.

A woman with frizzy blonde hair and sharp green eyes is waiting in the paved yard. The child calls out to her, 'Miss Ayerling, yuh coming back?'

She shields her eyes and waves to the child to return to the others. 'Can I help you?' she asks me. She has an American accent.

'My mother grew up here,' I say. 'I want to see her file.'

'Do you have an appointment?'

'I've come from England.'

'Well—' Her attention shifts between me and the child, who is still watching. She says she's only a volunteer from Chicago, but Sister Joy will know what to do.

I follow her into the cool, paved hallway filled with hazy morning light. Beautifully carved mahogany chairs are lined up outside a door. Silver-framed black-and-white photos of nuns with rows of posing children hang on the walls. We go up a flight of stairs to the first floor.

Miss Ayerling knocks on a black door and we enter a small study that smells of candlewax. Sister Joy, sitting at a desk writing with a fountain pen, is breathing hard, shine pouring out of her blue-toned, dark skin. She looks up, as if she's just risen from an ocean and is seeing the world again after a long time. She motions me to sit and Miss Ayerling steps back.

I tell Sister Joy about Muma.

'Our records go back a century—'

'Anything will do.'

'But we only hold them for five years. They're shipped to America, our main convent.'

'How about Sister Abike?' Miss Ayerling says. 'She's a walking archive.'

'Can I speak to her? I've come a long way,' I say.

Sister Joy lays the fountain pen on the desk. The sound of children's high-pitched, magnetic singing reaches us from somewhere in the building.

'Muma was a singer,' I say.

'She's passed?' asks Sister Joy.

I look down at my hands; they're shaking. I hold on to the children's voices. 'She disappeared when I was young.'

'I'm sorry you didn't grow with her,' Sister Joy says. 'I've only been at the convent for fifteen years, but perhaps Sister Abike will remember something that can bring you comfort.' She writes a note and gives it to Miss Ayerling, asking her to take me to Sister Abike.

I go with Miss Ayerling to a white-painted hall further along the corridor. It smells of furniture polish and the faint citrus scent of oleanders. Rows of swaying children in green checked shirts are singing on a large, semicircular platform at the back of the room, their voices feeding into the spaciousness of the hall. A young woman is directing them. The singing stops and Miss Ayerling introduces me to Sister Abike, who is sitting on a chair at the side of the stage by the window, her hands in her lap. A tiny, still woman; a figurine.

Miss Ayerling gives her the note. Sister Abike reads it and rises. Her dark, glazed skin seems outside of time. She could be fifty or seventy. She steps closer to me, scanning my face.

'Her name?' she says.

'Coral Anderson. Maiden name Thomas. Born June 1931.'

She walks to the wide-open window and beckons me over. A range of green mountains, sunlight illuminating them so they're almost translucent.

She stares at me in the light. 'Just look at you. Same eyes, mouth, everything of her.'

'You knew her? She was here?'

'So long ago, but yes.'

I lean against the window. A body of light holds me up, a fuzzed-out memory of me imagining this moment. 'Anything you can remember. Please.'

'This means a lot to both of us,' she says. She half-closes her eyes, a sliver of watery white between the lids. A memory tape, flickering.

The children file out of the room, talking and laughing, some still singing. Miss Ayerling and the other nun follow them. Me and Sister

Abike alone in the big hall among old resonances. We return to the chairs and sit down. Fierce afternoon light beams at us. Sister Abike closes her eyes, trance-like, as if she's resisting the pull of the sunlight, afraid it might transport her into black holes. Explosions in space, centuries ago.

She opens her eyes. 'I came here in 1945,' she says. 'Nineteen – an empty vessel,' she says. 'Your mother was thirteen or fourteen. She seemed older than me. Little Mother, we called her – always caring for the young ones.'

I'm a child again, holding in the crying. Wanting to be one of *those* children. I feel sparks in my eyes and a scalding wetness as tears stream down.

Sister Abike shifts her chair closer, holds my hands, and makes a soft noise at the back of her throat.

'She was the best singer here. Always saying she would sing her children into being. And here you are.'

'She said that? She wanted children? Me.'

'A husband, children, a home. Her own family. Very much.'

'Did you stay in touch?'

'She wrote often – at first. I knew she was married. That she had a girl – you. She wrote from Guyana once. That was the last—'

'Where in Guyana?'

'Forgive me' – she withdraws her hands and I realise I've been squeezing too hard – 'I should have kept her letters,' she says. 'But—'

'Don't you have any? Maybe they're with her file.'

She shakes her head. 'I seem to remember that wherever she was, the river was the only way in and out of the village. She wanted to see the world, to experience herself outside the orphanage.'

I'd never imagined Muma that way, an adventuress. It's another persona to add to the list of things that Irving and Oraca said Muma was – singer, nurse, party-woman, flirt, outsider, mother – just not much of a mother to me. But was she a mother who abandoned her child, or did we abandon her?

I tell Sister Abike I've been given so many different versions of Muma; if she could only use one word to describe her, what would it be? She thinks about it for a while. Says she can think of two: impulsive and shy. She says Muma bought her ticket for London the day after she heard someone talking about going. She was friends with only two of the other girls in the orphanage. She spent a lot of time by herself. But there was no sign of her shyness when she was on stage. 'She was another person when she was singing,' Sister Abike says.

'I need to track her journeys. Jamaica to London. London to Guyana. Guyana to where?'

Sister Abike looks towards the open window, staring straight at the mountains. The children's playtime voices on the veranda below reach us through the silence. A trace of Muma's child-voice in the outer layers of sound.

'She studied to be a nurse those last three years that she was here,' Sister Abike says. 'Then she went to London. She was training to be a midwife.' She tells me that she was surprised when Muma wrote from Guyana, asking her to look out for a house near the orphanage, big enough for the two of us.

'She was coming for me!' I say. I jump up, my legs shaking. Seconds, hours, millennia pass through the light. Air moving against my face, the feeling that Muma is standing between us.

'Don't cry,' Sister Abike says. 'I wrote to tell her that we found a house for the both of you. But she never replied. I assumed she'd gone back to your father.' She clenches her lips against tiny yellow teeth. 'I wrote many times.'

'What else did she say?' I ask.

She half-turns in the chair, looking away from me. 'Is he still alive?' she asks, her voice a whisper, amplifying the silence.

'My father? Yes.' The hairs on the back of my head are guitar strings, pulled taut. A tingling awareness. 'What is it? I must know everything.'

She's looking down at her lap and I hear what she tells me. That Muma had a relationship with a musician when she was married. I know this must be the trumpeter that Oraca told me about.

She says Muma married Irving because he was older, seemed worldly, although she later found out that he knew no more about the world than she did.

'His name?' I ask.

'I—'

'Maybe she's still with him.' I imagine Muma and the trumpeter on stage. His cheeks as big as globes as he blows comet-tail sounds from his trumpet. And Muma's middle voice emerging from the shadows, riffing just above his notes.

'She never used his name,' Sister Abike says. 'She was ashamed of what she was doing.'

I think of Monassa, the things he did to me, how I wanted to go out into the world like Muma and find myself. But instead, I split off, disintegrated, withdrew. I walk to the window and look down at the children sitting cross-legged on mats on the terracotta veranda.

'Shame can make you disappear,' I say.

Sister Abike joins me at the window. 'We teach the children to have hope for their futures,' she says. 'But if your mother were alive, we – you – would have heard from her before now.'

'I won't believe anything until I have facts. See for myself,' I say.

She says that she can't remember everything that was in the

letters. It was too long ago. And whatever she remembers is likely a mix of what was written and what she read between the lines.

'But she asked you to find a house for us in Jamaica. She must have decided to leave Irving.'

'Nothing was fixed. She must have changed her mind.'

There are three options: Muma was going back to Irving or returning to take me to Jamaica with her. Or going back to her lover. I ask how long Muma and the musician were together.

Now Sister Abike is fully turned away from me, looking at the empty stage.

'Was she seeing him before I was born?' I ask.

She doesn't answer.

I put my arm around her. She's crying.

'Could the musician be my . . . father?'

'Dates are difficult for me. So long ago. Those details. I can't tell you anything more,' she says.

'Please!' The white walls are moving in on me, blank pages.

Broken beats in my head. My body speaking tongues. If I'm not Irving's child it would explain so much. I tune inna my body, cos that's where truth is. Sonic matter and blood in the mix. All whoosh and hiss. Maybe it doesn't make any difference. Oraca and Irving are earthly mooma and poopa, all the earthly imperfections of brown clay matter; Muma and the trumpeter are spirit parents, the guiding purity of sound.

Sister Abike faces the door, clasps her hands in front of her stomach. 'I'll send off today for your files. This was your mother's home. It is yours too.'

She walks me to the stairs. I tell her where I'm staying and ask her to contact me there if she remembers anything else.

Her eyes half-close around a thin line of eyewater. A shard of memory.

I go out to the car and tell Carlton this was Muma's home; that's something, at least. On the drive back I pretend to be asleep, all the while wondering if the search for Muma is taking me closer to myself than to her.

I open my eyes as we drive past the river and remember what Granny Itiba said: *Black River falls in the dry season*. I wonder what season this is, because everything seems to be falling.

26

Bacchanal

Over the next two weeks, Miss Ermeldine and Fern are busy preparing for Christmas, putting up new curtains, red poinsettias with tinsel in every room, the house filled with the smell of rum and fruit cakes baking. I stay out of their way, spend the time reflecting on what Sister Abike has told me about Muma. Play it over and over, a mixing-down of characteristics. My mind empties itself of the syndrums and sirens. But just as soon as I feel that I have her more firmly in my mind's eye, there's a rhythmic fading.

Then cut-out.

There are more questions. Doubt.

I go into the yard and lie in a hammock slung low between ackee trees at the side of the house. In this heat, I have to remind myself that it's Christmas Eve. The fireflies are drifting away. The ripe, red ackee bulbs with black seed eyes hang like effigies. Dark mountains stand against the tinted glass of the sky. Blue smoke of hardwood, moving down from the heights, enters my body, winding like mixtape, spooling backwards.

Muma's voice: *Child, let me carry you across the sea.*

Clear as if she's standing right in front of me.

Then Fern's voice, coming from the kitchen, calling me.

Miss Ermeldine has returned from a Christmas shopping trip to Kingston and Fern has set the table on the veranda at the front of the house with green-glazed bowls of stuffed cho-cho and tureens filled with dark pools of oxtail, white beans and callaloo.

'People from Belize coming in two weeks, just after the holidays,' Miss Ermeldine says as Fern ladles food on to our plates.

'How many?' Fern asks.

'Three of them – archaeologists. They want meals, laundry, packed lunches for field trips.'

'Coming to dig up the cockpits!' Fern says.

'They're professionals. Knowledge is good,' Miss Ermeldine says. She blesses the table and we eat.

Miss Ermeldine says that she and Fern are going to her sister's tomorrow for Christmas lunch and she asks if I want to go. I say I'm happy to stay alone.

'Me can stay,' Fern says. 'Tek Yamaye swimming in the river.'

Miss Ermeldine pushes the horn-rimmed glasses on to the bridge of her nose and peers over her bosom.

'Maybe the coast,' I say. 'I haven't been to the beach yet. My Christmas present for Fern.'

Fern squeals, 'Yes, yes, yes. Please, oh please, Miss Ermeldine! There'll be Christmas parties on the beach.'

Miss Ermeldine says she'll call Carlton.

Fern drops her cutlery, goes to Miss Ermeldine and kisses her cheeks.

'Stop dat,' Miss Ermeldine says, but she's trying not to smile. Fern is not just a live-in helper; she seems more like a daughter to her.

'I'll clear the table,' she tells Fern when we've finished eating. 'Go pack your things. Carlton can come tomorrow.'

I go to my room and pack a small bag. Carol singing coming from the Anglican church a mile away. Sugar-pitched spirituals rising, falling, dissolving into the night. I imagine myself dancing on the beach. Sea spray cooling my body. The sun blazing red on the horizon.

Dancers whispering, 'Catch a fire.'

The next day, mid morning, Carlton packs our bags into the boot of his car. Miss Ermeldine presses some money into Fern's hands. 'Enjoy yourself.' We get into the back seat and Carlton drives through Marlborough Hill, past the old, abandoned railway station. The sun is scorching; it's the hottest it's been since I landed.

'Fiyah,' Carlton says, wiping his brow with his white handkerchief. 'You think this island is fiyah, but is pure water. Born from the sea. Rivers running under the land.'

Carlton talks all the way to Troy and Albert Town. He knows everything about the trees, herbs, flowers, birds. We stop at Rio Bueno and have ice-cold beers and fried fish studded with fiery peppers. We drive in silence along the coast to Runaway Bay.

The air is tangerine-coloured and sweet, the black sea spread out, empty. Lights and beats in the distance. Carlton follows the drums, just like Asase, Rumer and me tracked the bassline in search of raves, back in those dub-dancing days.

'Aie, aie, Missus Foreign, beach parties. Bacchanal,' says Carlton. 'Hear the drums?'

'Dem have the best Christmas parties here,' Fern says.

'Anyone can go?' I ask.

'Strictly freeness,' Fern says. 'Everybody just fling down dem bodies on the beach and sleep when them done.'

'What kind of a sinting is that for a woman from England!' Carlton says. He stops by a rum shack and a German couple ask him to drive them to Dunn's River. We take our bags out of the boot while he negotiates a price with them. And then he's off, tooting and waving his hand outside the window. We check into the small hotel in front of the beach, shower and change into swimwear and sarongs.

Irie Beach, Runaway Bay. A bombshell of fiery colours on the horizon. White cruise ships float in the distance like ghost ships.

A semicircular shore, the bay protected by red coral. I'm a runaway on the leeward curl of the island where slaves ran free to Cuba and Haiti. Thinking 'bout Muma and Charmaine. Women on the run. The chopped vocals of Black women coming in and out of the sound highways of history.

Incense from a pimento-wood jerk shack smudges the air with a prehistoric mood. Trade wind blowing as people wade through an ocean tinged with blood-red sunlight. The long, drawn-out sigh of the tide, seaweed spread on the shoreline like shadows waiting to rise. A track kicks in: tidal horns and primitive chants. Black, brown, bronze, white, half-naked bodies popping style on the sand. The DJ calls out, 'Beach-Rock-Reggae is what the people want. Yeah!' Flashing his locks, flipping switches, gyrating between three turntables, mixing dub, soca, disco and spirituals.

It's probably snowing on the other side of the world. I think of Irving and Oraca, alone in their empty homes. I'll write to them soon enough. Although right now I don't know what I'll say.

I'm too far from the crypts and shebeens, concrete and tempered steel. I'd dreamed of this kinda living with Moose, in Muma's fire-rush tropics. I breathe in the salt-encrusted air, thinking, *Yeah, Moose, I made it back for both of us. Dance with me.*

'Come on,' Fern shouts. 'What you standing there looking so serious for. This ah no England.' She pulls off her sarong and drags me into the sea, kicking up warm water. The sea is shallow a long way out. Ropes of floating seaweed. We wade out until the sand beneath our feet turns to jagged, slimy rocks.

Further still, and the current pulls me off my feet. I swim, dive beneath the bottle-green water. The ocean washes over and through me. The closer I get, the further away Muma seems, as if I'm right behind her now, but she's drifting further and further away. Down into the seagrass beds and coral reefs that are tarred with black algae.

I kick to the surface, shake the water out of my eyes, swim back to shore where Fern is dancing, winding her narrow hips in small circles. I crouch down and circle my arse, swinging on the off-beat. Dance myself into the spirit, my hands in the air.

'Eh-eh, Miss Foreign have moves,' Fern says. 'Watch me, nuh.' And she steps it up, squats, gyrates her batty one way and her shoulders another.

The DJ turns up the musical pressure, begins toasting:

'Watch me, nuh –
Me ah the Preacher DJ,
Come to sweet up the scene
Mek you jump and switch,
Tek you inna spirit
Inna spirit . . .'

'Dance, sister?' a bare-chested man in rolled-up jeans asks.

He tries to pull me close to his body, but I step back and he holds the fingertips of my right hand in his and we dance, free and easy, not rub-a-dub style.

'Ride the riddim, sister,' he says.

Dancers wade into the ocean. The beach is lit up with lights from rum shacks. We're in a trance, retracing the footprints of the first people of the island whose music and smoke rituals still burn in the air.

The music stops and I sit on the sand.

'Sister, that was irie,' my dance partner says.

He lights a spliff and blows ganja into my waiting mouth. I swallow dream-infused sea air. Feel the concrete, tempered steel and metal breaking up inside me.

He points to the horizon: reds, oranges, yellows, broiling. 'Sister, what you see?'

'History. The light of this island is full of it.'

'Seen, sister. You have de sight.'

I leave him and sit with Fern. We lean back on our elbows, watching dancers in the sea, their bodies glistening, aquatic, unearthly.

A waiter brings us a tray with cocktails, and I choose a Jungle Bird that has a single leaf of ganja floating on the top. He walks away without taking any money. I sip the bitter-sweet drink and the nerves in my face contract and fire flows down my throat. The beach tilts. I hear laughter and play-fight screams further down. In the distance, I see people in bikinis and swimming trunks dancing in dry, bony movements. The DJ calling out,

'Me a go keep you rockin' and swing
Love is all I bring.'

Two musicians, a saxophonist and tabla player, set up their instruments on the beach. One of them, an Indo-Caribbean woman, begins playing first, licking up a drumbeat, her tongue slipping on to her bottom lip, her eyes closed, like a blind person, happy to let go of colour and shape, giving up everything except sound. The saxophonist trills sharp soprano notes. And one long note that goes on and on into time.

The musicians walk around after their session selling cassettes of their music and I buy two, for me and Fern. We're talking to a group of Canadians when, way off in one of the rocky bays, I see a man with his back to me dancing with a small group. He's skanking in quick, crouching movements as if he's picking things out of the darkness. Trunks slung low on his hips, his broad shoulders narrowing into a tight waist like a warrior shield.

The body looks sickeningly familiar.

I walk slowly down the beach to get a better look. The man is still dancing, pulsing his batty bone, squatting low on his quads, arms pulling the air. He's winding like Monassa, but there's no way it can be him. I must be seeing things, my vision still fogged by fear. I walk back to Fern and we wade into the sea again, near the coral reef.

The musicians stop just before daybreak and the woman blows a conch shell. The sound rolls across the sea, away from the shore, like the island is saying: *staaaaaay staaaay.*

There's a juddering sound of thunder, lightning flashes and seconds later a tropical downpour sends everyone sprinting for cover. Me and Fern huddle inside the bar against the other wet, steaming, half-naked bodies. The man in the distance disappears into a cove.

'What you looking 'pon?' Fern asks.

'That man looks like Monassa, the man I'm running from.'

'Him see you?'

'No.'

'What you want fe do?'

'It can't be him. But let's go, before the storm gets any worse.'

We run back to the hotel in the rain. In our room we shower and put on white towelling robes and push the single beds together and climb in. The rain is lashing the windows, the wind howling.

In the island's light and with the sound of the sea, nothing seems real. It can't have been Monassa. Even if he was out of prison already, no way he'd have tracked me to Jamaica.

We order brandy, patties and roasted cashew nuts. A young man brings it to our room, and we lie on our backs in our twin beds.

'Do you have a boyfriend?' I ask.

'Once,' Fern says. 'Cameron. We lived together for a while. He was a country man.'

'Where's he now?'

'Him move to Kingston two years back to make music in one of the studios. Not a word since him gone. Cities swallow people.'

I tell her about Moose, our dancing nights. How he was killed. 'Cameron could come back. What then?' I ask.

'Me nuh want him now. Soiled goods.'

We laugh.

'You afraid of this man, Monassa?' Fern asks.

'I was scared – but afraid to admit it.'

'Mek sense to me.'

'But not any more,' I say. 'Not since Granny Itiba took me to Cockpit Country and I learned about the rebellions of magic, false footsteps and smokeless fires.'

The rain stops and I open the window which looks on to the ocean. Open my mouth for the blow-back of dream-infused air.

27

Control Tower

Christmas and New Year are over, and I spend the next couple of weeks at Miss Ermeldine's lodging house writing lyrics on the terrace and going for walks in the afternoons with Fern. Night-time is when the fear comes. In the darkness, I see Monassa everywhere, dancing on the beach or floating beneath the sea.

Everything looks better in the early dawn, when this island of water and light sucks the fear out of me, drains it into the red earth and the rivers below.

I'm rising. Rising.

At breakfast one morning, I'm sitting on the veranda with a mug of cocoa tea, looking out at the land: waterfalls of frothing white flowers hanging from trees; ink-blue plants strange as sea anemones; coral-coloured shrubs; mountain air cool as the ocean. I'm tuned to the power of this place; it's where I need to be.

Two of the archaeologists come out on to the veranda and drop their backpacks and equipment close to the steps – ropes, helmets, headlamps, wetsuits, harnesses and foil-wrapped meat patties and bullah cake that Fern has prepared. They arrived late yesterday evening; the clanking engine of their jeep woke me.

They introduce themselves as Leila and Cornell and Leila sits next to me, our backs against the French windows, looking out towards the land. She's tall, dark brown skin, long beaded hair and trenches on her forehead and sides of her mouth. Her body is packed tight into her T-shirt and khaki shorts, the muscles of her arms and legs defined and alert.

Cornell, a short, squat man with purple-black skin, a shiny, shaven head and a half-smile, sits on the left side of the table close to Leila. Fern brings a tray of coffee, tiny wooden bowls of cornmeal porridge, cornbread and pots of pawpaw applesauce. She lays them out on the red, flower-printed tablecloth.

Leila says she's from Belize and the founder of Everything to Dive For.

'You work with ArtConscious?' I ask.

'You've heard of us?' she asks.

'In Bristol. The Sugar Museum,' I say.

I tell her about Moose and his work with Kalihna. Cornell says that Zed, the other member of their team, knows Kalihna well, they've dived together many times in Cape Town and Florida.

'Holiday or relatives?' Leila asks me.

'Tracing my mother,' I say. 'She's been gone a long time.'

She tilts her head to one side. 'That's tough. There's always something left behind, a lead. No matter how long.'

Cornell says if they can be of help, just let them know.

It's nice to have company at breakfast. Fern and Miss Ermeldine are always busy in the mornings, cleaning, speaking with the men who farm the twenty acres of land surrounding the house.

Leila tells me they run a volunteer diving training programme and asks if I'm interested. They want more descendants of enslaved people to take part in their searches. Cornell says he's the lead scuba diver and it would be his pleasure to have me on board.

I tell them that right now I'm focused on finding out what I can about Muma. Whatever time is left is for music. We talk about dub and its roots in slave uprisings. Sacred rhythm breaking time. Re-appropriating history. Communicating stories of resistance.

It makes me wonder if Muma is dead and her voice is like the relics pulled from wrecks, coming through some rhythmic opening in time.

Zed comes out to join us. A thin, pale-skinned man with stringy limbs, tufts of red Afro studded like coral on his scalp. He has long pillow marks on one side of his freckled face. He stretches his arms upwards and leans from side to side. Flops into a chair facing Cornell across the table. 'Something about country air knocks me out,' he says as he yawns. He pours coffee into a mug and drinks in greedy gulps, his nose deep into the cup, his eyes on me.

They seem warm and relaxed with each other.

'You checking out the caves?' I ask.

'We're gonna scope out one or two before the main event,' Cornell says. 'Port Royal with the rest of the team next month – excavating a slave ship that went down about a hundred miles off the coast.'

'Sounds dangerous,' I say.

'Going deep has its risks,' Leila says.

Zed, who's been silent most of the time, says: 'We're interested in the networks of rivers below the caves, their routes to the sea.'

'Do they all lead to the ocean?' I ask him.

'All water is connected,' he says.

Leila drains her cup, stands up and shakes her legs out. 'And raising our ancestors is raising ourselves.' She says I'm welcome to join them for dinner in Port Royal one evening; they'll be staying at the Hummingbird Lodge.

Cornell and Zed follow Leila down the four veranda steps and I smell the ocean on their clothes, damp, briny. I imagine them in their diving suits, descending to the seabed, shape-shifting amoebas, like me and Moose when we skanked low, head-to-head-tethered, our bodies sinking. I see the divers getting close to the shrinking, splitting, crumbling white oak and slippery elm of a wreck. Floating red clay fragments, the green-glass water a magnifying lens on Black bodies that drift timelessly in smoky sediment.

Zed lights a cigarette and leans against the railing, offers me one. I shake my head and he asks if I'm going to the festival tonight. Fern has told me it's the annual celebration of the victory of the Maroons over the British. I'm going in the afternoon. The smoke coils tight as a fossil, then loosens into a chain that rises and disappears. I imagine them lowering themselves into caves on steel wire, zipping up and down like the lifts in the Tombstone tower blocks that shuttled our bodies between heaven and hell. I think of the bones of the Maroons – Africans, Tainos. In the flat-bottomed cockpits. Some flushed out to the sea.

Leila is by the jeep. 'Come on,' she calls to Zed. 'The caves won't be there forever, and neither will we.'

'Everyone says they've been here for millions of years,' I say. 'What does she mean?'

'The water is percolating downwards,' he explains. 'The ceilings of the caves are collapsing, pushing them higher and higher. Eventually they'll open up to the sky.'

'Another uprising,' I say.

'That's intense for this time of day,' he says. He laughs, says maybe he'll catch me at the festival or at breakfast tomorrow.

I watch them load up the jeep and they drive off in a spray of red dust.

By lunchtime the mountains are alive with drumming, chanting and the hollow-trunk sound of horns blowing. Yellow birds in the distance fly above star-shaped depressions and ephemeral streams. The sun disappears, and clouds, dark as burial mounds, move in.

Miss Ermeldine leaves in her small brown Lada to drive to her sister's in Port Antonio for the weekend. Fern tells me there'll be plenty to see at the festival. Drumming, invocation of the spirits, storytelling about the fighting tactics of the Maroons. She says she'll join me after she's finished her chores. Miss Ermeldine's made it clear that Fern has to scrub the archaeologists' clothes every night as she does not, under any circumstances, want bat guano in her house bringing fevers of the dead from the caves. Fern sees me off from the veranda and I walk along the country roads alone.

It's hot. Banana leaves are glowing with sunlight. The purple hills are inlaid with turquoise orchids. Cars, trucks and jeeps toot as they make their way to the festival. I flag down a small country bus. The road is lined with yellow-and-green stalls selling drinks, beads, Kente-print clothes. Ancestor warriors watching us from giant murals on whitewashed walls. Throngs of people camouflaged in branches are dancing. Pitchy Patchy masqueraders play rhumba boxes and shakkas. Megawatt sound systems on every corner. Oil barrels of smoking meat.

An illusion.

A cow-head masquerader in a calico and wire mesh mask with horns charges at me and dances around me in circles. I push past him, shay-shaying with the crowd. I buy a can of chilled beer and stand next to a sound system pumping dub. I rock with everyone, chopping the air with my hands.

I'm rising, rising.

I'm not underground. I'm rocking the riddims of my own revolution. I toast lyrics to the music as I dance, and the controller turns the sound down to hear me before calling over the mic:

'Come, foreign lady, mek we hear yuh.'

The crowd roar, blow whistles and push me forward.

I take the mic and the controller turns the volume up and down, timing it to my lyrics and the drums and bassline.

'right yah now people
Sonix Dominatrix at the control tower
cos me full a tactics
me know how fe dip
me know how fe give de bad bwoy de
slip
check them revolution style yah
wicked and wild'

The women take the lead, rippling hips, throwing invisible lassos in the air, pulling in imaginary partners, squatting down, leaning forward, shaking their arses in defiance. It reminds me of the day I drove Racer's car and escaped the police. The speed, the moves, the feeling of power. I give the mic back to the DJ.

'A yuh dat, daughter! Check us again,' he says.

I move on and stop at a stall selling beaded necklaces and wooden bracelets. The woman takes my hand and looks at my mahogany ring.

'Dat is craftsmanship,' she says.

'My man made it.'

'Yard man?'

'Yeah.'

In the periphery, a man in a devil mask with red horns and wire meshing prowls towards me. 'Baby, your revolution was way too loud,' he says.

Arrhythmic electricity in my body. I inhale a black storm. Separation of positive and negative. I become supernatural.

'If a man can't dance, he says the music ain't good,' I reply. My voice holds steady, but my legs are freakbeat shaking at the sound of his voice. Monassa's voice.

The devil mask laughs. 'You let the spirits skank you, baby?' He leans forward as if he's gonna kiss me. I turn away, disgusted. He grabs my arm and drags me off the street, pushes me against a white-washed wall, banging my head with the force.

'You're dread,' he says. 'Trying to blow me out?'

'Just getting outta your smoke.' I pull away from his hold, rub my head and cut my eye on him.

'So yuh run things?' he asks.

'Was I supposed to stay in the Safe House with ghosts?' I ask.

'Cool runnings, baby. You were afraid.'

It's not a question. His voice is tender, the breath behind it no more than could blow out a candle. He places a finger under my chin and tilts it upwards. His eyes have a warm-blooded stillness. I push his hand away.

'Heard your Shackles Shebeen night was maxing the massive,' he says. 'Why dig up from a scene like that? Why take my blood-claat money?'

A group of warriors covered in leaves dance past, a row of drummers behind them.

'Come on!' they call.

Monassa pulls me round a corner, off the festival road. Three Rastas are sitting on the steps of a house smoking a chalice. They look at us and nod. Their faces disappear in smoke.

He takes off the mask. The man's rinsed out. Face is gaunt, goatee and hair shaved, a bullet-path parting on his head, needle track lines on the sides of his mouth. We sit on white plastic chairs at a table where a woman has cauldron pots on a fire in the ground.

'You sitting there yuh have to buy food,' she says.

Monassa gives her some notes, and she ladles red bean soup into bowls and puts them on the table.

I take a few mouthfuls, tek time to think. 'Was I supposed to leave the money in the Safe House? For the Heartist, Christina or someone else to take it? I couldn't write to you in prison and tell you what I was doing.'

A tremor of sadness in his eyes, something I've never seen before. I feel repulsion, pity, hatred, confusion. All the things I feel for Irving and Asase.

'Where's the money?' he asks.

'In a special account. Three days' notice before I can get it out.'

His eyes narrow. 'You're dark, baby. Still waters and all that.' He takes a spoonful of the soup and calls out to the woman for pepper sauce.

'Dungle said you'd be on remand for a year.'

'I got bail, just after Dungle. They've still got Racer – in solitary.'

'And the Safe House?'

'If you're looking to skank me, this ain't the place to do it,' he says. 'I've made moves on this island before. I've got people here.' He sprinkles the red sauce in the soup, tastes it, smacks his lips.

'I've proved myself to you and your crew,' I say.

'I told you, remember? Once you move with us, you can't leave. You're inna our business.'

'What d'you want from me?'

'Did you enjoy the cocktail I sent over to you at the beach? Special mix.'

We get up. I walk alongside him, keeping him at arm's length. His hired jeep is parked on a side street close to the sound system where I was toasting. The DJ waves at me. His dub track is thumping, sirens and sync-drums blaring, people's synchronised hips swaying left to right like bells.

We get in the car and he drives down a track off the main road through the country. I give him my *poor-t'ing* face, but I'm faking. I'm tuned to the duppy rebels of this territory. Their fire is inna me.

'Don't give me that look,' he says. 'I haven't come to hurt you, baby-girl. I'm thinking on everything you've said.'

He stops at a rum shack filled with carnival revellers. Roots riddims pumping, people two-stepping, holding glasses of shots high in the air like torches.

The waiter brings a bottle of white rum and some mixers. Monassa pours and stirs. I sip. He's watching the drink, not me. I put the glass down, not sure if he's spiked it.

'How did you find me?' I ask.

'By tuning into you, baby. Pluckin' the guitar strings of your mind.' He plays air guitar: chengeh-chengeh. 'I used any little thing you told me 'bout where you came from. Where your family came from. Then chatting to the taxi drivers at the airport. They run their mouths like they run their cars. Yabbah yabbah yabbah.'

I look him bang in the eyes, let out a long, sneering exhalation as I say, 'Ooohhh. I'm afraid.'

'Don't ramp with me. I know the pattern of your breath, the temperature of your skin, the smell of you.' He puts his hand on my crotch and squeezes. 'Everything about you,' he whispers.

He drains his glass and pours another.

I stare into his brown eyes, a gene pool of shadows.

'The money's loose change,' he says. 'I've been working the streets since I was a boy. It's the principle, baby.'

'What do you want?'

He looks me up and down. 'Island suits you. You're darker, sweeter. Flesh on your batty. Something different about you.'

'I'm a 'trang woman,' I say.

'My mind ain't good in a cage,' he says.

'Take your money. I'm not going anywhere.'

'You're popping style on the island. You've set up this chase. It's dark, baby.'

‘I can walk from here.’ I get up, step quick.

He’s next to me, close as a quab. ‘What? Don’t you want me to escort you back to Miss Ermeldine’s lodging house?’

‘For fuck’s sake!’

‘Think I didn’t know that too? I’ll drive. I’m your protector,’ he says.

I get in the jeep, all the while thinking how I’m gonna psych the fucker out.

He puts on gold-framed Aviators, busts a rootsy riddim. The four car speakers on the doors are pumping hard, like a gang of heartbeats. We speed round the coiled mountain, descending into the burnished light of late afternoon.

‘You need me. Nah true?’ he says.

‘Blood-claat, no,’ I say.

He strokes his chin like he’s milking it for wisdom before driving directly into a crater-like pothole. The jeep skids. He looks at me and sees the worry on my face, then drives closer to the edge of the mountain.

I scream at him to stop.

I recognise the stench of his arousal: yeasty, earthy musk. Bile rises from my stomach and I gag.

He’s giggling. ‘Scream for me, baby.’

The man is high on my fear. I style it out, try to act cool.

People heading to the festival flash past in glistening cars, swerving and beeping at us to get into our own lane. Old trucks with heavy-lidded bonnets and bulbous front lights crawl by and the drivers wave and cuss.

‘Tell me you love me bad-bad-bad,’ he says.

‘Bad is the word,’ I say.

He takes the car right to the edge of the mountain and closes his eyes for a few seconds, opens them, closes them, again and again.

My feet are pressing on imaginary brakes and I've forgotten how to breathe.

He shouts, 'We're going over.'

I look down and see rocks, white as skulls, scattered amongst the green bush. I scream again, holding on to the sound of my voice going on and on and on.

He speeds around a tight corner and slams on the brakes. I smell burning rubber. The front wheel on my side is hanging over the edge and the car is rocking.

'Anything, anything,' I shout. 'I love you.'

'Bad,' he says.

'I love you bad,' I say.

He pulls hard on the steering wheel, brings the car back on to the road and speeds off again.

He's driving towards a small viewing area and I throw open the door and lean out, waiting for the right moment to jump as the jeep slows on the sharpest point of the bend. But he's got my right wrist in one hand, controlling the car with the other.

'Shut the door or I'm gonna bruck it,' he says.

I try to pull away, but he's bending my wrist backwards and I hear the joint crack and pain shoots up my arm.

I shut the door with my left and he lets go and I pull my hand from his. My fingertips are numb, wrist hurting so bad I can barely move it.

'The fight's done,' he says. 'Give up the pum-pum and let's have some fun.' He's laughing again, stroking his chin. I want to punch the side of his head with my other hand but I keep it on my lap.

'Miss Ermeldine will call the police if I'm not back tonight,' I say. 'She knows I'm here alone.'

He slows the car and turns the music down. 'Ah so?' he says. We cruise further down the mountain. There's a tropical downpour.

Rain sharp as poisoned arrows flies at the jeep, bounces off into the valley below. The air becomes the colour of stone and the drumming from the festival fades away. It stops raining by the time we get to the bottom of the mountain. We drive along the narrow, wet roads, past cane fields.

He pulls in at the top of the lane to Miss Ermeldine's house, turns the engine off. The light is lilac now, the air clear of petrol fumes.

He leans across and puts his hand on my crotch. 'I'm staying in the Blue Lagoon Cabana in Runaway Bay.' He revs the car. 'Hold that!'

'Full of moves, ain't yuh.'

'I want your batty there. We'll get the money first. I'll collect you in two days' time. The Anglican church we just passed. Midday. Tell Miss Ermeldine you're moving on. You've got two days to pack, sort the money, say your goodbyes. I'll get our tickets to Miami.'

'Miami?' I pull his hand away from my crotch, cross my legs.

'New scene, new riddims,' he says. 'I've got passports. New identities for both of us. A fresh start. You know it's what you've always wanted. Check it: me and you want the same things.'

I see dark clouds spinning off the skyline towards us. The scent of turned earth is in the air.

'Didn't know what I wanted till I came here,' I say.

'You need me,' he says. His voice makes shapes like open wounds.

'If I don't come?'

'Moose is dead. I'm flesh and blood. I've saved your raas once. Don't forget.'

'I've paid for that!'

'Don't gwaan dem ways. Tell the truth, you enjoyed the danger zones.'

'You're not in my head any more.'

'You and me have a connection, nah true?'

I think of him as a child on the streets, his mother running wild.

He looks like a boy now, his eyes wide and pleading, trying to style it out with an unconvincing sideways smile.

'You like all this,' he says, and he spins the wheel left and right, stops it spinning with his fist. 'Need to feel wanted. I get it.'

'You a psychologist as well?'

'I know women.'

'Not this one.'

'I'll chase you, kinky gyal. Be sure of that. Gwaan, get some rest. Don't wash. I like it fenky-fenky.'

I get out of the car and slam the door and he shouts: 'Don't sleep on your stomach. Duppies are liable to make their way in.' He's laughing, the noise coming from the base of his throat.

'I'll see you there,' I say, because this fight isn't just for me. It's for Muma too.

'Easy, my selector,' he shouts as he drives off.

The house is in darkness. Fern must be at the carnival. We'd arranged to meet there at three. It's just gone five. Daylight turning indigo. The archaeologists' muddy boots are scattered on the veranda by the side of the door, but their jeep is gone. The air smells of tomorrow's mist, this morning's smoke. Firecrackers explode in the sky far away. I go to the yard at the side of the house to watch them. Zed is sitting on a lounger, wicker chairs and circular table near to hand, maps and unopened cans of beer on his right. He's holding a can as he looks across at the mountains.

I go to the ackee trees where the hammock is tied and sit facing him.

'Been to the festival?' he asks.

'Earlier,' I say.

'Never saw you.'

'Too many masqueraders.'

'They're something else.'

I ask where the others are, and he says they're still at the festival. He walked back so he could explore the area.

I rest my back against the weight of the tree behind me, pull my legs up under me. Zed takes a beer and holds it up. I nod and he throws it to me. The beer spuzzles out when I open it. I catch the foam in my mouth, tip my head back and swallow a lot more. It warms my chest and soothes the throbbing in my wrist.

'You OK?' he asks.

'Kinda.'

The red-brown tufts of his Afro look like they were alight moments ago.

I start shivering. My body is bent out of shape, empty. I drain the can.

'Ever afraid of what you'll find?' I ask.

'From the wrecks?'

I think of me inside the empty wreck of the Safe House circled by Monassa's black, quick-moving thoughts, sinking inside his head.

'Shackles. An iron cannon. A bell furred up in white limestone. Hard to touch at first. There's something like dread. Then tenderness.' He laughs softly as if he can feel that tenderness now.

'Bondage. Fire. Sound,' I say.

I ask him where they were today, and he says they were exploring a cave. He talks about descending three hundred feet into an underground lake. Trying to find other ways in and out of the upstream system.

He offers me another beer. I get up and go to the table where the maps are. I ask if the cave is marked on one of them. He says, sure, take a look. I pick up a can and the map and go back to the hammock. The can is still cool. I press it on to my swollen wrist. Study the map for a while.

'How's your mission?' he asks.

‘Mission?’ I’m afraid that he’s reading my mind.

‘Your mother?’

‘Oh. Leila told you?’

‘Yes.’

I fill him in on what I learned at the orphanage, taking smaller sips of the beer. I glance up towards my bedroom window. For a moment I think a light has gone on, but it’s fireflies drifting around the shutters. Behind him, shadows from the trees reflect on to the house like criss-crossing rivers.

He drains his beer, opens another for himself.

‘Where in Guyana was she?’ he asks.

‘Nobody kept her letters. All the nun remembers is that the river was the only way out.’

Zed tells me that Kalihna, the Guyanese artist who made the model of a slave ship, grew up in Arapiaco, an Amerindian village near the Pomeroon River. The river was the only way in and out.

I swing my legs off the hammock. Breeze sloshing around my face.

‘There must be a thousand places like that in Guyana,’ he says.

We’re in darkness now. The headlamps of a car sweeping through the night like searchlights.

Zed says Kalihna’s mother told him about a group of women who came to help pregnant women – missionaries or charity workers. They brought medicine and supplies. Kalihna’s mother was pregnant with him. He was way overdue, didn’t want to come out and was born with the cord wrapped around his throat. Blue in the face. One of the women unravelled the cord, cut it, breathed life into him. That woman stayed on when the others left – moved from the village to the forest somewhere at the head of the Pomeroon River.

‘Alone?’

‘Yes. She became spiritual, or was having a crisis.’ He carries on, saying the woman caught malaria a while later and the villagers took her in a boat, heading for the coast. She was trying to get on one of the cargo ships heading who knows where. But she died on the dugout. The boatmen put her body into the river to be flushed out into the Atlantic.

He stops talking. Looks at me.

I can't speak. I'm thinking of Muma, with the bodies of the other Black women I see, pulling at the wrecks of ships, trying to get out.

I feel unsteady in the hammock, as if it's swaying under a force of darkness. I hold on tight with both hands. The beer comes up my throat, acidic, bringing the fear up from my guts.

'There were thousands – millions – of men and women who did things like that all over the world,' Zed says. 'This woman was a much older woman, old enough to be his grandmother. She wasn't your mother.'

'Why tell me?'

'Artefacts are open to interpretation. But they give us direction. That woman – missionary, aid worker, whatever she was – her story ended in the Atlantic,' he says. 'Your mother was born here. This is where you look. Focus on anything she left behind.'

'I've looked. The only thing she left is me,' I say.

He smiles. 'Start with you, then.'

I tell him that the flat where I grew up in England was like an archaeological site with all of Muma's things. Her mic. Bottles of perfume. Some records. Paintings of mountains, white ships in the distance.

'A scene of somewhere in Jamaica that she loved, maybe?' he says. 'A place that might be significant.'

I say it will be hard to check the paintings for a while. But I'll do it as soon as I can. He says he'll help with that whenever I'm ready.

'So you know the island well?' I ask.

'Well enough.'

'You can help with something else?'

'Anything.'

'I'm looking for a place to . . . retreat. Somewhere isolated.'

'How long for?'

'A few weeks. Maybe more.'

He tells me about an uninhabited cay that has clear waters and a coral-pink beach. A short ride from Port Royal. He says he'll take me there when they're in Port Royal next month.

I stand up. The earth is moving.

'Need some help?' he asks.

'No. I've got this,' I say.

As I walk towards the house, he calls out: 'Uranus turned retrograde.'

I turn back. 'What does that mean?'

'The planet of revolution and awakening,' he says.

'You believe all that?'

'Water, methane, ammonia. Sound like the right ingredients for a revolution,' he says.

'I need some of that,' I say.

I leave him lying there in the rising darkness. Up in my room, I lie on the bed. Headlights scan the building. Footsteps up the stairway. Fern calling my name.

She comes into the room and sits on the bed. 'Why you never come?'

I kiss my teeth.

'Is who trouble you?' she asks.

'Monassa's here. Spoke to him.'

'Jeggries!' She takes my hand in hers and looks up into the sky. 'Go to the sacred grounds. Protection.'

'I'll sleep on it.'

'No fret yuhself. Spirit watching you.'

I try to sleep. An undertaker's breeze sweeps down from the mountains. A faraway tide riffs through the night. I put the radio on. The broadcaster says something about low pressure, a storm coming in from the coast of Africa.

Muma's shadowy weight at the bottom of the bed. I look down and there she is: her tissue-twisted curls matted with seaweed. Sparkling salt-encrusted bones.

Them throw spells on us, Muma moans. *You can put death on a man too.*

It's the first time I've seen her. Her face has the transparency of water. Life pouring through it.

I try to speak, ask her where she is, what I should do. But words are backed up in my throat. I look in her eyes, they're yellow and strange.

I'm closer to her than I've ever been. I reach out to pull her roots from the darkness. She slips away.

28

Riffs

In the morning I look out the window and see a trail of destruction: ribcages of boards from the outhouses are scattered around the land, branches lie like broken bones, the hammock is a noose hanging from the tree. Two workmen, grey-haired and wiry, are picking up pieces of zinc and dragging them away.

After breakfast I stay on the veranda drinking coffee. The archaeologists have just left. Fern comes to clear the plates. She's wearing a long, jade-coloured, cotton dress with a sleeveless triangular bodice.

'Bad-breed storm, come tek what it needs,' she says.

'Miss Ermeldine must be upset,' I say.

'She can't stand disturbance,' she says. 'Carlton and she gone to Kingston to see about the insurance. She not coming back till everything tidy.' Fern pours coffee into two terracotta mugs and sits at the table. 'You did 'fraid last night when you hear the storm?'

'I was listening to the radio,' I say. 'Must have heard the worst of it in my sleep. It made me dream Muma. Like she was really there.'

'Time isn't the same here,' she says. 'Everything mix-up.'

'She was talking about spells, killing.'

'Ancestors speak in one voice,' she says.

'Don't know about spells. I should get a flight somewhere.'

'Yuh nuh tired of running? Ask the ancestors fe help.'

I don't want to run any more. Can't leave the island when I'm close to finding out what happened to Muma. I feel her more strongly here. An energy running through me. Not a haunting. A vibing pitch. Undistanced by each note unpicking time.

Fern says there's a daily tour of one of the Maroon towns where there are many more dead in the cemeteries than are living and where there are sacred grounds for dancing, singing, healing and possession by the spirits. She says the tour bus stops nearby, it's the only way of getting there today. I should go, ask spirits for guidance.

'The tourists go, but them don't take it seriously,' she says.

'Been hearing Muma all my life,' I say. A guiding force. No such thing as afterlife.

'Nuh tell Miss Ermeldine,' Fern says. 'She's Anglican. She'll throw licks after me if she find out.' She goes to call the tour people.

I watch her moving, her jade dress swirling around her ankles. I want to hold on to her, press my face against hers, feel the warmth of her skin.

The tour van pulls up two hours later. It's white with a red stripe along the middle. I kiss Fern goodbye, take my backpack and climb in. Six serious-looking tourists with sunburnt skin; the whites of their eyes are red. Three Americans – two men and a woman – a Mexican man and two Canadian women. They're kitted out in khaki, bottles and bags strapped to their bodies like ammunition. The guide is up front with the driver. Reggae booms from speakers secured to the doors.

The guide has dreadlocks hanging past his shoulders, thick as the roots of old trees. He's popping style with a red, yellow and green bandana tied round his neck, gold string vest over a black T-shirt and denim shorts.

'Earl,' he says by way of introduction. 'Y'all set?'

The driver turns the van and drives back on to the country road.

'Listen up, folks,' Earl says. 'Today's itinerary one more time for the lady. We're gonna pick up an old military trail heading south. Uphill all the way. The most outta-standing karst landscape anywhere in this ya world. Serious thing. Cockpits in the morning, come back, eat a little yard food. Then we check out some caves. Everybody cool with that?'

One of the American men responds in stilted patois, 'No problem, man.'

Everyone laughs.

Earl sounds like a poet preacher as he talks about cockpit towers and saddles, ephemeral river valleys, limestone crust, fossils of camelis and armadillos. His voice going loud and quiet, waving his arms around.

The American man asks if they can camp there overnight and be picked up the next day.

Earl says: 'Yuh can't go breezing off on your own. People can't ramp there. Me talking 'bout drops of three to five hundred feet if oonuh step outta place. Terra incognita, you overstand?'

The American whistles at the figure.

'Bases a quarter of a mile across, pure muddy clay,' says Earl.

Everyone stops talking. The man flicks his torch on and off.

Moisture-laden trade winds blow in through the window, the smell of last night's rain and woodsmoke. Skeletal, swaying bamboo floats by.

Flickers of silver taffeta light on the turquoise lagoons.

The tourists lean their heads against windows and neck-rests. Honey-coloured light drugs them to sleep.

We drive down a narrow, chalky track to the cave and get out of the van where three empty tour buses are parked. Everyone stretches their limbs, pulls bags apart in search of water, creams, mosquito sprays, cameras. We walk down a small trail with overhanging trees and vines crossed over us like a cage. The entrance to the cave is covered in green ferns. A metal gate, the sound of water rushing inside. Earl says there are sections of an underground river running through the cave and three entrances in the shape of a triangle. The stream entrance further along, the sinkhole entrance and this one, which has steps running down. We hear voices inside.

Earl says he'll lead the way to the Cockpits from here. 'Yuh have yuh things?' he asks me.

'I'm not going. I came for the sacred singing. I'll meet you back here.'

'Careful, sistah, no mess with dem things. Come nuh?'

I shake my head.

'Sistah, if you go inna dat business, yuh 'pon you own.'

The tourists cluster around.

'You've paid your money, you may as well get your money's worth,' a woman says.

'If she doesn't want to—'

'Spoiling it for the rest of us—'

'Whose responsibility—'

Earl breaks in, 'Listen up. This is Jamaica. Everything irie.' He shakes his head at me, and says, 'Gwaan, me will check you here at three when we finish de walk.'

I follow the signs to the sacred grounds, just as Fern directed. I come to an area where the land is broken up by yellow-and-white limestone. Towering mahogany trees surround a smallholding fenced off by corrugated metal. Chickens in the yard and two large, rusty-coloured dogs sleeping in the shade of fruit trees. Silver light slipping between banana leaves.

I call out. No one answers.

The wind blows, the rhythmic continuity of someone breathing. Thin, grey smoke coming from a pit in the ground. I think of the cave and the map that Zed showed me. The five hundred feet drop into nothingness.

I head back to the cave where Earl has taken the group. I go down the stone steps, holding on to the metal rail. The ground is slippery with bat guano. The sound of water rushing far below. The cavern is lit like a cathedral with kerosene torches that give off a blueish smoke. Dreadlock stalactites. Rocks compacted into the earth like dinosaur teeth. Pools of amber-coloured water. Earl and the others must be further inside. Two women in psychedelic-patterned bikinis are floating on their backs in a pool with their eyes closed. A group of local men are hitting bamboo sticks on stalactites and singing a song about a man being beaten but bouncing back again and again.

Deeper and darker than the Crypt.

I take off my shorts and T-shirt and slip into the pool in my bikini. One of the women flips forward on to her stomach and smiles at me. I close my eyes and try to float on my back. My body, as heavy as limestone, holding on to the shock waves of loss and death. A thousand fluids inside me.

You can put death on a man.

I've absorbed everything: Irving's quiet hostility, Asase's overpowering ways, Monassa's skanking.

I'm floating now.

Time extends hundreds of years. Far into the hollow of the afterworld. I'm in the spirit-world of ancestors. I feel them in the brackish light of the cave, bucking, flexing, driving themselves forwards between my world and theirs. Their voices singing backwards into my throat. I see my reflection in the water, my face camouflaged in limestone dust.

You can put death on a man.

I leave the cave and walk up the gravel driveway and on to a wider track that leads to the road. Catch a bus to Balaclava. Along roads that curve with the Black River, past blue-, yellow-and-orange-painted stalls of fruits, white stone houses and wooden shacks. At Balaclava I stop at a roadway hut and buy mango juice and a bag of freshly roasted nuts from a higgler before jumping on a bus, another white van, that drops me at Maggotty. I walk down the long dirt road to Granny Itiba's house and go up the steps on to the veranda. A broom is by the open door, leather sandals and a bucket of soapy water. I call out and step inside. Granny Itiba is crouched down on the floor by the window, the light falling on her as she rolls large leaves on a mat.

She stands up and her nutmeg face spreads into a smile. She's wearing a long, brown lace-bark dress.

'Daughter!' she says.

'I've come for the magic,' I say.

'Daughter, I been waiting.'

There are small bottles of blue water on a shelf. She takes one of the bottles and we sit at the wooden table. Holding my stare, she takes each of my hands into hers and squeezes them. She closes her eyes and sings. Her voice goes into my body, a feeling like my bones filling with the sea. She raises the bottle.

'Drop of the ocean inside this,' she says. She shakes the bottle and asks, 'What yuh see?'

'Ships,' I say.

'Me see a man,' she says. 'Dark as the depth of the sea. Darker.'

'He won't let me go.'

She leans forward. 'I have herbs for every purpose,' she says.

Her hands feel hot.

'I'm a true practitioner,' she says. 'My mother too. She used the name Fire Rush. She could find fire in yuh body, burn it down to de truth.'

'Fire Rush,' I say.

'A little horse bush will clean out a man's kidneys. Too much will kill him.'

I tell her what I know about Monassa, his mother, his life on the streets. The money I stole and how he'd tracked me down.

She knocks the bottle over and the seawater spills on to the table, spreading like a map of small islands.

'Him is like a duppy. They do everything they did when they were living: nyam food, sex a woman.' Little beads of sweat dapple her forehead, but she doesn't wipe them away. 'I bind his mouth, I bind his soul and his gods. Whoever comes to hurt you will not be a match for what you can now do. Here, take this.' She gives me a small plastic bag with a piece of tree bark. 'Touch it to his skin, hold it there. Him will swell up. Plenty will kill him. A likkle will leave him suffering. Whatever you want. Him won't trouble you after dat.'

'I can't go back to him.'

'Yuh must face him. We all have fe face our shadows. Me will blow the abeng horn tonight. The living and the dead will hear it.'

29

Last Dance

Fern left a pot of ganja tea on the bedside table to help me sleep. The pot's still warm. I mix in half a cup of white rum and drink it before getting into bed. The shutters are open. The air pressure still low, smoky breeze blowing in. I watch a red lake flow out of the red hibiscus on the table, through the window and into the night, where an abeng horn blows in the distance.

The sound of the horn travels into the dance-hall nights of the Crypt where Asase, Rumer and me are dancing out of our bodies into rainforests and black rivers.

I wake at ten the next morning, too late for breakfast. I dress in black tracksuit bottoms and a gauzy silver batwing top. I put Moose's tape into my Walkman, pack it in my silver bumbag and secure it around my waist. Put on elbow-length black leather gloves. Test the movement in my wrist.

Miss Ermeldine is in the kitchen by the large, black iron stove. It's more like a music deck, with six turntable hot rings, double ovens the size of record boxes and rows of knobs. She's at the control tower, mixing a pot of stewed peas, humming along to the long-wave radio station where a woman is singing about spells she's put on her man.

The yellow jalousies are open, grey-twisted clouds float in the sky.

She pulls her chin down when she sees the way I'm dressed. 'You running up and down too much. Hot foot good for nobody.' She wipes her hands on a tea towel, pours creamy Irish Moss from a blue enamel jug into a glass and gives it to me.

'Where's Fern?' I ask.

'Gone to town. Those guests have the girl buying this and that like there's no tomorrow.'

'Maybe there isn't.'

'Don't talk like that in my house. Is bad luck.' I swallow the creamy liquid in one go.

'Bammies and escovitch fish for dinner,' she says.

'I'm going out.'

She sucks her teeth and shakes her head.

She calls me but I don't turn back. I walk out into a misty morning, a slit-throat red line on the horizon. Walking along the country road. Cloud vapour circling banana bushes. White orchids hang like light bulbs from calabash trees. I wave to familiar faces along the way: barefoot toddlers in faded underwear running around in yards; girls in dresses with sashes and frills, playing with boys in old-fashioned drainpipe trousers; women with baskets of provisions balanced on their heads, humming and swaying; old farmers with machetes swinging at their sides.

I wait for Monassa, as arranged, outside the Anglican church with its burial ground of ancient, lolling gravestones. I check the Walkman in my bumbag. Last night I'd stuffed the thin slivers of tree bark into the spools of Moose's cassette and put it in the Walkman.

Twelve on the dot, he drives up in an open-topped jeep, bass thudding.

I climb in.

'Check you out! Leather gyal. Wicked and wild style, baby.' He leans across and licks my lips, leaving a beaded line of his spittle hanging between us.

I wipe it off. 'Please!'

'Give me a likkle overstanding, baby! Almost three months locked up. I'm horny as hell.' He's wearing a khaki T-shirt and army-surplus trousers. There's a blue coolbox and silver ghetto blaster on the back seat.

'Got my money?' he asks.

'They wanted ID. Miss Ermeldine locked my passport away for safekeeping. She'll be back at three.'

'I've got our tickets for Miami leaving tomorrow night.'

I think of the Maroons who terrorised the slaveholders and put their plantations on lockdown. I'm in the light at last. I'm not going to give it up.

'Tomorrow we'll be flying high. Miami nights here we come,' he says.

'Let's check out the area while we're waiting,' I say. 'The caves where runaways hid. Piece of our history.'

'I'm inna that, baby. Yuh know I can't keep my raas still for long.'

I direct him and he speeds along the potholed roads, swerving outside his lane to pass slow-moving trucks.

'Arawaks, slaves, pirates and thieves holed up in caves way back when. They had tactics,' he says. He makes a noise like an insect at the back of his throat.

He drives along hill-and-gully roads, through Maggotty, past Black River where people are having cookouts of janga and dasheen, rafting, swimming, the smell of frying plantain sweet in the air. Riddims thumping from ghetto blasters. I see the mangrove of hog plums and Granny Itiba's house. Light reflecting off the zinc roof. I think there's someone sitting on the veranda, a stick-figure like an insect embedded in amber.

'I've missed you, baby,' he says. 'Prison was rough. Nevah going back. Whatever it takes.'

'What about Racer and Dungle?'

'Every man for himself for a while. Prison was no joke. Man dem crying and screaming at night. Caged like slaves. No such thing as history. That shit's still playing out in real time. Believe!'

'Police gonna be tracking you when you don't sign on,' I say.

He barks and howls. 'Let them bring on the mastiffs,' he says.

I ask if the Heartist caught Charmaine and he says she's still on the run but his bredrin will find her and bring her back where she belongs.

'Forget 'bout her. Look.' He takes a card out of his trouser pocket. 'Bona fide fake ID. Shaved my hair. Pulled out the ruby in my tooth, watchya, nuh.' He opens his mouth and flashes his teeth. 'We're all alike to them. They'll never find us in ravers' paradise Miami.'

'Isn't that where your muma is?' I ask. 'You looking for her?'

He ignores me.

We drive through the ancient towns where chanting and the chengeh-chengeh of an electric guitar floats from wooden halls. There are only two cars parked outside the cave. We get out and Monassa marches ahead in his military boots, stepping like he's going to war.

The cave is exactly as it was drawn on Zed's map. A semicircular opening, thirty feet wide, on the southern face of a steep slope. The opening empties into a circular chamber about fifty feet in diameter. Monassa pays the entrance fee, and we put on yellow helmets and he takes a red torch. We step along the walkways into the main cavern, the biggest one. Giant arches, stalagmites, stalactites, rock formations like stone sculptures of death heads. A sign says: THIS CAVE IS USED FOR LATE-NIGHT DANCES AT THE WEEKENDS.

'A cave rave for runaways. What a dark scene,' Monassa says. 'We could set something up in Miami, a cave shebeen for runaways from the dark corners of the earth.'

'Whatever you want,' I say.

We go along the runway as far as we can. I step over the cordoned-off area where Zed and the others must have been the day before. We walk into a labyrinth of caverns. I use my belly as an anchor as I squeeze myself through a narrow gap, pulling between the slimy cave walls. Monassa follows and we walk along a dark passage that opens into a cranial vault, like we're inside someone's head. I hear a single note. The first of all time. Hanging like a stalactite.

I become sound. I become supernatural.

The ceiling is twenty or twenty five feet high, scarred with shallow cavities filled with roosting cave swallows. To the left is a broad ledge several feet above the cave floor. There are large piles of rock and rubble. To the right are two passages leading into deep recesses. Darkness relaxes my hearing, the sound of rushing water beneath us.

We walk further and further along the ledge into another cavern, through a narrow passage, the ceiling just a foot from our heads. Eroded limestone shifts beneath my feet. I walk behind him. Shadows on his back, a monogram of salt and fire and flesh. The burning stamp of the past; heat, a burden he carries inside. I see that now.

The wall on the left opens up, and there's the drop that Zed talked about. I look over the edge into the glinting water below. Charcoal on the ground next to me from an old fire. Darkness come from light.

A strange feeling in my stomach, a neglected space where pain, loneliness and fire are churning.

'You always have an escape route, don't you?' I ask.

'I flex with the dead.' He thumps his chest with his fist and says, 'I'm a night mover. It's my rhatid inheritance, a gift from my muma.'

The passage cuts back sharply to the left and I'm thinking I can't do it. He's too fast, too slippery. I imagine pushing him, watching him explode in the air and then dropping into the water.

And the words are out of my mouth before I can think. I say it with my tongue curled. 'This is a time-limited offer, baby. You booked the flights for Miami. Sun, sea, sand and . . . the rest. Let's fling it down here.' I unzip his trousers, put my gloved hands on his cock. Press him flat against the clammy wall on the right. We're face to face. Now it's me on top. To the left is a drop inna hell.

He moans, turns his head to the side, his eyeballs roll up in their sockets. I work my hand harder. He closes his eyes. 'What are you doing to me?' he asks.

'You'll be the writing on the wall,' I say.

'Baby, you know what I need.' He moans louder.

The devil says, *Gwaan, push him*. Truth is, I know his stalking speed too well. If my timing's off, we'll both drop inna nothingness.

I keep my right hand working, put my face closer to his cock and nuzzle it with my nose. He moans again and relaxes his body, waiting for the touch of my lips. I keep my face in position, rolling the tip of my nose against his cock as I pull the glove tighter on my other hand and open my bumbag. Press the Walkman open and push my finger into the spool, take a little of the bark – and then some more – and scratch it against the skin on his groin.

'Yes! Do want you want with me, baby,' he says.

His nostrils flare, and he roars with pleasure as he climaxes. His voice recedes hundreds of years back into the hollow of the cave.

He slumps against the wall, his breathing slow and laboured.

'Best leave now,' I say. I take the torch from his hand as he zips himself up.

He shakes his head. Looks at me, his eyes shining. 'A yuh dat, babes, flinging down moves like that. Gwaan!'

I shine the torch along the narrow passageway and walk on.

'I feel good. I'm charged,' he shouts. 'Let's get the cash, grab your things. Back to my hotel. Finish what you started.'

I walk faster, my lungs vibrating like soundboxes.

'Wait up,' he calls.

I turn back. He's walking slow, swaying.

'Faster!' I shout. He steps it up and I turn off the torch. Darkness rises like floodwater.

'Hey!' he shouts. I switch the torch back on. And off. And on. Shine it on him. His face is swelling, his eyes disappearing into slits.

The fire, the rage inside me, is burning acid. Floodwater.

Been there all along. Twenty-eight years. Four hundred years.

'Stop messing,' he says. 'The air's bad.' He drops on to all fours. 'Can't breathe.'

He vomits and rolls on the ground in guano shit.

'Get up,' I say.

'Can't move.'

I walk back, take the car keys from his trouser pocket. Carry on.

'Wait up!'

I turn.

'Get yuh raas here,' he says. He tries to get up.

'Life is a time-limited offer, baby.' I say it with my tongue curled: 'I'm leaving you for the devil.'

He pulls himself up to sitting. His head is deforming, his mouth moves, but no words come out. I run hard through the passageway without turning back. My chest crackles and sparks like a just-lit fire. I stop, draw deep breaths. *Gwaan, gyal,* I tell myself. I squeeze myself back through the narrow entrance. It doesn't feel as easy this time, my body is tense and the air feels heavier. I'm struggling to breathe.

Yamaye, you've been in tighter spots, gyal. Get your raas outta here.

I push through and walk the rest of the way, inhaling slow and long.

*

Twenty minutes later, I'm back on the walkway. I step over the rope into the main cave. A couple and two children are going out. I tag behind. The man at the entrance nods at us.

The couple get into their car and I walk to the jeep. Drive past cane and banana groves. Turn off the track and get out. This feels like the place where Granny Itiba and I walked. But I'm not sure. There are steep-sided hills sloping at sixty-degree angles. A clearing with red flowers that look like flames. Tin-roofed houses on a hill in the distance. I walk across an old track covered in leaves and red mud, slipping on rubbly stones. Vines and roots everywhere. Hovering mist. Marked trails appear and disappear. Networks of slit-eyed ferns are watching me.

The smell of ganja smoke coming from far away.

This is the right place.

Deeper: sinking streams.

Deeper: tropical bird colour flashing between cottonwood trees.

Deeper: rum-coloured moisture dripping from green canopy.

Brittle limestone covers bottomless caverns. One wrong step and I'll break through the limestone crust. But I'm not afraid.

One-hundred-foot-high trees cut off the sunlight here and there, like the light going on and off at the end of a dance when the DJ calls out: 'Last dance. Last dance. Grab your partners.'

The foliage casts an illusion over everything. Moose calling me, speaking rivers and trees. Nearer than he ever was in life. The first time I'm truly hearing him.

The ground beneath me trembles and I hear the rebels. One rising, ringing tone.

I'm sweating in the humid eighty-degree heat. Too hot to think properly.

Yes, I tell him. I'll go back to Maggotty. Rent a place near Granny Itiba. Tend the land with her. Help myself to grow.

When she passes, I'll buy a house near the sea. Set up a beach shack. DJ. Sing. Have open mics for women DJs and singers.

Flowers shaped like duppies hang in the shaded light, secretive, taunting. I imagine Monassa in the grave-dust darkness. His body will be swollen by now. Maybe he'll get out. Maybe he won't. If he does escape, he'll be more like a duppy than a living man. But then, he already was.

'Moose,' I call out. 'Muma!'

I listen for their voices in the feedback loop of rainforest sounds, the beat of his earth-riddim ancestry. I lie down, put my face to the ground. Hear the sounds of runaways from centuries ago, playing shakas, funde drums and duppy riffs. Cockpit Country's ghostly shebeen.

30

Audiotopia

B-SIDE/DUBPLATE, 45 RPM

Dread Time

No more running. You're Sonix Dominatrix, popping style on the decks. Headtop lyrics, sometimes singing. Dropping guerrilla-uprising riddims on the cay.

Lock-off!

More and more dancers arrive on speedboats. They throw themselves inna the mix.

The midnight sun hangs in the sky day and night. A gold disc of soprano notes. The sea throws up sprays of red seed notes and curling Cs.

Girrl, check you out: in dem black satin boxing shorts, silver trainers, silver chain vest, your Afro puffed out like clouds.

The beats of this cay go backwards and forwards in time.

Drum loops, drop-out, delay, space-echo.

Audiotopia.

Faces bubble up from the past: Moose, Asase, Rumer, Lego.

Cracking sounds like cannons going off on the coast. Electric wires drop from the sky, flashing supra-watt basslines on and off, on and off.

The singer comes back, she's singing:

'sending my dream
always be seen

night-moves mystery
tek yuh there
my girl
let me tek you to the sea'

You know who she is.

You ask her, 'Muma? Where are we?'

'Daughter, we're home,' she says. 'This is the oneness of sound.'

Separation of positive and negative. You become supernatural. Connect to the electric storm.

It's you that's the fire. Hurtling through the outtasphere of sound. Falling through sinkholes. Through time.

Floating. You're in the sea. Women bobbing on their backs, singing in ancestral tongues. Singing freedom. The sun beating down on them, their heads gold deadbolts in the ocean.

One by one you drop inna dub bassline. You're holding on to Moose as you all descend. Your bodies stripped down to shimmering core.

Moose's voice, a supra-watt pressure: 'We're all travelling like stars.'

Your bodies are black brittle stars in the rock-rubble riddims of the sea. Currents and smoke spinning into fire.

Eruptions exploding into a universe of sound.

Acknowledgements

I've been on a sixteen-year journey in the writing of this book, and I've drawn heavily on the female spirit – *nuh mus* – during its development.

Heartfelt thanks to my agent Niki Chang and my editors – Ana Fletcher and Željka Marošević at Cape, and Lindsey Schwoeri and Allie Merola at Viking – for the forensic and creative editing, for seeing all the layers in the story, pulling them apart and helping me to put them back together in ways I may never have thought of. I have learned so much from you.

Nuff Love Sistren mention for Desiree Reynolds and Leone Ross for their invaluable Jamdown straight-talking advice, support and guidance.

Special thanks to Averill Buchanan who has provided personal editorial support for the past five years.

I would like to acknowledge grants from the Arts Council England Developing Your Practice funding stream and The Society of Authors, which provided me with invaluable writing time to develop this book.

I have collaborated with a community of passionate writers, editors, activists, researchers, musicians and other artists in the writing of this book. Each of them has contributed a *likkle* bit of magic and I would like to thank them all for their unique offering:

Rong A

Melanie Abrahams

Sharmilla Beezmohun
Carol Bird
Bernardine Evaristo
Jenny B. Garcia Camacho
Maggie Gee
William Henry
Peter Herbert
Aditi Jaganathan
Marie James
Shaun Levin
Eva Lewin
Kat Lewis
Maria Masullo
Lucy McKay
Lorraine Mullaney
Alan Murdie
Sally Orson-Jones
Dub Plate Pearl
Anne Rainbow
Shivanee N. Ramlochan
June Reid
Polly Roger-Brown
Lynda Rosenior-Patten
Jacob Ross
Richard Skinner
Bibiana Timpanaro
Tyrone Wright
Wayne Wright
Alex Wheatle
Mad X

Also a shout-out to *Wire* magazine. I've relied on this eclectic monthly magazine as a valuable reference for the vocabulary of writing about sounds.

While this book is a fictionalised account of my life, I have also drawn on the following books and articles for research purposes; I'm indebted to the authors:

Gaston Bachelard, *The Poetics of Space*, translated by Maria Jolas (copyright © 1958 by Presses Universitaires de France; translation copyright © 1964 by Penguin Random House LLC. Used by permission of Viking Books, an imprint of Penguin Publishing Group, a division of Penguin Random House LLC. All rights reserved.)

Lloyd Bradley, *Bass Culture: When Reggae Was King* (London: Penguin, 2000).

Paula Burnett (ed.), *The Penguin Book of Caribbean Verse in English* (London: Penguin [1985] 2005).

M. J. Day, 'Natural and anthropogenic hazards in the karsts of Jamaica', in M. Parise and J. Gunn (eds), *Natural and Anthropogenic Hazards in Karst Areas: Recognition, Analysis, Mitigation*. Geological Society of London Special Publication 279 (April 2007), pp. 173–184.

Louis Chude-Sokei, '"Dr Satan's Echo Chamber": Reggae, Technology and the Diaspora Process', in *Popular Inquiry: The Journal of the Aesthetics of Kitsch, Camp and Mass Culture*, vol. 1 (2018), pp. 46–60.

Sarah Daynes, *Time and Memory in Reggae Music: The Politics of Hope* (New York: Palgrave Macmillan; Manchester: Manchester University Press, 2010).

Herbert G. De Lisser, *Twentieth Century Jamaica* (Kingston: The Jamaica Times, 1913).

Julian Henriques, *Sonic Bodies: Reggae Sound Systems, Performance Techniques, and Ways of Knowing* (London and New York: Bloomsbury, 2011).

Zora Neale Hurston, *Tell my Horse: Voodoo and Life in Haiti and Jamaica* (first published 1938; New York: Harper Perennial, 2009).

Simon Jones and Paul Pinnock, with photographs by Jonathan Girling, *Scientists of Sound: Portraits of a UK Reggae Sound System* (Bassline Books/Independently published, 2017).

Dawes Kwame, *Natural Mysticism: Towards a New Reggae Aesthetic in Caribbean Writing* (Leeds: Peepal Tree Press, 1999).

M. G. Lewis, *Journal of a West India Proprietor* (London: John Murray, 1834).

Riccardo Orizio, *Lost White Tribes: Journeys Among the Forgotten* (London: Penguin, 2001).

Chris Potash (ed.), *Reggae, Rasta, Revolution: Jamaican Music from Ska to Dub* (London: Books with Attitude, 1997).

Olive Senior, 'Cockpit County Dreams', in *Talking of Trees* (Kingston, Jamaica: Calabash, 1985).

Richard Skinner, *Dub: Red Hot vs Ice Cold* (London: NOCH, 2013).

Paul Sullivan, *Remixology: Tracing the Dub Diaspora* (London: Reaktion Books, 2014).

M. M. Sweeting, 'The Karstlands of Jamaica', in *The Geographical Journal*, vol. 124, no. 2 (1958), pp. 184–199.

Michael E. Veal, *Dub: Soundscapes & Shattered Songs in Jamaican Reggae* (Middletown, CT: Wesleyan University Press, 2007).

Joseph J. Williams, *Psychic Phenomena of Jamaica* (New York: The Dial Press, 1934).